Beautiful Days

Story Collections by Joyce Carol Oates

By the North Gate (1963)
Upon the Sweeping Flood and Other Stories (1966)
The Wheel of Love and Other Stories (1970)
Marriages and Infidelities (1972)
The Goddess and Other Women (1974)
The Hungry Ghosts (1974)
The Poisoned Kiss (1975)
The Seduction (1975)
Crossing the Border (1976)
Night-Side (1977)
A Sentimental Education (1980)
Last Days (1984)
Raven's Wing (1986)
The Assignation (1988)
Oates in Exile (1990)
Heat and Other Stories (1991)
Where Is Here? (1992)
Where Are You Going, Where Have You Been?: Selected Early Stories (1993)
Haunted: Tales of the Grotesque (1994)
Demon and Other Tales (1996)
Will You Always Love Me? (1996)
The Collector of Hearts: New Tales of the Grotesque (1998)
Faithless: Tales of Transgression (2001)
High Lonesome: New & Selected Stories, 1966–2006 (2006)
Wild Nights! (2008)
Dear Husband (2009)
Sourland (2010)
The Corn Maiden (2011)
Black Dahlia & White Rose (2012)
Lovely, Dark, Deep (2014)

Beautiful Days

stories

Joyce Carol Oates

An Imprint of HarperCollins*Publishers*

BEAUTIFUL DAYS. Copyright © 2018 by The Ontario Review, Inc. All rights reserved. Printed in the United States of America. No part of this book may be used or reproduced in any manner whatsoever without written permission except in the case of brief quotations embodied in critical articles and reviews. For information, address HarperCollins Publishers, 195 Broadway, New York, NY 10007.

HarperCollins books may be purchased for educational, business, or sales promotional use. For information, please email the Special Markets Department at SPsales@harpercollins.com.

FIRST EDITION

Designed by Michelle Crowe

Library of Congress Cataloging-in-Publication Data has been applied for.

ISBN 978-0-06-279578-6

18 19 20 21 22   LSC   10 9 8 7 6 5 4 3 2 1

to Greg Johnson

Contents

Acknowledgments

"Fleuve Bleu" originally appeared in *Kenyon Review*.

"Big Burnt" originally appeared in *Conjunctions*.

"Owl Eyes" originally appeared in *Yale Review*.

"The Bereaved" originally appeared in *Yale Review*.

"Except You Bless Me" originally appeared in *Salmagundi*.

"The Quiet Car" originally appeared in *Harper's*.

"Les beaux jours" originally appeared in *Alive in Shape and Color: 17 Stories Inspired by 17 Different Artists*.

"Fractal" originally appeared in *Conjunctions*.

"Undocumented Alien" originally appeared in *Conjunctions,* and has been anthologized in *Pushcart Prize: The Best of the Small Presses 2017*.

"Donald Barthelme Saved from Oblivion" originally appeared in *American Short Fiction*.

"The Memorial Field at Hazard, Minnesota" originally appeared in *Yale Review*.

Occasional lines from the work of Donald Barthelme occur in the story "Donald Barthelme Saved from Oblivion."

Beautiful Days

I

Fleuve Bleu

Mid-afternoon, late autumn, bars of spangled light on the river, he was crossing the bridge on the pedestrian walkway fluttering with flags when he'd first seen her, not knowing it was *her*. And the whimsical thought came to him, as such thoughts had often come to him when he'd been younger, and had lived alone and walked a good deal by himself in urban places—*I will marry her. That one.*

Except, of course, he was married now. He was long married, by now. The brash young man who'd walked for hours in cities, tireless, curious, thrilled to be alone, sometimes taking photographs but often to no purpose other than to walk on his quick, restless legs, had long departed.

SHE HAD GLANCED AROUND in that instant, as if he'd reached out to touch her. A leap of recognition between them like a blade of light on water.

Almost, he'd lifted his hand in greeting. But he didn't know the young woman and he was sure she didn't know him.

Afterward he would claim that their eyes had met, that first time,

and she would say laughingly—*I don't think so. I think I would remember, if that were so.*

HE WAS DRAWN TO THE RIVER. Swift-flowing ravenous waters
rushing close beside buildings in this old riverside mill town.

Le Fleuve Bleu it had been, once. At the time of the French settle-
ment in the 1730s. Now, just Blue River.

Yet strangely, by some logic a local historian might have explained,
the small riverside city itself was still called Fleuve Bleu—pronounced
in the flat nasal way of upstate New York, "fluuv blue."

On the farther side of the Blue River was Fort Winston, Ontario.

From the ceiling-high window of his office in the old brick Rutherford Building on River Street where often he sat dreaming he could
see massed trees on the Canadian shore less than a mile away, the
bulky silhouette of the single-span bridge that linked Fleuve Bleu and
Fort Cornwell, a stretch of waterfront—massive rusted oil drums,
warehouses, trucking yards, docks. Barges on the river moving with
surprising swiftness in the churning water like rhinos.

When he'd first come to work in this (family-owned) law firm he'd
brought a camera with him every day. He'd spend his lunch hour
roaming the waterfront, taking photographs. He'd climb out onto the
fire escape, taking photographs. Gradually in recent years he'd ceased
bringing a camera to work though something ached in him, a yearning, an emptiness, when he saw something, more often someone he'd
have liked to photograph—a distinctive face, a memorable gaze.

As he thought it—*A gaze to pierce the heart.*

It had come to seem an indulgence, his expensive cameras—(about
which his dear kind wife never spoke, never reproachfully)—and taking so much time, such exactitude, caring so much about images few
people would ever see. Of course his family and friends "admired" his
photography—how could they not? He was one of *theirs*.

More recently since his fortieth birthday to resist the camera, to resist making costly prints of his work—this seemed to him a kind of virtue.

A Tolstoyan virtue, of negativity. Not wasting money on photography. Not approaching the young woman on the bridge with whom, in that first, fatal instant, he was smitten.

FEARLESS SHE'D APPEARED TO HIM, at the bridge railing. Leaning just a little too far over the railing, as a reckless child might do.

She was staring down at the water rushing twelve feet below the walkway. *Le fleuve bleu* and so in fact the water appeared blue, dark cobalt-blue, heaving and bucking and throwing up spray, chill droplets tossed by the wind so that pedestrians squealed with surprised laughter—*Is it raining? No—not rain . . .*

It was a surprisingly warm November midday. A day to bask in sunshine.

First he'd seen her, her back was to the walkway. A white skirt of some thin material like muslin billowed about her legs that were slender yet hard with muscle. Crimped hair, dark-red like sumac.

Then, she looked around. Saw him.

Blood-red mouth, startling.

He felt a tinge of pleasure—*Do I know her? Is she smiling—at me?*

She was with companions—was she? Not alone.

The walkway above the river was crowded at midday. Festooned with cheery little flags alternating red-white-and-blue (U.S.) and red-and-white (Canada).

Thinking she might be Canadian. With friends, visiting for the day.

Yet: if she wasn't Canadian, not a stranger, she could turn out to be the young sister of one of his high school classmates in which case (he warned himself) it wasn't a great idea to approach her on the pedestrian bridge. Even a smile was risky.

And so, he'd continued past her. He had not hesitated for a moment. After that initial moment.

The thin white-muslin skirt lifted in the wind, almost touching his legs, he passed that close.

A PURELY WHIMSICAL THOUGHT of the kind that bombarded his brain through much of his waking life. Thoughts like giddy gnats he made no effort to curtail, knowing them harmless.

Yes. That one.

THE SECOND TIME, things happened swiftly.

Crossing Center Street in a sudden downpour, waiting for a red light to change, impractically dressed for such weather in high-heeled shoes. She was furious with herself. Could've whipped herself raw. Trying not to fucking cry. Overcome with self-disgust, dismay. For this was not right—she was twenty-eight years old. Her love for her children waxed and waned, was that normal? She didn't think so. She commuted to Fleuve Bleu to get away from them. She didn't love the father of the children. She was a textbook editor's assistant. She was God damn smarter than her boss—even he knew that. Smarter than so many people, but what had it got her?

Oh God. Forgive me, I am hopeless.

A new-model station wagon pulled up beside her as she stood at the curb in pelting rain, the driver's window lowered—"Hey. Get in. Wherever you're going, I'll take you."

THEY VOWED: THEY WOULD BE honest with each other.

Brutally, totally. No holding back!

"D'you think it's even possible?"—he asked.

"Yes. I think it is."

She told him it would be the *inside-out* of the rest of her life, her relationship with him. She hoped it would be the *inside-out* of his life, too.

She meant, what they had together was a counter-world. That

other world, the "real" world—that did not apply, between the two of them.

He wasn't sure that such exclusion was possible, or even ideal.

He said, "Yes."

"Because I'm always lying. In that other life. In my 'real' life. I tell people—I tell myself—'I live for my children. I adore my children.'" She spoke avidly, ardently. The blood-red mouth had been smeared in their eager lovemaking. She looked young now, uncertain. He was fascinated by her, the way she had of blundering forward, speaking as she was thinking, head-on, reckless, not censoring her thoughts to impress him, the man, or to shield him. There was no one in his life—no one else in his life—who plunged forward in such a way, heedlessly.

"Of course I love them—I am their mother. But I'm so much more than their fucking *mother*. When they behave badly, and it goes on, and on, and I can see that they don't love me much—I mean, children need you, it's *need* they feel for you, not love—I feel as if my heart is breaking, I think *Jesus! What a fool you were, to get into this*. And I mean it! The whole mother-thing, the woman-thing, the woman-body-thing—like quicksand. It's just that I would never tell anyone else, certainly not the father of the children. Not my mother, not his mother. Jesus!"

She laughed, too hard. A hectic flush had come into her face. He liked it that she was so brash with him, in these early days of intimacy. It was his experience that women took pains to seem "feminine"—but not this one.

Not beautiful but her frankness was a kind of beauty. And she wasn't as young as she'd first appeared to him—for which he was grateful.

When he was away from her, he found himself thinking of her obsessively. And in her presence that was hot, humid, close-up and magnified, he felt that he could almost not breathe.

Like a bold exuberant child pushing gifts at him he didn't know if he wanted—didn't know if he should accept—she was telling him secrets he wasn't sure he wanted to know. How she'd lain in bed exhausted as a young mother, at the age of twenty-three—hearing her baby cry in the next room, fretting, wailing, and she'd pretended not to hear. Her heart had shrunk into a hard little root, hearing the baby cry. She'd thought—*It will cease, finally. At some point.*

Milk had leaked from her nipples. The swoon of motherhood had been upon her, unspeakable pleasure in the baby's tough little gums sucking at her, and soon then she'd been unable to resist. Heaved herself from her bed. She'd never been able to let either of her children really cry, as abandoned children might cry.

He was quiet, listening. A faint roaring in his ears of warning.

They lay on the bed, a rough-textured coverlet twisted beneath them. Overhead, across the faintly cracked ceiling, a lattice-pattern of light like something undersea.

It was a room he'd acquired specifically for this purpose. Not a room with which he was personally associated but a room in a rental property owned by Rutherford, Inc. for which he was an officer.

"And how do you feel? Do you 'adore' your children, also?"

He didn't like her intonation—*adore*. He knew, she was being ironic, self-protective. But he didn't like irony unless it was his own.

Irony the double-edged sword. Take care wielding it.

Heard himself say, thoughtfully—"I love my kids. Of course. But we don't need to talk about them now, do we? This is our special time together."

He spoke easily, guilelessly. Each word he uttered was a true word, it was the sum of his words that was problematic.

She said, "I thought we wouldn't lie to each other. I thought that was the point."

"Why do you think I'm lying to you? I'm not."

"There are lies of omission. Some of the worst."

"Darling, I won't lie to you. I'm not lying when I say that I'm deeply in love with you, but I can't take my feeling for you back into my other life. It would be devastating."

"But do you really love that other life?"—she spoke wistfully.

He thought—*I will have to lie to her. She expects it.*

"Yes, I love my 'other life.' But it's this life with you, these times with you, that are special to me, that give me strength to endure the other life."

On her belly he traced an invisible trail. Her skin shivered beneath his fingertips. The flesh was a young flesh—taut, tight. He understood that he should not be thinking of his wife's body, his wife's far slacker, looser skin—he should not, and he did not. His fingers could feel what his eyes couldn't see—the faintest of birthmarks. In shape something like a leaf. Delicate, breakable.

Reading her like Braille, she thought. As no one had read her before.

SHE SNATCHED UP HIS FINGERS, kissed the knuckles. Had to let the man know, she wasn't a passive female. She didn't just *lie there.*

A GAZE TO PIERCE THE HEART.

He'd ceased looking. Ceased expecting to see anything that leapt to his eye. Long restless walks, most days—didn't hope to see anything exceptional.

Giving up the camera, you gave up the possibility of certain kinds of seeing.

More often on his walks he saw people whom he knew, or half-knew. People with whom he'd gone to school. Ex-teachers. Aging friends of his aging parents. Faces familiar as faces glimpsed in dreams. On the street, in parkland along the river, in restaurants and cafés he patronized as in the foyer of his office building at 55 River Street that surprised him and made him smile when he glanced up to see Gothic engraved letters in the granite portico—his family name, a very old name in Fleuve Bleu, detached from him and impersonal: RUTHERFORD.

"Really? That's your name?"

She'd laughed. Her teeth were not perfect teeth but her smile was a perfect teasing smile.

"It's like 'Rockefeller'—'Carnegie.' I mean, around here. You don't expect to meet anybody actually named 'Rutherford'—the feeling is, they must've all died."

He'd laughed. It was like being tickled with hard, unsentimental fingers. She wanted him to know she wasn't impressed, not much.

Sure, she was impressed. Her chic-vintage clothes from secondhand shops, faux-leather shoulder bag, faux-leather shoes, the less-than-perfect teeth you might call charmingly crooked, and something defensive in her way of speaking marked her—(Christ, he didn't want to think in such terms!)—as of a class distinctly below his own.

His notion that she might be Canadian had been totally groundless. In fact, she'd been born in the same hospital in which, twelve years earlier, he'd been born, in Fleuve Bleu. And she lived now, with her husband and two young children, in Rensselaer Falls seven miles east of Fleuve Bleu.

It wasn't *adultery,* he told himself. There was no encroachment upon his other, essential life. He would never be jealous of the (faceless) husband. He would never meet the (faceless) children.

And what was more crucial, she would never meet his wife, his children. That was understood.

HE BEGAN BRINGING HIS CAMERA. Not the old camera but the new, expensive digital Nikon.

But she said *No. Not that.*

He'd been surprised. Hurt and disappointed. But thinking—*She doesn't trust me. Maybe that's a good thing.*

HE WAS FORTY YEARS OLD. He was married, he was the father of two adolescent children. And he was happily married, his wife was a lovely, kind, intelligent and gentle person whom he would never wish to hurt. His life moved past in surges, like warm water through his fingers. It was the balm of domestic life—a rhythm of days, routines. He remembered when the children had been young and had clamored at his legs, demanded to be lifted in his arms. *Daddy!*—their cries had torn at his heart, the ritual cries of children. When he'd been with them, he'd sometimes found himself staring at them as if they were strangers. It was fascinating to watch his wife with the children, they'd brought out a particular patience and kindliness in her that caused him to love her deeply. He thought *They have made of us better people than we were meant to be.*

EVEN IN THE COUNTER-WORLD, there were anniversaries.

Day of the week they'd first seen each other on the pedestrian walkway: Tuesday. (At least, he'd seen her.)

Day of the week he'd sighted her on Center Street, in the rain, absolutely by chance, pulled boldly up to the curb and offered her a ride: Friday.

Day of the week they'd first made love: Friday.

This Tuesday and this Friday: six days apart.

At first, anniversaries were weeks. Then, months.

Sometimes they met publicly, as if by chance. Fleuve Bleu was such a small town, the downtown area scarcely more than a few blocks, the stately old Rutherford Building a five-minute walk from Fowler's Publishing, Inc. She'd laughed seeing him looking eagerly—anxiously?—for her.

"Hi!"

"H'lo!"

Crazy smiles. You feel your face rearranging itself in such smiles.

"Are you—?"

"Are *you*—?"

Taking care not to meet too often in the same places. Very shrewd, their caution.

Mostly, they met in the rental flat. He could walk there easily, and she could walk there easily, the apartment building was on a side street, not a street much frequented by pedestrians, always he would arrive first, as planned. He liked it that the place had no history, certainly no personal history. He wasn't even sure that she knew he owned it, or was one of the owners. The room, the bed, their bed—it was of that *inside-out* world, sequestered and secret.

It was weeks before he'd realized she didn't have a key, he had not given her a key, and she'd never requested one. For always, he was the first to arrive at the flat and would be awaiting her; sometimes she stood outside the door listening to him inside talking on his cell phone—words indistinct but tone clear, invariably her lover was in a good mood, laughing, at ease.

She hesitated to interrupt him. No—she felt a small thrill of anger, striking her fist on the door to interrupt him.

Email messages, text messages—these he received in a continuous stream, she could hear the tiny *ping!* in his cell phone.

But when they were together, seriously together in their room, in their bed, their cell phones were turned *off.*

Shiny little screens blank-black, dead. No life inside.

Later, when they were separate, and their separate lives had resumed, the little screens were relighted.

STILL IT WASN'T *ADULTERY.* He didn't think so. Though he had to deal with his feelings of resentment, unease, mild panic when she was away from him, when (for instance) she'd been unable to meet him for most of a week, or when (a worse instance) she'd kept him waiting in the rental and hadn't answered his cell phone calls and called him finally after twenty minutes to say tersely she was sorry, she had to cancel and would explain later.

He'd said, "Look. That isn't how we're doing this. No explanations are needed, and no explanations are wanted."

He wasn't (for instance) going to drive out to Rensselaer Falls, to see where she lived. Wasn't going to make inquiries (not in even the most casual way) about her with Gerry Fowler whom he'd known in high school, whose family owned the textbook publishing house, and who might plausibly have some connection with . . . But no: God damn he would not.

For one thing, he couldn't utter her name aloud to anyone.

To himself, and to her, he could utter this name. But never to anyone else, for that would be a violation of the deep intimacy between them, that was like no other intimacy in their lives.

Oh, this strange panic-sensation, that she'd abandoned him! She had left him behind in his own dull bell-jar life, to suffocate.

Abandoned him for her life with her family about which now she rarely spoke. Driving seven miles home to a place he'd never seen. (Though he knew the address. He'd memorized the address.) The mysterious husband, the mysterious children, many years younger than his children who were, strictly speaking, hardly "children" any longer.

There is a point when your children are no longer *young*. Painful to acknowledge, you are no longer a *young parent*.

"We could begin again. Our own children."

(Had he uttered these ridiculous words aloud? He hoped not!)

Out of inertia remaining late at the office, leaden-limbed, melancholy, the last person to leave the office but even then—though he knew they were waiting for him at home—he went down to the waterfront, to brood; not the renovated tourist waterfront with the brisk bright flags snapping but the older and shabbier waterfront, that was shrill with the aggrieved cries of gulls. He wanted to breathe the knife-sharp winter air, wanted to feel his senses quiver with life and with yearning. Overhead the night sky pulsed with its own mysterious life. Futile to point out that the stars you see are long extinct—their light was not extinct, dazzling the eye.

He stared at those rippling lights reflected in the part-frozen Blue River and wondered what would come of him—what would come of *her*.

Almost, he thought, it would be better not to see her again. Or maybe, better if they had not met.

If she were ill. If she—died . . .

Stray, senseless thoughts. Cruel and stupid thoughts. Yet, he could not help himself. Unless he concentrated fiercely on his work, unless he was with *her*, he was bombarded with such thoughts.

Where she lived, where he might've driven. Seven miles east of River Street, approximately. Rensselaer Falls was a village adjacent to the small city of Canton. He knew people who lived there, but no one well. No one whom he might've visited. Except her, whose address he'd memorized: 44 Eagle Street.

Yes but he had not, had he? Not yet.

Instead of going to bed that night. Joining his wife in bed. (It was her custom to go to bed as much as an hour and a half before he did.) Instead, slipping outside and in the SUV driving darkened streets east and north of Fleuve Bleu. And along the moonlit highway Route 17 to Rensselaer Falls. And beside the road, for a mile or two, the Blue River. And in the distance, not visible except to his dreaming mind, the great St. Lawrence. And in the Village of Rensselaer Falls he would seek Eagle Street and on Eagle Street he would seek the numeral 44 and in front of the darkened house at 44 Eagle Street he would park his vehicle . . . At dawn, the house would begin to awaken. Lights upstairs: she'd said she wakened early.

She would find him there, in the SUV. She would be astonished, she would come quickly to him . . .

What are you doing here! My God.

Her eyes wet with tears of surprise and emotion. In the early-hour before the sun had fully risen.

"But that hasn't happened. It has not."

His voice was reproving. Pleading.

HE FELT HE WOULD LOVE HER less desperately, after this.

And he would blame her, and resent her, after this.

"HELLO!"

"Hello . . ."

Gently at first he pushed against her on the pedestrian walkway.

His mouth sought her mouth, fastened upon it, sucking.

A hungry kiss, a kiss that says *Just don't stop me, don't interfere with what I am doing.*

It was not late: scarcely 7:00 P.M. But very dark, a November evening, and the bridge deserted.

Above, a smudged-looking moon. Heavy-lidded lewd eye.

She felt the railing against her back. Still she lifted her arms to him. His knuckles against her back that couldn't but hurt, and he knew this, and she felt her mouth forced open, she was laughing too, breathless and laughing, laughing against the force of his sucking kiss that left her weak, dazed.

Still, the kiss continued. Her jaws felt unhinged, she was exhausted, yet it was a playful sort of kiss (she wanted to think this) meaning how much he wanted her, how powerful his desire for her; and close by on the railroad bridge freight trains were thundering past, even now at this romantic hour, even now.

IT WOUNDED HIM, the old mill city was gradually shrinking.

Losing population, since the 1970s.

When he'd graduated from high school Fleuve Bleu had contained

22,800 people; now, the latest census indicated just 16,300. The mills had closed, the factories along the Blue River, fewer trains came through, fewer barges. He'd lived downstate for several years, and he'd done well enough—but he'd returned for family reasons, and then he'd married a young woman from a prominent family in Canton. Now family held them tight as in a web.

He told her: for eighteen months after law school, working for a law firm in New York City, he'd lived near the Verrazano Bridge. Crossed and recrossed the Verrazano and he'd never tired of admiring its beauty.

Strange to hear a man say that word—*beauty*.

She loved to hear him speak in this way. That dreamy look in his eyes after they'd made love. What had been combative and edgy between them spent. She could deceive herself, he'd take her with him if ever he returned to live near the Verrazano Bridge again.

She said, she didn't think she'd even seen a photo of the bridge. And so he showed her, on his cell phone.

Of course, you can't see it, so small. Check it on your computer.

She asked why he'd returned home, if he'd made the break?

He said no break is permanent. Like a bone that heals crooked, still it will heal.

GOOD BREEDING.

Tall, good bones, fair-skinned and fair-haired, he'd learned to expect the attention of others, and in some, the most subtle gestures of subservience. The name RUTHERFORD was a kind of shield, of which he needn't be conscious. His own name—"Tom Rutherford"—suggested a kind of modesty, self-effacement. One of those who wants to be liked and is furious when he isn't, but you aren't likely to know.

By the age of eighteen he'd grown to a height of over six feet. Already in grammar school he'd been a tall boy, he'd taken for granted the unspoken authority of the tall: the deference of others, sometimes even adults. He'd become an individual who has only to step into a room, a space, a dimension in which there are other, less-tall individuals—basking in an unacknowledged royalty. Ridiculous of course. He knows.

Yet he wonders if women experience something of the same. Half-consciously, even resentfully, acknowledging the presence of the beautiful woman in their midst: the not-beautiful, the girl-with-bad-skin, the too-heavy girl, the too-short girl, the too-tall girl. These assessments are quicksilver, involuntary. That they are unjust and ridiculous doesn't alleviate their power.

He'd seen men glance at her when they were together. And women. Sexual jealousy. Nothing more lethal.

He wasn't jealous, he was sure.

THAT DAY WALKING TOGETHER on Cartwright Street. Not grip-ping hands—not in public!—but their hands touching, brushing to-gether like tiny whips.

He was saying—

She was saying—

And near the intersection with Seventh Avenue a woman stepped precipitously out between two parked cars and was struck by a vehicle—fortunately, a minivan that had been slowing to a stop at a red light—not more than a glancing blow along the side of her body, but the woman was thrown to her knees screaming in surprise and pain, and immediately he'd run to her, Tom Rutherford had run to her, and crouched beside her asking if she was all right, should he call an ambulance?

So quickly this had happened. And so publicly.

She had followed him, to offer help as well. Then hesitated and held back, staring.

She saw the stricken woman, helped now to her feet by the tall fair-haired Tom Rutherford. She saw the woman's tear-smitten face, and how Tom Rutherford spoke to her, and supported her. She saw how Tom Rutherford went to gather the woman's handbag and packages, that had been scattered on the street. And by this time others had gathered. And the minivan driver, dark-skinned, agitated, had joined them. He had forgotten *her*, or nearly.

The street was slushy with part-melted snow. Dirty snow, and the stricken woman's clothes were wet, the palms of her hands had been scraped. Tom Rutherford was saying maybe he'd better call an ambulance, just to make sure.

The woman who'd stepped blindly into the street was talking loudly. She did not want to be taken to the ER. She insisted that she was all right. A woman of youthful middle age, with an excitable voice. Had she hurt her knees? Had she sprained a wrist? Pedestrians were gathering. Tom Rutherford stood among them, tall and responsible. How long this continued, might've been ten minutes, there on the sidewalk at the intersection of Cartwright and Seventh Avenue where traffic was moving normally again, moving around the minivan parked haltingly in the street. There was a look of haphazard, something gone askew. Very soon, a Fleuve Bleu police officer would arrive.

By this time, when Tom Rutherford glanced around, he saw that he was alone.

Of course. We can't be seen together. In an emergency, we can't be together.

IT WAS A REVELATION: in an emergency, each would have to flee the other.

She thought—*If I'd been the one hit by a car. Would he have stayed with me? Would I have sent him away?*

NEXT TIME THEY MET, they'd decided to forget how swiftly she'd departed from him.

And how readily he'd understood, and had not judged her.

THE BLUE RIVER HAD FROZEN SOLID in January. And now the Blue River was thawing, in late March.

A river thaws from the middle outward. Dark-churning-rushing water bracketed by ice.

There's a look to a late-winter river of something prehistoric: jagged ice-boulders piled up on the banks, like an avalanche.

With his camera he went outside in the fierce March wind. Left his desk at mid-morning, heaped with work. Contracts, documents. He was a tax lawyer, basically! He hated it, his life had come to this subservience in the maintenance and increase of others' estates.

His professional life. In which he was very successful.

Well—moderately successful. In Fleuve Bleu terms, he'd done well.

Earnestly he was telling her, trying to explain—*If I'd failed at law, it would've been better. Just walk away. Tell my father. Tell the family. But things have gone differently. I've always been God-damned good at what I do—that has been my curse.*

WITH THE THAW BARGES HAD RETURNED to the river. Upstream, downstream. Sometimes you could see their cargo—mounds of coal, gypsum, potash, sand. His law firm worked with river- and lake-freighter companies, drew up contracts, dealt with tax problems. The Great Lakes freighters had been steadily losing business for decades—once several hundred freighters, now scarcely more than one hundred. The Blue River had once been a prosperous waterway, now no longer. Yet Tom Rutherford would prevail, the family law firm would prevail, even as the waters diminished. Corks float: corks of privilege, opportunity.

He wanted to tell *her*. Explain to *her*.

This isn't my life. What people see. My life is only what you see—what you touch. That is my life, my soul.

That, and his photography. Hundreds of pictures he'd taken in the past several years in his computer he hadn't examined, hadn't sorted out, edited. The work of photography isn't the picture-taking but afterward. Art is a solitary matter.

SHUDDERING OF THE OLD RAILROAD BRIDGE. Locomotive and freight cars thundering above the river. Something sexual in the pounding of the rails, a deep-blooded beat, he felt the gathering tension in her body. Where she gripped him most intimately, where he thrust into her, the stiffening of her body like a delicate watch that is being wound ever tighter, tighter . . . Her body bucked, heaved; a cry was strangled in her throat; she clutched at him as a drowning swimmer would clutch at a rescuer, a hoped-for rescuer; clawed and moaned in delirium, such genuine anguish she seemed drawn out of herself, terribly exposed, vulnerable and violable; like nothing he could experience himself, or would risk.

IF SHE LOVES ME SO MUCH, *how will we end it.*

THE FLOATING SENSATION OF LIGHT in a room. Light in a room, where you are sleeping. Light penetrating your (shut) eyelids.
My dear one, my darling you have made me so happy.

HE WAS READING TOLSTOY. The late, embittered Tolstoy: *Resurrection, The Kreutzer Sonata.* Twilight of scx-dcsirc. Bleak stoicism of a life without erotic love. An elderly man raging against the young, with a pretense of Christian morality. The rage of old men, hoping to legislate the desire of the young. Abstinence! After Tolstoy had rutted and groveled in the female body for decades, impregnating the much younger woman who was his wife at least thirteen times—belatedly then, in his old age, Tolstoy came to feel a hypocritical revulsion for what he called the carnal life.

Yet in a fascination of his own, he read Tolstoy. Wanting to protest *No—no! It is nothing like this. Love is nothing like this.*

SINCE CHILDHOOD HE'D HAD a recurring magical dream. Bright cloudless winter morning and he was gliding along a roadway, beside a river, sensing that if he turned to look that's all he would see—a blur.

"This is the strange thing: the place is so open and light-filled and yet so secret. It's the place I long for where something wonderful is waiting on the other side of the river."

"But it was the bridge, where we met."

"The bridge! Yes of course—it was the bridge."

ABOVE THE LOOSE-JOINTED BED, a rectangle of floating light. Filmy curtains stirring in the breeze. She never wanted the window shut and locked but always open at least a quarter inch, otherwise the (steam-heated) room became too hot and stale-smelling. While they were gone, sometimes away for days over a weekend, rain was likely to be blown into the room, the mattress was likely to be damp, pillows and coverlet damp, curious little leaves and parts of dried leaves blown about the room . . . He was mesmerized by light falling not onto but into her hair, light shining out of the coils of her dark-red hair. He licked her body with his tongue, her nipples, the shallow of her belly, the birthmark that reminded him too of a leaf, the tight little belly button, that made him laugh.

She protested, Oh!—so sharply, it was a kind of sexual pain.

He gripped her wrists, he turned her wrists. An unexpected cruelty in him, the woman seemed to provoke. His wife was so kind, so sweetly placid, so readily dispirited, discouraged—a *nice woman,* and not brash and tough like this woman—he could never have touched her in such a way.

Just the thought of touching the other wife with such raw impatient desire—not possible.

Thinking—*You can't live with this. Must back off, soon. You need distance.*

You both need distance.

IT WAS NOT OFTEN, in fact it had been very rare, she'd fallen asleep in that bed.

Stealthily then taking her picture. Three times, quickly.

SHE SAID, "Y'KNOW? I want you to love me."

He said, "But I already love you!"

She said, "I mean in a way to last. In a way to take home with you. A way that enters your dreams."

He said, faltering, "You are already in my dreams."

THEY WERE AUDACIOUS, DARING. They went together to a place that, if they were seen together, there could be no explanation except the obvious.

A late-afternoon film at the art museum. A film she'd intended to see by herself. She'd told her husband she wouldn't be home until at least 8:00 P.M. so he should feed himself and the children, she'd left a meal for them in the refrigerator. (Telling him this for what reason? he wondered. Did she think it gave him pleasure to be forced to envision the husband, the children, the meal she'd prepared to be served in her absence; to be forced to envision such domesticity, such intimacy that excluded him as surely as if he'd been standing at the door to that house and the door had been shut in his face. And did she not know?)

The film was in fact several short films made in the 1940s, of dances by Martha Graham. He'd never seen Graham dance, and was struck by her strange defiant beauty, the angularity of her face

and body, the forcefulness of her movements. In "Lamentation" she
wore a purple gown, a kind of cloak over her head. Sitting beside
the woman who was his lover, whom he had no right to be seeing
in this public place except he'd forced her, he'd insisted. And she'd
resisted at first, then gave in. And clasped his hand now, thrilled
to be seeing Martha Graham dancing, thrilled to be seeing Martha Graham dancing in his company, sharing. "It's so beautiful. I'm
crying—don't know why." She touched her fingertips to her eyes. It
was strange, it was exciting to him, she was crying, though he tried
to laugh at her—"Why are you sad?" She said, "Well, I'd wanted to
be a dancer, see. I've danced, I've taken lessons, years ago. It's over for
me now, I'm a spectator now. But that's not why I'm sad, I think."

There was Martha Graham moving in her tense angular way, as
if pushing against a substance denser than air. Suddenly you could
see the space about her yearning body: how it resisted her, how she
defined her body in resistance to it, ever pushing, pressing. The eerie
precision to the dance, that would have seemed to him, at another
time, in other circumstances, loosely free and improvised.

"I think—I'm thinking of us. How we'd be seen, seventy years
from now. If someone was filming us. Recording us." She laughed,
whispering. She was embarrassed by her emotion, as he hadn't seen
her. He wanted to console her, make light of her remark—except it
wasn't a remark that indicated fear, or unhappiness—rather, it was
matter-of-fact.

She knew nothing of the surreptitious photos he'd taken. He had
sequestered them away in his computer. A naked woman, a naked
woman so trusting she'd fallen asleep, mouth slightly open, mouth
damp . . . She'd have been furious, and possibly she'd have been offended in a deeper, more primitive way, as if he'd stolen something
from her she hadn't even known she had lost.

When they left the little theater, she'd made a gesture of walking
ahead of him, stepping singly out into the lighted lobby, but he'd

been close beside her, gripping her hand. She said, "I'm so happy that I could share this with you. But I think—I think this is something of a mistake, a blunder, I mean the risk . . ." She pulled her hand from his, and he gripped it harder. There were only a few people in the lobby, he had to know they might be women who might know his wife, might be women who knew him, yet stubbornly he accompanied her out to the street, some measure of the dancer's defiance had entered his spirit, the hell with risk, the hell with caution.

"In seventy years we'll both be dead. So?"

HE SAW HIS WIFE STRUGGLING with the kitchen door. She was outside, and struggling to unlock it. She was holding two grocery bags awkwardly in her arms, her face was vexed, peevish. Her eyeglasses glared with light. Had he locked the damn door against her? Had she gone away and locked it against herself? For a moment he held back, considering. Then quickly he came to the door, quickly he opened it and took the grocery bags from her.

"There you go."

There. You. Go.

LATE AUTUMN, WINTER, LATE WINTER and spring—(as usual, the cold-grudging spring of upstate New York)—he didn't want to calculate the months, the anniversaries they were beginning to forget, Tuesday, Friday, the several times they'd had to cancel meeting in the room; her cell phone ringing in distress, his cell phone ringing in distress. Less than six months swallowed up in the more than twenty years of his marriage as a shrinking ice floe is swallowed up, melting, disappearing into the ravenous rushing Blue River.

She'd been saying in her mock-wistful way what about a life elsewhere, downstate. She'd been saying lately that her work at Fowler's that had so bored her initially was now engaging her, assisting the editor on an introductory college linguistics textbook. "I thought I didn't care for this job, I'd been resenting it, it's just a job, part-time, there are so many other things I'd hoped I could do with my life, but—I'm sort of fascinated by this—language, syntax—the way words emerge out of nowhere, you could say—the way words fit together and are in a sense 'objects'—in some languages especially. There's a chapter on visual speech, written language, cuneiform—'pictographs'—how these were replaced by another kind of alphabet—and became extinct . . ." The wonder of it seemed to grip her, as if no one had had such thoughts before.

She was thinking (maybe) she would work as an editor somewhere downstate. Or (maybe) (he didn't want to ask) she was envisioning returning to college, taking courses in linguistics—"It's like that's the key to so much of being human."

(There was this side of her he didn't quite recognize. Intellectual, aggressive. Dissatisfied, as she was ambitious. Not a hint of this in the girl he'd seen on the pedestrian walkway, sexy blood-red mouth and white skirt lifting in the wind about her hips. But she'd allowed him to know, with disarming casualness, that she'd gone to a very good university—in fact, Cornell. She'd had a scholarship covering full tuition. Studying psychology, economics. Had to drop out junior year, return home to help her mother deal with her demented, slow-dying father.)

(*He* had gone to Colgate, later transferred to Syracuse and got his law degree at Cornell. But their years in Ithaca had not overlapped.)

When they'd first met she had confided in him recklessly, dazzling him with secrets, now she confided in him in the way of a needy person, to sink hooks into him. (He was thinking.) It wasn't sexually provocative now, this candor. He didn't find it attractive.

He was beginning to be frightened of her, of what she could wreak in his life. His was a *Rutherford life,* no matter how lightly he took it. Being *Rutherford* you had to acknowledge how whatever you did could cast ruinous light on others with that name; you

had to acknowledge, if you weren't too full of yourself to understand, how you owed it to others bearing that name a measure of
discretion. It frightened him to think how casually, how idly, how
randomly the woman might destroy his life that might look to her
shining and solid as a great suspension bridge but which he knew
to be precarious as a miniature bridge made of cards.

He thought—*But she doesn't really mean it. She doesn't want to
break up our families. She is just testing me.*

HE'D BEGUN TO NOTICE: she wasn't so poised as he'd thought.

She was a good-looking woman but not a beautiful woman.
Something almost coarse in her laughter, the snorting flaring nostrils, bared wet teeth. The way she straddled him, which he'd liked
originally, now he liked less, it had come to seem to him predictable,
plotted. And she was heavy, for a slender woman. Muscled legs and
thighs, and shoulders strong as a swimmer's.

More often now they walked together. If anyone observed, they'd
become friends: Tom Rutherford and the dark-red-haired woman
who was no one anyone knew, not likely a lawyer or paralegal from
his office though probably not one of the office staff either, judging
by the way she behaved with him, laughing up into his face.

He saw eyes moving onto them. He thought so.

And he'd begun to notice: she wasn't so secure as he'd thought.

She was jealous of his interest in other people, fleeting as it was.
Jealous of his decision to pause on the street or in a park, take a photograph of—whoever. As they walked together often without speaking. Or, if she was speaking to him, he wasn't listening but glancing
covertly about.

It was his nature, he wanted to protest. Couldn't help his curiosity!

She observed him squatting to exchange remarks with a toddler,
as the child's mother looked on. Beautiful little caramel-skinned

girl and the mother fleshy-bodied and pretty—dark Caribbean face, eyes shining with excitement. A stranger can make another stranger happy, so quickly.

She felt a tinge almost of rage. Her lover was promiscuous in his soul.

HE'D WANTED TO BE a great photographer. He'd traveled to Rochester, to Buffalo, to New York City to see photography exhibits. Not for years now, but when younger. Cartier-Bresson, Man Ray, Robert Capa, Irving Penn his heroes. Garry Winogrand, Bruce Davidson. Just the fact of lifting a camera, fitting his eye to the lens was exciting to him, or had been.

Happiness is being in one place. The picture fixes you in one place.

HE WASN'T A PARENT of young children, as she was. His children were adolescents, no longer very interested in him, unimpressed with Dad. Neither had the slightest inclination to follow him into law. Neither took photography seriously though both took pictures with their cell phones, constantly. He thought—*Still, they respect me. They would be devastated if our family broke up.*

The wife remained brave, blind. The wife remained resolute and unknowing, blind as the carved figure on the prow of a ship braving all weather.

TENTATIVELY SHE SAID, I think we should stop.

He didn't hear. Didn't reply. Didn't refute.

ALL THOSE WE ARE HURTING, *if they knew. Those who believe that we love them exclusively. If they knew but of course they don't know, we will never tell them. Because we love them, when we are with them. As we love each other, in this place.*

SHE THOUGHT—*None of this has happened. Not in my real life.*

SHE COULD NOT BEAR IT, the intense sexual sensation. It was a kind of seizure. Dark-feathered wing falling sharply in her brain, and then oblivion. In that second she was gone, she could barely move.

He said, Hey. He was concerned, edgy.

He said, Darling? I've got to get back. OK?

She felt a rush of hatred for him, that he could speak so casually, in his ordinary voice. That he could speak at all.

Darling is such a cheap word. Worn like a copper penny, that smells in the hand.

In the bathroom she fumbled dressing. Why didn't he go alone and leave her here, did he think she'd steal something, or leave a demented message on a mirror for someone to discover and raise an alarm. Always waiting for her, she had to use the damned toilet, she knew he was restless thinking of driving home. At a certain point, the man's brain prepares itself for the next sequence of actions, the next scene. The old scene begins to fade.

God damn she'd dropped something, out of her bag. Groping for her toothbrush on the floor that was gritty and needed cleaning. (Why was she always dropping things? Was this new?) (She was frightened: that creeping numbness, sometimes, in her upper spine.)

"Darling? Are you all right?"—tapping at the door, though he'd never have been so rude as to try the doorknob to see if she'd locked it against him.

IN A SICK FANTASY, he'd seen a woman naked in a bathtub sprawled and moaning, and the bathwater rosy with blood from her slashed wrists. He'd seen the bathwater splashed onto the floor. He'd tried the doorknob but the door had been locked against him.

My God my God my God! This can't have happened.

ONCE SHE SAID SUDDENLY, Are you comparing me with her? You promised you would not.

Shocked he protested, Of course I am not! I would not—I could not do that . . .

You are not of her world. She is not of yours. It would be like speaking two languages.

HE'D READ AN INTERVIEW with an executioner at one of the Texas penitentiaries. Capital punishment—(as it was euphemistically called: not capital murder)—was exacted in that state by "lethal injection." It was administered by more than one person, but one man alone was the official executioner; he was the person who delivered the death warrant to the condemned prisoner, incarcerated on death row. All very proper, ritualized! No doubt, there is solace in ritual, at such times. For both executioner and condemned man.

Except, the executioner was retiring. Still relatively young, in his early fifties, but he was retiring—"It catches up with you."

Couldn't bear it, so many condemned men. So many ritual-deaths.

And he, Tom Rutherford, was thinking—"It catches up with you."

He loved her too much. He was distracted from his wife, his children. So distracted from his work, he believed the office staff talked of him worriedly.

The first to know *Something is wrong with Mr. Rutherford!* will be office staff.

The idea of love, a secret love, illicit love—it seemed quaint, precious. The small gemstone you'd found by the shore, of no actual value but flashy, like mica, slipped into a jacket pocket and fingered, held in the hand, secretly, from time to time—"For luck."

If someone asks, what do you have there, in your hand?—you open your hand to display, on the palm, the small gemstone of no value, and you say: "Just something I found by the river."

HIS WIFE IS UNWELL: he can't leave her.

His wife is emotionally fragile: he can't leave her.

His wife has cancer: he can't leave her.

He rehearses, his lips move silently. Any words that can be uttered are but mere *words*—easy to speak, but not so easy to retract.

He doesn't tell her any of this, exactly. But she seems to understand. She is upset. Then she tells him she won't be emotional again. Won't break down again. Won't be weak. I *promise.*

He has made her beg. He is shocked at himself, dismayed. He can't forgive himself. But there is pleasure in it, very likely it will happen again.

DELIRIOUS SMELL OF THE CALLA LILIES she'd brought to the room.

Entering giddy and thrilled, more beautiful than he'd ever seen her, snow melting in her hair, in her eyelashes. Wanting to celebrate, feeling high, giddy and thrilled, for some sort of undisclosed good thing had happened in her life, family-life, work-life, she didn't care to reveal laughing at the expression in his face as she came to him.

TRYING TO BREAK THE SPELL, just a little.

Trying to mitigate the feeling.

Trying to see the woman apart from "love." How another might see her, coolly assessing.

Her clothes, her shoes. Tried to dislike her footwear. Boots, worn at the heel. Chic-stylish clothes from vintage clothing stores, always colorful, a clash of stripes, yet she seemed to calculate the effect, or usually.

Eventually he discovered that she wasn't a very careful or even clean person, for a woman. *His* fingernails might be finely ridged with dirt, truly it meant nothing, only that he'd been doing something involving some sort of dirt or oil, but *her* fingernails finely ridged with dirt looked wrong.

Sometimes, he saw spots or stains in her clothing, that hadn't come out in the wash or in dry cleaning.

None of it mattered. That was the truth he discovered.

He loved her, anything else was trivial.

Wanting to tell her, assure her—*If I am not begging you to leave your husband and marry me it is only because I know you would not— ever—do this. I know that I must not ask you because it would begin the break between us. I am remaining with my wife because my wife needs me, and because I love her, I will always love her though not as I love you.*

If my wife were to say to me, I don't need you—go away; I would go away, at once. And I would beg you to come with me.

THEY MADE LOVE AVIDLY. They made love less often, and so with an air of desperation. Each time they made love she thought— *This is the final time. He is preparing me.* They made love on top of the damp coverlet, or kicked it aside impatiently. They made love as he sat, bare-legged, naked, on that bed with his legs spread, upper thighs not so hard-muscled as he recalled, and she straddled him, determined, but whimpering, his hands cupping her small buttocks, that felt like a child's; it was not a good feeling, it was a cruel sudden feeling; he felt he might injure her, so deeply thrusting into her, as into her belly, the soft moist vulnerable body of the exposed and vul- nerable female. *Oh! oh!*—each outburst like a cry for help, it would be cruel to acknowledge.

Love is what can't be helped. When it waxes, and when it wanes.

Love is what happens when you've been looking another way.

Love is that sensation of something on the back of your neck, tell yourself it's nothing, a strand of hair, at last you touch it and discover it's an insect—you cast off with a curse.

HE DID NOT SAY, finally—*I can't do this much longer. I don't want to hurt you but—there are others I am not able to hurt who mean more to me than you do.*

IT WAS FIVE MONTHS, three weeks, six days from anniversary to anniversary. No formal good-bye, one afternoon she simply failed to show up at the place on Cartwright Street.

He'd been desperate, badly upset. Thinking—*Where is she! I'm so crazy for her.*

He called her cell phone, and she did not answer. Called her repeatedly. Called Fowler's Publishing, and asked for her, and was told that she no longer worked there, she'd quit.

"No longer works there? Are you sure?"

What a question! *Are you sure?*

He would call again, hoping to speak with another party, and hoping for another answer. Only afterward realizing that in so doing he'd spoken her name aloud for the first time, to another person: "'Juliane Deller.'"

A faint smell of calla lilies in the room. Faint rancid-rotting smell, all but imperceptible.

⁂

Like a bone that has been sprained, even broken, but beneath the skin, invisible inside the skin, the marriage healed, and was stronger. So he told himself, plausibly. *Stronger.*

IN A WAKING DREAM he saw her: the lean, angular figure, swathed in purple. The movements of her limbs that were both awkward and graceful, of utter sincerity. Aloud he named: "'Lamentations.'"

All that day, he would recall the dream. Not its specific vision but the emotion it engendered in him of loss, grief, profound remorse.

TELLING HIMSELF—*She must have wanted it, too.* For he'd never heard from her since.

He'd tried to contact her, she had not once tried to contact *him*.

He'd tried to remember their final meeting, which he hadn't guessed was to be final. He wondered if she'd known, at the time. Or if, recollecting their conversation, in retrospect seeing something in his face he hadn't known was there, she'd decided precipitously— *That's it. No more.*

He recalled their lovemaking, now from a little distance. Seeing, as if for the first time, the dimensions of the small room that had contained them, like a gemstone smoldering with radioactivity, in a sealed box.

The oblong window, the wetted wood, damp coverlet on the bed, and a pattern in the coverlet like ferns. And those bits of broken, dried leaves that had blown into the corners of the room, sticking to the bare soles of their feet. The faint-rancid lily-smell.

And her thick kinky-crimped hair, sticky against the nape of her neck. The necklace of carved beads, earthen-hued, he'd bought for her, resting against her neck, damp-glowing skin as she lay beside him sprawled, unclothed—in an ease of intimacy that had come quickly to them, possibly too quickly to be sustained.

She'd smiled happily, stroking the outsized beads, that had been crafted by Ojibway (Ontario) Indians.

"Thank you!"

ADULTERY OF SOME GENERATION preceding his own, when the world was sepia-toned and there were rules, expectations. A world in which it was assumed you knew the statutes.

Like his old cameras that required film, he'd relegated to the back of his photography equipment closet—that was *adultery*. Quaint, outmoded. "Obsolete."

The old way of a sequestered love, marriage, a wife whose happiness depended upon your remaining faithful, children whose "respect" for you was at risk—he hadn't the cruelty (or the courage, that amounted to the same thing) to walk away. He had not.

(SHE'D NEVER ASKED HIM for money, he was thinking.)

(But why, why such a low mean thought? This wasn't worthy of him.)

MONTHS PASSED, A SUMMER—he wasn't waiting to hear from her, not exactly. And now September, and nearing November—the anniversary of their first encounter.

On the pedestrian walkway, the white-muslin skirt lifting around her legs. A stranger, back to him, dark-red hair and no one he knew, why hadn't he walked past, why had he lingered, hungrily his eyes moving on her, even before she'd turned to expose her face—the blood-red mouth, dark bemused eyes. *Of course I see you. I see you seeing me.*

She'd denied it, however.

Many times he'd returned to the bridge, with his camera. Looking for—what?

SHE'D GIVEN HIM JUST A SINGLE GIFT, a DVD of several Balanchine ballets, soon after they'd seen the Martha Graham film. Since he'd expressed enthusiasm for the Graham film.

In her ardent girl's voice that had so charmed him, and then, by degrees, so annoyed him, she'd said that he would "love" the Balanchine dances. She'd expressed the (wistful) wish that they might see some Balanchine together, that summer possibly—the New York City Ballet performed at Saratoga Springs each July.

(He'd thought: What is she thinking? Where would the husband and children be? Where, my wife?)

He'd thanked her for the Balanchine DVD. He'd meant to play it, but had never gotten around to playing it. Probably, he'd never taken it home, he'd find it one day in a desk drawer in his office, or, after his death, clearing out his office, his wife might find it and wonder: Balanchine? Why?

SEARCHED FOR THE PHOTOS he'd taken of her sleeping. Her unclothed body partly covered by a rumpled sheet. Crevices, shadows. A strand of hair across her forehead.

In his computer he searched for the photos until at last, he gave up. Where?

THE STORY WOULD END, he thought. He had to see her again.

Months later when he'd forgotten her, the lovemaking in the damp bed, the sharp sweet smell of calla lilies in his nostrils, their languorous limbs tangled together—months beyond the anniversary of their first meeting he began to think of her so keenly, he could not sleep.

His wife, his children—at the epicenter of their lives he felt famished, diminished as a husk. They never saw *him*.

A year, and more. And then one day in early summer he drove impulsively out of Fleuve Bleu on Route 17 east into the rolling hills of the Adirondacks, to the Village of Rensselaer Falls.

He hadn't called her. He hadn't wanted to risk calling her.

He made his way to Eagle Road. (Not Eagle Street—he'd misremembered.) His heart was beating quickly in the exhilaration of great danger though he told himself, consoled himself—*At any time, I can turn back. I will turn back.*

Eagle Road was a narrow winding road at the edge of the village. There were sidewalks on Eagle Road but they were sunken, overgrown with weeds. At 44 Eagle Road a gravel driveway dipped down to a stand of straggly pines and beyond the pines an idiosyncratic house of stucco, brick and wood, 1950s Frank Lloyd Wright–inspired "modern" that looked as if it had been built by an untrained hand.

There were vertical panes of glass, a front door of hammered copper. He recalled that she'd mentioned her husband having some talent for carpentry, but she had not elaborated and he hadn't inquired.

The house was both eye-catching and shabby: a property its owners couldn't maintain as it was meant to be maintained. Like other lots on Eagle Road, this lot was thinly wooded and had no proper lawn; here were wild-growing ferns, tall grasses and shrubs. A meandering gravel walk led from the driveway to the front door of the house.

There was an attached garage with a battered-looking overhead door. Scattered in the front yard were scrap-metal sculptures: horse, pig, parrot on perch, windmill. Some of the sculptures were rusted and others were brightly painted in patchwork colors, as a child might have painted them.

His heart contracted—*She lives here? Here.*

It had not occurred to him that by this time, Juliane and her family might have moved away.

In his vehicle at the top of the driveway he sat, uncertain. He didn't want to attract attention, yet it didn't seem, in this neighborhood of scattered houses, that his car was likely to attract attention.

And then he saw the garage door lifting, slowly. And a figure appeared, a female figure, thinner than Juliane had been, he was sure—a daughter? This person was ushering a younger girl out of the garage. They were headed for the top of the driveway. (Were they going to bring recycling bins back to the house? He saw emptied bins at the curb.)

He saw then, the individual he'd thought was a girl was Juliane. Walking hand in hand with a child of about eight. Oh, but she was far thinner than he remembered—she wore a shirt, jeans, sandals. The shirt fell loose from her shoulders and the jeans fell loose from her hips as if it might be held in place by only a belt. Even at this distance he could see the hollow at the base of her throat. She was bareheaded and there was something wrong—her hair wasn't stirring in the wind, it was much shorter, thinner. Her beautiful dark-red hair! He felt a stab of sheer horror, she'd been ill and he had not known— was that it? She'd kept herself hidden from him in her illness.

These months, now a year they'd been apart and not in communication—he'd imagined the woman coldly indifferent to him, or angry with him, that he had not loved her as much as she'd hoped to be loved; he had not loved her as much as she'd loved *him*. All that time he'd imagined her healthy. He could not have thought of her as other than healthy. It had been painful to him, a blow to his masculine pride, that the woman had been the one to walk away from *him*.

Now, he pressed his foot on the gas pedal. (Was she looking up at the road? Had she seen?) Quickly, he drove away.

No idea where he was going. His thoughts beat wildly in his head like panicked bats.

For a while he drove blindly. He hadn't meant to come to this place and now—he was desperate to escape. Yet, he didn't leave Rensselaer Falls. He found himself parked beside a stream, a rocky creek or narrow river on a road that intersected with Eagle Road, in a region of boulder-strewn hills. He wondered if this was the Blue River—Le Fleuve Bleu? He tried to imagine the geography. A map of Lawrence County.

He thought—*But why am I here! What does it mean, I am here . . .*

THEY'D ROLLED THE RECYCLING BINS down the driveway. Yellow plastic for cans and bottles, green for paper, cardboard. Rolling the bins was noisy, reckless. It wasn't a good idea, the plastic bins dented easily.

In the house she felt faint, breathless. She was switching on lights, for dusk had come early.

She hadn't seen him at the top of the drive. Or rather, she hadn't realized that she'd seen him.

Had it happened again, as it had happened on the bridge over the Blue River? She'd seen the man, but not clearly. He had seen her—that was certain. She'd felt the impact of his seeing her. In a haze of sudden alarm her eyes had passed over him, the SUV at the top of the drive, a stranger's car, and the driver was a stranger, behind the wheel. For she had no expectation of seeing the man, ever again. She had no wish to see him. He had not loved her enough—he had loved her, but not enough. The shock and terror and exhaustion of her illness, and her need to deny the seriousness of her illness to the children, had ravaged her as fiercely as the months of chemotherapy had ravaged her, and left her burnt clean of desire. Her bones felt lighter, as if the marrow had been sucked out. She did not fear what would happen next, if the cancer recurred. For she had already considered her death, she'd come to think of it as *her death*, unique to her. But it would not be a violent and surprising death, not that. Not the death of action movies, that leaves the victim screaming in terror. The cancer-death is slower, slow-paced. The cancer-death is mitigated by medication that is a kind of lethal injection, a numbing that rises along the spine, into the chest-cavity, the throat and the brain. It is a numbness that is peace as you see that your death is not separate from you but is you in the way that nourishment taken into your body is transformed into you.

In the fatherless house the children often bickered. The girl was eight and small for her age. The boy was eleven, wiry and sharp-elbowed. The one was a handful of feathers, the other a handful of pebbles. Now, seeing the mother's face, they paused and stared. The girl came to her, wanting to be embraced. The boy held back, too old now for embraces, and too sharp-elbowed. For a year they'd been frightened of their slow-speaking mother, who'd once been so fluent and so funny, but they had not—ever—thought that she could die, for that was an unthinkable thought. That was not a thought you allowed in the window, that was a thought you kept outside the window as a screen sensibly keeps out hornets, flies, mosquitoes. Absolutely sensible, that is what you do—you keep such things out. That is what she did. And the father, the children's father, of course that is how he behaved—*You can't die. Won't die. It's treatable. We both know—well, we know—lots of people who . . . We know, and they didn't die. Most of them.*

And once he'd said to her, in anguish—*You're selfish! You're letting this happen!*

In the end the children's father hadn't been able to bear it. She had been such a young beautiful woman, he couldn't bear to see the change in her. And so she'd sent him away, taking pity on him. He hadn't wanted to go—he'd protested—yet in relief he'd left the house at 44 Eagle Road. He returned when she invited him for dinner, and he visited with the children and took them to children's movies, child-meals, in neutral territory. He returned if she beckoned him, but he did not beg to return permanently. He hadn't suggested a legal separation, still less divorce. Each was thinking—*Why? Our time together is ending of its own volition.*

Now she hears a vehicle at the top of the driveway, another time. The coppery taste of chemicals at the back of her throat has grown sharper. She thinks—*But he wouldn't! He has let me go.*

She is frightened, but she is resolute. She steps outside shivering in her shirt and jeans. The children have been drawn off, to TV. The wind has picked up. She has lost nearly twenty pounds, her clothes hang on her. Badly she has missed the Blue River, the smell of the river, the wind whipping her thick crimped hair. She'd ended her job with the textbook publisher, she'd told him about the cancer, the biopsy and the surgery and the chemo, eight months of chemo that lay ahead. She had not told anyone else in Fleuve Bleu.

She was thinking of him, Rutherford—the first, hard kisses that had taken away her breath. The randomness of it, love as haphazard as playing cards blindly dealt. He'd seen her above the river, and a second time he'd seen her, in pelting rain. She must've seen him, of course. She is smiling, remembering. His hand, his playful hand, fingers clasping hers and gripping tight, so she can't pull loose. Oh, she misses him!—she has missed him. Her heart is beating painfully, she is having difficulty breathing. Then she sees him again, at the top of the drive. He hasn't turned into the driveway, his SUV is parked on the road where she'd imagined him, how many evenings at this time. The headlights are on. He has climbed out of the vehicle and is standing now at the top of the drive. Tentatively, as if he isn't sure who she is, or whether she will remember him, he lifts a hand to her in greeting. Furiously she calls out to him—"Go away, God damn you! Go away please." Her voice is weaker than she'd anticipated, she isn't sure that he has heard her.

He is going nowhere. She sees that, at the foot of the gravel driveway, wind whipping the thin fabric of her jeans around her tensed legs.

Big Burnt

From the start the plan had been to include a woman. Not *the woman* but *a woman*.

Yet it hadn't been clear if the woman would be a witness or whether the woman would be involved in a more crucial role.

"DON'T PANIC."

Her eyes glanced upward, in alarm. Somehow, without her awareness, the sky had darkened overhead. The temperature was rapidly dropping and the wind was rising.

At the wheel of the small rented outboard boat the man pushed the lever that controlled its speed and the boat leapt forward slapping against waves in a quasi-perpendicular way that was torture to the woman though she was determined not to show it.

"We're not in trouble. We'll make it. Just hang on."

The man spoke almost gaily. Quickly the woman smiled to assure him—*Of course!*

They were only a few minutes out onto the wide wind-buffeted lake when lightning flashed overhead in repeated spasms like strobe lights and there followed a deafening noise like shaken foil, many times magnified.

The lake was the color of lead. The first raindrops were flung against their faces like buckshot.

The woman, shivering, was sitting so close beside the man, she could easily have lifted her hand to touch his wrist, that was covered in coarse dark hairs; she might have touched his shoulder in a gesture of (wifely) solicitude. If the situation were not so desperate she might have—(playfully, provocatively)—pressed her hand lightly against the nape of the man's neck.

He liked her to touch him, sometimes. Though he rarely touched her in such casual ways. His sidelong glance at the woman would be startled as if she'd touched him intimately.

(But is not all touch intimate?—the woman reasoned. For her, *touch* was the most intimate speech.)

For the past two and a half days the woman had been calculating how to make the man love her. The man had been calculating how, when the interlude at Lake George was over, and he'd returned alone to his home in Cambridge, he would blow out his brains.

EARLIER THAT DAY, when they'd taken the boat to Big Burnt Island, several miles from the marina at Bolton's Landing, the lake had been calm, even tranquil—*glassy*. Vast lake and vast sky had reflected each other in an eerie and surpassing beauty that made the woman's heart contract with happiness.

"What a beautiful place you've brought me to, Mikael!—thank you."

The woman spoke warmly like a heedless child. In an instant she was the ingénue Nina of *The Seagull*. She heard her voice just too perceptibly loud, rather raw, over-eager. Yet the man who did not smile easily smiled then with pleasure. Yes, this was what he liked to hear from a woman's mouth. For indeed the vast lake surrounded by pine trees was beautiful, and *his*.

Now, a few hours later, the glassy surface of the water had vanished as if it had never been. All was agitated, churning. The wind made everything confused for it seemed to come from several directions simultaneously. The sky that had been a clear, pellucid blue that morning was bruised and opaque.

"Christ! Hang on."

"What?—oh."

The man was white-lipped with fury. On their left, out of nowhere, a large motorboat bore upon them like a demented beast. In normal daylight this twenty-foot boat would have been dazzling-white like their rented boat but the light was no longer normal but dimmed, shadowy. In normal weather boaters on Lake George were courteous and respectful of others but with the approaching storm, no. In the wake of the larger boat that crossed their path their boat shuddered as if rebuked. *Thump-thump-thump* the small boat slapped against waves sidelong, slantwise.

Don't panic. He will hate you if you panic. You are not going to drown.

She had an old terror of collision, chaos. A childhood terror of dark water covering her mouth, a panicked swallowing of filthy water. The sensation of water up her nose, recalled from swimming as a girl in a school pool amid a flailing of arms and legs of other girls, thrashing, splashing, sinking, gasping for air, and yet there came water up her nose and into her head feeling as if it were about to explode.

The woman gripped the seat beneath her. Tightly with both hands. Crazed waves in the wake of the rushing boat were making her head pitch forward, and then back; forward, and back. She was being shaken like a rag doll. Her neck ached alarmingly—whiplash?

Frothy water was beginning to wash into the boat, onto the woman's feet, wetting her legs, her hair and her face.

Deftly, or perhaps it was desperately, the man turned the wheel, that the boat might roll with the waves. Always he was shifting the speed lever—forward, back. And again forward, and back. The boat jerked, bucked crazily. But no sooner was one danger past than another boat, not so large as the first, but large enough to stir waves like punitive slaps against the smaller boat, crossed their path from the right, at a fast clip.

Just. Don't. Panic.

She'd resisted the impulse to press her hands against her eyes, in a childish gesture of *not-seeing.*

Surely they would not be capsized on the lake? Surely they would not *drown*?

She didn't think so. Not possible. Well—not *probable.*

This was Lake George, New York, in late August. This was not a remote region of the Adirondacks. Or a third world country vulnerable to typhoons or tsunamis where thousands of people died in the equivalent of a key-click. There had to be rescue boats in a severe storm—yes? The equivalent of the U.S. Coast Guard?

The woman was determined to smile, that the man would see how she *was not panicked.* The woman recalled her children, when they'd been young. They too had tried not to show fear, sorrow, grief when these emotions had been perfectly justified. They had tried *not to cry broken-heartedly* when their daddy departed with a (vague, guilty, unconvincing) promise to return. The woman who was their mother had loved them fiercely, seeing this: stoicism in such young children! Surely this was a kind of child abuse.

On the island, the woman had seen flashes of heat lightning in the sky, in the distance. Silent flashes, like illuminated nerves or veins. The man had taken no notice, most of the sky had been clear at this time. But the woman had noticed other boats leaving the island and had asked—"Will there be a storm? Should we leave now?" and the man had merely laughed at her.

"Don't panic. We have plenty of time."

Once they were in the boat, however, he'd seemed surprised by the quick-gathering thunderclouds. The rapidly increasing wind, the drop in temperature and the first raindrops chill as hail striking the bow of the boat, the windshield, their faces. He'd asked her to retrieve their nylon rain-jackets from the back of the boat, and the bulky bright orange life vests he'd disdained earlier in the day.

Being taken by surprise was upsetting to the man, the woman could see. She had not ever known any man who'd liked surprises unless the surprises were of his own doing.

Now came rain pelting like machine-gun fire pocking the water's surface. Amid the churning waves visibility was poor. There were drifting mists. The woman peered anxiously ahead—she had no way of telling if the boat was making progress.

Beside her the man was steering the boat with the fiercest concentration. His face was tense with strain. His jaws were clenched. He was enjoying this frantic race across the lake—was he? In his mostly sedentary life in which he gave orders to others, subordinates, and was not accustomed to being challenged or questioned let alone actively opposed, this lake crossing to the marina at Bolton's Landing had to be an adventure, the woman thought. Several times he'd admonished her not to panic, she had to surmise that it was panic the man most feared, in himself as in others.

He'd told her when they'd first arrived at Lake George that he knew the lake *like the back of my hand*. This was not an arrogant boast but rather a childlike boast and so the woman had smilingly questioned whether a person did indeed know the back of his own hand, and could recognize a picture of his hand among the hands of others?

But the man hadn't heard her (quite reasonable, she'd thought) query. Or if he'd heard, he disdained schoolgirl paradoxes.

The woman had examined the back of her own hand. Her hands. She was shocked to see—what, exactly?— had her hands, already in her early forties, begun to age, to betray fine, faint lines, odd little discolorations, freckles? Or was she imagining this? But there was no doubt, she couldn't have identified her hands pictured among the hands of other women her own age.

Sometimes, glimpsing by chance her reflection in a shop window or a reflecting surface, the woman thought with a quizzical smile—*But who is that? She looks familiar.*

The man had no time for such caprices. His mind was not a mind to "wander" but was rather a problem-solving mind, or rather brain, sharp and fine-tuned and galvanized by challenge. When he ran, he ran—for a specifically allotted amount of time. When he walked, he walked—swiftly, with a minimum of curiosity. Driving a vehicle he drove swiftly and unerringly though consumed in thought, *thinking*. In any public neutral space through which he was merely passing Mikael Brun had no time to waste merely *seeing*.

As he'd claimed to know the vast lake *like the back of my hand*—its inlets, its shoreline, its myriad large and small islands, the mountains in the near distance (in particular Black Mountain)—so too he knew the little fifteen-foot outboard he'd rented that morning at the marina in Bolton's Landing for he'd once owned a near-identical model, trim and compact and dazzling-white with a canopy and a sixty-five-horsepower motor, purchased in the bygone days of a marriage now disintegrated like wet tissue.

Did the woman dare ask the man about this marriage? She did not.

The man had come to a point in his emotional life at which he had no need to articulate *My marriage* but only to feel the edginess and dread of one who has come too close to a precipice, without needing to give his fear a name.

Intuitively the woman understood. The woman was adept at reading the secret lives of others, that are presented to us in code; she could sense the man's fear of something not to be named, and would make herself indispensable in combating it.

That morning the man had deftly steered the small boat between color-coded buoys on the route to Big Burnt. He'd had no trouble avoiding the trajectories of other boats. To his admiring companion he'd pointed out landmarks onshore, and mountain peaks in the distance. But now in heavy rain he was having difficulty steering a course to take him to the inlet that contained the marina—though (of course) as he drew nearer, he would begin to recognize crucial landmarks.

Unless, as in a nightmare, he'd forgotten these landmarks. Or the landmarks had ceased to exist.

When the rain had first begun, they'd put on light nylon rainjackets, with hoods. But now, as rain and wind increased, the man conceded that they might put on life preservers also.

When the woman had difficulty adjusting the bulky orange vest that was much too large for her he'd tied it for her, in a lull in the storm, to see that it was properly secured.

The gesture had been curiously tender, protective. The woman was touched, for the man did not always behave toward her in a way that signaled affection, or concern; often, the man seemed scarcely aware of her. She wondered if when he'd secured the ties of the life preserver the man was thinking of his children when they'd been young, as she often thought of her children, not as they were at the present time but as they'd been years ago, requiring their mother for the simplest tasks.

Impulsively she thanked her companion with a quick kiss on the mouth. He laughed as if surprised, and a flush came into his rain-wetted face, that had a slightly coarse, just slightly pitted skin as if it had been abraded with some rough substance. "Mikael, thank you! I feel like"—the woman hesitated, not quite knowing if this was the right thing to say—"one of my own children. Years ago."

To this feckless remark the man did not respond. She had noted how, frequently, it was his way to smile stiffly and in silence when another's remarks baffled or annoyed him.

I can love enough for two. You will see!

The storm-lull had ended. The boat was bucking and heaving and the man had to grab the steering wheel, quickly.

It was at that moment that the woman happened to glance behind them, to see to her horror that water was accumulating in the back of the boat: backpacks, towels, articles of clothing, bottles were awash in water; the back was alarmingly lower than the front. But when she nudged the man to look he brushed her hand away irritably and told her there was no danger, not yet for Christ's sake, and *not to panic.*

"Are you sure? Mikael—"

"I've told you. *Don't panic.*"

If the small boat were to capsize, or to sink—if it were swamped, and they were thrown into the turbulent lake—they would be kept from drowning by the life vests. Still, the woman was frightened.

She recalled a canoeing accident at a girls' summer camp in the Catskills years ago when she'd been eleven years old and away from home for the first time in her life; inexperienced girls had been allowed to canoe, and one of the girls in her cabin had drowned—the canoe she'd taken out onto a lake with another girl had overturned, she'd fallen into roiling water screaming and within seconds disappeared from view as if pulled down by an undertow.

Lisbeth had been in another canoe, staring in horror. No one seemed to know what to do—no one was a good enough swimmer, or mature enough to attempt a rescue—by the time an adult came running out onto the dock it was too late.

She'd never been able to comprehend what had happened except that one of her cabin-mates was gone and the camp shut down and sent all the girls home, a week early. Soon after she returned home she could not recall the name of the drowned girl.

Yes but her name was Fern. Of course you remember.

She could cling to the overturned boat if that were possible—if the boat didn't sink. That had been the drowned girl's mistake—

she'd panicked, tried to swim, failed to grab hold of the canoe as the other girl had done. Lisbeth's own terror she would transform into the sheer stubborn hopefulness of one who *would not drown.*

Oh but where was the marina? How far away, the southwestern shore of Lake George? She did recall a narrow inlet—passing close by land on their way out into the lake—but she had no idea where this was and she did not dare ask the man another time.

She remembered an American flag stirring in the wind, high above the marina dock. Vivid-red-striped, white stars on blue background, triumphant in morning sunlight like something painted in acrylics. The flag was so positioned, she supposed, to reassure persons like herself uneasy on the open lake, that they were nearly safe, returning to land. Her eyes filled with tears of yearning, to see that flag again and to know that the ordeal on the lake was nearly over.

THE MAN'S NAME WAS MIKAEL BRUN. The woman's name was Lisbeth Mueller. They were forty-nine and forty-three years old, respectively.

Each was unmarried. Which is not altogether synonymous with *single.* Between them they had accumulated three ex-spouses. And five children of whom the eldest (nineteen) was the man's and the youngest (seven) was the woman's.

The two were—technically—lovers; yet they were not quite friends. It was painful to the woman (though knowing that this was a thought the man wasn't likely to have) that they were not a *couple* but *two.*

A casual observer at their lakeside motel in Bolton's Landing, at the marina that morning or on Big Burnt Island through the day— (obsessively the woman would afterward contemplate such "pictures" frozen in time as a way of trying to comprehend the man's motives in behaving as he'd done)—might plausibly have mistaken them for a married couple: middle-aged, in very good physical condition and just slightly edgy as if they'd had a recent quarrel and wanted to avoid one another. The woman, quick to smile. The man more likely to frown, glancing about as if distracted.

He is looking for someone. Something.

That is why he has come back, to look.

Were the two long-married, thus invisible to each other? Or were the two not married, nor even lovers? The casual observer might have noticed how the man held himself aloof from the woman, as if unconsciously; though meaning her no ill will, he simply forgot to hold open a door for her, for instance, so that she knew to come forward quickly behind him to press her hand against the door, to hold it open for herself in a graceful gesture lost to the man; when the man conferred with the lank-limbed boy at the marina who was preparing the boat for him, the woman stood by alert and attentive, though neither the man nor the boy would acknowledge her. The woman had perfected a small smile for such limbo-situations in which, though in physical proximity to her companion, she somehow did not exist until he recalled her.

In the light wind, the woman's tangerine-colored scarf blew languidly over her face. Somehow, without her knowing, she'd become the sort of woman who wears such scarves even before there is a need to hide a ravaged neck.

The man wore a baseball cap to shield his eyes from the sun. The man also wore (prescription) sunglasses. His jaws glittered with a two-day beard that gave him a look of mild debauchery. Yet the man was speaking quietly, wistfully to the marina attendant:

"I first came to Lake George forty-six years ago—that is, I was brought as a small child. My parents camped on Big Burnt for weeks in the summer. I've come back often—though I've missed a few years recently . . ."

But why did the man feel obliged to tell this to the lanky-limbed teenager in shorts and T-shirt, how did he expect the boy to respond?

The woman was embarrassed for her companion, that he spoke so frankly to a stranger. Clearly, this was out of character. Mikael Brun barely spoke to *her*.

"Same as my dad, I guess," the boy said, not looking up from what he was doing in the boat, "—except he lived here year-round."

"You've camped on Big Burnt?"—eagerly the man asked.

"Some islands we camped on, I guess. But I don't remember their names." The boy paused, shifting his shoulders uncomfortably. "Hasn't been for a while."

Lived. The man had not heard the boy say *lived*. The woman sensed this.

In Cambridge, Mikael Brun was often stiffly formal with strangers, and even with acquaintances and colleagues; his manner was never less than civil, but he wasn't a naturally friendly man. As a prominent scientist at Harvard he'd cultivated the poise of a quasi-public figure who, even as he seems to be welcoming the interest of others, is inwardly repelling this interest.

When they'd checked into their lakeside motel Mikael had engaged the proprietor in a similar conversation about Bolton's Landing, Lake George, and the Adirondacks generally; he'd asked the proprietor questions intended to establish that they knew some individuals in common in the area. And the proprietor had certainly known of Big Burnt Island though he had not ever camped there.

Lisbeth had thought of her companion—*He is lonely. Lonelier even than I am.*

She felt a surge of hope, knowing this. For the weakness of the man is the strength of the woman.

He'd called her out of nowhere, to ask her to accompany him to Lake George for a few days at the very end of August. It would make him very happy, he said, if she would say *yes*.

Astonished by the call, needing to sit down quickly (on the edge of a rumpled bed in her bedroom) as faintness rose into her brain, the woman had murmured *Yes maybe*—she would have to check her schedule.

She scarcely knew Mikael Brun. She'd had an unfortunate experience with the man the previous year, which she would not wish to repeat; yet, when she'd heard his voice on the land line, she'd felt a stab of hope, and happiness. She'd thought—*He has forgiven me.*

Lisbeth Mueller was an actress, or had been an actress in regional theaters and on some daytime TV, whose primary source of income came now from teaching in the speech and drama departments in local universities. Of her recent projects she was most proud of having staged a multi-ethnic production of *A Midsummer Night's Dream* conjoined with an original, collaborative drama of the sociology of urban immigrant life from the perspective of first-generation American-born undergraduates at Boston University.

Among Lisbeth's fiercely loyal circle of theater friends and acquaintances in the Cambridge-Boston area, ever-shifting and diaphanous as the trailing, undulating tendrils of a great jellyfish, it was believed that her considerable talent as an actress had never been fully realized. Married too young, children at too young an age, two divorces, numerous men who'd exploited her trusting nature, career missteps, misjudgments—how swiftly the years had gone, and how little, except for the children, and her reputation for stubborn integrity, Lisbeth had to show for them. It was difficult for her to believe, waking in the early hours of the morning as if an alarm had rung somewhere close by, that her career wasn't still in its ascendency: the next audition would be the catapult to long-delayed recognition . . . And there was always teaching in which she threw herself with the zeal and enthusiasm of a seasoned ingénue, always the hope that, experience to the contrary, she would be offered a more permanent contract than simply the three- or one-year contracts given adjunct instructors like herself.

"'Adjunct'! I don't think we have 'adjunct instructors' in our department. I know we don't have anything like 'adjuncts' at the Institute"—so Mikael Brun had remarked, like a man discussing a rare disease.

How did you meet Mikael Brun?—the woman who'd accompanied him to Lake George would be asked. *What did you know of Mikael Brun's state of mind?*

And she would say, for this was the awkward truth, that she had no clear memory of when they'd first met, only a (vague) memory of their being (re)introduced to each other, at one or another social gathering in Cambridge. Not frequently, but occasionally over the past several years since Lisbeth's separation and divorce they'd "seen each other" in interludes of varying intensity. Lisbeth berated herself for being (nearly almost) always available to the man. (Of course, she saw other men in the interstices of seeing Mikael Brun. Always she was hoping that a relationship with another man would take predominance in her life, that she might forget Mikael Brun altogether; but this had not yet happened.) Once he'd brought her a dozen blood-red roses after he'd seen her in *The Cherry Orchard* and they'd been drinking together in her house when Mikael said, in an outburst of emotion, that lately he'd been feeling the *need to try again* . . . And this too, in the faintly bemused, faintly incredulous tone of a man describing a rare pathology.

He had not stayed with Lisbeth that night, however. Or any other night.

And then, he'd been furious with her when she'd had to leave a dinner party to which he'd brought her, having had an unexpected call from a friend who'd had a medical emergency that day, and could not bear to be alone. Livid with indignation Mikael had said to Lisbeth, not quite in an undertone, that, if she left the dinner, she shouldn't expect to see him again; Lisbeth was stricken with regret and tried to explain that she couldn't ignore the call, a plea for help— "Please understand, Mikael. I'd rather be here. I would rather be with you." Her oldest friend in Cambridge had had a sort of seizure, perhaps a small stroke; the woman simply could not bear to be alone that night, and had called Lisbeth out of desperation.

Lisbeth had smiled at Mikael Brun most winningly, like Desdemona beguiling Othello. But the man had been unmoved. It was astonishing to her, he'd been unpersuaded by her appeal; for wasn't Mikael Brun renowned as a man of generous instincts, himself; wasn't he a legendary figure with students, post-docs, younger scientists? Lisbeth had said, faltering, "Well—I won't go. I'll call Geraldine and explain that I can't see her until tomorrow." But Mikael said, "No. Go to her. Whoever she is, go. I'm leaving, myself." Others at the dinner had seemed not to be listening to the two as they spoke rapidly together in an adjoining room.

In the end, Lisbeth left the dinner, her host having called a taxi for her. By the time the taxi arrived, Mikael Brun had departed.

How stunned she'd been by the man's fury! It had been in such disproportion (she thought) to the situation. He'd looked as if he'd have liked to hit her.

She'd wondered if it meant that Mikael Brun was in fact attracted to her, and possessive of her; or whether his behavior was just mean-spirited male vanity.

I'm sorry, Mikael. I don't think I want to see you again.

Or simply, *I'm sorry. I don't want to see you again.*

These terse words Lisbeth prepared, but Mikael Brun had not called her.

It was the story of her life! Lisbeth Mueller was the radiantly smiling person to whom others turned in desperation, like stunted plants in need of sunshine. Patiently she listened to them, like a therapist; unlike a therapist, she didn't charge a fee. (Though if she'd been a therapist she might have had a steady income, at least.) She was kind, generous, unjudging. She had not the personality for the rapacious competition of the stage. She was never ironic and may even have not quite understood what "irony" was—as she'd been accused of by more than one man. Possibly it was easy to take such a woman for granted, even to betray her, who seems to demand so little from others, while freely offering so much.

But then, after several months, Mikael Brun called her. His voice was tremulous over the phone. He made no acknowledgment that months had passed since he'd last spoken to her as if he'd forgotten the circumstances but he did sound contrite, hopeful.

"You will, Lisbeth? You'll come with me?"

"I said—I'm not sure. If the children can stay with their father a few more days . . . They're at Aspen."

"You're—free? And you'll come with me to Lake George?"

Had he not heard? *Children, their father. Aspen.*

"Well, yes, I think so. Yes."

Impulsively she spoke, overcome by emotion. She would not have been prepared for her reaction to the sound of the man's voice.

Mikael Brun continued to speak, excited, near-ecstatic. Through a buzzing in her ears Lisbeth could barely make out his words. Had she been mistaken, all these months?—had the man been waiting to hear from *her*?

After they hung up Lisbeth remained sitting on the edge of the bed, somewhat dazed. Her heart beat sharply, quickened. Her heart had not beat in this way for a long time.

Afterward she would realize that she'd been waiting for the phone to ring again, and for Mikael Brun to decide that he'd made a mistake and would have to cancel their plans after all. For he'd called the wrong woman.

ELABORATE PLANS HE'D MADE for the weekend, which had to include the woman. A woman.

And the Monday following, when he'd have returned home.

Last things he'd prepared with care. So long he'd contemplated these, with the thrill of toxic bitterness, it was a relief when the *last things* were finally executed.

At the time, in his fiftieth year, Mikael Brun was a distinguished scientist, professor of psychology at Harvard and director of the Harvard Institute for Cognitive and Linguistic Research. In Cambridge it was generally believed that Brun was on an extended sabbatical leave from Harvard, freeing him to spend all his time at the Institute; in fact, the leave was unpaid, and open-ended, while Brun was being (secretly, by a committee of professional peers and high-ranking Harvard administrators) investigated for "suspected improprieties" in his research. A former post-doc in Brun's laboratory had reported him for having purposefully misrecorded data in a number of experiments, subsequently published in leading professional journals. Vehemently Brun had denied the charges; he had no doubt that he had not committed "scientific misconduct" (as it was primly called) either willfully or inadvertently; yet, the effort to clear his name would be demeaning, exhausting; he thought of Shakespeare's Coriolanus, he would not lower himself to the level of the rabble, to save his own career. And his disintegrated marriage, and the disenchantment of his children—he was weary of the effort of trying to make his fickle daughters love him again, and prefer him to their mother as they'd once done.

To the north. I will go to the north. The words haunted him like words from a song of long ago when life had been simpler and happier.

Of course he would never do it, that way—so crudely . . .

Blow out my brains was a phrase he sometimes heard himself say, with a bluff sort of heartiness. There was a Chekhovian ring to such a remark, melancholy, yet bemused. A joke!

Still, he would not *blow out his brains* for such a trifle as the meretricious investigation at Harvard. And it was an absurd cliché to ascribe suicide to the breakup of his family, that was hardly a new development in Mikael Brun's life. It was infuriating to him, that others might interpret his suicide in such petty and reductive terms.

Who dies for what is quantifiable dies in shame. The suicide soars beyond your grasp as beyond your ignorant understanding.

One final time, he would return to Big Burnt. He would put his things in order before driving north so that, when he returned, he would not be confronted with the responsibility. He'd come to realize that all the places he had lived had been spoiled for him by the experience of living in them, except for Big Burnt Island.

Impulsively, he called a woman whom he'd known casually, in the years following his divorce; a woman whom he found attractive or in any case sympathetic, an intelligent woman, an uncomplaining woman, with a local reputation as an actress—Lisbeth Mueller. And when he heard the woman's startled voice over the phone he'd thought—*She is the one.* He heard himself ask Lisbeth if she would like to come with him to Lake George, in the Adirondacks, over the long Labor Day weekend.

In an instant he'd felt certain. Something like a leaden vest had slipped from him. There'd been other women he called, or left messages for—(this, Mikael would never tell Lisbeth, of course!)—but Lisbeth Mueller was *the one.*

She was a beautiful woman, or had been. He saw other men appraising her, and took solace in their looks of admiration and (maybe) envy. Several times he'd seen her onstage (only once in a play of substance, by an Irish playwright whose name he'd forgotten) and would scarcely have recognized her, her ivory-skinned face illuminated by stage lights, flawless as her carefully enunciated words.

In actual life, Lisbeth Mueller was not so assured. Often there was faint anxiety in her face, even when she was smiling—a "dazzling" smile. Her manner was gracious, and seductive; she was a woman who is always *seducing,* out of a dread of being rejected. A woman always slightly off balance, insecure. Mikael quite liked it that Lisbeth was always in need of money for the man should provide the money, binding the woman to him for as long as he wished her bound to him.

Seeing Lisbeth Mueller enlivened in his presence, made happy by *him,* he'd laughed with relief and pleasure. Often there was a kind of skin or husk over him, that made relating to others difficult, even breathing in their presence difficult; but that was not the case when he was with Lisbeth, who seemed never to judge, and always grateful for his attention.

It was crucial to Mikael, or had once been—that others might be made happy *by him.* For so long he'd been an outstanding son who'd made his parents happy or in any case proud of him. All of the Brun family, proud of Mikael who'd received a scholarship to an excellent university (Chicago) and had the equivalent of an M.D. (that is, a Ph.D.) from another excellent university (Yale). And now he was a professor at the greatest university of all (Harvard)—in fact, he was the director of his own research institute (though it wasn't clear to the relatives exactly what Mikael was researching).

There'd been a few women whom he'd made happy, if not for long. And the children—for a while.

For a long time he hadn't had a reasonable expectation of happiness for himself. Maybe something like *gratification*—being elected to the National Academy of Sciences at the right time, before most of his rivals; being awarded million-dollar grants, in the days when a million dollars meant something. And of course seeing his ambitious experiments turn out successfully, results published in the *American Journal of Cognitive Science* and elsewhere.

Not happiness but relief. Shrugging off the leaden vest.

As if his lungs were filled with helium. He *could float.*

Neatly laid on the desk in his home study were these items: *Mikael K. Brun Last Will & Testament*; a manila folder containing financial statements, including IRS records; the title for his Land Rover, which he was leaving to a cousin (whom he had not seen in fifteen years); an envelope containing a final check for the Filipina woman who'd been cleaning his house—soiled laundry, stained sinks and toilets, sticky tile floors, carpets—on alternate Mondays for nearly twenty years; envelopes containing detailed instructions for his young laboratory colleagues, who would be devastated by their mentor's death; and envelopes addressed to several former students containing letters of recommendation.

He had tried, and failed, to write letters to his son and his daughters. He had not tried to write to his former wife (whose address he no longer had) nor had he tried to write letters to his own relatives. For words of a personal, revelatory nature did not come easily to him.

Was he hoping that the woman would change his mind in this late stage of his life, that was a possibility but—*no.*

No more than a terminal cancer patient could have a reasonable hope that vitamin C shots will alter the course of his disease.

Had he hoped for the woman to change his mind about the possibility of his being amenable to his mind being changed by any woman—*No. Not that either.*

∽

"Here we are."

At last they'd come to Big Burnt Island. Lisbeth was prepared to find the island remarkable in some evident way, unusually "scenic"—but of course it closely resembled nearby islands, as it resembled the densely wooded Adirondack mainland surrounding the lake. Tall pines, deciduous trees, a hilly landscape, what looked like dry, slightly sandy soil—"It's very beautiful," she said uncertainly.

"Is it!"

Mikael Brun laughed. She supposed he was laughing at her—for having said such banal words, with an air of surprise.

Mikael had been in an exalted mood since early morning. Lisbeth had never seen him so happy, and was grateful for his happiness; he was a man of moods, mercurial and unpredictable. Not happiness itself but the relief of the other's happiness was crucial to her.

At first she'd been uneasy in the rented boat. It did look—*small*. And Mikael had made a droll comment that it wasn't *teak,* only just fiberglass—"Minimally adequate." She could not control a faint shudder as she stepped down into the boat, that immediately rocked beneath her weight, assisted by Mikael and by the lanky-limbed marina attendant. She'd never felt comfortable in any boat for invariably she was forced to recall the canoeing accident of her childhood about which she hadn't wanted to speak to Mikael Brun—of course. He'd have laughed at her for worrying that a fifteen-foot outboard might be as easily overturned as a canoe.

Mikael had rented a boat with a canopy, to protect them from the direct sun. Lisbeth was relieved to see oars and bright orange life preservers stored in the rear.

On their way to Big Burnt Island Mikael kept to a reasonable speed even as other boats rushed past. He was in very good spirits. Lisbeth thought—*How close we are! How intimate.* Seen from a little distance they were certainly a couple.

At Glen Island, where, at the ranger station, Mikael applied for a single-day permit for Big Burnt Island, as at Big Burnt Island itself, he had some initial difficulty securing the boat to the dock. In both cases Lisbeth was pressed into helping him, awkwardly looping a rope around a pole. In both cases the helpless *thump-thump-thump* of the small vulnerable-seeming white boat against the wooden dock was distressing. Lisbeth saw her companion's jaws clench as if he were feeling pain.

But then, at last, at Big Burnt the boat was secured. There were a few other outboards in the small inlet but none at the dock for which Mikael had a permit. Happily he sprang out of the boat and reached down to grasp Lisbeth's hand, to pull her up onto the dock. His fingers tightened upon hers to the point of pain. She laughed breathlessly and protested—"Please! You're hurting me."

Sorry! He hadn't realized, he said quickly. He was wearing a cap with a visor pulled low over his forehead, and dark sunglasses that obscured his eyes. His skin was just slightly coarse, pitted. He seemed excited, mildly anxious. But happier than Lisbeth had ever seen him.

How easy it would be to love such a man, she thought. And easy to be loved by such a man.

It was a foolish, feckless thought. Such thoughts plagued the woman in times of stress in particular, seeming to come from a source beyond her.

In their backpacks were sandwiches, Evian water, towels and the morning's *New York Times*. Mikael intended to swim, and hoped that Lisbeth would also—"I don't enjoy swimming alone." He was scornful of her mild addiction to the daily crossword puzzle but she'd thought that in these circumstances, in protracted intimacy with a man she scarcely knew, focusing on the crossword puzzle would be a way of focusing her excitement.

On land, Mikael took Lisbeth's hand in his and led her briskly uphill. There was no evident path but Mikael's way was unerring through stands of scrub pine—he might have made his way blindfolded.

"This was our campsite. On this promontory."

Mikael's face fairly glowed with excitement and his voice seemed higher-pitched, tremulous.

Fortunately no one was camping on the site. There was a clear and unimpeded view of the lake. Happily Mikael pointed out to Lisbeth mountain peaks in the distance—Black Mountain, Erebus

Mountain, Shelving Rock Mountain. Lisbeth shaded her eyes and stared.

They left their backpacks on a weathered picnic table which, Mikael told her, had been the table his family had used. He was speaking warmly, intensely. Lisbeth knew better than to interrupt as he reminisced of the summers he'd come to the island with his family—"Until everything ended."

"And why was that?"

"Why was *that*?"

She'd said something wrong—had she? Was he angry with her, in an instant?

"I mean—did something happen? So that you stopped coming here . . ."

"Yes. Of course 'something happened.' It's in the nature of our lives that something invariably 'happens'—isn't it? You do something for a finite number of times, but you often don't know when you will do it for the last time. In our case, we knew."

Mikael was speaking matter-of-factly now, as if he were lecturing, and not accusingly; after a while he said, relenting, "It was more than one thing but essentially, my father died."

Lisbeth asked how old he'd been when his father had died and Mikael said, with a shrug, "Too young for him, and too young for me."

Lisbeth touched his wrist in silent commiseration. She did not intrude upon him otherwise for she saw that he was deeply moved. Behind the dark lenses his eyes were rapidly blinking and evasive.

Another time she thought—*He is such a lonely person!*

She thought—*I will make him love me, and that will save him and me both.*

It was another of her bizarre feckless thoughts, that seemed to come to her from a consciousness not her own.

Several times Mikael circled the campsite. He might have been seeking the entrance to an enclosure—a tent? His expression was pained, yearning, tender. He took pictures with his iPhone. He squatted on his heels, oblivious of Lisbeth who stood to the side, waiting uneasily. Indeed it was a beautiful setting—the campsite with an open view of the lake, and the pale blue sky reflected in the lake. She was touched, that Mikael Brun was sharing this private place with her and that they would be bound together by this sharing.

It was a fair bright warm morning on Lake George. As midday approached, the air grew brighter and hotter. There was the likelihood of rain sometime later that day—(so Mikael had mentioned to her at the motel, casually)—but for now, the sky was clear, luminous. Lisbeth noted the abrupt drop beyond the campsite—not a very good site for children. She noted how clean the island was, so far as she could see. Visitors to the islands were forbidden to leave debris and garbage behind; they were required to carry it back with them to the mainland. In that way overflowing trash cans were avoided. The air was wonderfully fresh and the lake water, as Mikael had several times said, was pure enough to drink.

Was it! Lisbeth wondered at this. Hadn't acid rain fallen in the Adirondacks, in recent decades? Was the lake so pure as it had been in Mikael Brun's childhood? Lisbeth noted that they'd brought bottled water with them, in any case.

A thrilling idea occurred to her: she would suggest to Mikael that they camp on Big Burnt sometime, together. Was that possible? Would Mikael be touched by this suggestion, or would Mikael resent her intrusion? *Was* it an intrusion, if he'd brought her here? Lisbeth had no great love of the outdoors, still less camping, but if such a romantic interlude would appeal to Mikael . . .

We decided that Big Burnt would be our honeymoon. Beautiful, remote, Mikael's boyhood place . . .

After some minutes Mikael returned to Lisbeth, walking unsteadily. His cheeks shone with tears. He seized her hand again, as if he'd feared she might be easing away. For a moment she was frightened that he would do something extravagant—he would kiss the back of her hand and cry out that he loved her, like a Chekhov hero.

That was when we knew. Where we knew. Big Burnt.

Instead he led her along a path above the lake, speaking excitedly. Big Burnt was the largest of the Lake George islands, he said—thirty acres. It was so called (his father had said) because Native Americans had once burnt the trees to clear fields for planting.

Now they were beginning to see campers at other sites, in colorful tents. Mikael waved at them, called *Hello!* Lisbeth tried to see how living in a tent on this remote island might be romantic—to a degree. She tried not to be distracted by the cries of children. She tried not to notice campers staring at her with something like envy. (Was this so? But why? Was it so clear that she and Mikael Brun were only day-packing, and not camping here?) To every remark of Mikael's she was smiling, enthusiastic. She did not listen to everything he said but she gave the impression of devoted attention. He was pointing out to her the varying merits of the several campsites, which she would never have seen for herself—some had open views of the lake, some were farther inland; some boasted shady trees and privacy, others did not. Proximity to the lake, proximity to a marshy area, frogs at nighttime, gnats and mosquitoes, morning sun, evening sun, camping platforms, steep ledges, flat rocks, sandy soil—proximity to outhouses. These varying features had to be weighed carefully in choosing a campsite, Mikael said gravely.

"Which would you prefer, if you were camping here?"

"Which would I *prefer*? The campsite my father chose, of course."

What a naïve question Lisbeth had asked her companion! She wondered if she should apologize.

Lisbeth asked if Mikael had brought his own family to the site and Mikael paused before saying vaguely yes, a few times he had.

Mikael paused again as if there were more to say, but he did not say it.

Not such happy times. Not often repeated.

Lisbeth was thinking, she should have known better than to ask Mikael Brun about his ruinous marriage. For a man of such pride and self-regard, any reminder that he had failed at anything would be devastating to him.

He'd become quieter now, walking slightly ahead of his companion. He was thinking—he was *not thinking*—of what awaited him after Lake George.

The *last things*. Boldly and brashly he'd executed the *last things*, that would outlive him, so he had no need to think at all, now.

Now, no question *Why*. For him there was only *how, when*.

Hand in hand they walked along the edge of the island for some time. It had been rare in their relationship that Mikael Brun had ever taken the woman's hand in quite this way—certainly, she could not recall Mikael having done so. By another route they returned, steadily uphill, in the increasing heat, to the picnic table at the Brun family's old campsite. It was a mild shock to the woman, that their backpacks and other items were there—as if indeed they were camping here, and were returning to their temporary home.

Mikael had bought lunch at a deli in Bolton's Landing and had been very particular about the sandwiches he'd ordered; but now, the multi-grain bread was badly soggy, the lettuce limp. The tuna fish salad tasted as if it had been laced with something sugary and the coleslaw, in little fluted cups, was inedibly sweet. Still, Mikael ate hungrily. He had not shaved for two days—(it was a custom, he'd told his companion, that he ceased shaving as soon as he left Cambridge and headed north)—and his beard had come in graying and steely, a surly half-mask. At Lake George, he said, his appetite was always "prodigious."

He saw that the woman was eating sparingly, as she'd eaten sparingly at breakfast. She was having difficulty with the large, damp sandwiches that leaked watery mayonnaise. Each time she drank from the plastic water bottle, she took care to wipe the opening with a paper napkin. But she removed from a plastic bag the several ripe peaches Mikael had bought, offering him one and taking a smaller one for herself.

The peach was delicious. Juice ran down Mikael's chin. His mouth flooded with saliva, the taste of the sweet fruit was so intense.

Shyly, yet with an air of recklessness, the woman was saying that she thought she might like to "try camping" again. She hadn't been camping, she said, for a long time.

Mikael laughed, not troubling to disguise his disbelief. "You camped, at one time? Really?"

"Not in a tent but in a cabin. Just once. I mean—for about a week. When I was a girl."

"Where was this?"

"*Where*? Oh, nowhere—important . . . Somewhere in the Catskills, I think. It wasn't nearly so beautiful as Lake George." Embarrassed by Mikael Brun's bemused scrutiny the woman wiped her mouth. She'd given up on the soggy tuna fish sandwich. She'd used all the paper napkins she'd been allotted. In the dappled shade at the picnic table her face looked appealingly young yet strained.

He did not want to hurt this woman, who had been hurt by other men. Without her needing to tell him this, he knew. For she seemed to open herself to such hurt, and to recoil from it belatedly, like a kind of sea anemone that is exquisitely beautiful but fragile. You begin in awe of such beauty but soon become impatient with it and want to injure it.

"Nowhere I've been has been quite so beautiful as this," the woman said, as if her point had been contested. "You must have been so happy . . ."

"You think that children are made 'happy' by beauty? You should know better, you have children of your own. Children are blind to beauty."

They were silent for a moment. The woman surely felt rebuffed. But she persisted, as if reluctantly—"A terrible thing happened when I was at camp. A girl from my cabin died in a canoe accident . . ."

"It wasn't a canoe. It wasn't an accident."

Mikael spoke with such authority, the woman looked at him. Her smile was faint, quizzical.

"What do you mean? Why do you say that?"

"There was a girl, and she died—she'd been murdered somewhere on Big Burnt. But it wasn't a canoe accident. I was very young and all that I knew was what I could overhear from adults speaking . . . This was in 1972."

The woman was silent, staring at him across the badly weathered wooden table. Her eyes were widened in perplexity and yet in a distrust of her perplexity—should she know what her companion was talking about?

He spoke sometimes in a kind of code. A kind of poetry. Elliptical, elusive. He left me behind. Probably—he left us all behind.

The silence between them was strained for silence between individuals, in an island setting, is far more awkward than on the mainland.

Mikael could not think of more to say because he'd just realized that the subject of the *murdered girl* had been a forbidden subject about which he should not have known. The memory of the girl (whose family had been camping at a site not far from the Bruns at the time of her death) was both scintillant and fleeting like a fish seen in murky water, that has no sooner emerged into sight than it has vanished.

Sylvia. The forbidden name came to him, though he knew not to speak it aloud.

He had not thought of *Sylvia Delacorte* for years. He was sure, it had been most of the years of his adult life.

The girl hadn't been so young, actually—sixteen. To Mikael, at age five, that had not seemed young.

A man had strangled Sylvia Delacorte. Or had he beaten her to death with a rock.

Somewhere in the woods it was rumored to have happened, in the dense interior of the island where no one went. He, Mikael, had been too young to be told what had happened, why the park ranger boat had come to Big Burnt in the early morning bringing such disruption and upset and why adults had stood about in small stunned groups speaking quietly together. His young mother he'd seen embrace herself as if she were cold, and shivering, and when he'd seen her, and she saw him seeing her, she'd frowned at him with a look he'd interpreted as angry and told him to go away, back into the tent.

For the remainder of the summer he'd had trouble sleeping in the tent. In the child-sized sleeping bag which he'd so loved.

Later he'd learned, when he was a little older, that the murderer of Sylvia Delacorte had been a boy of just seventeen. He too had been a camper on Big Burnt, with his parents. One of those boys Mikael had probably seen on the island, older boys whom he'd envied, barefoot, dark-tanned, fearless swimmers off the docks, loud-voiced and jeering, oblivious of a five-year-old.

Mikael was staring at his woman companion whose name—for just a moment—he'd forgotten as he'd forgotten what the thread of their conversation had been, before the subject of the murdered girl had derailed it. Dappled light gave the attractive fair-skinned woman an underwater look as if seen through a scrim of water of a depth of just a few inches.

The woman was telling Mikael how much she'd like to camp on Big Burnt Island, and how much her children would love it. This was a bold statement, Mikael knew. But what could he say in response?— the *last things* determined that, after Labor Day, Mikael Brun would cease to exist.

How vulnerable this woman was!—how perishable, the human

body. That was the human tragedy, that no one could bear who dared to confront it head-on, without subterfuge and hypocrisy.

He was touched that Lisbeth Mueller—(for that was her name, of course he knew it)—had trusted him, coming to Lake George with him on this impulsive venture, and to Big Burnt; he was obliged to protect her, since she had so trusted him.

Yet still it was so—*She too could perish, in the woods. Whatever has happened to one, can happen to another.*

HE ANNOUNCED THAT HE WAS going swimming, and hoped that Lisbeth would join him.

She had told him earlier, in fact several times she'd tried to explain, that she did not much like swimming, and had not swum in years.

Yet he seemed almost not to hear her. When she told him that she didn't think it was a good idea to swim so soon after eating Mikael laughed at her. "That's ridiculous. An old wives' tale."

Zestfully he stripped to his swim trunks, which he was wearing beneath khaki shorts. His legs were covered in coarse dark hairs and were hard-muscled and tanned from the knees downward; his thighs were pale, his torso and upper arms so pale you might imagine you could see veins through the skin. His body was reasonably lean yet flaccid at the waist; his chest and back were covered in wispy, graying hairs. Lisbeth had not seen the man so exposed—that is, on his feet, a little distance from her.

"C'mon! Come with me."

"I didn't bring a bathing suit. I told you . . ."

"Then wade in the water. You won't get your shorts wet. And if you do, a little—so what?"

Because I don't want to! Damn you leave me alone.

But she was laughing, for Mikael meant only to tease.

Lisbeth accompanied Mikael to the edge of the lake, directly below the promontory; she would take iPhone pictures of him swimming, as she'd taken pictures that morning of the lake, the island seen from the lake, the mountains across the lake.

Pictures of herself and of Mikael Brun in the rented boat, taken by the teenaged marina attendant who surely thought the two a married couple. *Thanks!*—Lisbeth had thanked the boy brightly.

You want a record, a commemoration of an interlude so intensely lived. You believe that you do.

Below the promontory there was no beach, only a few misshapen boulders strewn amid sandy soil. Boldly Mikael stepped into the lake and waded out until he was staggering waist-deep in the thick-looking water and then, as Lisbeth watched with some unease, he pushed himself out as if plunging into the unknown and began swimming.

He was a good swimmer, as he'd boasted. Fortunately he seemed to have forgotten about urging her to wade by the shore. A stronger breeze had arisen and the lake was now reflecting a pale-glowering sky.

For some minutes Lisbeth stood watching her companion swim in large, loose circles like a freed child. She smiled to think how totally oblivious of her he was—and yet, she could understand that he wouldn't want to come to this remote place alone.

It was a relief, her companion was swimming so well. Other campers, if they happened to glance in their direction, would think that the middle-aged husband was a competent swimmer but the middle-aged wife standing onshore looking on with a vague smile, probably not. She had no need to think, wryly—*What if he drowns? How will I get back home?*

Lisbeth returned to the picnic table, and began the *New York Times* crossword puzzle. What a relief, to be alone! To be free of Mikael Brun's laser-like attention, if for just a few minutes!

Of course the crossword puzzles were trivial and a waste of time but there was solace in such brain-activity, that blocked unwanted thoughts. Even so, Lisbeth often left the puzzle unfinished. As (she thought) she left so much of her life unfinished. And now, she could not concentrate. It did seem ridiculous to be in this beautiful place and to be focused on a mere puzzle.

Her attention was drawn to the figure in the water, diminished at a distance, vulnerable-seeming, and yet somehow stubborn.

The man was her lover, but not her friend. She had trusted him well enough to accompany him on this end-of-summer trip to the Adirondacks, but in fact she could not trust him, she knew this. In his bemused indifference to her was the promise of betrayal to come. She could not risk this, not at her age.

"I will risk it. Mikael Brun is worth it."

Onstage it is not uncommon for solitary individuals to speak aloud. The convention is that the audience overhears, and the convention is that the audience pretends it is plausible that a solitary individual, brooding, musing aloud, would think so coherently and succinctly. Badly in her adult life Lisbeth yearned for the protective confines of a play—a script. Chekhov, Ibsen, Shakespeare. Recently, she'd performed in a locally praised production of Synge's *Deirde of the Sorrows*—which Mikael had seen, and seemed to have admired.

It was the invention of original speech, spontaneous and unrehearsed speech, that had been so difficult in her life, and had propelled her into a succession of misunderstandings and mistakes.

Farther out, she saw one of the ungainly predator birds Mikael had pointed out from the boat. A prehistoric-looking creature—"great blue heron"—though its feathers were gunmetal gray, not blue. The heron's sharp beak was perfectly suited for aquatic hunting.

At last, after about twenty minutes, Lisbeth saw to her relief that the swimmer was turning back. Streaming water down the length of his body, stumbling just a little, Mikael emerged from the water. He seemed to be searching for her, staring. (He'd removed his dark glasses before entering the water.) She saw the pale torso slick with wet hairs, that looked thin and wispy; the soft, fleshy knobs at the waistline; the legs, that appeared just slightly tremulous after the strain of energetic swimming. When Lisbeth came to him with a towel he was short of breath.

His skin felt cold, clammy. His fingers were chilled. Lisbeth embraced him in the towel and rubbed him vigorously as she might have done with one of her children until he took the towel from her to dry himself. He insisted that the swim had been "terrific" and that next time, Lisbeth would come with him—"You're a good swimmer, after all."

"Not me. You're thinking of someone else, Mikael."

"I'm thinking of *you*."

His mood was brusque, jocular. But still he was short of breath. Ascending along the steep, scrubby path to the picnic table he surprised Lisbeth by leaning on her, just a little.

Almost, her companion seemed to be feeling faint. Lisbeth took hold of his arm, and held him as he walked, in such a way that it wasn't apparent that she was supporting him, if he chose not to notice.

Returned to the picnic table Mikael drank bottled water thirstily, and insisted that Lisbeth drink as well. He asked Lisbeth what she'd been doing while he was swimming and she told him nothing really, for she'd been watching him—"Watching and thinking."

"Yes? Thinking what?"

"How lucky we are to be here, in this beautiful place."

He was regarding her closely. Again, she'd uttered the word *beautiful*. She did not know if *beautiful* was a word that conveyed genuine awe or whether it was merely banal, over-used; she dreaded Mikael Brun disliking her, for the shallowness of her soul.

His soul, she supposed she could never grasp. He was right to be bemused by her efforts to understand his work. When they'd first begun seeing each other she'd tried to read some of his scientific publications—*A Short History of the Anatomy of the Human Brain*,

Cognition and Its Discontents: The Linguistic Wars. She could not read more than a sentence or two of his scientific papers, filled with the terminology, figures, and data of neuroscience. She understood that Noam Chomsky had long been a mentor of Mikael Brun, and had tried to read work by Chomsky on linguistics, biological determinism, genetically transmitted principles of language. But when she'd tried to speak to Mikael about these subjects he'd listened to her with such an expression of patience, if he didn't laugh at her outright as he might have laughed at a bright, naïve child, she'd soon given up.

"Yes. You are correct, Lisbeth. Our lives are purely 'luck'—we are borne along by the current, and imagine we are the ones in control."

In his elevated, jovial mood Mikael pulled Lisbeth with him, to a secluded place beyond the campsite. He'd returned from the arduous interlude of swimming—and from the bout of breathlessness— with a desire to make love, Lisbeth surmised. She chose not to suppose that, in his exalted state, Mikael Brun would have made love with anyone; she chose to believe that he did in fact desire *her*. He was not always affectionate in lovemaking, and seemed more playful now. She wasn't comfortable with the quasi-public nature of this lovemaking but there appeared to be no one within sight. And so she did not resist but returned his kisses avidly, and ran her fingers through his thinned, damp hair. His skull was hard, bony as rock; his breath still came short, but his skin that had been clammy from the water was warming. Soon, it would be aflame.

She had not ever made love in any place quite like this. On the ground—which was hard, uncomfortable against her back—and the sky abruptly overhead—the sky not fair and tranquil as it had been but thicker-textured and bunched together, like blistering paint. Mikael was kissing her eagerly, pressing his mouth hard against her mouth as if wanting to devour her. His unshaven jaws were harsh, abrasive. He was much heavier than she, his limbs longer, dwarfing her as he held her down, in place; a moment of panic came to her, that the man would hurt her, he would suffocate her, half-consciously perhaps, for having intruded in this childhood paradise with her distracting questions. Clumsily he pulled at her clothing, pushing aside her hands though she meant to help. She felt like prey gathered in the beak of a great predator bird, without identity even as the life was being annihilated in her. She was thinking *He has planned this. But not with me.*

Afterward she asked him if as a boy camping on the island he'd had fantasies of bringing girls here and he said curtly, as if the question were offensive to him, "No."

"Really? Not even when you were an adolescent?"

"Big Burnt is like no other place."

He spoke disdainfully, and would say no more.

By quick degrees he fell asleep, one of his arms outstretched and the fingers twitching. Lisbeth tried to lie beside him, in the crook of his arm, not very comfortably. Her breasts, her lower body ached. Her mouth throbbed as if bruised. At a distance she heard the voices of campers, and at a distance the sound of a boat on the lake. Her eyelids were heavy yet her brain was alert, brightly awake. She had not yet slept beside this man for in his sleep he was restless, sighing deeply, shrugging his shoulders, pushing her away if she came too near. Now she was wondering if she would ever sleep beside him, in any normal fashion. In a house, in the confinement of a shared life.

Lovemaking. Making-of-love.

As if love does not generate itself but has to be made—by the effort of two.

She was sitting up, and had adjusted her clothing. Her hair was matted. Her skin felt sticky. Gnats circled her damp face, her hair. She took one of the man's hands in hers—gently. She saw with curiosity that his thumbs were precisely twice the size of hers. The backs of his hands were covered in thin dark graying hairs. On the third finger of his left hand was the ghost of a ring—(she thought); the wedding ring he'd worn for years, and had, as he'd told her with a harsh laugh, "tossed away" after his divorce.

She did not want to wake her lover for he seemed drawn, fatigued. Like the swimming, lovemaking took a good deal of energy from him. His face that was usually so alert, handsome in alertness as a predator bird, was slack now in repose. His mouth was slightly open. A glisten of saliva in the corner of his mouth. She wondered if she could love the man sufficiently, to compensate for his not loving her. Or perhaps, in some way, out of weakness perhaps, he would come to love her.

In time, he stirred and woke. His eyelids fluttered, he was seeing her. "'Lisbeth.'" The name seemed strange on his lips, a memorized name that made him smile in a kind of dazed wonderment as if the glowering sky was partly blinding.

Lisbeth leaned over him to kiss him. "Welcome back to Big Burnt, Mikael."

It was not a naturally caressing name—*Mikael*. Yet in Lisbeth's soft throaty voice, it had the effect of a caress.

Overhead the sky appeared to be dimming. The air was humid but a cooler wind was rising. Lightning leapt among the clouds like exposed nerves but it was only "heat" lightning—so far away, its deafening thunder had dissipated to silence.

"DON'T PANIC—HEY?"

Another time he spoke playfully yet she understood the severity beneath—*Don't you dare become emotional, not in my presence.*

At last with a single sixteen-ounce plastic Evian bottle she'd begun to bail water out of the back of the boat, that had risen to a depth of— could it be six inches?—for Mikael Brun had decreed finally, bailing might not be a bad idea. Pelting rain and waves sloshing steadily into the rear of the boat so that the rear was much lower than the front did indeed cause Lisbeth to feel panic which (she hoped) she was able to disguise from her companion.

He'd insisted that the boat was "unsinkable." He'd insisted that she should not worry, he would bring them back to the marina safely. Yet Lisbeth thought Mikael was probably relieved, that she'd begun to bail water even as he hadn't wanted her to think he thought it was necessary.

Their things in the back were awash in churning water. The backpacks were thoroughly soaked. The oars were floating. Awkwardly in her seat Lisbeth was turned in a desperate attempt to bail out water. At least it might be possible to keep pace with the water coming into the boat though the sixteen-ounce bottle was much too small, absurdly impractical. She had never worked so hard, and so frantically, at any physical task. Emptying water out of the bottle, over the side of the boat; submerging the bottle (horizontally) into the water in the rear, allowing the bottle to fill, and again emptying it over the side of the boat . . . The continuous jolting and rocking of the boat, the agitated motion of the waves, not rhythmic but chaotic as if being shaken in a madman's fist was making her nauseated. She felt as if she might vomit but would not succumb.

Directly overhead were flashes of lightning, vertical, terrifying, so close that the deafening thunder-claps came almost instantaneously and she could not keep from whimpering aloud.

"If you hear the thunder, you're all right. You're *not dead*."

Mikael was trying to be funny, even now. She supposed that was what he was attempting—to be funny.

Ever more desperately she was bailing water. Like a frenzied automaton, bailing water. Whatever she could do was not very effective—the rear of the boat seemed steadily to be sinking. But she could not give up—could she? If she gave up she would crouch beside the man with shut eyes, pressing her hands over her ears, catatonic in terror.

She was thinking how good it was, thank God her children were nowhere near!

Still, she continued to bail water. Numbly she smiled, bailing water.

Her clothing was soaked. Her hair hung in her face. She was shivering convulsively. Yet her heart beat hard in determination. One day, she and Mikael Brun would look back upon this nightmare and laugh, in recollection.

Crossing Lake George in that storm we realized if we survived, we could survive virtually anything. Together.

At the steering wheel of the boat Mikael kept on course. Tried to keep on course. His mood had shifted. He'd been elated at the outset, pushing off from Big Burnt, and then he'd been grim, abashed; but now again he was feeling elated, even reckless. They could not drown, after all—impossible! This was Lake George which he knew like the back of his hand. He had no doubt that he was going in the right direction and might have been a quarter mile from the marina.

He'd been so happy that day!—he could not surrender that happiness now.

On Big Burnt he'd felt as if he had come home. Yet it was a home from which others had departed. He'd felt like one who has opened his eyes in a strange place that is also a familiar place—a familiar place that is also a strange place. One of his lurid fantasies, that his father was buried on Big Burnt . . . Melancholia like an undertow had had him in its grip all the days of his life but now the raging lake was making him happy again, holding his course on the raging lake was making him happy again, bringing the woman back safely to the marina, not harming the woman as he'd vowed he would not do though it was within his power—as a child is made happy he was being made happy in sudden random gusts, waves.

Of course, he would not blow out his brains. Ridiculous!

There are ways less melodramatic. Ways that emulate natural causes. Whiskey, sedatives. He was a distinguished neuroscientist, he knew to obliterate consciousness the way a blackboard is cleaned. So many "sacrificed" animals in the Brun lab, so many years. The scientist's hand would not waver at obliteration.

Though possibly: he'd direct his lawyer to file a counter suit.

He'd fire that lawyer and hire another, better lawyer. He would not slink away in disgrace. He would not slink away at all—*he would never resign his professorship.* He would certainly never step down from the directorship of the Institute which he himself had founded. Instead, he would appeal the university's (hasty, ill-advised) decision if it went against him. If the appeal failed he would sue. He would sue the dean of the college, and he would sue the chair of his long-time department. He would sue each of the committee members. He would sue the president of the university who was *ex officio* on the committee.

He could marry again if he wished. It was not too late.

He would not make the same mistakes again. If he could remember these mistakes that had not seemed to be mistakes at the outset.

He could marry this woman—Lisbeth. She loved him, and would grow to love him more deeply. He would give her no cause not to love him as he'd done with other women, out of distrust of female weakness and subterfuge. But what was the last name, he'd forgotten . . .

Wide is the gate, and broad is the way, that leadeth to destruction. . . .

Strait is the gate, and narrow is the way, that leadeth onto life.

These biblical words came to him at the wheel of the little outboard, he had no idea why. He was no admirer of the Bible. He wasn't even certain which of the gospels this was—St. Mark? Matthew? Carefully he'd explained to anyone who asked, to interviewers, he was not by nature a religious person yet, as a neuroscientist, he understood that probably religion is hardwired into the human brain.

Wide is the gate . . . That was the problem: the lake was too vast, "broad"; it was the narrower inlet he sought, to bring them to safety.

This inlet was close ahead. A few hundred yards perhaps. In a few minutes he would be close enough to the mainland to see exactly where he was.

Already it seemed to him that the waves were less severe. He was nearing land—was he? To his left, a small familiar nameless island would appear; to his right, the rocky mainland. He would see—(was he seeing?)—lights on land; he knew where this was, very close to the marina. He had only to keep on course, even with this poor visibility he could not miss it.

And yet, there was a thinness, almost a transparency now to the mist. Everywhere he stared was imbued with a kind of radiance. It was the illumination of the finite, that filled him with melancholy, but also, strangely, a great happiness, hope . . .

And then, out of nowhere, there appeared a boat—a rescue boat?—and a male voice calling to them *Did they need help*?

A Lake George ranger boat, suddenly beside them. Mikael was both immensely relieved and terribly disappointed.

Out of the heavy rain a flashlight beam was directed at them, at the man's grimacing face.

"Hello? D'you need help?"

"Yes! Please! We need help!"—the woman cried.

He was furious with her, in that instant. But he did not contradict her. Abashed, he followed the ranger's directions. He followed the larger boat, that accompanied them to the marina. To his dismay he saw that, as he'd anticipated, the marina was directly ahead. He would have brought the boat in safely himself, within ten minutes.

Neither he nor his female passenger would see the flag at the end of the dock, high above their heads, hanging limp, sodden, unrecognizable as an American flag.

There, in still-pelting rain, amid flashes of lightning and claps of deafening thunder the man and the woman were greeted by the young teenaged marina attendant in a yellow rain poncho. "Great! Great job getting back, mister"—the words were flattering as they were insincere. The young man secured the boat for them, that was bucking and heaving beside the dock; he helped each of them out of the boat, the woman first, then the man, with as much solicitude as if they were elderly or infirm, and their bones fragile. "Careful, ma'am! Sir! The dock is slippery."

RETURNING IN THE CAR to their motel several miles away, the man was silent in his soaked, sodden clothes as if abashed, brooding. The woman could not stop exclaiming how wonderful it was to be out of the boat, off the lake, in the car and out of the rain! She was delirious with gratitude, relief. How happy she was, and how determined never to step into a boat again in her life! If she was expecting the man to protest such an extravagant statement, he took no notice. Halfway to the motel the man abruptly braked the car on the shoulder of the road and asked if the woman would mind driving?—he had a migraine headache, all the muscles of his upper body ached.

Gratefully the woman drove the rest of the way, still in rain. How she hated rain, in the Adirondacks! She'd been shaken for just a moment—thinking *He is disgusted with me. He will make me get out of the car and walk back in the rain.*

Of course, he was not angry at her in the slightest. He too was relieved—obviously. Several times he embraced her, kissed her roughly on the mouth as soon as they entered their motel room.

Their nostrils pinched, the room smelled musty. Outside the sliding glass doors to their little balcony the vast lake was invisible in rain, mist. Perhaps there was no lake at all, they'd been under a cruel enchantment. There was no "visibility" from the windows of their room, they had only each other.

In revulsion for their soaked, soiled-seeming clothing they took lengthy showers. The clothing was hung to dry, by the woman. When Lisbeth came out of the shower she saw Mikael hunched over his laptop, sitting on the edge of the king-sized bed. At last the terrible storm was lifting. Rain came less ferociously. Lisbeth returned to the bathroom to dress and when she emerged again, she saw Mikael on the phone, on the balcony. She heard his lowered voice. She heard him laugh—somehow, this was disconcerting. For he had not laughed with her.

How lonely she felt, he'd moved so quickly beyond her! She understood by the way in which his gaze slid over her, appraising, bemused. He told her he'd decided to return to Cambridge a day early, they would leave in the morning. Early Sunday morning—"We'll beat the traffic."

Tenderly he stooped to kiss her. Rubbed his rough beard against her cheek. As if it had all been a joke of a kind and their lives had never been seriously at risk.

"Hey. You saved us with all that bailing."

SHE WOULD PROTEST AFTERWARD, he'd given no sign.

No sign. No hint. Not a word.

He hadn't been unhappy. (No more than any of us are unhappy!)

Many people would contact her. Most of them were strangers. Brun's family, ex-wife, relatives. Colleagues at Harvard and at the Institute. Journalists. She'd been unable to keep confidential the (shameful, incomprehensible) fact that Lisbeth Mueller had been the companion of Mikael Brun for several days before he'd returned to his Cambridge home and killed himself. She'd had to give statements to police. She could give only a faltering, uncertain testimony that altered each time she gave it. She did not lie but she neglected to tell all that she might have told. What had been intimate between them, she would never reveal. She would not show anyone—not even the grieving Brun children—the pictures of Mikael Brun alone and with Lisbeth Mueller—on her iPhone. Nor could she bring herself to reveal to anyone that among the final words Mikael Brun had said to her were these playful, not-very-sincere words—*Hey. You saved us.*

For she had not saved them, had she.

She was furious with the man, and came to hate him. She was

devastated. She was in love with him, and wept for him, in a frenzy of grief she could not reveal to anyone. She could not sleep for she was pleading with him—*Why? Why did you do such a thing to yourself, and to me?*

It was clear, Mikael Brun had prepared his *last things* before he'd left for Lake George. All had been neatly organized, awaiting his return from Big Burnt. That seemed to be incontestable, she would not contest it. Her heart was lacerated by the realization that, in his last hours, her lover had forgotten her entirely. Not one of the *last letters* had been addressed to her.

She could not think of any words she might wish to utter to anyone. She had not an adequate language, she had no script. And so, eventually she gave up trying.

Owl Eyes

F ifteen."

"Fif*teen*. That seems young."

It is an inane remark. He steels himself for more.

In the advanced calculus class at the Math Institute twenty-six university students regard him with curiosity. Unmistakably, Jerald Tabor is the youngest individual in the room. His cheeks smart with an obscure sort of shame as the late-middle-aged professor continues in a vague kindly manner:

"Well, it is true in math there is no 'young'—no 'old.' In math all ages abide equally . . ."

The professor is a renowned mathematician, Jerald knows. Has been told.

Though the professor's name is not one Jerald will readily recall as he will not readily recall the man's face if he happens to encounter him outside the classroom.

Still less is Jerald Tabor likely to learn the names of other students in the class, or their faces. In the six-week summer session he will scarcely glance at them at all as in the public school he has attended for years he has made little effort to learn the names and faces of classmates. Jerald is unsentimental and pragmatic: memory is precious, not to be squandered on what is inconsequential.

In this class as in other classes Jerald feels "islanded"—uncomfortably distinct from the other students. As often he feels "islanded" in life.

As if—almost—he can see a shimmering aura surrounding him, setting him apart from others.

They see him, or some variant of him. Always from the outside, at a little distance.

Sometimes these others are friendly. More often, they are not so friendly. They can be cruel, crude, indifferent, curious. They can be unexpectedly kind. Sometimes they are resentful as the undergraduates in this class are likely to be resentful of a skinny lanky-limbed fifteen-year-old high school junior with math skills (allegedly) sharper than their own.

Jerald's mother has told him many times that he is *special*. He understands that he has no choice in the matter.

THERE!—THE OWL-EYED MAN. Staring at Jerald so strangely.

Not often is Jerald aware of his surroundings, still less of strangers in public places. Yet he notices this man.

A startled look in the stranger's face. Eyes magnified behind thick lenses.

Is this someone Jerald should know? Someone who knows *him*?

It is frightening to Jerald, who rarely goes anywhere alone, whose mother has overseen much of his life, to realize that he has seen this man before: at the train depot, on campus, in the vicinity of the Math Institute.

Jerald is a shy boy, too shy even to turn away quickly from a rude stranger as another boy might. Instead he stands irresolute at the foot of the math building steps as other students pass around him. His heart is beating rapidly. He'd had a triumph in the calculus class, the professor standing at the green board had directed a curt nod of approval in his direction—*Good work.* No words, just the nod, and the joy in Jerald's heart, glaring up quickly, in gratitude.

The stranger might be in his mid-fifties, or older—Jerald has a vague sense of adult ages. He wonders if it is someone who knows his mother?

It is the eyes that frighten Jerald. So fixed upon Jerald's face, intense and glaring behind the lenses of his glasses—*owl eyes* . . .

Quickly Jerald moves on. In the wake of a noisy cluster of undergraduates as if he were one of them.

IT IS TRUE, JERALD TABOR is fifteen. But not a mature fifteen.

He is thin, underdeveloped for his age. Fairly tall—five feet seven—but with narrow shoulders, the face of a bright evasive-eyed eleven-year-old.

His mother selects his clothes for him. Lays out his clothes for him. If he has distractedly misbuttoned a shirt she buttons the shirt correctly. It is rare for her to chide him. She does not at all mind his dependence upon her. She brushes his stiff pale hair which he is likely to have forgotten but she has no need (at least) to remind him to brush his teeth—that Jerald never forgets for the sensation of bits of food between his teeth is disagreeable.

Much of his waking life Jerald is at his computer. If he is away from his computer he is immersed in his iPad.

The actual world is blinding to him. A maze. But if there is a way to be memorized through the maze, Jerald will memorize it.

The great adventure of Jerald's young life until now: commuting to the Math Institute at the University each weekday afternoon for six weeks, mid-June through July, to take a course in advanced calculus.

Five days a week Jerald takes the 11:47 A.M. train—alone—for fifty-three minutes to the University which brings him there well in time for his 2:00 P.M. calculus class. Five days a week his mother drives him to the train depot and will be waiting to pick him up when he returns at 6:09 P.M.

On the Saturday before his first class Jerald's mother and he rehearsed the trip to the University in every particular. Travel from home to the Math Institute, and back, can be divided into seven distinct steps and these steps Jerald has memorized as in a game of chess in which all moves are known beforehand.

It was Jerald's high school math teacher Mr. Edelman who arranged for Jerald to receive a summer scholarship at the Institute. "How far you can go in math isn't for me to say, Jerald. But I know that you are already beyond me." Mr. Edelman had spoken affably, frankly. You could see in his face the relaxation that comes with knowing one's limits.

Jerald has seen his math teacher at the mall with his young children and has understood that there is happiness in Mr. Edelman's life, in the life of the family, that has nothing to do with the mathworld. This would be beyond Jerald, he thinks. He will have to content himself with the higher life.

Though sometimes it frightens him, there might be no higher life.

How Mr. Edelman acquired a scholarship for Jerald at the prestigious Math Institute Jerald does not know though (he supposes) his mother has to know, for she'd had to approve.

Jerald is enrolled in Calculus II for credit. Jerald is not merely *auditing* the course, he is *enrolled* in the course as if he were (already) a university undergraduate.

You must not fail, Jerald. You must not embarrass us.

These are unspoken words of course. Jerald's mother would never speak so openly.

The University is a very elite school. Often this is said, with an air of subtle reproach. As if *very elite* were an insult directed against those who are not, who cannot be, will never be *very elite*.

Jerald's mother has sometimes spoken of the University and all that the University entails with an air of reproach. Or rather, with an air of bitterness and chagrin. For she'd once been a Ph.D. student, and an instructor, at another university of nearly the same prestige, in another state.

Now that Jerald who is her only son and indeed her only family has been given a scholarship to the Math Institute she is not so bitter though she is still wary.

She is proud of Jerald, of course. Yet she is anxious for him.

. . . must not fail. Even if no one knows but us.

Failure preoccupies Jerald's mother. Much of life, most of life, for most people, is *failure*. For *failure* is measured by a significant *lack of success*.

There is much in their lives about which Jerald's mother does not speak to him. So much that Jerald does not hear. Yet anxiety pervades the household as a faint chemical odor sometimes pervades the air of the small suburban community in northeast New Jersey where they live.

In the calculus-world all anxieties rapidly fade. It has always been the case that while doing math, even simple arithmetic when he'd been a child, Jerald has forgotten the ordinary anxieties of his life; he forgets even his mother whose pride has kept him leashed close to her, in an old dispute (about which Jerald knows little) with the man said to be his father.

The location of Jerald's father is not clear. Not even the man's exact name is known to Jerald for it is (evidently) not Tabor—this is the maiden name of Imogene's mother. It has not (yet) occurred to Jerald to question his mother who has assured him that his father has cut off all ties with them and is so remote from them as to inhabit another "galaxy."

Sometimes his mother's pinched mouth refuses to utter so much, the unspoken words become a din like nocturnal insects in the dry heat of summer that keep Jerald awake at night.

But the calculus-world is another world. It is both distant and contiguous with this world, into which Jerald can pass like a child stepping through a transparent wall.

"HELLO. IS IT—JERALD?"

He has not eased away in time. Saw Owl Eyes approaching him on the walkway after class and now too late.

It has always been painful to Jerald, to give pain to another. To seem to be, still less to *be,* discourteous to any adult.

So, now. Trapped.

"I think we know each other? At least, I know you—'Jerald Kovacs'—"

The stranger speaks with a faint accent and with an air both hesitant and eager. Such yearning in the voice, Jerald wants to flee.

He is not at ease with the emotions of others particularly adults. It is frightening to him to be *responsible.*

"Not 'Kovacs'?—has your mother changed your name?"

Changed his name? He has no idea. The possibility has never occurred to him.

Shyly shaking his head *no.* For indeed—literally—with the unyielding logic of the computer—*Jerald Kovacs* is not his name.

Owl Eyes seems not to register *no* and steps nearer. Owl Eyes risks a smile.

A hot midsummer afternoon yet the owl-eyed man is wearing a brown cloth jacket with pleats and buttons, over a white cotton shirt. His trousers are of a texture too heavy for summer. On his feet are leather sandals that expose waxy-white toes with gnarled and discolored toenails.

"But it is 'Jerald'—isn't it?"

Jerald ducks away vaguely shaking his head. It is not like him to be rude but he has panicked, he must escape.

Hears Owl Eyes call after him—"Jerald? Wait, please . . ."

No no *no.*

On lanky-long legs near-running. His heart is a frantic fluttering in his chest like a trapped bird.

THE STRANGER SEEMS to know him: *Jerald.*

He is *Jerald.* He is not ever *Jerry.*

He is a shy boy but he is also a vain boy, he thinks well of himself. He has been taught to think well of himself, that he will not despair of himself.

You are special, Jerald. You are special to me.

Many times he has been warned by his mother: do not speak with strangers. Do not let strangers speak with you.

Yet (he is thinking) his mother would have wished him to behave more courteously with Owl Eyes who might be (Jerald sees this now, with a stab of chagrin) a professor at the University, a person of importance not to be so rudely dismissed.

Politely might've said *Sorry sir my name is not Kovacs. That is not my last name.*

Might've said *Sorry sir but I have to catch a train . . .*

This is how another more responsible boy would have responded, Jerald supposes.

Another boy, or a girl, his age, approached by an owl-eyed stranger with a faint accent, carrying a briefcase.

Jerald will tell his mother of course. Jerald's mother always questions him closely about the University, whom he might have met there or at the train depot.

It is late afternoon, a waning hour, temperature above ninety degrees on this midsummer day. University undergraduates are wearing shorts, torn jeans, T-shirts, sandals. All are older than Jerald and yet they seem younger than he, more carefree, careless, exuberant. Like glittering minnows they move in waves. Their eyes pass through Jerald Tabor for he is invisible.

It is a comfort to him, to be invisible. That is the promise of the math-world.

He has slowed his pace. No need to run!

What time is it?—only 4:35 P.M.

His train home doesn't leave until 5:16 P.M. He hopes that the owl-eyed stranger will not follow him to the train depot for (he believes) he'd seen the man there at least once . . .

The train arrives at the University depot at 5:12 P.M. and departs just four minutes later but Jerald always boards well before this. These precise times Jerald's mother wrote down for him but of course Jerald has no need to consult her notes for Jerald memorized them immediately, it is no effort for Jerald to memorize even complicated notations and Jerald is very anxious about arrivals and departures, *away* and *home*.

By a circuitous route—(in case Owl Eyes is following him after all)—Jerald arrives at the depot nearly a half hour early.

Few passengers here at this time. No one who looks familiar.

No one who glances at him with more than passing interest.

Jerald has his ticket purchased that morning by his mother. Several times he checks the ticket in his wallet just to make sure.

Jerald's stop is the first stop. Soon he will be home.

What can go wrong? Nothing can go wrong.

His mother will be awaiting him at the depot. His mother will probably be in her car, awaiting his train. He will see the car first. He will feel a stab of comfort seeing the gunmetal-gray compact car awaiting him.

Comfort in this knowledge certain as mathematical certainty, or almost.

Awaiting the 5:12 P.M. arrival Jerald sits on a bench at the farthest end of the platform facing the track where no one is likely to approach him. His iPad is open, he has lost himself in the calculus-world where no one can follow him and no one is named.

JERALD'S MOTHER HAS SAID she'd left the university world just in time.

Escaped with my life.

Jerald has asked few questions of his mother for it is not very real to him, a time before his birth. A time before his mother was *his mother* is neither comprehensible nor desirable to contemplate.

Jerald understands that his mother "works"—as other adults "work"—but Jerald knows little of the nature of her work and has not been encouraged to ask about it.

Nine to five, five days a week, a routine job in an office, a job requiring little thinking and little decision-making for she'd *Put all that behind me when I'd lost my nerve.*

Nerve is what you need for a certain sort of life. But one day she'd had enough, she said. At the prestigious university in another state.

No more books, no more thinking. Not the kind of thinking that requires *nerve*.

Jerald's mother had vacated her small office shared with several others. She'd set out on a table armloads of books with a sign FREE BOOKS PLEASE TAKE! Psychology, computer science, math, economics, analytic philosophy, biology, even art history. These books had caused her to think too much, and had made her sick.

Essentially it was whatever was inside the books that had made her sick. Prying open such books with your fingers, trying to read, underline, comprehend and assimilate—what a risk! Like biting into a sandwich in which there is broken glass. Or something poison. Rotted.

When Jerald's mother thought obsessively (she'd told Jerald) she had trouble breathing. Trouble sleeping. Strangers "tramped" through her dreams. The solution (obviously) was to give away the toxic books that had once meant so much to her when she'd been young, hopeful, and stupid.

It was not like Jerald's mother to speak like this to him. Afterward Jerald (who was twelve at the time) would find it difficult to believe that his mother had ever spoken so openly about her personal life, and at such length.

She'd described how she hated that the books began with particular sentences which excluded all other sentences. This made the books incomplete. What was incomplete was a lie. What was a lie was an insult. What was an insult would do harm, like a wound.

The solution was to give away all that tied her to her old self, to cut her ties with the past and make a new life.

There was no information about the father. Or about other men who (Jerald very vaguely recalls) had appeared sometimes in their home and at mealtimes.

Shyly Jerald had asked about *father*. He had not said *my father* but rather *was there a father?*—in a voice so soft his mother seemed scarcely to have heard.

If a man appeared in his mother's life, and if a man disappeared out of his mother's life, there was no available information. There was no language, only just silence.

It is very easy to forget silence.

Yet Jerald's mother has kept a few books from that long-ago time before his birth. Mostly paperbacks, textbooks. Surreptitiously Jerald has perused them in the damp basement of their house. He'd been younger then, no more than nine or ten, curious. He had not yet imagined that curiosity might be wounding.

In one of the textbooks he'd seen a passage outlined in yellow marker—

Life on earth is believed to have evolved from a single primitive species, a self-replicating molecule that lived more than 3.5 billion years ago. The agent for evolution is *natural selection*.

Numerically, he understood *billion*, as he understood *million*. But in no actual way.

He'd asked his mother what *billion* meant. With a quick smile she'd drawn a graph on a sheet of paper in which one half-inch represented 100,000 years and so *1,000,000,000* would leap off the page and onto the wall, around the corner and onto the hallway wall. Jerald's mother laughed at the child's perplexed face.

"Of course you can't *imagine,* silly. No one can."

JERALD DOES NOT tell his mother about the owl-eyed man who has (mis)identified him as *Jerald Kovacs.* Jerald will keep a watch at the University and try to avoid Owl Eyes.

He had not liked Owl Eyes saying *your mother.*

What right had a stranger to say those words—*your mother!*

It is understood that Jerald tells his mother everything—or nearly. Not about his math classes which have become too abstruse for her to follow but other, easier classes, and always about people, adults and classmates, who have "interacted" with him. But Jerald has no intention of telling her about Owl Eyes because (he believes) she will become upset, agitated and (possibly) report Owl Eyes to University authorities.

A stranger has made unwanted advances to my son who is only fifteen years old . . .

Jerald's mother has access to his computer, his iPad. Not a nook or a sliding panel or a shadowy crack in Jerald's life is inaccessible to his mother though (in fact) (so far as he knows) his mother does not often investigate his online activities which are math- and science-related almost exclusively.

Jerald's mother is not jealous of others in Jerald's life—(classmates, friends)—for there are no others.

It's a paradox, she has said. Pronouncing the word with care—*paradox.*

Nothing matters except family—the bond of mother and son. This tie will prevail when all other ties fail.

Yet, all that is merely personal in life is transient and of little intrinsic worth. Jerald's mother is enough of a scientist/mathematician to understand this.

"You will live in both worlds, Jerald. No matter how far you go in the math-world you will always return to your mother."

"AFRAID YOU'RE ON THE WRONG TRAIN, son."

These words most dreaded by Jerald Tabor.

He has given his ticket to the conductor as usual but this time the conductor frowns at it for there has been an error, it is Jerald's error, in an instant Jerald breaks into a clammy sweat and is rendered helpless.

Seeing the stricken look in Jerald's face the conductor takes pity on him and explains that the train he has boarded is an earlier train running seventy minutes late due to a breakdown and the train he should have boarded is running just four minutes late.

And so it has happened that Jerald boarded the train at the correct time but the train he boarded was not the correct train.

Fortunately the conductor assures Jerald that the train he is on is stopping at the University in any case.

"I can accept your ticket, son. But just for your information—you are on the wrong train."

Jerald murmurs thanks. He is weak with relief.

As the conductor moves away Jerald feels a wave of shock, that his mother should have been so careless, and failed to protect him. Very easily it might have happened that Jerald had boarded a train that would take him far from the University, to a distant place . . . She'd driven him to the depot that morning as usual and had taken it for granted that the train that pulled beside the platform at the "right" time was the train Jerald should have been taking.

Though the conductor accepted Jerald's ticket as if it were the correct ticket, and though Jerald didn't miss his calculus class nor was he even late to arrive at the University, yet the experience has shaken him. He is thinking he can't trust the trains, he must double-check his ticket each time. Can't trust his mother.

TERROR IN THE MAGNIFICATION of the stranger's owl eyes.

That a stranger might see so intently, peering into another's soul. *His* soul.

"I was your father, Jerald. For more than four years."

Jerald is not sure that he has heard correctly.

Father? Owl Eyes is claiming to be—his *father?*

The man is explaining. Providing dates. Jerald is not hearing these words clearly.

". . . your mother was separated from her husband, her first husband, when she became pregnant—"

Jerald flinches at such words. *Pregnant!*

"—with you. With the child that would be you. She and I were together at that time, though we hadn't been living together . . . ."

Owl Eyes is speaking haltingly, awkwardly. Clearly it is very difficult for him to utter these words that seem like stones in his mouth.

In a moment of weakness Jerald has allowed himself to be detained outside the Math Institute—*If we could speak for just a few minutes, Jerald. Please.*

He has seemed to acquiesce, that he is indeed *Jerald.*

Seated on a stone bench outside the Math Institute, less than three feet apart. Jerald doesn't recall sitting.

Staring at the man's moving mouth, uttering such words. Jerald wants to jump up and walk rapidly away. Run away. Lose himself in the swarm of undergraduates crossing the quadrangle.

But as in one of those nightmares about which he never tells his mother he can't move.

There is something wrong with Jerald's breathing. A sensation like a coarse rag yanked through his chest. He is light-headed, an insufficient quantity of blood flows to his brain.

If you feel faint when I am not around lower your head between your knees. You know how to do this, and why. Do it.

Doesn't dare lower his head between his knees for Owl Eyes is regarding him anxiously. He does not want Owl Eyes to touch him.

The man has provided a name but already Jerald has forgotten the name. Strangers' names do not interest him.

He is a visiting fellow at the University, he explains. He has a permanent position at _____.

Jerald sees the man's mouth move but hears only a fraction of his words. Jerald's own mouth is shut tight as his throat is shut tight and he is sitting very still gripping his backpack in both hands.

The man has been telling Jerald how he and Jerald's mother (whom he calls Imogene) had lived together intermittently for several years in the early 2000s. When he, Jerald, was a small child they'd traveled together as a family. They'd visited museums, planetariums. They'd gone to concerts and hiked along the lakeshore with binoculars, observing birds. He and Imogene had lived in separate residences but continued to be *together*—a couple.

"It was taken for granted by us—by Imogene and me—that you were my son, Jerald. You'd been born after Imogene had separated from her husband of the time, a man named Kovacs; though in fact, Imogene had not been divorced from Kovacs yet. She was excited by our having a child together and would study pictures of me when I'd been a child, to identify the 'likeness' between you and me. She was adamant that you *were not* the child of her former husband. Neither of us questioned the assumption of paternity. At least, I didn't question it."

Imogene. Jerald has rarely heard his mother's name, and never from a stranger. There is something disagreeable in the very sound, uttered so familiarly in another's mouth.

Kovacs is not a name Jerald knows. The only name he has heard, attached to his own, is *Tabor.*

"The three of us—your mother, you, and me—lived isolated lives for years. I was a university professor, your mother was a Ph.D. candidate in computational psychology, a brilliant woman. Brilliant but 'nervous'—that was said of Imogene. Yet, for some reason I never understood Imogene did not want to marry me. Her first marriage had made her very unhappy, she'd said. She did not even want to live together openly. We rarely appeared together in public. Your mother was not a social person, she had no friends. She was estranged even from her closest relatives. Eventually she had what must have been a nervous breakdown and dropped out of the Ph.D. program. She blamed me for the breakdown, and she blamed you—you were three or four by this time. She would say that being a mother had been a mistake, and for the mistake she would have to be punished. But still—in her way—she loved you. It was a burdensome sort of love, an obsessive love, a weight around her neck that made living with her almost impossible . . . Whenever we tried, and we tried many times, it soon became hopeless. Your mother created complications in all lives that touched hers. She was a beautiful woman in a way not every man would appreciate. She was beautiful to me. (I have not seen Imogene in more than ten years. I would not be able to bring myself to see her again, she'd so badly wounded me.) I loved her deeply but could not really understand her. Even when she made an effort, when she most insisted that she loved me, she seemed to resent the fact that I was close by—that a man was close by. Propinquity was painful to her. Her skin seemed to smart as if she were allergic to me—to us. You and me. She had breakdowns, illnesses. She refused to seek medical help. She was anxious about you, always anxious about you, for she didn't really want to be a mother to you, and so she had to be extra cautious, she said. She was terrified that she would hurt you. *The temptation to hurt the helpless is too strong. You can't be weak, to resist such a temptation*—she'd said."

Faltering, hesitating, yet the owl-eyed man continues. Now that he has begun he cannot be stopped. He is leaning forward as Jerald, in a kind of trance, remains unmoving, paralyzed.

"Her focus shifted to you, Jerald. Obsessively. Imogene no longer trusted me to be alone with you even for a brief while. She'd run back to me after twenty minutes desperate to see you—to see if you were all right. She'd check your breathing countless times a day—and at night—when you were an infant, terrified that you would stop breathing. As if breathing isn't autonomous and has to be willed. It was she who had accidents with you, not me—dropping you on the stairs, overturning a pan of boiling water so that some of it splashed onto you, household accidents . . . When we went out together as a family she became particularly high-strung, accusing. For a long time she'd said that we would be married when her life was more 'stable.' But when her life was stable she became quickly bored, she couldn't bear peacefulness. She threatened to 'harm' both herself and you. I made the mistake of putting pressure on her to acknowledge me as your legal father and to allow me to spend more time with you—but she refused."

The owl-eyed man pauses. Jerald tries to think of something to say, to ask. But his throat is shut tight. He is mortified by these disclosures, even as he cannot believe that they are true.

"Yet—though it sounds unbelievable—we did many things together as a family. Our lives were bound fiercely together. I loved you and your mother so much—you were the center of my life. You were a remarkable child with your own sort of dignity. You were exceptionally quiet and watchful. And very bright. Even in preschool you were precocious. You had not much interest in other children as other children had not much interest in you. I think it must be the same way now, judging from what I've seen of you on campus . . . You are a very dignified boy but dignity must come at a price, of loneliness.

"It was about this time, when you were four years old, that I made a mistake out of exasperation and despair. I wanted you to have my name. I wanted your mother and me to be married, finally. But your mother reacted in a kind of panic. She became very unreasonable. She threatened to report me to the police, and accuse me of harassment. Suddenly she was insisting that you were not my son after all. She'd made a mistake, she said. She arranged for a DNA test to establish the fact that I was not your father . . .

"This revelation was devastating to me, heartbreaking. For years your mother had behaved as if I were your father and she was very happy with my being your father but now it seemed that I was not your father after all. Nor was her first husband your father . . . Somehow, it seemed that another man, whose name I would never be told, was your biological father; but this man, according to Imogene, had no knowledge that he was your father, didn't even know that Imogene had had a baby, for there was no connection between them. Even now it's impossible for me to comprehend that your mother had deceived me so cruelly. Why at first she'd insisted upon convincing me that I was your father but a few years later changed her mind and wanted me out of her life—I never understood . . ."

In silence Jerald has been listening to these terrible words. His eyes have misted over with tears of disbelief, rage.

"It was purely chance that I saw you at the Institute, Jerald. I recognized you at once—of course! Though it has been eleven years . . ."

Earnestly Owl Eyes speaks as if he has no idea how Jerald is trembling with emotion.

"If you don't believe what I've been telling you, ask your mother. As if she remembers—"

Again Owl Eyes speaks his name, that Jerald seems not to hear.

There is a buzzing in his ears like cicadas, deafening.

(But does Jerald remember? A man . . .)

(There have been men in his mother's life. In his own young life. But so young was Jerald at the time, his memory is discontinuous and blurred as in a dream.)

It is too confusing to Jerald, and distasteful. He does not want to recall any of it. At least he knows that his name is not *Kovacs*.

Seeing that Jerald is about to break away from him the owl-eyed man says again urgently, "Ask her. Please. Your mother. If she re-members—"

Jerald wants to murmur *Leave me alone.* But all he can manage is a near-inaudible—*N-no.*

Stammering he has to leave, he will be late for his train . . .

Turning to run, without a backward glance for the flush-faced man seated on the stone bench gazing after him with an expression of hurt and yearning.

"AM I ADOPTED?"

It is a bizarre question. Out of nowhere Jerald hears himself ask his mother.

"Adopted? Of course not."

His mother laughs, this is too ridiculous.

"Considering that we look so much alike, you and I, adoption is not very plausible, is it?"

Jerald has no idea why he has asked his mother this question. Yet, he has no idea how he might have asked her another question.

Was there once a man who loved me, who believed he was my father, why did you send this man away . . .

Jerald's mother continues on the subject of adoption. Her initial amusement is shading into something like impatience, annoyance. For it is not like her son Jerald to ask stupid questions, still less questions lacking some point.

Jerald is somewhat shocked at the suggestion that he and his mother *look so much alike*. Never has Jerald noticed this.

His mother reaches out to touch Jerald. It is her prerogative to touch her son at any time but on long deft legs Jerald outmaneuvers her and exits the room.

SEARCHES HIS MOTHER'S THINGS when his mother is at work.

But his mother is not like other mothers, Jerald must know this. Consequently she has accumulated few "things."

As she owns few books so she owns few articles of clothing and virtually no jewelry. Few letters, few documents. No photographs.

Doggedly Jerald rummages through the drawers in his mother's bedroom with a rising sense of self-disgust.

Of course, he finds nothing.

(What is there to find?)

(Resents her, for having so little.)

(Resents *him,* stupid Owl Eyes!)

Jerald has been told that he has a father, for of course he has a father, but *your father* has never been a factor in *our life together.*

His mother has explained. Or rather, his mother has not explained but has told him all he needs to know.

Not a factor in our lives.

Still, Jerald seems to know that the man presumed to be his father lives in another state. Whether a nearby state, or a distant state, Jerald does not know.

This man (whose name is Kovacs?) (whose name is not Kovacs?) has never contacted Jerald. Or so his mother has claimed.

This man who'd been Imogene's first (and only?) husband and who is not Jerald's father has never been interested in Jerald—of course. Jerald has never given any thought to the man lacking a name, a face.

This man *is not* the owl-eyed man. But Jerald does not recall the owl-eyed man either.

(But Owl Eyes would have been younger then, eleven years before, and he would have looked different.)

That night Jerald wakes from a confusing dream of rushing faces and muffled cries and realizes that yes, he remembers the owl-eyed man very well.

He had not thought of him as Owl Eyes. Not then.

Remembers the man's deep voice, the voice bearing a faint accent that has not changed in eleven years. Remembers the man close beside him reading a storybook, with illustrations. A rhythmic accent to the voice, a kind of buoyancy.

Memory is tonal. This tone, Jerald remembers.

Soon then Jerald recalls a museum with high ceilings, hard-shining floors, echoing sounds. A hall of dinosaurs.

Enormous skeletons. Flying reptiles.

Nighttime sky, a planetarium, a long line of children, an exhibit of aeronautical inventions. A man with dark hair loose to his shoulders, dark eyes. A man who laughed often.

Took hold of the little boy's hand so that on the stairs the little boy would not slip and fall.

Hiking in a pine woods. A beach of hard-packed sand.

Peering at shorebirds through binoculars—*sandpipers.*

Memories return in waves, overwhelming. You can drown in memories.

"Jerald! Wake up."

Jerald's mother is surprised and disapproving, Jerald has slept so long. It is not like her son to sleep past 8:00 A.M. on any day of the week but especially on a day he will travel to the University for Calculus II.

Jerald sits up in bed. He is fully awake, his eyes are open and staring. Yet he is very tired, as if he has not slept at all.

JERALD TELLS HIS MOTHER that he will be staying later at the Institute that day, in order to attend a lecture. He will return on the 6:12 P.M. train. His mother is surprised to hear this since Jerald has not mentioned any lectures previously but she checks the University calendar and indeed it's true that there is a math lecture that afternoon at 4:30 P.M. at the Institute.

In the privacy of his room Jerald packs his laptop into his backpack as well as his iPad. He packs his charger cords. He packs a single change of clothes. Underwear, socks. He folds his clothing into tight squares, as tight as he can to force inside the backpack. He has some money, in cash in his wallet. He does not have a credit card.

Before he boards the train he double-checks the number of the train and the number on his ticket. Hears his mother call to him from the parking lot and remembers to turn to her, to wave good-bye.

After calculus class that afternoon Jerald lingers in the vicinity of the Math Institute waiting to see the owl-eyed man but does not see him.

Walks slowly to the train depot on the far side of the University and there waits beyond his usual train, that departs at 5:16 P.M. Shyly he peers at strangers standing on the platform waiting to board this train but the owl-eyed man is not among them.

Rapidly he calculates: two weeks, three more days in the summer session. These thirteen days can be broken down into a small infinity of seconds. Jerald will wait.

Except You Bless Me

Hag lady. Aint you hot shit.

Those boots you wearin they are shit.

Open yo mouth yo tryin to talk to us. Think we gon hurt you.

White bitch needin more then red grese on that mouth look like some-body some man want.

A PERSON WHO HATES ME has entered my office. Fourth floor, Starret Hall of Wayne State University.

I have been waiting for her, so I am not surprised. Her name is on my appointment sheet—*Larissa Wikawaaya. 6:35 P.M.*

Larissa is late for the appointment by about eight minutes. I have the idea that she has been out in the corridor for a while, hesitant to enter. Twice previously, she failed to show up for an appointment with her Composition 101 instructor, to discuss her work; but now in the final, rapidly passing weeks of the fall quarter she has taken a begrudging interest in the course—that is, in her grade.

Hag lady. You ugly got to know it. We just laughin at you hard as you try be PRETY.

It is a marvel to me, Larissa Wikawaaya's bravado. This swaggering young woman enters the office as she enters the classroom, sulky, stiff-faced, resentful. She is carrying a bulky quilted coat and a hefty shoulder bag in her arms. Her hair is tight narrow braids, cornrowed. Her manner is imperial. She doesn't exhibit the slightest unease, still less any concern, or guilt—that her instructor has guessed she is (surely) the person who has been leaving hate-notes shoved beneath this office door. *Mz Rane you plain ugly. You pitful. Everbody wonder how you don t kill youself lookin like you.*

Her hatred for me, the (white, woman) instructor, must be a shield: it will protect her from harm.

Since class ended that afternoon at 5:20 P.M. I have been seeing students for more than an hour, in twenty-minute sessions, and I am feeling slightly dazed. A ringing in my ears of unease, anxiety, that has been mounting, with the prospect of confronting Larissa Wikawaaya at 6:35 P.M., the last conference of the day. The students who've preceded her have not been difficult or disagreeable but each has presented a singular problem, as most students enrolled in this remedial composition course, in the night-school division of the university, are "problematic"—their writing skills, so-called, don't meet the university's basic criteria. Yet their problems are navigable, and I believe that I have been teaching them to write—to a degree. What we love in teaching, if we love teaching at all, is this conviction of progress: spontaneous exchanges, sudden insights, smiles and even laughter.

But I have not been looking forward to Larissa Wikawaaya. Here in the confines of my cramped office, there is no one for either of us to look at but the other.

Since the nasty notes were left for me, slid beneath my door with (misspelled) MZ RANE crudely hand-printed on the folded sheet of paper, I've been obsessed with determining who has written them even as I have instructed myself not to care.

I have not told anyone. I think I am ashamed, and I have certainly been humiliated. Even, reading the hate-notes carefully, like one picking at an abscess, I've been frightened—does this person hate me enough to hurt me? Am I missing a threat, am I making a terrible mistake not to report this?

I've decided no. There are no actual threats in the notes, only just hatred, derision, contempt. *White bitch* is a signal that the hatred is about race.

Hate-notes shoved beneath my door which I have read, reread, discarded, and again pulled out of the trash, to be studied like Zen koans. *Do I deserve this? Such hatred, contempt? Why has this been directed at me?*

The hate is racial but it also seems sexual. A distinctly female sort of sex-hatred, I think. Each of the several notes has jeered at my appearance, my hair, clothes, efforts to be "PRETY."

This is not a situation I can discuss with anyone. It is too racially charged—too personal, hurtful. To speak of race at all in Detroit, in the aftermath of July 1967, is to invite misunderstanding, rage. I am not a person who is comfortable with confrontation, let alone disputation. The individual who is tormenting me might sense this—I am not going to seek her out, I am not going to "punish." My strategy, if you can call it a strategy, is simply to wait, to endure. To wait, and prevail.

I can't confide in my husband who has expressed disapproval of my teaching at beleaguered Wayne State, a quasi-white island amid the predominantly black and rapidly depopulating city of Detroit; I have not told any of the few night school colleagues whom I see, mostly by chance, who might sympathize with me, probably—and have lurid stories to tell of their own. (Failure is drawn to failure. We are all adjunct instructors with little hope of promotion, benefits, a future at

Wayne State. I could not bear their commiseration!) Certainly I have not informed the associate dean of Continuing Education who has hired me, who seems to like me, yet who might interpret my predicament as deserved in some way, and in any case an ugly situation with no good resolution.

For how could I accuse Larissa Wikawaaya when there is no proof? All I know—I think that I know—is that the individual who has left the notes is one of my more obviously dissatisfied Composition 101 students, and of the twenty-six students still in the class, there are seven low-achievers who might be in that category; of these seven, five females and two males, sulky semi-literate Larissa Wikawaaya is the most likely.

Larissa's awkwardly handwritten compositions contain some of the misspellings and tortured syntax of the notes, though she has tried to disguise her handwriting by printing the notes in an exaggerated way, as a child might. (Using her left hand?)

The first note was a terrible shock, and an embarrassment. I'd entered the fourth-floor office in Starret Hall in the early afternoon of my teaching day—(in the room are three desks, of which all three are shared)—and one of the other composition instructors was there conferring with a student; an older woman, face drawn with fatigue even as she smiled, smiled, smiled whenever she thought anyone was observing her; this very courteous woman told me that she'd found "something for 'Mz. Rane'" on the floor, when she'd unlocked the door—"I put it on your desk, but I didn't read it. I think—it must be for you."

Lamely then another time, with her faint, unconvincing smile—"I didn't read it . . ."

I took the folded note from her. I thanked her. I seemed to know beforehand by glancing at the stiff-printed words MZ. RANE, that seemed to contain a kind of pent-up venom, that this was a communication that would not be flattering, and might well be read in private.

If anyone asked me, that afternoon, which student in my composition class could possibly have written such a vicious note to me, immediately I'd have identified Larissa Wikawaaya.

There have been just five notes, since the start of the fall quarter. All obviously from the same person.

Initially, it looked as if this problem-student might drop the course. Clearly she was unhappy with my response to her written work. She was absent from class once, twice—three times—but returned with a perfunctory mumbled excuse. Much of the time she seems bored and disengaged but at other times, to my chagrin, she has been so insolent in class, whispering and giggling with friends at the back of the room, smirking at me as I speak, it's as if she scarcely cares whether I know she's the author of the hate-notes. When I suggest that she should raise her hand if she has something to say, and address the entire class, Larissa smirks at this suggestion too. She has managed to alienate most of the other students, who seem embarrassed by her. There are "good"—black, Hispanic, Asian—students in the class who sit nearer the front of the room, and have nothing to do with Larissa Wikawaaya. I've come to wonder if she might be mentally unbalanced, or on some mood-elevating drug—her anger and disdain are in such excess of the situation, her hatred of her composition instructor so disproportionate to anything I could mean to her.

Hag lady. White bitch.

Got to know how ugly you.

It's true—I am obsessed by Larissa Wikawaaya as I would be obsessed by a cyst discovered in one of my breasts. The terror is that the little tumor is malignant—the desperate hope, that it is benign. Yet you procrastinate having a biopsy, out of dread of knowing your fate.

My position as an adjunct instructor at the financially strapped state university is nearly as precarious as the position of a day laborer in the financially strapped city; I am one of numerous late-hire adjuncts working without a contract, with but the vaguest promise of being "seriously considered" for a position in the spring. Though I have a master's degree from the University of Minnesota, I am a woman—this disadvantage, in 1974, is considerable.

And so, my heart is suffused with a plaintive sort of hope, even now. My smile at Larissa is pleading—*Why don't you like me? What have I done to offend you? I have been hired to "teach" you—why won't you let me do that? Can't we both try?*

Am I hoping that somehow it will be revealed that I've been mistaken about her, these several weeks?

Somebody else hates you, Mz. Rane, see? Not me.

All this while, Larissa has been standing just inside the door, staring at me as if bemused, uncertain whether to come all the way inside, or whether to depart. She's breathing hard, she's a fleshy girl and easily out of breath, and quick to become overwarm, in this steam-heated old building.

"Larissa, please close the door over, and please take a seat . . ."

Please take a seat. The words strike me as hopelessly banal, even foolish. In Larissa's presence I'm forced to hear my own voice, its forced cheer, its perfunctory rhythms. My mouth moves clumsily, for in those derisive eyes I see myself as in a distorting mirror: pallid white skin, creased forehead and eyes crinkling at the corners from excessive smiling. My facial skin feels as if it's drawn tight—as if a stocking has been pulled over my face. Like other adjunct instructors who hope to make a good impression I'm wearing conventionally dressy clothes—white silk blouse, narrow-waisted gray flannel skirt, leather boots to the knee. (Yes, these are the boots the author of the hate-note derided, but I want to protest—*They are good leather boots! They are not inexpensive.*) My pale crimped hair is shoulder-length, brushed behind my ears, fastened with a tortoiseshell clip and not yet threaded too visibly with silver. Though the hate-notes have derided my effort to appear "pretty" I am—probably, one might say—an attractive enough young (white) woman of some ambiguous

age—twenty-eight?—thirty? My face is carefully, though not lavishly made-up; it would have seemed, in 1974, to administrators and
colleagues, as well as to students, a subtle violation of female convention, to have not "made-up" my face—a kind of disrespect, like not
combing hair, or wearing rumpled clothing. It has seemed particularly unfair, the hate-note derided *red grese* on my mouth, when the
only lipstick I own is Revlon's Plum Shadow.

My slightly rounded shoulders in the dazzling-white blouse and
the angle of my head betray my (naïve, stubborn) wish for this difficult student to *like me,* despite the history between us.

Or, at any rate, not so obviously dislike me.

To my remark Larissa grunts a near-inaudible reply—*OK, ma'am.*

Or maybe Larissa has muttered, shrugging—*OK, man.*

With a show of reluctance, or indifference, Larissa partly shuts the
office door. She tosses her quilted coat onto one of the other desks.
Her shoulder bag she drops to the floor. Firmly she grips the back of
a lightweight vinyl chair to position it more squarely in front of my
desk. She sits.

Larissa Wikawaaya is a heavy young woman for whom the act
of *sitting* is a conscious and aggressive act she wants me to observe.
She isn't tall but she is broad-shouldered, big-boned. Her weight has
given her an aggressive sort of confidence.

I remember girls like Larissa Wikawaaya from grade school, high
school. Physically belligerent, eyes snatching at mine in locker rooms,
restrooms. Places where adults could not protect a girl like me.

*Think you hot shit well you can brek. Like breking some chiken neck
that be that easy.*

I am smiling as I speak with this young black woman who hates
me. Like the older woman-colleague who smiles, smiles, smiles I am
smiling to disguise the strain I feel, that has caused a pulse to beat
in my head, on the brink of pain. I am sitting with clasped hands at
the utilitarian aluminum desk shared with other instructors, whose

teaching schedules don't overlap with mine. The chair in which I sit isn't made of lightweight vinyl but of wood: a hefty wooden chair with rungs, seat worn smooth by the buttocks of strangers. Calmly I am smiling at this brash woman with the exotic name as if I haven't the slightest suspicion of her, or have not lain awake for hours in dismay of how she has injured me; as if I haven't held in my trembling hands the cruel little hand-printed notes in black ink that have entered my brain like burrowing ticks.

". . . hoping that you'd come to see me this afternoon, Larissa. It would be a good idea, since we have only three weeks left in the quarter, if we could go over your newest assignment . . ."

. . . *good idea, since grades, go over, assignment.* I have prepared these conscientious words but confronting Larissa Wikawaaya's mock-neutral gaze on my face is unsettling. I am still in a way disbelieving—naïvely—that anyone could dislike *me.*

I have tried to rationalize her dislike: clearly it is rooted in race. To Larissa, *white* is the enemy. *White* is the oppressor. In this case, *white* is the instructor who will pass judgment on her, and "grade" her.

No one wants to be "graded." That is utterly natural.

Nor am I really comfortable about "grading."

There'd been mild shock waves in the class, when I'd handed back the first writing assignment. Larissa's work had been careless and confused from the start. I hadn't graded the weaker compositions but "corrected" them lightly in red ink, with suggestions for revising; from then onward, Larissa smoldered with resentment.

Had she wanted praise? Had she expected me to ask her to read her compositions aloud to the class, as I did with some of the others?

Instead I'd written on her papers—*Promising ideas here but please see me to discuss revision.*

Now Larissa is breathing audibly, as if she has hiked up three flights of stairs. A gleam of oily sweat on her forehead. Without smiling she continues to stare at me, rudely, or rather indifferently, as I pretend to be glancing through my grade book, searching for her name. (In fact, I know Larissa's record by heart.) To break the tension I ask her about her name—"'Wikawaaya'—is it Hawaiian?"—and see by her stare that this is not a welcome query. Larissa shrugs and mutters something inaudible. (Maybe the name is an appropriated African name? Maybe Larissa has no idea of the history of her family name?)

It is difficult to resist smiling at least faintly when others smile at us but Larissa is strong-willed, defiant. I can guess that she has been brought up by strong-willed and defiant black women who have disciplined her and that she senses, in me, a woman who will not, or cannot, discipline her, for which she feels yet more contempt.

The corners of Larissa's mouth are downturned, like fishhooks. Her forehead is furrowed. Her thick-lashed dark-brown eyes might be beautiful except for their smoldering derision. Often I've heard her laughter in the corridor outside our classroom, her jocose banter with friends, and so I know that Larissa's hostile manner in my presence is not natural to her.

Or, if it is natural to Larissa, it is natural to her only in the presence of her (white) instructor.

"Did you bring your composition, Larissa? Good!"

My voice is nervously upbeat, cheerful. My smile is in danger of splitting my lower face in two.

Slowly Larissa spreads out several sheets of tablet paper on the surface of my desk. We ignore the fact that these have obviously been crumpled in someone's fist in fury and afterward opened up, and smoothed out, to a degree. With her fingertips Larissa pushes the handwritten composition toward me as if she's loath to touch it.

It should be noted: Larissa's showy long fingernails aren't merely polished or painted. Each fingernail differs from the others, not only in color but in design: one nail is zebra stripes, another nail is tiny golden suns, another nail is a rainbow swirl . . . When I compliment

Larissa on her nails she accepts my remark with a tight little smile, and makes no comment.

Ma'am I don't want to like you. Don t you be tryin to make me like you. Just—go to Hell!

Larissa's matte-black hair too shows evidence of much painstaking effort on someone's part. Narrow tight-braided cornrows that pull the skin back from her petulant young face and bristle like snakes.

(I see Larissa glance at my nails, which are not only unpolished but also uneven. Perhaps there is a kind of cultural revulsion here, which Larissa feels at the sight of my nails, which she is suppressing out of unusual politeness.)

Larissa's grievance with me, that is, with her unsatisfactory performance in our course, has to do with the fact that I haven't been giving grades to any students who have not been writing at a minimum level—*C*. Below *C*, I don't give any grades at all until work has been revised, since I didn't want to discourage anyone. Larissa is trying to coerce me into giving her a grade—which grade would be, in her case, *F*; yet of course she doesn't want *F*, or even *D*—she wants a higher grade.

Her voice is edgy, scratchy, whining; she expects to be contradicted, but I don't contradict her; I am sympathetic, for that is my role. I understand—Larissa has been ill-prepared for college, even for Continuing Education at Wayne State, which is open admissions. She has been passed along through grade school, middle school, and high school; she has a degree from a notorious inner-city high school that is all but worthless. (Though no white educator can say this, in public.) As Larissa leans forward, I can smell the rich ripe odor of her hair. I can see the pale scalp between the tight-braided cornrows, an elaborate maze. Her body is young, hefty. Her breasts strain against her red sweater, that's decorated with tiny white stars; the faint aureoles of her nipples are palpable beneath. Her waist spills out in fatty roles over the belt of her tight slacks. Straining thighs, hips, belly—

Larissa's flesh exudes a warm, humid abundance. When she forgets to be angry with me, or resentful over her work, she seems childlike, impulsive, pleading. There is something plaintive in the way she repeats, for the second or third time, as if merely repeating these words will force me to placate her, that she needs to pass the course with a *B*—"For my av'r'ge, see, for the nurse school."

B! This isn't likely. Larissa will be lucky if she can raise her grade to *C-*.

And it has occurred to me that an individual so ill-tempered, so easily provoked, and so (seemingly) racist as Larissa Wikawaaya, is not a promising candidate for nursing school.

I shudder to think of Larissa in a nurse's uniform. Approaching the bed of a (white, helpless) patient.

The smoldering fury that provokes this young woman to leave hate-notes beneath a teacher's door could have catastrophic consequences in a hospital setting.

"Nursing school! That sounds—promising. Is there anyone in your family who's a nurse, Larissa?"

Larissa shrugs. Her response is a muttered nasal *Nah.*

"The Nursing School here has an excellent reputation. The Medical School . . ."

I am trying to be friendly, conversational. It isn't my role to discourage any of my students.

With my bright smile I tell Larissa that it isn't too late for her to revise the assignments, and to work hard on the final assignment which is an abbreviated term paper (with footnotes and bibliography!—surely useless pedagogical exercise for students like Larissa, but this is the curriculum requirement). I suggest topics from our anthology—civil rights, women's issues, impact of war, impact of slavery. Alone among the students in our class Larissa has never handed in any revisions. Very likely, she has crumpled and thrown most of the papers away that I'd so painstakingly annotated.

Note: this is an era before word processors and printers. It is not an era before electric typewriters, but only one student in the class seems to have access to an electric typewriter—a highly literate Hispanic woman who is a part-time secretary. The visual clarity of a typed paper might help struggling students compose coherent sentences, out of which coherent paragraphs might be composed, but even manual typewriters seem to be in short supply among my students. Larissa's papers have all been handwritten, on lined sheets of paper raggedly torn from a tablet.

"Mz. Raine, see—I got to pass this course. If . . ."

Larissa is earnest now, anxious. As we've been conferring together for the past several minutes, her bravado seems to have subsided.

"Larissa, writing isn't about 'passing a course.' Writing is about communicating. I'm sure that, if we go through this paper line by line . . ."

"I done that."

"All right, well now we can do it together. Each sentence, line by line . . ."

"Yes ma'am! You say so ma'am!"

Larissa laughs vehemently. Is she genuinely amused by my optimism, or is this adolescent sarcasm; is she disgusted with me, or is she actually hopeful? I invite Larissa to move her chair closer to the desk, and I edge my chair nearer as well. Together we look at her creased tablet papers, that glower dully in the fluorescent light; outside the high-ceilinged, not-clean window the November sky has turned to granite, dark and textureless. There has come a sudden light snowfall. Carefully I read Larissa's faltering sentences aloud, and help her re-phrase them; working in this way, orally, Larissa isn't so confused, nor so defensive. She seems to understand the nature of what a sentence and a paragraph are, at least while we're working together.

This is going surprisingly well. The conference is really not so difficult or so arduous as I'd anticipated. I make suggestions, Larissa repeats the sentences, decides if this is what she means, and takes notes. Like an overgrown child she frowns and grunts with effort. It is not natural for her to focus so intently, I think. To use her eyes, to *read*. She grips her pen oddly, at an awkward angle in her right hand, the colorful fingernails impeding her ability to write, to a degree; but she perseveres. If she were another student I might joke about the glamorous fingernails that must get in the way of her using her fingers easily. I feel like a mother teaching a young child to walk, grasping her child's wrists firmly; not daring to let go.

How old is Larissa Wikawaaya? Her mature-woman's body with heavy hips and breasts make her appear older than her age, I think. She has probably been attractive to men since early adolescence. I'd thought she might be nearly my age but now I can see that she's much younger, no more than twenty.

They seem less destructive, now—the hate-notes. If Larissa Wikawaaya is so young.

I seem to have decided not to bring up the subject. Not to accuse her. Not even to hint at what I suspect, or know.

It has begun to occur to me that Larissa Wikawaaya's writing problems might be essentially reading problems, for she seems to have difficulty deciphering her own handwriting. I open our essay anthology, and ask her to read a few paragraphs from an essay we'd studied in class recently—from James Baldwin's *The Fire Next Time*.

In Detroit, in the aftermath of July 1967 when the black inner city erupted in flame, this classic essay has particular resonance.

"Nah." Larissa's skin flushes darker, her eyes dampen with resentment.

In a coaxing voice I say, "Please, Larissa. Just a few paragraphs. Just try."

Larissa sighs loudly. She is looking very *put-upon*.

It seems clear that she hasn't read the Baldwin essay. It is all utterly unfamiliar to her. Reading words aloud as if blindly—as if she has no idea what she is reading, what the words mean—she seems about to burst into tears. So haltingly does she manage to get through a paragraph, so frequently does she stammer and come to a full stop, I realize that she must be dyslexic.

Perhaps this is the root of the problem, the animosity Larissa Wikawaaya feels for her (white, woman) instructor is the animosity she feels for reading, for school and its frustrations and humiliations.

Miserably Larissa says, "Ma'am you lookin at me so close, that make me—nervous, like . . ."

I ask if she has had help with reading, any special classes in school, and Larissa replies with a shrug, maybe yes, maybe no, as if she doesn't recall. She's defensive now—she has graduated from high school, isn't that sufficient?

"You may have a reading problem, Larissa, that's essentially a neurological problem. You could get help, I could make arrangements . . ."

Larissa is looking embarrassed. Her brightly decorated fingernails are touchingly silly now, as she grasps the heavy paperback anthology in both hands, like a child who isn't sure if she is loved. Her smooth forehead is crinkled in concern.

"'Ner-o-'—what is that? Like, in the head?"

"'Neurological.' 'Dyslexia.' It's very common, Larissa—a condition that scrambles letters and numerals and makes it difficult for you to read."

"Jesus! That like—brain tumor?"

"No. Not at all. When you speak, you don't seem to have much trouble organizing your thoughts . . ."

Larissa laughs, harshly. "They gon let me 'speak' my tests at the school here?—hell they ain't."

Larissa has been strangely restless during our conference. I think it isn't just the intense concentration but another distraction—she has been glancing over her shoulder, at the door, increasingly as the minutes have passed.

As if she half expects someone to be there, in the doorway, or outside in the corridor.

The office door is closed over as I'd requested, but not shut. Figures have passed in shadowy silhouettes against the frosted upper pane of the window set in the door, but no one has approached the door, that I've noticed. By degrees, as students from late-afternoon classes have departed, sounds in the corridor have abated.

"Got to leave now, I guess. You be goin home now . . ."

It is true that my office hours have ended, a few minutes ago. But I have not suggested to Larissa that I am impatient to leave, or want her to leave.

This is puzzling: Larissa both wants to leave my office, but seems hesitant to leave.

I wonder if someone is indeed waiting for her. Out in the corridor, or downstairs. Outside Starret Hall. Somewhere.

Beyond the sprawling university campus with its tall arc lights is a war-zone urban neighborhood intersected by highways. Acres of land abandoned after the "riot" of July 1967. Broken pavement, boarded-up burnt-out buildings, vacant lots reverting to jungles of overgrown trees and vines. There is a particular sort of tree that grows in such detritus—ginkgo. A kind of tough garbage tree, dropping smelly, slimy seeds, plant-equivalent of catfish and other bottom-feeders. Yet the ginkgo is a survivor-tree—a living fossil. And its leaves can be beautiful in spring.

Abruptly at an embankment above the John Lodge Expressway the campus ends. There, a twelve-foot wire-mesh fence against which years of litter have been caught, and calcified.

Yet the human spirit is not extinguished even in such a place. Through a haze of gathering migraine pain, exacerbated by the subtly flickering fluorescent tubing overhead, in the presence of this person who, so unfairly, hates me, I believe this.

EARLY THAT AFTERNOON on a TV in the faculty lounge was news footage of Muslims rioting in a Middle Eastern city. I hadn't time to look, hadn't wished to see. Twenty or more people gathered around the TV, staring and appalled. What was this? Where was this? A man burned alive? We had all seen such footage at the time of the Vietnam War. We had seen too much, our souls have been sickened. On TV now, anything might be shown. There is no protection from it.

A tire had been thrown over a screaming man pursued by a crowd. The man was believed to be a native of the region, a Christian Iraqi. The tire had been doused with gasoline and set on fire by the shrieking mob, the man had died a hideous death: why?

Always, there are reasons. Reasons will be provided.

I had not looked. I rarely watch TV. My husband and I don't own a TV at this (idealistic, naïve) time in our lives.

There was talk in the faculty lounge of a public stoning by Muslim fundamentalists, that had been broadcast recently as well. An "adulterous" couple, young man and young woman, very young, buried in the sand to their heads, killed by their fellow villagers by being struck with stones, rocks. How long would such a death take, you wonder. You hope it would be quick, a quick concussion, skull fracture and the oblivion of death.

You hope. You don't want to know.

The horror of such violence washes over me, though I have not seen. I don't want to know, still less do I want to see. Horror of such hatred, blind wish to punish, to kill, to annihilate—terrifying to me, and leaves me weak.

Hag lady. Think we gon hurt you.

Always there are reasons—"provocations."

The TV commentators will explain. Professors at the university will explain. Ancient feuds, tribal hatreds, religious disputes, political disruption, refugees. This *why* is the account behind the immolation, and the stoning. Hatred of the Christian, and of the "adulterers."

Stories that end where you think they should end are false stories. The only true story is the story that seems to have gone wrong, and resists its ending.

It is past 7:00 P.M. Arc lights penetrate the smoggy dark outside my single office window, amid a flurry of snow. Preparing to leave my office, Larissa moves slowly as if dazed. She is distracted and anxious. She mutters to herself, rubs at her eyes. She has put on her quilted purple coat with iridescent threads, but has not zipped it up, and now removes the coat, muttering it's too hot. The paper we'd examined closely together she folded neatly, and put inside her shoulder bag. She has wanted me to see, to take note. But again I wonder—is Larissa mentally unbalanced? Is she drugged? Her young, heavy flesh doesn't seem altogether healthy, possibly she has diabetes. Maybe she doesn't know she has diabetes. She has been glancing anxiously at the door as if convinced that someone is out in the corridor.

Starret Hall at this hour is all but deserted. There is just one security guard on the first floor, I think.

When I say "Good night" to Larissa, she takes a faltering step toward the door, hunches her shoulders, and begins to cry.

In a sudden stricken convulsion, her body shuddering, and her face contracted like a baby's—Larissa Wikawaaya begins to cry.

I am surprised—shocked. I ask Larissa what is wrong, but Larissa is trembling too badly to answer me.

"Oh, Larissa—what is it? Are you afraid of—someone?"

Vigorously Larissa shakes her head, *no*. She wipes her eyes, her runny nose. She is shivering, and sobbing.

I offer her a tissue—tissues. She is deeply embarrassed, and deeply agitated.

By now I am on my feet, alerted. I am taller than Larissa, and I feel older. I am obliged to be older.

Larissa insists *no, no*—it's nothing. Larissa doesn't intend to confide in me.

Says she's damn sorry. Got to go, now.

"Please—would you like to tell me about it? Larissa? What is—making you unhappy?"

Larissa shakes her head more vehemently—*no*.

Somewhere she has to be, she says. Somewhere she's late getting to.

Or—somebody who's waiting for her. She's got to get there right away . . .

I am thinking that Larissa might not have anywhere to go? Or, wherever she has to go is not a place she has chosen?

I ask her to tell me what is wrong. I ask her if I can help her. I don't offer to call authorities—I know that would be a mistake. Inner-city blacks are not comfortable with the Detroit PD.

In my months teaching at Wayne State, nothing like this has happened to me before. In my entire teaching career of five years. A sudden emotional outburst in my presence, for no clear reason.

Though I have fantasized a confrontation with Larissa Wikawaaya, rehearsing appropriately dignified and irrefutable words, now that an emotional storm has broken, I am at a loss for words. I'm uncertain even what to do—whether to remain behind the desk that is a kind of protective shield, or to step out from behind it, and approach the stricken girl.

My instinct is to touch Larissa Wikawaaya, to clasp her hand or arm even as there comes a warning voice—*Don't touch! She doesn't want your sympathy or pity. It will be a very bad mistake for you to touch Larissa Wikawaaya.*

As if she hears this coolly admonitory voice Larissa mutters something apologetic. She is disgusted with—herself? She is deeply embarrassed. She has decided to bundle herself into the bulky quilted coat after all, that makes her look like a colorful upright dirigible. She fumbles with a glove, that falls to the floor.

Larissa is too bulky in the coat, to stoop for the glove. I pick up the glove and hand it to her. I tell Larissa that her coat is very becoming, and must be very warm.

Larissa stares at me as if she hasn't heard me. Her eyes are widened with a kind of animal fright.

"I'll walk with you, Larissa. It will be all right. I'll walk with you downstairs . . . We won't take the elevator."

My teeth are chattering too. The fright is contagious!

The two of us in Starret Hall, fourth floor—not a good idea. Two women, and all of the offices and classrooms shut up for the night. More than once the thought has come to me in this dreary desolate place—*How vulnerable I am, in this old building. At this hour of night. Who could get to me in time, if I needed help? Who would even hear me?* But now, with Larissa Wikawaaya, I'm determined to walk her safely down three flights of stairs.

We won't take the elevator. It's slow-moving, its interior covered in graffiti, always breaking down and used mostly by handicapped students in wheelchairs. And ill-smelling.

And someone might get into the elevator with us on the next floor down.

In the corridor Larissa heads blindly for the EXIT sign—the stairs.

No one is here. At least, no one is visible.

A corridor of darkened offices, fluorescent lights wanly burning. At the far end of the corridor, a shadowy dead-end. Fourth floor of Starret Hall is a kind of no-man's-land: no classrooms but only the (shared) offices of adjuncts.

I am wondering: Should I touch Larissa? (Just her shoulder, a wrist?) Is this a mistake? Or—not a mistake?

My hand reaches out to her—I am touching Larissa's shoulder. Not firmly, only tentatively. Not sure that she has even noticed, in the bulky coat. (But of course she has noticed. The touch is startling, unexpected.) Larissa is still sobbing, muttering to herself. She is insisting that there is nothing wrong, and that I don't have to come with her any farther. She is sounding a little angry, now. Indignant. Embarrassed. Apologizing for "bawlin like a damn baby"—and I am telling her there is nothing to apologize for.

Still, she's afraid of something—someone. Staring down the stairwell. I'm wondering if I should lead her. If I should take her hand.

And this is what I do: I take Larissa Wikawaaya's not-compliant hand, which is a warm, pudgy hand. We descend the stairs together, two more flights down. The stairs are littered, gritty. The fluorescent lights flicker. Someone shouts below, and we both flinch—but it is nothing. I am telling Larissa about the next essay assignment in our class, which I think will be of interest to her—Maya Angelou's *I Know Why the Caged Bird Sings.*

As we descend to the first floor, where there are more night school students, Larissa begins to seem embarrassed that she's being noticed. Her tear-glittering face, her halting manner on the stairs. She pulls her hand from mine. Her eyes are downcast. She hopes not to see anyone who knows her. Walking with me, her (white, woman) instructor! At the outer door, she hesitates. The cold air strikes our faces. Larissa's breath steams faintly. She is eager to slip away from me, and yet hesitant; her narrowed dark eyes dart about, as if she's looking for someone out there . . . When I ask if I should walk with her to a parking lot, or a bus stop, she shakes her head *no.* When I ask if I should call a taxi, for which I will pay the fare, she shakes her head emphatically *no.*

Then she's outside, walking hurriedly away. Purple quilted coat, knee-high boots, cornrowed hair bristling around her head.

"Good-bye! Good night . . . ."

Larissa doesn't glance back at me but lifts her gloved hand in a gesture of acknowledgment and farewell that seems to me friendly, almost sisterly.

But I will be so very disappointed: Larissa Wikawaaya never returns to our class.

2. MARCH 1985. EDSEL PARK, MICHIGAN

At Quest Laboratories on Woodward Avenue, just above Eight Mile Road in the Detroit suburb of Edsel Park, I am told to take a number and wait.

How busy the place is! The waiting room is alarmingly crowded.

There's a smell of disinfectant, panic. Children fretting, and several crying. From where I am seated I can see a child of three or four screaming in terror as a nurse tries to draw blood from his tiny arm.

It's a painful sight. The mother and the nurse try to hold the child down. The mother pleads with him, scolds. This won't hurt, don't be a baby, the nurse is using a baby-needle, see?—but the child, knowing better, continues to scream. As I wait for my number to be called, another child begins to cry. I am being made to feel shaky, anxious. I am thinking *Children should be protected from such fear. We should all be protected.*

Why am I here! It is a mistake, I think.

Yet, I won't leave. I dare not leave. I have a prescription for blood work that is already dated twenty-two days ago.

"Ma'am? Is something wrong?"

One of the medical staff approaches me, warily. In an unwitting gesture of dismay I've hidden my face in my hands.

Quickly and courteously I say no, nothing is wrong.

I smile to indicate that I don't mind waiting. Or—I might mind waiting, but I am determined to be stoical.

I've brought work with me, I don't intend to waste time. Hoping to blot out the cries of terrified children. The air of barely constrained chaos in this crowded place.

I no longer live in Detroit, but I have returned to Detroit for the spring term 1985 as a visiting "distinguished" professor at Marymount College. There, I've been teaching a graduate seminar in "Linguistics and Gender." I am no longer a young woman but I am no longer a desperate young adjunct instructor uncertain of a future.

At Marymount, I have a number of excellent graduate students. Several members of the faculty are auditing my seminar. At the same time, I am writing a paper for a linguistics conference later in the spring.

For this semester I am living apart from my husband. Carefully we've explained that being "apart" doesn't mean "separated."

Sometimes I am overwhelmed with a dizzy sort of elation at this living-alone, this strange "freedom" in the midst of a marriage of almost twenty years. But sometimes I am so very lonely, it feels as if the marrow of my bones has turned to ice.

I am determined to live an independent life. I think this is why I have come back to Detroit, to try again in this place in which I was so often desperate, now with more strength and conviction.

Those of us who married young can never know how we might have fared without marriage. How reckless we might have been, how fortunate, or unfortunate. My husband has seemed to understand—*I think you need to make these explorations. I think this will be your best time.*

He hasn't discouraged me. But he hasn't encouraged me. His love for me is such that he wants for me whatever it is I believe that I want even when (as he has said) he believes that whatever it is I believe I want will turn out to be mistaken. Yet, he wants me to make this discovery for myself.

Such love makes me feel humble, unworthy. I am not sure that I am capable of such selfless love, in return.

Such thoughts distract me from the hyperactivity in the blood-drawing room. I think I must have come at the wrong time, in late morning—so many frightened children!

Though this is Edsel Park, one of the older, working-class and "integrated" suburbs of Detroit, most of the medical staff seems to be black including the supervising nurse, and most of those who've come to have blood drawn are black.

I haven't told my husband about being prescribed for blood work, for I don't want to worry him needlessly. Whatever might be wrong with me is probably quite minor—anemia, possibly. I've been anemic intermittently since adolescence.

I don't want to think that illness at this time might force me to return to my husband prematurely, nor do I want to think that illness might force my husband back to me . . . My husband is a person of integrity and generosity and would never abandon me if I were seriously ill. But I don't want to think, either, that good health would free him.

Much of the time, I don't *want to think* at all about what you would call personal, not professional, matters.

"Ma'am? Comin with me, OK?"

The nurse to whom I have been assigned is a husky dark-skinned woman in her early thirties. She is brisk, matter-of-fact, friendly-seeming as I stumble in her wake staring in amazement: is this Larissa Wikawaaya?

Her hair isn't braided in cornrows, her manner isn't so petulant and irritable. She is actually smiling at me, just slightly impatiently.

Does she recognize me? Mz. Rane?

"Ma'am? Somethin wrong?"

Hesitantly I say, feeling blood rush into my face, "I—I think we know each other—'Larissa'?"

The nurse smiles harder. Indentations in her dark, sturdy cheeks. Cups her hand to her ear as if she hasn't heard clearly.

"Your name—it's 'Larissa'?"

"Nah, ma'am. No name like that, see. 'Bettina.'" With a roll of her eyes the nurse indicates a laminated ID around her neck, identifying her as BETTINA SMITH.

I am sure, this is Larissa Wikawaaya. She's eleven years older, not so heavy as she'd been; her features are less boldly defined, and she is no longer seemingly hostile. And she is exactly the right height.

I tell her that I'm sure she was once a student of mine—at Wayne State? In 1974.

"No, ma'am."

Bettina laughs. She is determined not to be annoyed by me, for she has become a nurse; or possibly, she is a nurse's aide, trained to draw blood expertly. She is a professional medical worker in a white nylon uniform, white smock, white slacks, white crepe-soled shoes. Her hair is not flamboyantly cornrowed but flattened against her head. The striking fingernails have been replaced by ordinary-sized nails polished a dark plum color.

I'm not sure of Larissa's last name, how to pronounce it—"Wi-kawaaya'?"

"What yo' sayin, ma'am? 'Wikki'—what?"

Bettina laughs as if she has never heard this exotic name before and might reasonably wonder: is it a familiar name? show-business name? Motown? Some sort of joke?

Or is it indeed her name, or was once her name, which she no longer wishes to acknowledge?

Carefully I pronounce the name: "'Larissa Wikawaaya.'"

"Nah, ma'am. Never heard 'Wikkiwatta' before, f'sure."

Medical workers at Quest are accustomed to exchanges with patients. No doubt, many of their patients are eccentric, elderly or infirm, and some are likely to be mentally unbalanced—you would expect such, at Quest Laboratories in Edsel Park just across Eight Mile Road from Detroit, Michigan.

I am determined to make it clear to smiling Bettina that I am not one of these individuals. She can see that I am an intelligent woman, presumably educated; possibly, a teacher. I am serious, and I am not mistaken or deluded. With a courteous smile, I persist: "Are you sure? You aren't—a former student? You look so very much like Larissa—she was about twenty at the time, in 1974. Are you sure that you never took a composition course with me, in the night school, at Wayne State . . . My name is Helen Raine."

"Ma'am, I am sure. For sure, see, I'd remember *you*."

Bettina is amused. Bettina is unhesitant in her denial. Bettina is very busy, she indicates; as I can see, the waiting room is crammed.

"It's just that you look so—so much like her . . . Do you have a sister? A cousin . . ."

Briskly Bettina has led me to a cubicle. I feel a sensation of dread, not wanting to enter, and to sit in the chair. Not wanting to have Larissa Wikawaaya draw my blood.

Bettina asks if I am feeling faint? If I am anxious about having my blood drawn? Though I assure Bettina that I am fine, Bettina isn't so sure. For Bettina sees something in my face, and sees that I am shaky, and have been walking unsteadily. My lips feel cold, as if bloodless.

I assure Bettina, or Larissa, that I am fine, maybe a little tired, just slightly sleep-deprived, worrying the night before about having my blood drawn, but fine—"Not faint. I don't faint."

Is this meant as a joke? It has come out wrong.

Close by, terribly loud—the child continues to scream. I want to press the palms of my hands over my ears. I am indeed feeling faint, feeling sick. I want to rush out of Quest Laboratories and never return.

"Ma'am, you sit, OK?"

Bettina is poking my left arm with deft fingers. If this is indeed

Larissa, she gives not the slightest sign; as a practiced medical worker she is both kindly and just slightly vexed. "Eh, ma'am, look like you sweatin. But you cold. Yo' veins so small, you forgot to drink water this mornin, did you? Nobody told you, you got to drink water, make your veins get bigger?"

I am feeling devastated: no one told me! I've had blood drawn in the past, and no one had ever suggested drinking water beforehand.

"Ma'am, better you come over here with me."

Frowning Bettina leads me away from the screaming child to a quieter cubicle in a farther corner. Here there is a chair that is a kind of recliner with a crossbar, like a baby's high chair, presumably to prevent the subject from toppling over in a faint. Weakly I'm protesting that I don't need this—I am not, truly, going to faint! Yet, Bettina seems to know better. I would not have imagined that I could be made so anxious by mere nerves—having to hear those screaming children—and yet, it seems to be so. I am feeling the floor shift beneath me, and I am feeling distinctly light-headed. This is a common symptom of anemia, the doctor has told me.

Bettina settles me into the recliner-chair, and fastens the bar across my midriff. She tightens a blood-pressure cuff around my upper arm, and frowns at the result—"Ma'am, you just eighty-nine over sixty. That *low*."

The supervisor is consulted. It's decided that I should wait for a few minutes, then Bettina will take my blood pressure again. This time, it isn't so low—"One hundred over eighty-seven."

How passive I am feeling, like one who has been hypnotized! A strange lassitude has come over me. As if I am already in the hospital, and Larissa Wikawaaya is my nurse.

But does she recognize me? Does she know *me*?

Frequently in the intervening years I've thought of Larissa Wikawaaya, always with a tinge of emotion—wondering what became of her, if she returned to school, if she managed to get into nursing school after all. It was something of a shock to me, she'd never returned to my class after our conference that had seemed so constructive. But she hadn't failed the course since she'd officially withdrawn with a grade of *I*—"Incomplete"—which meant that she could take the course again, with another instructor.

I've never told anyone about Larissa Wikawaaya, except in the most general terms. A difficult Wayne State student, dyslexic, whom I wanted to think I'd helped . . .

In the recliner with the crossbar securing me in place, I am urged by Bettina to try to "relax." At the same time, as Bettina ties a rubber band tightly around my upper left arm, I am told to make a fist— "hard." Bettina pokes at my veins with her forefinger, frowning. Several times she tries to sink her needle into a vein, and secure the vein, but each time she fails. "Them itty-bitty veins just *slide away* . . ." I am trying not to flinch with pain and discomfort.

I am thinking *Of course this is Larissa Wikawaaya. This is her revenge, of which she has no conscious knowledge.*

Bettina tries higher on the inside of my arm, and again fails. The needle hurts! Now I have become taut with dread. Trembling with anxiety. Bettina sighs in exasperation—(that is Larissa Wikawaaya's sigh, I would recognize anywhere)—gives up on my left arm, and tries my right. Again—"Ma'am, c'n you make a real tight fist? Try'n relax, ma'am."

She isn't scolding me. You could say that she is scolding my narrow veins, or one of her medical worker colleagues who failed to advise me to drink water before coming here.

I am thinking that I can't bear this. Like the stricken children, I will be screaming in another minute. Scream and scream for Larissa Wikawaaya to stop this torment so that I can flee from this terrible place.

I feel a wave of faintness rise from the base of my skull, a sensation of utter desolation, despair.

"Ma'am? You OK?"

Mutely I nod *yes.*

"You doin real well, ma'am. I'm gon find a vein right now."

Not right now, but in a few minutes, at last on the tender inside of my left wrist, Bettina manages to secure an elusive vein.

By this time I am breathing quickly, shallowly. My vision is splotched and wavering. On Bettina's short upper lip I see a film of oily moisture. Such strange intimacy between us—I think *For the second time in our lives.*

Now, the ordeal is just to keep conscious. As the needle draws little vials of blood. Three vials!

I shut my eyes, and with the fingers of my free hand I grip the edge of the chair arm, tight. I am thinking—how lonely I am! How badly I want my husband, and not this aloneness.

Gently Bettina encourages me to relax. Almost over now, ma'am, she says.

At last, the ordeal is finished. Bettina seems proud of me, that I have been such a "good brave" patient. "Nobody like bein stuck, that's f'sure." Bettina presses a gauze square against the tiny puncture wound and instructs me to apply pressure to it.

"Just sit here till you feelin stronger, ma'am. You OK, see?"

I am immensely grateful to Bettina, now that the needle has been removed. Now that the ordeal is over. Almost, I could cry—I am so grateful.

I fumble to remove the crossbar, pushing at it with the need to get away.

"Ma'am, you gon hurt yourself, you doin that . . ."

It's too soon for me to stand. My knees are weak, my head is swimming. Bettina urges me to wait. She grips my hand in hers. She is comforting me—squeezing my hand. She is inches shorter than I am, and some years younger. She helps me to my feet.

Bettina's strong fingers, gripping both my arms at the elbow.

Faintly scolding Bettina says: "Now you ain't gon faint on me, ma'am, are you? Now it's all over?"

I tell her *no.*

"You got anybody here with you, waitin for you?"

Now I see: the eyes that are thick-lashed, very dark, kindly and yet evasive. *She knows me. Something in my face, she knows.* And quickly I assure her *yes,* there is someone waiting for me, in our car in the parking lot, my husband who will drive me home. For I don't want to distress this woman any more than I already have.

Before I leave, I use the restroom at Quest. I run cold water to splash onto my face that looks splotched, oddly flushed. I am forty-one years old, I feel as if I am at the midpoint of my life. At such times, the midpoint of vast and impersonal and unchartable life itself.

Recalling how after that session in my office in Starret Hall, I never again received another hate-note shoved beneath my door.

The Quiet Car

Nowhere are we so exposed, so vulnerable, as on an elevated platform at a suburban train depot.

In balmy weather, choosing to stand outside to await the 11:17 A.M. to New York City instead of huddling in the depot with its stained floor and malodorous restrooms and incongruously pew-like benches.

Even if "known"—that is, even if an individual of considerable accomplishments, not famous but (certainly) admired in some quarters.

Seeing then, by the purest chance, for he rarely looks around in such circumstances, a person staring at him—unmistakably.

And this person, a woman, amid a gathering of passengers oblivious of him as they are oblivious of each other.

Quickly he looks away. Is the woman someone he knows, or has known? Someone who seems to know *him*?

A startled expression in the woman's face. A long horsey face, doughy-pale skin, an impression of long teeth bared in a half-smile, or half-grimace, of something like disbelief, yet recognition; clearly the woman (middle-aged, stolid and nondescript, with gray-stippled hair) is surprised to see him, but isn't brazen enough to call out to him, in the moment before, casually, without acknowledging that he has seen her, he turns away.

It's a risk of being "known"—if only to a very small subset of literate Americans.

Rarely does R___ lose his poise, in such circumstances. For sometimes it does happen, more often in a museum, that a stranger will stare at him as if trying to place him, and if the stranger is reasonably attractive, whether female or male, of some possible interest to R___, he may smile, and acknowledge the recognition; might even, depending upon his mood, shake hands, exchange a few words. *I'm an admirer of your writing*—these words he has heard a gratifying number of times in public places, deflected with a murmur of thanks and a modest smile.

This morning on the train platform, in a bright blaze of unsparing autumn sunshine, the horse-faced woman isn't attractive enough to merit a second glance.

And the train is arriving at the depot, exactly on time.

SO ACCUSTOMED HAS R___ BECOME to the New York City train arriving at Track 1, he has half-consciously memorized the exact place on the platform where the door to the Quiet Car, which happens to be the first car, will line up.

Briskly he steps inside, and takes his usual seat near the front of the car, left side of the train; lays his raincoat beside him, to discourage another passenger from sitting there. (Though, in the Quiet Car, it isn't likely that anyone would sit with a lone passenger unless there were no other empty seats.)

In the Quiet Car, a tense sort of quiet prevails. For where there is a generic prescribed quiet, even subdued murmurs and whispers are jarring; of course, cell phones are forbidden, and fellow passengers are vigilant to uphold the rules.

From time to time an unwitting passenger will blunder into the Quiet Car talking to a companion, or on a cell phone—the occupants of the Quiet Car will glare at him but (usually) will not say anything in the hope that the conductor will come by quickly, and restore order.

In all things, *order* is maintained by authority, which is a kind of force. *Disorder* is the default.

It is not an exaggeration to say that R___, who loves few things about his life, loves the New Jersey Transit Quiet Car. He loves the isolation, the solitude, the "invisibility" of quiet; the understanding that no one will speak to him, and that he need not speak to anyone. If a friend or acquaintance comes into the Quiet Car it is protocol for them to sit alone, with no more than a nod or smile of acknowledgment. Here, eyes shift away. Most people have brought work. Even the conductor will murmur politely, if speech is required.

R___ had not willingly moved to this suburban place. He had not willingly left the city. Financial constraint determined the move which (as it has turned out) was a very good idea though it is (still, after years) not an idea that brings pleasure and so he rarely thinks of it and if he does, if he is obliged to think of it, it is the Quiet Car in which his abraded soul takes sanctuary.

As the train pulls out of the depot he resists the impulse to glance around, to see if the horse-faced woman has followed him into the Quiet Car. He does not think she would dare sit with him—surely not—but it would be as annoying to him if she were to sit across from him, or behind him. If she'd taken a seat in the Quiet Car a few rows back, to study him from afar.

At last, steeling himself he glances around—and doesn't see her.

Relief! Yet (he has to concede) mild disappointment.

For now he will never know why the woman, seemingly a stranger, had looked at him so strangely. As if she hadn't just recognized R___ but had been startled to see him.

On the trip to New York City he usually reads that day's *New York Times*. If he reads slowly enough, with the obsessive care of one with a surplus of time on his hands, the entire seventy-minute trip will be taken up by the paper, which he (more or less) forgets as he reads, and which he can then jettison at Penn Station.

He has brought along "work" as well—notes he has been taking on a new project that hovers just out of sight like a shimmering mirage that, as he approaches, retreats . . .

Flatlands of New Jersey. Rears of crumbling buildings, rooftop water towers, fences topped with razor wire. Open fields and wetlands, trees growing out of mounds of rubble . . . By Elizabeth the air has turned sour like fermentation. By Edison the white-hued autumn light seems to have dimmed. He has not been thinking of the horse-faced woman but suddenly he remembers her: Carol Carson.

That bland, generic name! He recalls what a strain it had been to feign interest in the earnest young woman, who'd seemed even at the time, at least twenty-five years ago, on the brink of middle age; one of a dozen students in a graduate seminar he'd taught at a distinguished university in a time he'd come to consider, in rueful retrospect, the very pinnacle of his career.

R___ had a visiting professorship at the university, in fact he was to be invited to teach there several times. Overall he was treated very well by the university—that is, the Humanities Program in which he'd been hired—and yet he'd never been offered a full-time position with tenure. His was a quasi-glamorous career navigated at the periphery of the academic world, a matter of prestigious but finite appointments; endowed professorships that, for all that they were well paid, ran their course within a semester. Of course R___ understood: he had not the formal requirements for a permanent position with tenure, for he had only a master's degree in comparative literature. He had not (probably) the professional commitment to an academic vocation that would require much beyond the teaching of advanced seminars and the giving of a few public lectures. His name had some currency, as merely academic or scholarly names did not; he was an attraction midway between "popularity" and "obscurity" though (to R___, at least) it was something of a joke that anyone might regard his career with envy, supposing that his books *sold well.*

Still, he'd published in the *New York Review of Books,* the *New Yorker,* and the *New York Times,* a trifecta of sorts, interpreted as glamour by those who'd never published in journals with circulations beyond a thousand. For a brief vertiginous while he'd published a "witty"—"scathing"—column in *Vanity Fair* in which, with the zestful ferocity of a state-appointed torturer, he'd castigated the overly talented for their ambition. And he'd always been grateful, which is a kind of innocent vanity, as if sensing at the time that such achievements, like a career as a tightrope walker, might be tied to the energies of youth, and would run their course in time.

As a young man R___ had acquired a *certain reputation* in New York literary circles. Like "indelible" ink a *certain reputation* does indeed fade with time but does not quite vanish.

In the seminar, with its intriguing title "Dystopian Visions," each student had been carefully selected, by application, for more than fifty students had applied for twelve openings, and, as a young instructor at the time, R___ had taken the responsibility seriously.

She, the woman, one of only three young women in the seminar, had intrigued R___ only initially; he'd been impressed by the writing sample she had submitted, a close reading of texts by Kierkegaard, Rilke, and Camus. But as soon as he realized which student she was, which of the young women, he'd been disappointed, and bored. Of course he made every attempt to disguise his lack of interest in her as he made every attempt to be courteous to all of his students and to seem not too obviously to favor some over others— those who impressed him as sharp, bright, possibly brilliant; those who turned out to be "good" but not extraordinary; those who were touchingly intimidated by him, yet did not fawn; and those who were annoyingly intimidated by him, and did fawn.

He recalls: a glinting-red-haired young woman, almost a beauty except for oddly wide nostrils and a sharp nose; a heavyset young woman with skin that resembled foam rubber; and the horse-faced girl, "Carol Carson," who seemed so clearly in awe of R___, if not in love with him, he'd found it difficult to look at her. He couldn't decide if she was amusing, or embarrassing; gratifying (to his ego), or exasperating. Though not so heavy as the other young woman she was far from slender, an athletic-looking girl except she moved with a plodding sort of deliberation; when he happened to see her in the corridor of the humanities building, unaware of him, she was likely to be staring down at her feet as she moved, a small fixed insipid smile on her lips.

In the seminar, Carol Carson seemed to accept a minor role from the start. Diligently she took notes, shyly she gazed at R___ at times with parted, moist lips. She never disagreed with anyone even when (R___ sensed) she might have had something to say. He grew impatient with her, cruel—"And what do you think, Miss Carson? *Do* you think?" The others laughed, eager to align themselves with their young professor; Miss Carson blushed, and bit her lower lip.

If R___ persevered, she might finally speak; it was as if (he eventually realized) this annoying student required his permission to speak in his presence, each time. Often then she contributed astute and original remarks about Dostoyevsky, H. G. Wells, Aldous Huxley; when he asked her to read passages from one of her papers, the others were impressed as well, if but temporarily. In any group there are those who must be acknowledged, and admired; there are those who make no demands upon us, for whom we feel a kind of gratitude, that they expect little from us and so will not object when it is little we give them, in our zeal to give the others what they demand.

Especially, unlike even the other young women in the seminar,

Carol Carson lacked the edgy feistiness, or flirtatiousness, of those female students who might have been identified as nascent feminists; she seemed to belong to another, earlier era when plain-faced females did not aspire to much beyond their station, neither muses nor creative artists themselves. When R___ took up Robert Graves's blunt remark "A woman is a muse or she is nothing" no one in the seminar took particular issue with it, and even the women laughed, if uneasily. She, Carol Carson, had shaken her head in a kind of giddy mirth, at the mere prospect of a woman who might brashly aspire to creativity.

She'd worn dull, dour clothes of no discernible hue. Wide-hipped, with a flat chest. It may have been a small gold cross she wore around her neck—R___ had never looked closely. The long face exuded a mournful air and the often bared and damp teeth a look of childish trust but the eyes—(he was remembering now with a quickening of interest)—were thick-lashed, amber and beautiful; intelligent eyes, yet without confidence. It was typical of Carol Carson, he thought, that, though she was one of the more impressive students in the class, she did not behave as if she knew this; in fact, she seemed to shrink from such knowledge, like a tall person who tries to minimize his height. It exasperated R___ how the girl deferred to the least talented (male) student in the seminar, as if such deference were his due.

One thing was clear and unwavering: Carol Carson's fixation upon *him*.

Had the other students noticed? R___ supposed so. No one seemed to be a friend of hers, who might have suggested to Carol Carson that she was making a fool of herself; though perhaps, so far as R___ knew, it was all utterly harmless, schoolgirl behavior—just slightly incongruous in a graduate student of obvious intelligence. She'd allowed R___ to know, however obliquely, and shyly, that she had to travel an absurd distance to attend his seminar on Thursday afternoons, the sole university course she was taking at the time;

for she was the caretaker of an aging, ailing parent in a small town beyond the upscale suburban setting of the university. She'd been a graduate student in some obscure subject—an amalgam of linguistics and psychology; for some unclear reason, she'd taken courses at the seminary attached to the university.

R___ had asked if she intended to become "a woman of God"—(the expression had seemed comical to him)—and Carol Carson had answered solemnly, "Oh no, Professor. I couldn't be that," as if the prospect were too grand. She added, "I want to know all that I can know about God, I don't want to be a theologian." And then she'd blushed fiercely, for having uttered a statement that so conjoined the pretentious and the preposterous.

After the three-hour seminar, when R___ was eager to depart, there was Carol Carson lingering in the wood-paneled room, slowly packing her things; glancing toward R___ with lips parted in a fragile smile, awaiting a kind word from him—"Excellent work today!" or better yet, "Would you like to have a coffee, Carol?" Of course, R___ would never utter such words; it was all R___ could do to smile toward the awkward girl with gritted teeth and without quite seeing her, muttering, "Good night!"

Before Christmas break she hauled into the seminar room a bag of hardcover books revealed to be, after the other students had departed, copies of R___'s first two books, and in a paroxysm of shyness she asked if he would mind inscribing them: "I'm giving just special books as Christmas presents this year." R___ had been gracious, if somewhat embarrassed. (He would think afterward that no one else in the seminar had purchased a book of his, so far as he knew, though they'd all seemed to admire their young professor very much.)

Recalling now the dour, doughy-skinned face flushed with pleasure when he handed back a paper on which he'd written in red ink *Very promising. Thoughtful & original. A.*

Yet—something had gone wrong. What was it?

Twenty-five years ago. No, longer—at least twenty-eight years ago . . .

When he'd still been married. Before he'd become estranged from both his children.

When he'd been in the heedless ascendancy of his career and not (as he could not not concede) as he was now, in its long slow afternoon of decline.

Carol Carson—(barely can R___ tolerate that name, it has become ever more grating in its banality)—had made an appointment to have a conference with him in his borrowed office, to discuss her final paper; and R___ had forgotten. Or rather, an acquaintance had come to town, an editor of a distinguished literary journal whom he'd hoped to cultivate. (Or had the editor hoped to cultivate R___? In such relationships in mimicry of friendship there is invariably a gentleman's quid pro quo which no one would be crude enough to acknowledge, still less to name.)

All these maneuvers, these transactions, or plotted transactions, which had held such promise to change his life for the better, had come to nothing much; or, perhaps to something, that had turned out to be, for all the excitement in their contriving, nothing much. The intense, heightened, thrilling and occasionally risky alliances he'd made in New York literary circles, the quickly forged bonds, broken promises, minor betrayals and feuds for life, embittered recriminations in an era before email when a letter might be an investment of hours to be recalled for decades—most of these turned gossamer-thin, faded and forgotten.

Worse yet—(he is remembering now, like one who has flung open a door so wide it can't be easily shut)—he'd disappointed the girl another time, at least; not his fault, was it?—for Carol Carson so pursued him, in her plodding, deliberate way, a figure of pathos in graceless snow boots like hooves, a scarf tied hastily about her head, eyes downcast as she'd trudged through a blizzard to the humanities building bearing more of R___'s books for him to sign; though she must have known, as any child would have known, that no faculty member was likely to be in the department at that time, on Friday afternoon in a blizzard.

The departmental secretary was the only person on the floor, and she'd been preparing to shut up the office early that day. With sly cruel humor she would report to R___ how Carol Carson showed up with books for him to sign and had lingered outside his door in a little puddle of melted snow from her boots—"Forlornly, poor thing."

Carol Carson had asked the secretary if R___ had been there and the secretary said, "I'm sorry, I don't think he has. I wouldn't expect to see him until next Thursday."

Of course, it had been some foolish misunderstanding. R___ had (probably) misheard Carol Carson's request for a conference at that particular time; or he'd heard, without troubling to write it down. The blizzard was entirely fortuitous.

How exhausting, another's adoration! By the end of the semester R___ had had quite enough of the lovestruck girl who seemed never to be hurt if he was short with her in class, or failed to smile at her in the corridor, or amended her grade of A with a slash of a minus.

It was not his fault. At the end of the term he'd been confronted with an embarrassment of very good work. Never again would he invest quite so much enthusiasm, energy, and zeal into any university course as he did in this, with the result that virtually all of the twelve students handed in worthy papers; yet, he could not hand out A's to more than half the seminar, with a sprinkling of A-; and so he'd given Carol Carson a B+, downgrading her final, ambitious paper ("Dystopian Visions Through the Eyes of Virginia Woolf") along with work by the other young women, and the weaker male students—leaving him with a respectable spread of grades from C+ to A, to which no dean could object. One or two of the young men had complained, but none of the young women; certainly not Carol Carson who accepted her fate and retreated without a murmur.

It had been a triumphant semester, of a kind. R___ had quite enjoyed his Thursdays at the suburban university. Invited to dinners most weeks by distinguished faculty at the university and at the Institute for Advanced Study close by, where his *certain reputation* guaranteed a general interest among even those who rarely read books by living writers.

That year, one of R___'s books received full-page, laudatory reviews in the *New York Times Book Review* and in the *New York Review of Books;* he acquired a Parisian publisher. He was short-listed for a major book award in that ambiguous area of non-fiction categorized as cultural criticism, but failed to win; in subsequent years, though he would write better books (in his opinion) he would not be nominated for any award. Who can understand such things? In the decline and fall of others we see a natural, inevitable trajectory; in our own, a bafflement, an injustice and an outrage. Sand and pebbles slipping beneath his feet, despite the care with which he strode along the walkway gripping a railing . . .

Had Carol Carson written to R___, after that semester? Not to accuse him of treating her unfairly, of course, not in reproach, for reproach is not the way of the Carol Carsons of the world. Rather, she had written flattering letters to him, thanking him again for the "wonderful, unforgettable" semester that had "changed my life"; plying him with requests for reading lists, suggestions for graduate schools, advice. She'd dared to ask if she might meet with him in New York City, just once. Of course, she'd asked him for a letter of recommendation to be "placed in my file."

He had not answered. Vaguely he'd meant to answer but—he had not. His relationship with the distinguished university had become clouded. He could not punish anyone on the faculty but he could punish, however obliquely, one of their students. Nor had he any interest in a pen pal relationship with an earnest, deeply boring and unattractive girl however bright, imaginative, and adoring of him. Soon, the letters ceased.

He'd totally forgotten her. Not one minute of one hour of thousands of hours since he'd last glimpsed her a quarter-century before (in the humanities seminar room, slowly assembling her books and papers, only just daring to glance up at R___ with shy amber eyes aswim with moisture as he talked and laughed with the glinting red-haired girl standing very close to him) had he thought of "Carol Carson."

So all things pass into oblivion, and are not mourned. As the train to New York City passing through the nondescript New Jersey countryside is a kind of moving oblivion. You see, but you don't *see.* Your eyes glance at, but don't retain. The brain is not involved. Attention is elsewhere. Concentration is too precious to squander.

In Penn Station, the journey ends abruptly. In jangling darkness that yields reluctantly to dimness, then to (muted) (underground) lights.

R___ is lost in a reverie, and has not finished even the first section of the day's paper. Yet, he will toss all of the paper out. He doesn't want to be burdened with carrying even a newspaper. He feels a sudden revulsion for what is called *news.*

By this time he has been thinking so intensely of the horse-faced woman, he finds himself looking for her when he leaves the train. Hordes of strangers, hurrying past him; that air of clamor and impatience; he calculates that the middle-aged woman who'd once been his young, hopeful student had probably boarded the car just behind the Quiet Car, for she was standing at that position on the platform . . .

And now, again, he sees her through a gap in the crowd: on her way to the escalator, but pausing to stare at him.

Indeed it is Carol Carson, in her fifties. Grown yet more plain, thickset. Someone's mother. Grandmother. Unless, more likely, she had never married.

Yet the eyes are still striking, moistly amber, thick-lashed and fixed on him.

"H-Hello! Professor—" Her voice is hoarse, wavering. She calls him by the old, formal title though he has not been a professor in years. "I think you saw me looking at you, I'm sorry but I was surprised—" She pauses, embarrassed; she is a clumsy woman, and tactless; graceless; she wears a hideous "pantsuit" and clunky shoes; she could be a minister, a teacher, a public defender, a social worker; there is that air of service about her, a grim persistent service that thrusts itself upon others, to their despair.

"I'm sorry, Professor—I—I guess—well, I"—again she pauses, with a fleet, fatuous smile—"I'd heard you had died . . ."

"'Died.' Really."

He is shocked. He is deflated. His eyes blink rapidly, as if in a bright blinding light.

"I mean, obviously—I thought I'd heard . . . I don't know if I had *actually heard* . . ."

The silly, maddening woman! R___ would like to turn away, stride briskly away without a backward glance. Yet there is something in the woman's expression that holds him, the look of girlish yearning in her eyes, and bafflement, wonder.

On the platform beside the Quiet Car he is trying to recover. His old poise, equilibrium. Though he is not so young and resilient as he'd once been, in his professorial days, in the days of the Dystopian seminar when a young woman had trudged through a blizzard on his behalf, and had not for a moment blamed him for scorning her.

With a cool smile, like a performer in an Oscar Wilde comedy, R___ says archly: "Well! What did you feel, when you'd heard that I'd died?"

Smiling at the silly woman through a haze of pain, an imminent headache. Yet it is crucial to continue to smile as if nothing at all were wrong, on the platform at Penn Station, as strangers pass around him and Carol Carson impatiently, like a rough current in which they are fixed as bodies trapped between boulders in the stream.

"'What did I feel?'"—The woman pauses as if seriously thinking, frowning. "Well. To be frank I guess I didn't feel anything much." Adding then, as if such a fine point might be appreciated by her listener, "I'd never known you well, Professor. When you were alive."

The Bereaved

"We should go away. Separately."

Separately. Rhymes with *desperately.*

Distinctly she'd heard her husband speak. But his back was to her—(it seemed now, her husband's back always was to her: she would have to imagine a face imposed upon the back as in a Magritte painting)—and so, she could easily feign not-quite-hearing. For much of marriage is an affable not-quite-hearing.

If the husband had wanted the wife to hear precisely what he'd said, he'd have faced her. So the wife reasoned.

Also, the wife's right ear was infected. She'd been putting drops into that ear for days. So, if the husband said *My head is filled with mucus* the wife heard *My head is filled with music* and smiled at the thought—for it was certainly a happy thought, like a rising balloon.

Not mucus, music.

Not separate, desperate.

"Yes. You're right. Oh yes—but where shall we go?"

It was not subtle, this *we.* With the bright blind confidence with which she often addressed the husband, that so grated his nerves, the wife spoke as if *we* were singular and indissoluble as a fist-sized chunk of Kryptonite.

Quickly adding, before the husband could turn to her, and protest— "Somewhere she'd never been. Somewhere without memory."

IT WAS THE SLAIN DAUGHTER of whom they did not speak.

Slain because she had died so suddenly, the wife imagined the violent sweep of a scythe.

"Yes, thank you. Thank you for calling. Yes, Daphne was my stepdaughter. You know she was my stepdaughter, why do you ask? Max's daughter, and my stepdaughter. Thank you for your condolences but no—I don't think that's a good idea right now. Max has no interest in speaking to you."

Thank you and go to hell. Never call again.

Soon it would be the first birthday after the death. Was there a particular, Latinate term for such an anniversary?—not the date of the (step)daughter's death which had been October 11 but the date of the (step)daughter's birthday which was December 19.

The two dates would compete now, the wife thought. Birth-date, death-date. And the two numerals in perfect equipoise: 1992–2014.

Since that night in October when the terrible news had come to them they were orphaned parents. The little boat of their marriage had come unmoored. The daughter had been their only child and the opportunity (the wife freely conceded) for the wife to have been essential in the marriage, in helping to raise the "difficult" daughter.

Like putting your only egg in one basket, and dropping the basket.

The wife did not utter this inanity aloud. The wife's head was a Niagara Falls of inanities whose din seemed to be increasing but these were interior, private.

Yet somehow, the wife understood that the husband sensed her words, and was repelled by her. For she felt obliged to turn all that she could into nervous jokes.

"A maker of witticisms, a bad soul"—someone weighty had said that—Pascal, possibly.

It was years since the wife had read Pascal's *Pensées* in an advanced French course. In times of crisis she reached for Pascal as one might grope for a life jacket that turns out to be flawed or faulty in some way.

The wife was not the mother of the slain girl but the wife had married the husband when the daughter was very young and when the husband had required a new wife with whom to raise the daughter.

"Yes, thank you. Yes, I am the stepmother. No, the 'birth mother' is not living, we think. Thank you so much, you are very kind, but no—that's not a great idea. Max is too distracted to speak to you right now."

To be a *stepmother* is to feel like a figure in a fairy tale. Not a benign but a wicked figure.

From the first the wife had anticipated such an impasse. To put it bluntly, the "difficult" daughter had not much liked her though with the passage of time, not unlike erosion, the girl's particular dislike for the stepmother had softened, in the face of the stepmother's protracted and indefatigable campaign to win her heart.

She had loved the girl, or had tried to. Badly she'd wanted to love the (step)daughter!

At the same time it was true, she'd badly wanted to have a child with the husband. Yes, you might have said *A child of her own*, or rather *A little sister or brother for Daphne*. But the husband, all but overwhelmed by the lone daughter, had been adamant in opposition.

"One child is enough! As William Blake says, 'Enough? Too much.'"

Max had joked but Max's jokes were sharp-edged as the fancy Japanese knives he owned, displayed in his kitchen though rarely used.

The wife saw nothing funny in such jokes. The wife rarely saw much that was funny in other people's nervous jokes.

As a young, uncertain wife she'd foreseen the possibility of loss. Nothing mattered to her so much as her marriage, more profound to her than the love she felt, or believed she felt, for the husband who made the marriage possible.

If she dies, we die. If but one, then—none.

"And now there is—none."

The wife felt a rush of fury and resentment that the husband had denied her, the second wife, the consolation of her own child. *Their* child.

Becca was nineteen years younger than Max—a generation, and more. He'd been forty-six at the time of their marriage, she'd been twenty-seven. The daughter who was to be the *stepdaughter* had been eight years old but precocious as a child twice that age in the more subtle skills of manipulation.

Precisely what had happened to Max Needham's first wife, Becca had not been told. A late marriage for him, a mistake from the start. A bright, even brilliant young woman, a Russian translator and poet for whom having a child had been a disaster, much bitterness, separations and reconciliations, finally a departure so abrupt that the husband had returned home early one evening to find the forlorn child, five years old at the time, waiting alone on the front stoop of the house and her mother gone—"One day, I will tell you more. But no one must tell Daphne."

Suicide, Becca thought. The possibility made her shudder.

Futile to make inquiries of Max Needham's friends and colleagues for either they knew, and protected him; or did not know, and protected him. All that was understood about the first Mrs. Needham was that she'd "disappeared"—"abandoned" her family.

Badly Becca had wanted to be married to Max Needham, nothing else meant much to her.

There were reasons for this, no doubt. She didn't want to look into *reasons.*

She'd had a career of some promise. So it was said.

She'd been a graduate student in Max Needham's seminar on the psychophysiology of linguistics at MIT when she'd dropped out of the program to live with Needham, and eventually to marry him.

"Yes, that's correct—Max's daughter is my *stepdaughter*. If you're wondering about the mother, I can't help you. Maybe ask Max."

It had been a challenge to love the willful little girl, but Becca had succeeded, to a degree. For Becca was no delicate orchid but a tough, resilient cactus, that could survive in arid and inhospitable places without complaint. At least, she'd succeeded in convincing Max that she loved Daphne, and could care for her like a proper parent; while Max was urgently elsewhere, teaching at MIT and lecturing across the country, moderating panels on PBS, serving on the president's bioethics advisory committee, Becca was on hand to drive the child to and from a succession of private schools, child psychiatrists, medical appointments, and "activities"; Becca was the parent to intervene with school administrators, to hire tutors, and arrange for "playdates."

In this role the wife was never heard to complain. Always the wife was cheerful, upbeat as the female lead in a Broadway musical. With a smile declaring to the daughter *I love you, sweetie!*—and not seeming to mind when the daughter muttered evasively—*Yeh. OK.*

In the early years of the marriage there'd been far too much emotion focused on the girl. The husband's fevered attention was like a blinding light shining into her face and how could the child not be—blinded?

The wife had learned not to interfere with most household decisions, particularly those involving the daughter. Not to express an opinion even when, for Max Needham was a publicly committed liberal, a staunch supporter of the rights of women and minorities, he invited her to speak "freely and openly." Max's love for the daughter was so suffused with guilt and something like remorse, it was not possible for Becca to suggest that such love was not healthy for either the girl or the father—or her.

The wife understood that if the husband were forced to chose between the daughter and the wife he would choose the daughter—inevitably. This seemed to her altogether natural and not to be regretted.

The wife also understood that it was not the daughter's fault that she'd grown into adolescence without comprehending that the universe did not revolve around her, whether for good or ill. As there are no "bad dogs"—(so the wife, who'd grown up in a family of dog-owners, knew)—but only "bad trainers." The daughter had lied to both parents equally, and raged at both equally, and, when she was young, injured herself so frequently in falls, collisions, and household accidents, Becca worried that authorities might suspect the parents of child abuse.

"Yes, there is child abuse in our household. Not abuse inflicted on the child but by the child."

Such witticisms the wife uttered to friends who were not likely to repeat them to the husband.

After some years the wife gave up telling the daughter that she loved her. For there was never any response except an embarrassed smile or frown or smirk and the evasive mumble—*Yeh. OK.*

(Did anyone notice? Did Daphne notice? Certainly, the husband would not have noticed.)

Eventually, Daphne graduated from one of the prestigious private high schools in the Boston area to which she'd been sent at considerable expense. Though she'd been tested with an I.Q. of 153, and had been admitted to Wellesley, her grades were erratic at college and she dropped out after her sophomore year. She had spells of anorexia, and lost so much weight that her collarbone nearly protruded through her skin; she contracted hepatitis, and her beautiful pale skin turned sallow; her thick lustrous wavy dark hair turned thin and brittle. The following year she enrolled at Boston University but after a single unhappy semester dropped out again. It was not unusual for the daughter to disappear for days and to be indifferent to the parents' anxiety over her. The wife suspected that the daughter was involved with drugs but did not dare tell the husband for she knew that the husband would denounce *her*.

Jesus, Becca! Try to love Daphne, at least.

Try to be on the girl's side for once.

The wife had learned: you do not, ever, intervene between a parent and a child. If you are not the parent, and the child is not your child, you dare not presume, for both will despise you.

Alone sometimes the wife wept bitter tears for the child—*her* child—she'd been denied by the husband. The difficult, exhausting daughter had made a second child unimaginable.

And yet she loved the husband, and could not imagine ever leaving him. (Though in weak moments she fantasized how, one day when she was no longer so urgently needed by him, the husband might leave her.)

In the twelve months before her death the daughter was living with friends in a loft in TriBeCa, university dropouts like herself who worked at low-paying quasi-glamorous jobs in fashion, art, or the theater; with financial assistance from her parents she was taking courses at the Parsons School of Design, or so they believed. It was rare for Daphne to call home, or even to email or text her parents, and often it was impossible for them to contact her except to write to her at the Varick address, enclosing checks.

It fell to the wife to make out the checks and mail them. Thinking— *You can't ignore us! You need us for this.*

Even so, the daughter rarely thanked the wife. The wife imagined the daughter eagerly ripping open the envelopes and extracting the checks without noticing the handwritten little notes inside.

So far as they knew Daphne was living, working, and taking courses in New York yet when the call came announcing her death it would be revealed that she was living in Jersey City, and had no current job; she'd never enrolled at the Parsons School, but must have kept the tuition for herself; she'd been involved with an unemployed actor named Jorge of whom she'd spoken from time to time—"My stalker." She'd thought it funny, her parents' alarmed reaction.

Three nights before her death Daphne had called home and left a rambling and incoherent message for her father to call her back; the wife had been hurt and annoyed that the daughter had wanted to speak not to her but to the husband to whom she referred in her childish whining voice as *Dad-dy*. Angrily the wife had deleted the message. So many years of enduring the daughter's indifference, or scorn; so many years of *trying to be loved* as a mother and not merely tolerated as a stepmother; so many years of disguising her hurt, resentment, and her dislike—*I am so tired of you! Go to hell, you spoiled little brat. I am finished with you.*

The wife hadn't meant this of course. It was but one of the thoughts that flashed through her brain many times a day, an expression of exasperation, impatience, self-disgust—of no significance except its timing.

After the daughter's death the wife checked the voice mail in a trance of horror. Several times listening to the tape terrified that the husband would discover the message, which had been for him; the message would have been Daphne's last words, to her father. But the message had vanished as if it had never been.

Details of Daphne's death would remain unclear. She'd been struck and killed on I-278 south of the Verrazano Bridge at 2:30 A.M. of a weekday in October. Witnesses reported having seen a young woman jump from a minivan that braked to a rolling stop on the shoulder of the roadway a few minutes before, but no one could describe the minivan or could recall the license plate numbers; the minivan had immediately sped away. It was a night of mist and a lightly falling rain. No one could explain why the young woman had stepped onto the roadway where she was believed to have died instantaneously of injuries sustained when a vehicle traveling at a high speed struck her except—"She'd been looking around kind of confused. Like she didn't know where she was, or couldn't see well in the fog. Or she thought the guy in the van would come back to get her, and she wanted to get away from him."

There was no preventing the disclosure, in the press, that the twenty-two-year-old woman who'd died in the rain on I-278 had had traces of alcohol and amphetamine in her bloodstream.

The driver of the minivan, eventually located, had not been named "Jorge."

There had been a "Jorge" with whom Daphne Needham had been staying in Jersey City—not *living with,* but *staying with* as he'd made clear when questioned by police officers. This "Jorge" refused to meet with the Needhams nor would he speak with them on the phone.

The wife meant to console the husband, who was inconsolable. Yet the wife could not herself comprehend that the daughter was *gone.*

"I keep thinking she'll call. The phone will ring, I will pick up the receiver . . ."

The wife seemed not to know: did she grieve for the daughter, or was she (secretly) relieved that the daughter was gone? If she fell into fits of sobbing it wasn't clear why.

But now we have no daughter. Now there is—none.

She saw how the husband regarded her, across that abyss. Somehow it had happened, they were on opposite sides of the abyss.

She was sick with grief but also with (secret) shame. The knowledge that she'd deleted the message, in fact she'd deleted other, earlier messages from Daphne, from time to time, over the years . . . Max would never have forgiven her if he'd known.

She'd thought they would grow old—older—together. They would laugh together at muddled words. Not long before the catastrophe as in another lifetime the wife had said *asparagus* and the husband who was hard of hearing in one ear had heard *Asperger's*. The wife had said *charisma* and the husband had heard *miasma* and they'd laughed together as if nothing could be funnier.

Yet, Max resisted getting a hearing aid. His reasoning was, he was *too young.*

Becca had laughed at him, and kissed him. He was quite right, he was *too young.*

Among their wide circle of friends there'd been several abrupt, seemingly senseless and unanticipated breakups of marriages that had seemed as secure as their own. More secure than their own.

Fourteen years the daughter had pulled at her, like gravity. And how often she'd hoped that the daughter would simply—*go away.*

There'd been an interregnum of some forty minutes after the daughter had died on I-278 before the parents had been notified. The land phone ringing in the night, such a rarity they'd scarcely registered it for their crucial calls came now by cell phone; there was not even a land phone extension in their bedroom.

Eventually, the wife had stumbled from bed to answer the phone, in another room. She'd been so convinced that the call was a wrong number, she'd hardly reacted when the speaker asked if she was Mrs. Needham? Mother of Daphnc Needham?

In this way, for those ignorant moments, they'd been unwitting survivors of the daughter. It was shocking to think that the daughter had died, *and they had not known.*

The wife felt tenderness for the bereaved man as one might feel for a wounded animal and yet the wife felt some fear, for the wounded may lash out in confusion, pain, and rage.

The husband did not wish to speak of their loss. He was a very private person, as he was a quasi-public person; if Max Needham had medical problems, he would not confide even in family members, let alone friends and university colleagues. And he would not have forgiven his wife if she'd violated his privacy.

Only to others did the wife speak of the loss of the daughter, in a voice of incredulity.

"No premonitions. No 'omens.' Not a thing!"

The wife spread her fingers wide as if to indicate—look, nothing hidden! The wife's fingernails, that had once been neatly filed and polished a pale tasteful pearly-pink, had been allowed to become uneven and brittle.

Now when it was too late she was becoming superstitious. She noticed that her hands sometimes shook. (Was this punishment? For deleting the message? For not calling Daphne back? Almost, she hoped so.) She could not bear looking into the future, any future—it was like confronting your reflection in a too-brightly-lit mirror. *No! Don't look. You will be damned sorry if you do.*

Yet, she would plan a trip for them in December. A kind of honeymoon, to Central America. This trip the husband had wanted to take *separately,* the wily wife would conspire to appropriate. They would be out of the country at the time of the daughter's birthday. Maybe—(the wife's brain spun crazily)—she could arrange travel across time zones, to avoid December 19 altogether.

Each night the husband came to bed at a later hour, and each night the wife was waiting up for him, a light shining in her eager face.

"Max? I have an idea."

"Yes?"

It was the coolest, most neutral of responses. Not a question really for it expressed no curiosity.

"It would be good for us, as you suggested. To be away—away from here—by mid-December."

She had not said *by her birthday*. The husband must have felt some relief.

In the dark the wife dared to touch the husband as she would not have touched the husband by day. Her hand moved onto him—the slope of the man's shoulder, his smooth broad back that was turned to her; the warm curve of his body, that had grown unfamiliar with time.

In the dark in their bed the wife and the husband would appear to be together. Something had struck them a cruel blow, they had fallen and were lying very still in dread of being struck another time.

As younger lovers the wife and the husband had lost themselves in each other's bodies but with the passage of time each had become opaque to the other, and impenetrable. She knew that Max would have liked to sleep in another room, and not with her, but that he was too gentlemanly, too kindly, to hurt her; even if he didn't love her, he did not want to hurt her. She would take advantage of this!

Becca whispered, "Max? Darling? Please talk to me, I loved her too."

She felt him stiffen. She could imagine how his eyes flashed with hatred of her. What had she said—*loved*?

"I mean—I miss her—so terribly . . ."

Invisible in the dark her eyes brimmed with tears. Her hand blundered onto the husband's thigh. She was dazed with love for him, her husband. A terrible need for him. She would explain herself to him, how frightened she was of what had happened and how frightened she was of losing him for if she lost him, she was not sure that she could bear to continue. She had failed as a mother, in the end she had been a *stepmother* merely, and that could not be amended. And he would understand, and he would forgive her. For there was so little time now. For time was running out, soon it would be mid-December.

With the boldness of desperation she would touch the husband, caress him, slide her arm around him—she would stroke his stomach, and the slack skin of his lower belly, and between his legs . . . But he pushed her hand from him, with a little grunt of irritation.

"Go to sleep, Becca. It's late."

2.

"There they are: right out of Diane Arbus. Look, Max!"

It was a cruel witticism. The wife could not resist.

The wife spoke in a lowered voice, an aside to the husband who smiled thinly, scarcely glancing up from the *Ecotourist's Guide: Panama & Pacific Coastal Islands* in which he'd been making annotations, to see the family of fellow tourists approaching.

It was unfair, the wife thought. Sometimes the husband appreciated the wife's acerbic wit, other times he seemed to be inwardly wincing.

Once he'd laughed heartily at her jokes, even her silly, childish jokes. Now, he was likely to regard her as if he'd never seen her before—a woman who happened to be seated at his table in the ship's dining room, or who boldly sat beside him on the deck when it was clear he preferred to be alone.

A woman who followed him into their cabin, when it was clear he preferred to be alone.

Why do you try to make me laugh? Do you think that will make me love you?

She did not think so. But yes, she must have thought so.

Hard to resist a cruel, cutting remark, to make someone laugh. The less likely the person was to laugh, the more desperate the joke.

The wife understood the psychology of the stand-up comedian: *Though I am nothing, a black hole, please acknowledge that I am alive— laugh, clap. Laugh.*

Swathed in sunscreen, in crisp long-sleeved white shirts, mosquito-repellent cargo pants and wide-brimmed hats, the bereaved wife and husband were seated in wicker chairs in thinly white tropical sunshine on the third-level deck of a small cruise ship called the *Boca Brava*. It was the second day of the six-day cruise: they were somewhere in the balmy waters of the Gulf of Chiriquí, off the western coast of Panama.

The wife had made virtually all of the arrangements. In their marriage it was the wife who oversaw such routine tasks as paying bills, renewing subscriptions, the reliable cycle of household maintenance and repairs. (It was the wife who'd dealt with the funeral home on Massachusetts Avenue, the funeral arrangements, the purchase of a grave site and a small granite marker. It was the wife who would oversee giving away the daughter's clothing and other possessions to the local Goodwill in a few months' time.) The wife had not dared to trouble the husband with many queries—if there'd been the slightest difficulty with their travel plans the husband would have insisted upon calling off the trip. She'd had to go alone to a medical clinic for immunizations (typhoid, yellow fever, hepatitis A and hepatitis B, malaria) since the husband was sure, having traveled to Asia and Africa within the past several years, and having been immunized then, that he didn't need these renewed.

The daughter's birthday—the first since the death—was in two days. It was possible—almost—to think that the birthday, like the death-day, was a matter of geography: now they were no longer in freezing Massachusetts but in tropical waters off the coast of Panama, approximately eight degrees north of the equator.

Travel is relocation, *dis*location. The wife found herself unaccountably happy at times—like a new, young wife on a honeymoon with a husband who is (yet) a virtual stranger—their shared history thin as a sickle moon.

They'd traveled a number of times with Daphne to England, Scotland, Ireland and to Europe. But not to the Caribbean, and not to Latin America. These waters were pure and unsullied by memory.

Not going away from home, but returning. The wife realized suddenly—*That will be the hard part. The emptiness.*

In waves panic swept over her. It was the terror of utter, irrevocable loss: she would never see the daughter again as she would never feel the exasperation, frustration, hurt, and hope the daughter had roused in her.

And it was panic too, that their lives had been changed irrevocably. Bizarre that they should find themselves, indistinguishable from other affluent American tourists with a fashionable interest in "eco-tourism" on the dazzling-white *Boca Brava,* an attractive married couple of middle age, unencumbered by children, childless.

"D'you mind if we take this chair? Thanks!"

In a bright grating voice the rotund little woman addressed Becca even as her heavyset daughter rudely dragged an unoccupied chair away from the Needhams' table. There was something aggressive in the way the girl appropriated the chair as if she were snatching it from the wife and the husband against their wishes, to bring to the table where her parents and younger brother were sitting.

"Of course not. Please take it. You're welcome."

The wife spoke with thinly veiled sarcasm, for the girl had already taken the chair without even acknowledging her. What was bizarre was that the girl's tongue protruded from between pursed lips as if the act of taking the chair, gripping it and hauling it away, required extreme mental concentration. The wife's heart beat hard, as if her territory had been invaded; how did the rotund little woman know that the wife and husband had no one else coming to join them, thus no need of the chair?

It was so petty! So annoying.

The husband had taken no notice—of course. An exchange so fleeting and trivial had not the power to break Max Needham's concentration on his reading.

In times of stress, and at other, quite ordinary times, the husband disappeared into such intense spells of reading, as into his work. To the wife this was a place not unlike a black hole into which she could not follow nor even peer inside—it was *his*.

As if to spite the wife, who found them painful to look at, and more painful to listen to, the family out of a Diane Arbus photograph— (there were several families on the *Boca Bravo,* affably smiling, relentlessly friendly, attractive adults and adorable freckled children, who looked as if they'd stepped out of a Norman Rockwell illustration for the old *Saturday Evening Post;* there was only one family Arbus might have photographed)—had not moved farther along the deck to an area where there were unoccupied tables and chairs, but had decided to sit close by the Needhams. So close, the back of the husband's chair was being jostled by the brother, so that the husband, with a flicker of annoyance, moved his chair forward, and continued to read.

"Should we move somewhere else? Max?"—the wife leaned forward to murmur in the husband's ear.

"No. Just relax."

Just relax. As if the wife were the cause of her own discomfort!

The obtrusive family were obviously Americans, though there was something "foreign" about them, too—an obese couple with an obese young-adult daughter and an obese pubescent son who took up a good deal of space even outdoors. The wife had sighted them within the first hour of boarding the *Boca Brava,* and seemed all too often to be seeing them since. They were always together, like a colony of biological organisms. You looked from one to the other to the other as in a four-way mirror, sensing something wrong with each of them, a shared genetic flaw.

The father was tall, big-shouldered, big-headed, with a protruding belly carried high like a drum above his belt; he didn't walk so much as lumber from side to side like a collision about to happen. He might have been in his early fifties, but he appeared much older, petulant and querulous, like one who is accustomed to getting his way, yet wary of insubordination. Each time Becca had seen him, he'd seemed displeased about something. His pudgy face was flushed and his rimless eyeglasses gave him the look of one who can barely contain his rage. He wore boxy striped sports shirts of a kind no one had worn for decades, and Bermuda shorts that fell below his knees; on his immense feet, Birkenstocks with white socks. His voice, addressing his wife, his daughter, or his son, often in rebuke, resembled a low-pitched aggrieved barking.

The mother, who barely came to the father's shoulders, was a very stout woman who wore her faded-brown hair in braids tightly wound about her head as in a Grimm's fairy tale, and over these a sun-visor of dark green plastic, that cast a faint, lurid-green shadow on her moon-shaped face. Her skin was flushed like the father's, but relatively unlined; her eyes were small, close-set, and lashless. Her figure was a single, soft-solid mass like something that has melted—bosom, waist, hips. It was impossible to imagine this woman as a girl, let alone a sexual being; she must have been born middle-aged. She wore beltless shifts—muumuus?—that fell to mid-calf and on her small, fleshy feet open-toed sandals. Her public expression was one of strained affability—she was the one of the four to glance about smiling, hoping to make eye contact with strangers, that she might exchange greetings and pleasantries. When the father addressed her in his aggrieved barking voice she stood very still and cast her eyes down like one who is receiving instructions, or chastisement, from above. She did not reply to the father (at least, so far as Becca had seen) except by nodding meekly. In the family, it was the mother to whom much was entrusted—everywhere she went she carried a shiny tote bag filled with articles of clothing, towels, sunscreen, camera equipment, tissues, antibacterial hand sanitizer, bottled water and snacks. The others were always requiring something from her which she handed over with a smile, and for which (at least, so far as Becca had seen) she received no thanks. The mother's upper arms, exposed in the sleeveless shifts, were raddled and slack and terrible to behold and so Becca turned her eyes from the sight as from the head of Medusa.

The obese boy of eleven or twelve resembled the father to an uncanny degree—oversized head, fleshy face, peevish expression—though he was wearing a snug-fitting T-shirt, khaki shorts and running shoes without socks, as a normal American boy might wear; his toad-like lower face seemed to have melted into a succession of chins but his eyes, small in the fatty ridges of his face, were alert and attentive, fixed on the tiny screen of his iPhone, which he took care to hold below the father's sight.

"*Ee*-gor! Put that away and look up here. This is the 'Gulf of Chir'quíi'—out there is the Pacific Ocean."

Ee-gor—Becca supposed the name was "Yegor"—paid little heed to the chiding mother.

But it was the obese daughter who made the family a Diane Arbus family, in her mimicry of her parents as in one of those psychology texts of the 1950s in which the photographs of generations of genetically impaired individuals were published in a parody of a family tree. Here was a defiantly homely girl of about twenty who squinted through thick glasses rudely at strangers, and furrowed her forehead, and, when she grimaced, which was often, her plump pink moist tongue emerged out of her mouth like a sea creature out of its shell. Like the father she was tall, big-shouldered and big-headed, and seemed often perturbed; like the mother she had small close-set lashless eyes and a shapeless body—breasts, belly, thighs and hips run together like a sinewy gelatin. Her brown hair was limp and lank, brushed behind her ears and fastened with bobby pins. (Bobby pins! Becca had no idea that bobby pins were still sold.) Her ears were prominent, with pointed knobs. Like the mother the girl wore a sleeveless and beltless shift but it had become too tight for her heavy thighs and haunches, and rode up to her massive dimpled knees as she sat; like the father she wore Birkenstocks with white cotton socks. In repose her face was round and blank as a plate with a suggestion of mental retardation or idiocy yet when she spoke, often irritably, to the brother, she appeared more or less normal; the small wet eyes flashed with sisterly dislike and indignation.

"Becca?"—the husband nudged the wife.

"Yes? What?"

An embarrassed expression on Max's face suggested that Becca was—what?—staring too intently at their neighbors? But Becca had not been staring at them at all, she'd been reading the paperback *Endangered Species of Central America* she had brought from their cabin.

Reading and rereading the same paragraph on the Panamanian golden frog which was now believed to be extinct in the wild, though specimens were preserved in captivity in North America.

Becca wanted to protest to Max—she felt immense pity for the obese girl. She wasn't *staring*.

Thinking what a nightmare it must have been for the obese girl to have endured an American childhood looking like *that*. Imagine—middle school, high school!

Yet she felt too something crueler, and cruder—a kind of physical repugnance, and resentment. *How ugly she is! How can she bear her life*—

Something slipped from Becca's hands, and fell to the deck—the book she'd been reading, or trying to read.

At the next table the rotund little woman made a sympathetic little *cluck* with her mouth, the equivalent of a maternal nudge, and at once, with a grunt, the obese girl shifted her haunches in her chair, leaned over awkwardly and picked up *Endangered Species of Central America* to give to Becca. So quickly she'd obeyed her mother, you could not tell if she was resentful, reluctant, or—simply clumsy. Her forehead furrowed and her plump pink moist tongue protruded between her lips as in a parody of concentration.

"Here, mam."

Becca was taken entirely by surprise stammering—"Oh—why—thank you."

She would recall later, in the aftermath of shock, how the four of them were staring at her—the freak-family whom Diane Arbus might have photographed.

∞

Next morning dinghies took passengers from the *Boca Brava* to a succession of islands in the Gulf of Chiriquí. To Becca's relief, the obese family hadn't been assigned to their dinghy.

In the ship's dining room that morning the wife had resolved not to seek out the freak-family. She feared the husband's awareness of her obsession with them—it would be one more wifely flaw in his eyes. Yet, to her dismay, without knowing how it had happened, she found herself staring at the obese girl in the buffet line, slowly shuffling along heaping eggs, sausages, waffles, French toast, syrupy prunes and large croissants onto her plate. There was a terrible, obscene hunger in the girl's face, as if she had not eaten in days. And what was she wearing?—not a beltless shift (like her mother, also in the buffet line) but ridiculous bib-overalls, that emphasized her immense belly, thighs, hips.

As Becca stared in fascinated horror she saw the girl's tongue protrude as she poured maple syrup onto her plate . . . Fortunately Becca was sitting in such a position that she couldn't see the girl and her family at their table in another part of the dining room.

She'd noticed that others in the dining room watched the obese family too. The father in striped sports shirt, Bermuda trousers, Birkenstocks and socks attracted attention not for his clothes but for his complaints to the head waiter about something that had displeased him, and his curt, cutting remarks to his family. Particularly young people, teenagers, followed the obese girl with appalled eyes . . . She had to be aware of people staring at her, Becca thought. Poor thing!

Later, to Becca's dismay, the obese girl rudely cut in front of her to grab a life vest from one of the bins, as passengers queued up in preparation for a trip to the islands.

The life vests were bright orange. The obese girl in bib-overalls was an extraordinary spectacle tying her life vest carefully in place over her large sloping breasts; quickly Becca looked away, chilled as the girl's tongue emerged wetly from her mouth.

The girl had to be mentally retarded. Mentally "disabled." There had to be some sort of neurological deficit to account for such a bizarre habit.

Becca secured a life vest for herself, and one for Max. She saw how the girl's father and brother were also pushing to the bins, with a pretense of not noticing how they shouldered others aside; only the mother stood apart, with her affable, silly half-smile. (Becca took care not to look too pointedly at the mother for fear the woman would greet her happily and try to strike up a conversation like one trying to start a fire with two dull damp sticks.)

Then, Becca's anxiety that the freak-family would turn up in their dinghy, that turned out to be unwarranted.

It was a windy humid day in the Gulf of Chiriquí. The open boat rocked, pitched and bucked in choppy waves of the hue of Coca-Cola. The Indian guide assured them there was no danger—"No sharks, *sí?* Just hold tight."

Was this a joke? Most of the passengers laughed, nervously.

The previous day, returning in the dinghy to the ship from the islands, the boy who operated the outboard motor had spoken excitedly in Spanish to the guide, pointing—about thirty feet away were a half-dozen fins slicing the surface of the water.

"Just baby sharks. No worry!"—the guide bared his teeth in a smile.

And was this a joke? Were the fins those of other, less dangerous fish? The wife saw bafflement in her fellow passengers' faces though everyone laughed as if the guide had said something witty.

The guide's name was—(neither the wife nor the husband chose to acknowledge this painful coincidence, refraining from exchanging a glance)—"Jorge." He was of medium height, compactly built, with smooth dark-stained skin and shrewd eyes; he wore a khaki-colored shirt and khaki shorts and it wasn't difficult to imagine a bandolier of cartridges slung across his chest and in his powerful-looking hands a rifle.

Jorge had told the group that he was of Guna Indian descent and that he was from the Guna Yala archipelago which, unfortunately, they would not be visiting on their tour.

The wife thought—*He is a descendant of the Spanish holocaust survivors.*

She'd been appalled reading of the "aggressive colonization" of this part of the New World by Spanish invaders. Sixteenth-century *conquistadors* had looted treasure in Bolivia and Peru and brought it to Panama to be shipped to Spain and along the way they'd practiced what would be called in a later era "genocide"—slaughtering directly or in some way causing to die most of the indigenous tribes of Central America. She was familiar with the ugly history of the European colonization of North America and its genocidal wars against the native population but the Spanish conquest seemed to have been worse—more widespread, more brutal and in the zeal of its Roman Catholic mission more "religious." With so ugly a past it was no wonder that ravaged countries like Panama focused now on fashionable global "ecotourism."

And very expensive tours these were, the wife had discovered. For part of their mission was to preserve the ecology and environment of the tourist places.

Each of the *Bocca Brava* dinghies was named for an island creature—*Howler Monkey, Sea Turtle, Sea Lion, Boobie, Albatross, Dolphin.* Each of the dinghies was marked with a cartoon likeness of one of these. The Needhams had been assigned the *Howler Monkey* dinghy which was comprised mostly of couples not unlike themselves—middle-aged, Caucasian, clearly educated and well-to-do, "fit." There was an older, retired couple, and there was a biracial couple with very well-behaved young children. Everyone was friendly with the possible exception of the tall lanky-limbed reticent Max who seemed oblivious of his companions, fussing with his camera lenses or staring into the distance as Jorge lectured the group on the evolutionary history of the islands.

The wife was embarrassed by the husband's aloofness. Fortunately, no one on the *Bocca Brava* knew who they were.

Please excuse him—my husband doesn't mean to be rude. He is in mourning for his daughter who was the only person in the world he loved without qualification.

Perhaps this wasn't altogether true. Perhaps the husband had often been angry with the daughter, disappointed and frustrated. He would not have confided in the wife.

Please excuse my husband. He is in mourning for his own lost life.

Onshore, the husband gradually drifted away from the group. It wasn't that he wasn't interested in what the guide had to say, he'd explained to Becca, but that the questions and comments of others in the group exasperated him. He'd been spoiled by decades of teaching at MIT where students were not likely to ask uninformed questions of Professor Needham.

The wife stared after the husband with eyes that ached from the white-rayed tropical sun even when the sky was overcast. She felt a pang of hurt, that the husband was no longer her companion and friend.

The cloud-layered tropical sky and the churning sea surface were indeed beautiful but the island was an astonishingly ugly place comprised of immense, grotesquely shaped lava-rocks that produced a sensation of vertigo in the wife's brain.

*Dis*located. Prone to thinking—*But why am I here? Am I so desperate? What is this place?*

In precise English the Indian guide was describing the history of the lava islands that had been formed by volcanic eruptions many thousands of years ago. The surrounding waters were rich with nutrients but only a relatively few lizard and reptile species had managed to establish themselves on the volcanic islands—"It is estimated that as many as ninety-nine percent of species have become extinct." The wife didn't know if the guide meant only just species of animals on this island or in the Gulf of Chiriquí generally—or all species, globally?

The great drama of nature scarcely involved humankind at all. The great drama was evolution in which human effort—"civilization"—was but recent, and fleeting. There should have been a grim satisfaction in the knowledge that the primitive creatures of these islands—lizards, snakes, sea turtles, crabs, insects, iguanas—shorebirds perched on rocks amid pyramids of whitish droppings—would outlive *Homo sapiens;* but of course, there was not.

The wife thought—*Each of us thinks, I will be spared! I am someone, something special.*

Even thinking such a thought, the thinker is seduced, and deceived.

"Take care, *señora*!"

Sharply Jorge called to her, as she'd been about to step onto a foot-long lizard with a serrated back and a flicking tongue that so mimicked the lava-rocks in both the texture and color of its skin you could barely discern it.

Peering up at the hillside, the wife saw that the terrain was alive with such creatures, virtually invisible. Most of them were immobile as sculptures but if you looked closely you could see—life . . .

"I'm sorry, Jorge! He is so beautifully camouflaged."

It was a curious thing to say—*Beautifully camouflaged.*

"Yes, *señora*. It is why he is still with us."

The wife laughed uncertainly.

The ecotour guides were not ordinary tour guides but individuals with educational backgrounds in biology, ecology, and marine life. The husband had been impressed with Jorge, he'd said. Though he had not ever uttered the name—"Jorge."

The wife wondered if Jorge was thinking bemusedly—*It is why some of us are still here, señora. And why we will outlive you.*

"ARE YOU HAPPY WE'VE COME? I am."

How pathetic, the wife's brave announcement! As if embarrassed for her the husband avoided the yearning eyes in the mirror above the bureau and murmured a vague gracious assent.

"The islands are beautiful. Fascinating. Each in its own way . . ."

Weakly the wife's voice trailed off. She had never been an articulate person and now following the daughter's death she heard her voice often from a little distance as if her skull were empty, and the sounds echoing within.

It was true that the Panamanian islands were very beautiful to her. Each day's excursions left her exhausted like one who has tried to see, to hear, to smell and to taste too much.

This is your last chance. When you return from this, it will all be over.

She'd wondered what accidents commonly befell tourists. The dinghy landings on the islands were unexpectedly arduous, even younger and more able-bodied passengers had to take care stepping from the boat into a rocky surf. And climbing down into the dinghy from the *Boca Brava*, on the outside of the ship, required coordination and concentration.

She'd wanted to ask Jorge if there were occasionally "accidents" in the islands. A careless tourist touching one of the venomous creatures, a sudden sting or bite, an allergic reaction, cardiac arrest . . . Attacked by a stingray or a shark while snorkeling . . .

And the *Boca Brava,* like all cruise ships vessels of possible contagion. Susceptible to epidemics of flu, dysentery, pneumonia, salmonella, norovirus.

The wife smiled to think how astonished the husband would be if she told him not to bother shipping her body home, if something happened to her. *Whatever is usually done with a body in circumstances like these—that would be all right with me. Really.*

In their cabin in the *Boca Brava* the wife and the husband were rediscovering the physical awkwardness that precedes intimacy. Once the cabin door was shut behind them, and had to be shut firmly in order not to swing back open, the wife felt the mild panic she'd felt as a young girl when she found herself alone—by accident, or by design—with someone male. It was a kind of sexual claustrophobia, a sudden powerful wish to escape.

Awkward and embarrassing, to use the single, so very small lavatory close beside the bed. The sink was small as the sink in an airplane lavatory and the toilet had to be flushed several times to be effective. The shower was a narrow stall behind translucent strips of plastic. The husband, six feet two inches in bare feet, had to crouch in the narrow space and invariably left a puddle of water on the floor which the wife sopped up with a towel thinking—*Tears! Cold tears.*

This was a new intimacy in the marriage, the wife thought. The intimacy of the unspoken, forbidden. The intimacy of physical closeness like that of conjoined twins. Yet it was not an emotional intimacy.

Nights in the cabin, in the uncomfortably low, lumpy bed that appeared to be just slightly smaller than a double bed, were as arduous as days spent hiking on the islands. The ship's engines seemed louder in the night—ceaselessly humming, vibrating like a great shuddering lung. And the ceaseless rocking motion of the ship was much more noticeable at night, like a great heartbeat you could not not acknowledge. Like most of the ship the cabin was fiercely air-conditioned. The wife had managed to shut vents in the ceiling to deflect some of the air currents directly over the bed but still the air was very cold and though you took shelter beneath bedclothes you were susceptible to thinking unwanted thoughts—*Mortuary. Cold meat. In the tropics.*

The wife was aware of the husband beside her with his back to her stiff and unyielding as if he did not dare sleep—not so long as she was awake. Of course, she did not dare acknowledge the husband's wakefulness; she did not dare touch him, as she'd touched him that last time, and been rebuffed. But each night she did wait for him to speak to her, or turn to her—possibly, this could happen. *Becca? Are you awake? I've been thinking—we should talk* . . . Sleep came suddenly, like the flash of a shark's fins; yet, like the flash of a shark's fins, sleep was fleeting. Alternately shivering and sweating through the prim flannel nightgown like the nightwear of an Amish wife the wife slept and woke and slept and woke again with a mouth so parched it was painful for her to swallow—but she did not want to disturb the husband (who was asleep by this time, breathing audibly, a nighttime sound that might be mistaken for sobbing) by slipping from the bed, though it was not a bed one could adroitly "slip from"—(rather more, you would be cantilevering yourself upward, with considerable strain to the knees)—entering the dwarf-bathroom and pouring bottled water into a cup from which to drink. (Of course, they dared not drink the ship's tap water. Only bottled water was safe for the tourist-passengers of the *Boca Brava*.) Near morning there came sleep heavy as those leaden vests you are obliged to wear when being X-rayed and sometimes this heavy sleep induced a headache in the wife who had been taking ibuprofen in secret since the start of the trip, as much as she dared along with motion-sickness and anti-diarrhea medication. And in the morning pulling open the blinds covering the windows that comprised most of the outer wall of the cabin the wife would exclaim, "My God! How beautiful!"—for invariably, this was true.

Streaks of the most exquisite color in the eastern sky, and the vast sea of "waves"—a phenomenon so profound, it can scarcely be registered by the human brain.

And in the distance, the shore—the "isthmus"—emerging out of mist.

Already the equatorial sun had begun to ascend. You had to have faith that it would not expand to fill the entire sky in a fiery blinding glare that consumed all things.

The wife was touched, the husband had come to stand beside her. It was as if—(the wife told herself, knowing she must be kind to herself in this vulnerable phase of her life)—the husband was accepting from her a gift of the beauty and strangeness of the tropical place to which she'd brought them.

"Yes. It is beautiful." The husband spoke haltingly, as if unsure what his words meant.

"So hard to believe, it's 'December.' Only think what 'June' would be like!"—the wife spoke eagerly.

Better to have remained silent but the wife could not resist such remarks in mimicry of the romantic days of their early love—the young, naïve wife, the older, informed husband.

But to speak of "December" had been a mistake. The wife had failed to realize what "December" would mean to the husband.

The birthday of the slain daughter was this very day. It was to pass unacknowledged—that was their (tacit) agreement. The wife felt a wave of faintness, she had made such a stupid blunder.

She was thinking not of the birthday but of the death-day. The birthday had been erased by the death-day. And—(it was the damned air-conditioning in the cabin, that could not be modified)—she was thinking of that terrible morning weeks ago when in a trance of horror they'd driven to Newark, New Jersey, to the county mortuary to identify the daughter's body. It came back to the wife now in a rush—the shock of such a small body.

The mission was to identify, and claim. Arrange for the "remains" to be brought to Cambridge, Massachusetts, to what is called a *funeral parlor.*

What a quaint term! Why, the wife wondered, is such a place a *parlor*?

She laughed. The sound was ghastly, like the prelude to a coughing fit.

"Becca? What's wrong?"

Quickly the wife said, "Nothing." Though she was so cold, her teeth had begun to chatter.

They were about to leave the cabin. The wife felt faintly nauseated at the prospect of breakfast—(at home, the wife rarely ate breakfast and never such a large breakfast)—but it was not possible to skip a meal on the ship for reserves of strength were needed for the strenuous hikes.

"Max, did you try to contact her?—Daphne's mother?"

It was a sudden and impulsive question. Like a poison toad it leapt from the wife's mouth without warning.

"Did I 'try to contact her'—no. I did not."

The husband stared at the wife as one might stare at a person who has suddenly reached out inappropriately to touch him. His face that had softened with commiseration had tightened and his voice was flat and unyielding.

The wife had no clear idea how to interpret these words and so stood awkwardly smiling at the husband like one confronted with a riddle.

"I only meant—if—if you'd had any idea where she might be, or could contact her—somehow . . . If"—the wife stammered, and swallowed, and pressed blindly onward—"if she was still alive, she would want to know about . . ." The wife's voice trailed off for she could not bring herself to say *her daughter's death.*

"That woman has not been alive to any of us for some time, Becca. And now, I think we should change the subject."

"Even if you hate her, if she's alive she should know. Even if Daphne hated her, she should know."

But Max had turned away, and left the cabin firmly shutting the door behind him. His face had turned ashen and his voice had begun to shake and Becca knew it would be unwise to follow him too quickly.

In the first months of knowing Max Needham she'd been given to assume that his young daughter's mother was no longer living, though neither Max nor any of his friends had told her so, directly. She had even wondered if Daphne's mother had killed herself in some way that involved the child as a witness, but of course no one would speak about this to her. Yet now, seeing how Max had regarded her with a look of loathing, she had the unsettling idea that perhaps he was lying after all, and his first wife was still alive.

She didn't know if this possibility filled her with dread or with an irrational hope.

NOW IT BEGAN TO SEEM as if the Diane Arbus family was following *her.*

In the ship's lounge where she was sitting with a book in her lap reading of the Coiba Island penal colony that had been closed only in 2004, an infamous Panamanian site of brutal executions, tortures, human misery dating from 1919 which they were to visit briefly on the next-day's tour, there came the girl, the brother, the mother—talking loudly among themselves, the obese girl accusing in a whining voice, the obese boy denying in a whining voice, the obese mother trying to placate them making her maddening *cluck-cluck-cluck* with her tongue; and instead of sitting on an unoccupied sofa in another part of the lounge, to the wife's dismay the three sat down just behind her, and continued their inane chatter that mimicked human speech as the chatter of monkeys mimics human speech without being intelligible. Though the wife could not actually see the obese girl, she could imagine the girl's plump moist tongue protruding between her lips, and she could imagine the expression on the boy's face that was both aggrieved and petulant. And the mother must have taken out of her shiny tote bag the ubiquitous hand sanitizer for the wife smelled the sudden sharp odor of the antibacterial disinfectant and could not concentrate on her book for fear of being sick to her stomach.

Thinking how strange, though the daughter had not died in a hospital the wife had a clear memory of smelling such an odor in association with the daughter's death. The daughter had been brought to an ER in a Newark hospital—that is, her broken and lifeless body had been brought to an ER—but she had not died there, they were told that she had died in the roadway approaching the Verrazano Bridge, in the rain.

Yet, the wife felt a surge of nausea, at the smell of the disinfectant. Blindly she pushed to her feet, and stumbled away, in dread of being overcome by a fit of vomiting.

Behind her, the Arbus family continued to bicker. The wife's nostrils pinched with the powerful smell of disinfectant even after she was free of them, gasping for breath outside on the ship's deck.

"God, help me. Help me to keep going."

After the dinghy returned them to the ship late each afternoon Max dropped off his hiking gear in the cabin and disappeared. He did not invite Becca to accompany him. Once, wandering the ship with a book in her hand as a prop, Becca discovered her husband in a deck chair at the prow of the ship where sunbathers lay sprawled on lounge chairs; Max Needham was the older man facing the ocean, his back to the others, in a long-sleeved white shirt, khaki shorts and wide-brimmed hat. Becca saw that he too had a book as a prop but that he wasn't reading his book, he was staring at the ocean and hearing the sound of waves washing against the ship's side—*Nothing, nothing, nothing. Take comfort.*

The husband wouldn't initiate divorce proceedings, she knew. He was too kindly, and thought too highly of himself—he wasn't a man who would stoop to cruelty. He wasn't a man who wished others to think of him—*Max is divorcing Becca? How can he, the poor woman will be devastated.*

Like many men who are distinguished intellectuals, whose work has been largely cerebral and has taken them far from their roots, Max Needham was highly aggressive; but in his relationships with individuals, his aggression was masked by a perverse sort of passivity. He would so shut Becca out of his life, he would so starve her emotionally, she would be forced to initiate divorce proceedings against *him.*

So painful was the thought, Becca felt her tongue numb and tingling in her mouth like a living thing. Her tongue, prodding against her lips. For the first time understanding how natural it was, that a tongue might emerge from a mouth in a ferocity of concentration.

NEXT MORNING, ON THE ISLAND OF COIBA, again she saw them—the Diane Arbus family.

Of course, there were many other ecotourists—and tourists—on Coiba, which was the largest island in Central America. There were dozens of ecotourists from the *Boca Brava* crowded about the site of the old penal colony, reconstituted now for tourists as a UNESCO World Heritage Site with a gift shop selling souvenirs and picture books of the prison. (Becca had read of the horrific tortures and executions in the penal colony during the regime of the dictator Noriega and wondered how the books might picture these.) Yet, even while Jorge spoke to his group in a grim voice of the history of the prison in which so many Panamanians had died Becca was nervously aware

of the obese family—father, mother, sister, brother—in the corner of
her eye.

Such rage she felt for them! These were the sort of people who
should have been imprisoned in the penal colony, and hidden away
from sight. Obese clowns, who provoked reasonable people like
Becca to fits of exasperation.

It couldn't be that these terrible people were following her. She
knew! For often it happened, ironically, it was she who seemed to be
following them.

The tourist-group to which the obese family belonged was the *Al-batrosses*, who sometimes followed the *Howler Monkeys* on an island
excursion, and sometimes preceded them. The *Albatrosses* were led
by an Indian guide younger and more personable than Jorge with a
moustache, a red headband, and a dashing look reminiscent of Che
Guevara. This young guide laughed often, and evoked eager laughter
amid his group of tourists. Becca could not help glancing back at the
obese girl, who stood close to this guide, head cocked in concentra-tion as he spoke; Becca could not see if the girl's hideous tongue was
protruding but she could see that the girl was wearing one of the belt-less, shapeless dresses in which her rubbery young flesh was encased
as in a loose bandage, and on her pudgy feet Birkenstocks and white
cotton socks.

"Many thousands of prisoners died here and are buried in un-marked graves in the cemetery"—solemnly Jorge spoke with a wave
of his hand indicating a desolate area stretching behind the old
prison; but in her effort to hear what the handsome young *Albatross*
guide was saying, Becca scarcely heard. She was thinking—*She has
fallen in love with him. She will be heartbroken.*

Next, the *Howler Monkeys* were taken by bus to another part of
the island. Three hours hiking in an ancient forest in rising heat and
the wife worried that both she and the husband—but particularly the
husband, who took less care than the wife with such precautions—

would suffer from insect bites, for the strong-smelling insect repellent they were wearing was sweating away on their skin, and stinging insects were everywhere. But their eyes were dazzled by gorgeously colored butterflies, dragonflies. Overhead in the tall trees macaws of all colors—vivid scarlet, vivid blue, vivid yellow, vivid green. Swarms of smaller birds and hummingbirds so tiny, you could barely see them in the green-tinted humid light.

Yesterday had been December 19. They had lived past the birthday, the wife thought. A small smile twisted the lower part of her face, she hoped the husband would not see.

(Of course the husband would not see. The husband walked ahead of the wife as if he were alone, staring intently into the forest, camera poised at chest level.)

Jorge was lecturing to them about frogs—"endangered amphibians"—the "catastrophic decline" of amphibian populations worldwide. Frogs, toads, snakes, lizards. They must proceed with caution and not step off the trail for venomous reptiles were plentiful in the rain forest where there was intense competition for food, and a great range of predators. Despite the rising heat and a din of tiny insects in her ears the wife tried to listen to Jorge explaining the phenomenon of toxic creatures and the mimicry of toxic creatures by species that were not in fact toxic but were designed to appear so to elude predators. "It seems as if all of life is eluding predators, unless you are one"—the wife heard herself make this trenchant observation to Jorge though (she was sure) she'd never been one of those annoying individuals who makes clever inconsequential remarks in such circumstances to draw attention to herself.

Fortunately, no one seemed to have heard except Jorge, who nodded in polite agreement. How clever, the *señora*! The husband had drifted farther ahead, camera raised now to eye level.

Becca had read about Panamanian golden frogs (in fact, the creatures were toads) that were poisonous, and had become extinct in the wild. She'd read about poison dart frogs. She was prepared to engage Jorge with informed talk of such creatures, as well as sloths, monkeys, and sea lions—but hesitated for fear of being mistaken for a desperately lonely American woman of still-youthful middle age whose husband was shaking her out of his life in the way of a man shaking something off his shoe at which he does not wish to look.

Among the *Howler Monkeys,* sloths were a hit. Many clever remarks were made about sloths, and many pictures were taken. And, farther into the forest, packs of monkeys: mantled howlers, white-headed capuchins. These were the most popular creatures of all though they kept a cautious distance from the human *Howler Monkeys* eagerly taking pictures of them.

In some parts of the world, the guide told them, monkey meat is a delicacy. In Africa, apes are eaten: "bush meat." But the monkey population in Central America was protected.

The capuchins were fretting and shrieking at one another. Were they angry? Excited? Frightened? Showing off? Were they well aware of their human observers, and mocking them? Becca felt her heartbeat quicken in imitation of the frantic-seeming creatures who flung themselves through the air in ceaseless agitation. It was upsetting to watch them, yet impossible to look away. "Something terrible is going to happen"—the little monkeys seemed to be screaming this warning and the wife meant only to be amusing in translating it aloud. Fortunately, no one seemed to hear.

After the forest, which left the wife drenched with sweat and feeling oddly disoriented, as if she'd been granted a profound vision (of animal ancestors?) that had come to nothing, they were driven by van to a rocky shore with stretches of sandy beach where dinghies from the cruise ship had landed. As the guide lectured entertainingly on the courtship rituals of sea lions the wife felt a clutch of dread that the Arbus family would be there, inescapably—though at first she didn't see them, amid a pack of tourists taking pictures of cavorting sea lions and their young.

And then, there they were. Big-headed big-bellied father and son, obese mother and daughter in sleeveless beltless shapeless dresses.

How they ruined the primitive beauty of the setting! The sea lions, and seabirds . . . Everything was ruined by their presence. The wife believed that others felt the same way, and looked upon these people with exasperated pity.

It was particularly upsetting to see how the brother was wading in the surf much too close to the sea lions, as visitors were warned not to do. Becca considered calling to him—*Be careful! A sea lion can slash you with its claws.* She watched to see if the sea lion would attack the brash boy . . . The boy's mother made a futile effort to call him back but the boy took no notice, stamping and hooting in the surf; the father took no notice, frowningly absorbed in his videotape camera. The obese girl was also barefoot, having removed her sandals and socks, wading in the surf with an imbecile look of intense frowning concentration, tongue protruding . . .

Soon then as the wife looked on in horror the boy, the girl, and the mother began to strip to bathing suits as other tourists were doing, for swimming and snorkeling were allowed in this cove.

The wife looked on in amazement. Such ugly ungainly individuals voluntarily removing their outer clothes in public! Only a few yards away was another family—(in fact, one of the Norman Rockwell families)—attractive adults, beautiful young children. These were normal, undeformed bodies from which no one would look away in disgust.

From what she'd overheard on the ship Becca gathered that the Arbus family was from Long Island. Both parents were educators of some kind—high school? community college? It was not possible to believe that they were university faculty. In the ship's lounge Becca had overheard the big-headed father talking importantly about Central America to another passenger who must have been amused by his fatuous arrogance. And the obese girl—her name was something like "Nadine"—"Natalie"—was still in school, it seemed.

The wife wanted to call out to the girl's mother, to warn her— *Don't! Don't let your daughter expose her body like this! You can't know what you are doing . . .*

There came the heedless fat boy running in the surf, making a yodeling noise to frighten away seabirds; his chins, torso, stomach and thighs jiggled. And there was the girl in a pink floral bathing suit with a little skirt like the skirt of a ballet costume that exposed her enormous lard-like thighs, her swelling belly and hips, her hideous sagging breasts like an obscene fruit . . . The mother sat in the shade of a great rock, tote bag on her lap, watching with a frowning sort of affection; the father sat heavily on a low rock with his fat legs outspread, enormous groin scarcely contained by the crotch of his Bermuda shorts, taking pictures of his hideous children wading in the surf. What was astonishing was that the family *seemed to be having a good time.*

The obese girl seemed truly not to know how ugly she was. Cavorting in the waves, breathless and panting like a young child as the brother splashed her, and she shouted and splashed him in turn. A kind of wildness came over the two, as in the white-headed capuchins in the rain forest. The wife wanted to shout at her *How on earth can you be happy? Don't you know what you look like?*

Indeed the wife wasn't the only person taking notice of the two. There were others casting scornful looks. A bare-chested boy of about fifteen and an older brother—both of them good-looking boys whom Becca had noticed on the ship, talking and laughing with other teenagers. It was the girl who drew the most derisive stares and yet—perversely—she seemed not to notice.

On the beach the wife stood, staring. A murderous rage overcame her. That the beautiful slain daughter was dead, and this obscenely ugly daughter was alive—it was unbearable. The raging words of Lear came to her—*Why should a dog, a horse, a rat have life? And thou no breath at all?*

The sun seemed to be swelling in the sky. White sun, white-vapor sky. In thin trickles sweat ran down her body inside her clothes and left her shivering.

Where was the husband? Why was he not beside her?

The wife felt strength drain from her legs and suddenly she was on her knees, and then on her stomach, fallen forward in the hot gritty sand.

"Ma'am? *Señora?*"—Jorge was bending over her, concerned. Other faces approached. The husband was absent but the rotund little Arbus mother had heaved herself to her feet with a grunt and hurried over on fat legs; she and the guide helped Becca sit up. Then, the rotund little woman in the beltless bare-armed dress took a cloth out of her tote bag which she dipped in the surf and brought to Becca to press against her overheated face. "Lower your head, dear. That will help. If you lower your head, blood will flow to your brain and you won't be so faint."

And, "It's the 'vagus' nerve, that can cause a blackout. In this tropical climate you could have heatstroke so you should be very careful not to become dehydrated."

And, "My name is Gladys, dear—'Dr. Gladys.'"

Unhesitating the wife obeyed Dr. Gladys. The wife was very weak, and did not push away the bottled water the woman lifted to her lips though (she guessed) someone else had been drinking from it before her.

High on the trail above the cove, not visible from where the wife sat spread-legged on the sand, the husband continued to ascend the trail, oblivious.

3.

"My name is Nathalie."

"Oh yes—'Nathalie.' Thank you."

It was late afternoon of the final full day of the tour. The wife had entered the library on the lower level of the *Boca Brava*, which was usually deserted, and had been dismayed to discover the obese girl there, alone.

As if waiting for me. But of course that can't be right.

Against a wall was a table of light refreshments: instant coffee, tea, cream and sugar packets; small cellophane-wrapped nuts and candies. The wife had intended to peruse the shelves of books but the obese girl misunderstood, and moved aside for her to approach the refreshments table. "Some of these?"—with a shy sort of pushiness the girl offered her a package of pistachios.

"No thank you . . ."

Smiling, the girl announced her name: *Na-tha-LIE*. She spoke with a faint lisp. Her manner was just slightly coquettish, the wife thought uncomfortably.

"'Nathalie' is a—pretty name . . ."

"Thank you!" The smile broadened. Moist pink gums were exposed. In the fleshy cheeks, sharp dimples.

And now—was there something missing? Something wrong?

She was feeling uneasy in such close quarters with the girl—with "Nathalie." Only later would the wife recall that she'd failed to tell the girl her name. She had not even thought of saying *My name is Becca.*

Close up, the obese girl was obviously younger than twenty. A child trapped inside the ungainly mammalian-female body.

Nathalie was slightly taller than Becca, and must have weighed one hundred pounds more than Becca. Like her father she seemed to loom and lurch dangerously. Her young forehead was lined and creased from frowning and like her mother's, her eyes were curiously bare. (Had she been ill? When Daphne had had hepatitis her hair had grown brittle and thin but her eyelashes had not fallen out, so far as Becca remembered.) She was wearing the unflattering bib-overalls with a mustard-yellow T-shirt beneath—Becca had the impression that the girl's enormous young breasts were bare inside her clothing, with no support. (How was this possible? Didn't the mother monitor the girl's clothing? Didn't the mother *see*? Becca felt a rush of maternal indignation.) Nathalie was nervous and self-conscious yet seemed pleased to be talking with Becca; she had the manner of a child who is accustomed to being praised by adults. Excitedly she spoke of a project she was doing for her Earth Science class at school and Becca had no choice but to ask her about it: a little book of photographs Nathalie had taken on the islands, with a text and captions: "The title is 'Birds and Animals of the Panama Islands.'"

"Isn't a bird an animal?"—Becca spoke lightly for she hated to be dogmatic.

Nathalie giggled. "A bird is a *bird,* and an animal is an *animal.* Like—a *mammal,* with four legs and fur."

Becca smiled uncertainly. Without wishing to be rude she was eager to escape the girl who stood uncomfortably close, and breathed and panted warmly against Becca's face.

Since Becca's near-collapse of the previous day on the beach at Coiba Island she'd been feeling chagrined, and not so critical of the girl's family. She had tried to blot out entirely the vision of the mother, the girl, the brother in swim suits—it was too awful to recall. She would still avoid them, if she could; but she had to concede that "Dr. Gladys" had been very nice to her.

Still, the father and the brother were physically repugnant. And poor Nathalie who was gazing at Becca with unabashed yearning and sucking at her lower lip—*She is brain-damaged, somehow. A neurological deficit.*

The wife felt a wave of sympathy for the girl. How terrible it must be, to be *her*.

As Nathalie spoke excitedly she pressed forward, and Becca stepped back. It was unfortunate that no one else was in the library to deflect the girl's over-intense interest in her, that did not seem to Becca altogether normal. Where was Dr. Gladys? Where was Yegor? The big-headed big-bellied bully-father? Becca saw that the girl's face might have been attractive if it hadn't been so fleshy, broad and round as a moon; the forehead and cheeks were stippled with small pimples, or insect bites, some of which she'd scratched until they'd bled. Her lusterless brown hair was parted in the center of her head and had been brushed slickly back, like the glistening fur of a seal. And she was smiling weirdly, or grimacing; as if a particularly intense thought was forcing itself through her brain the hideous tongue emerged from between her lips, plump, pink, and moist as a skinless snake. Becca stepped back, startled and repelled.

"Excuse me! I have to—have to meet my husband upstairs . . ."

With no effort to disguise her eagerness to escape, the wife fled as poor Nathalie stared after her with widened, hurt eyes.

"I LOVE YOU, BECCA, and I respect you"—these words, gravely intoned, struck chill in her heart.

He had not misrepresented himself. From the first, he'd said that he was not eager to remarry. He doubted that he would ever remarry, in fact—"I think you should know that, dear Becca."

It wasn't a matter of love or respect but he was older than she, and older in his heart than she could know; he had lost the capacity for surprise and for wonder he'd had when he was her age.

(And what had been Becca's age, at this time? Twenty-five?)

He would not speak to her of the debacle of his first marriage except to say that it had been a mistake, and that both he and his former wife had paid dearly for their (mutual) mistake. He would not speak to her of the treacherous wife who had abandoned not only her husband but also their five-year-old daughter—"Daphne is the center of my life, but it isn't enough for her that I am the center of her life. A child needs more than one parent."

He had taken her hand in both of his hands and led her to sit with him in an odd, exceptional place—on a rattan sofa in a glassed-in porch at the rear of the handsome old stone and stucco house in Cambridge, Massachusetts, in which he lived alone with his young daughter.

Max Needham was the most gracious of men. Max Needham was the most gracious of men so long as he was in control as the driver of a racing car is in control: the speed, the danger, the risk all his. If you are a passenger in such a car you have no choice but to submit to the speed, the danger, the risk in prayerful silence.

By this time they'd been lovers for more than a year. Most nights they spent together, at Max's house; Becca helped to prepare dinner for Max and Daphne, and often spent time alone with Daphne. She'd remained in graduate school but had ceased being Max Needham's student and rarely encountered him at the university; if they met, Max was coolly cordial to her, and did not encourage her to behave toward him in any way that suggested a personal relationship. Once, when she'd met her lover by chance on a Cambridge street and had too warmly greeted him, he'd stepped back from her with a look of disdain; when she called him that evening he had not answered the phone. Only several days later, after Becca had left several apologetic messages, did he relent.

And now, he'd sensed in the ardent young woman a feeling for him to which he was not—quite—equal. And he felt concern for the young woman, and wanted to explain more clearly that he didn't want to take advantage of her; at the same time, he understood that a beautiful young woman like Becca would want her life to be stable, and so—(and here Becca steeled herself for the terse, terminating words she would carry with her to the grave)—"If you feel that you can be a loving mother to Daphne, then—perhaps we could be married."

Quietly he spoke. As if, if Becca had not heard, he could very easily retract his words. Adding, before Becca could reply, "But know what you are getting into, dear Becca."

OF COURSE, SHE KNEW.

Of course, she had no idea.

4.

What was that, ahead?—the wife drew back, uncertain.

Alone and anxious she'd been walking on the dimly-lit lower deck of the *Bocca Brava*. The upper decks were populous tonight for there were strolling musicians, complimentary drinks, bright lights; the lowermost deck, which smelled of diesel oil, or what the wife supposed diesel oil might smell like, was deserted as usual. The wife felt the need to walk—to walk swiftly—sometimes, since no one was a witness, to break into a run—as thoughts bombarded her brain like shrieking shorebirds. *Know what you are getting into, dear Becca.*

At last it was the eve of their departure from Panama. Six arduous days and six arduous nights had not gone rapidly but seemed now to be too rapidly drawing to a close. In the morning there would be a final excursion to one of the islands and then passengers were to be ferried to the mainland, and taken by bus to the airport at Panama City. A day and a night of tiring travel and the wife and the husband would be returned like luggage to the stone and stucco house in Cambridge, Massachusetts, where the husband had set the thermostat at fifty-five degrees.

Here, the equatorial sun that had made the wife's eyes ache during the day had faded at last behind a mass of clouds like dirty red-stained gauze. There was a chill, sinister wind out of the gathering darkness. In the tropics the sun dropped with startling abruptness beneath the horizon, the wife found herself staring mesmerized and helpless as it vanished. That it was the earth's motion, and not the sun's, did not dispel the sense of dread—*Something terrible is going to happen. You will not know when.*

Now that their departure from the *Bocca Brava* was imminent the wife had ceased thinking of the Diane Arbus family. She'd glimpsed them in the dining room earlier that day, or rather she'd heard the father speaking sarcastically to the silent abashed girl, and unwittingly she'd turned to see who this cruel parent might be, but immediately turned away again. *No! No more.* She was thinking now of the return to the refrigerated house, and the emptiness of that house.

Almost she'd thought—*The emptiness of that life.*

Exactly where the husband was, the wife did not know. He wasn't in their cabin—she had checked several times.

After the final excursion of the day Max had looked unusually fatigued. He'd asked Becca if she greatly minded, if she might leave the cabin so that he could try to have a nap before dinner.

This was utterly unlike the husband who regarded daytime naps as decadent and a waste of time. Becca would have touched Max's forehead to see if he was running a fever (though his face appeared oddly ashen, not flushed) but Max frowned and turned aside, not rudely but unmistakably, and so she retreated at once and left him alone as he'd requested. But when after an hour she returned to the cabin, very gently opening the door, she saw that the rumpled bed was empty, the cabin was empty, though the blinds had been drawn against the shimmering sun.

His cell phone lay on the little table beside his side of the bed. The wife knew that the husband had been sending emails—that is, try-ing to send emails, for it wasn't likely that any could go out while the

Bocca Brava was so far from the mainland—and wondered to whom he was writing, and about what. For a long moment she considered whether she should look into his email, see what had accumulated in the outbox . . .

She went away. Shut the door firmly so that it locked, and went away.

There were few places on the cruise ship that Max found tolerable and one of these was the prow on the uppermost deck where often the wife had seen him, leaning on the railing, gazing out at the ocean—a lone stiff-backed man of late middle age who communicated a sort of radar warning to anyone who might be considering approaching him—*No. Please. Not now, and not me.*

Becca had noticed that Max had taken his suitcase out of the closet, and laid it, open, on a chair. How eager he was to pack, and to disembark.

It was the husband's custom to pack his suitcase with its many zippered compartments with such deliberation you would think—(the wife had once joked about this, and the husband had laughed)—that he was packing for the afterlife.

The wife laughed, recalling. The wife wiped at her eyes for there was a sharp odor of oil in the air that seemed to sting.

She'd been walking swiftly, half-running—seeing now, ahead, at the rear of the deck where the engines throbbed loudest, and lights overhead were dimmest, an unexpected sight: about fifteen feet away the girl in the bib-overalls appeared to be crawling on hands and knees like an ungainly dog and moaning to herself—*Oh oh ohhh.*

At first the wife had no idea what she was seeing. Was this— Nathalie? But what was Nathalie doing?

Then the realization came to her—the girl might have tried to throw herself over the railing but lost her nerve, or wasn't strong enough to lift her ungainly body and had fallen back onto the deck, sobbing and panting. Her fleshy face was mottled and streaked with tears. Her enormous thighs strained the material of the overalls nearly to bursting and her heavy young breasts swung loose to her waist.

"Nathalie! What on earth are you doing . . ."

Quickly the wife came forward. She knelt, and tugged at the girl's fingers that were tightly clenched around the railing.

But Nathalie didn't seem to recognize Becca. She resisted her as a wounded animal might resist a rescuer, moaning loudly, trying to butt with her head, and biting at Becca's hands, as Becca tugged at the girl's wrists. "No! Nathalie, no! Let go of the railing, take my hand, lean on me, let me help you up . . ." But Nathalie continued to resist. Becca was astonished: was the girl hysterical? Insane? Was it dangerous to touch her? Yet Becca didn't want to relinquish her hold on the girl for fear that the girl would fling her off and manage to get to her feet and throw herself over the railing . . .

As Becca pleaded with her the girl continued to moan loudly, clutching at the railing as if her fingers had locked onto it and rocking from side to side. Her young forehead was creased, her small bare eyes leaked tears. Horrible to see, the plump tongue began to protrude through pursed lips. Becca could not bear looking at the girl, or smelling the sharp rank animal-odor of her unwashed hair and body, yet Becca could not abandon her.

"Please! Try to stand, Nathalie. I can't help you if—if . . ."

The girl's sobs were not the sobs of a child but the howls of a wounded beast. Becca wondered why no one heard and came to help—whether observers had in fact approached and seen the struggle with the bawling girl on the deck and quickly retreated, not wanting to be involved.

At last Nathalie released the railing but now seized Becca's knees and begged her not to leave her. She seemed to be wailing what sounded like—*Afraid! Afraid* . . . Becca tried to lift her, but the girl would not cooperate and was far too heavy for Becca to lift. Her body was a dead weight.

Becca was pleading: "Nathalie—please! You're safe now, no one is going to hurt you . . ."

She wondered if someone had been tormenting the girl? The teen-aged boys who'd smirked and leered at her on the island?

But now someone was approaching them, shouting—"Get away! Get away from my daughter, you!" It was the obese father, lurching and blustering. His face was livid with rage. His shirt was open, his fatty hairless chest was slick with sweat. Astonished Becca would wonder afterward if the father had been standing at a little distance observing the girl—and then Becca—for some time before announcing himself.

In his aggrieved barking voice the father accused the girl: "God damn! Making a public spectacle of yourself! You—will—be—sorry." He'd seized the screaming girl by her upper arm as Becca tried to intervene and with a muttered curse and a swing of his free arm, as one might fling aside a protesting child, the father knocked Becca to the deck.

She fell, hard. The side of her head struck the wooden floor. The father stood over her blustering in indignation: "Leave my daughter alone, you! *You* are not her friend. *You* have no right to interfere in my family."

For a moment Becca could not think where she was. Something inside her head was ringing like a cracked bell. She managed to protest, "Your daughter tried to hurt herself. She's very upset—hysterical . . ."

"*You* are hysterical! Get away from us! Before I report you to the ship's captain . . ."

The father yanked the whimpering girl to her feet. The girl did not dare resist him as she'd resisted Becca nor did the girl try to speak as the father berated her at length in his harsh, barking voice. Becca managed to get to her feet but dared not approach the wrathful father who glared at her as if he'd like to strike her with his fists.

"Nathalie? Are you—all right?"

Becca's voice was faint, hesitant. Scarcely audible above the throbbing of the ship's engines and the curses of the father and so Nathalie did not hear or, hearing, paid no heed. She did not betray the slightest awareness of Becca standing uncertainly a few feet away.

The father turned to Becca, furious: "I've told you—you are interfering in my family. *Get away from us.*"

Still Becca persisted: "Sir, I need to know if your daughter is all right. I think your daughter needs medical attention . . ."

"I won't tell you again, you! *Get the hell away.*"

In the father's grip Nathalie dared not writhe and squirm as she had done, nor did she dare to scream or protest. Her face looked swollen, and oily with tears. She was staring vacuously at Becca as if she'd never seen her before. Bizarrely, her lips twisted into a dazed smile. Her lips parted, and the plump pinkly moist tongue poked shyly out.

Becca retreated. Becca fled.

Panting and agitated, head throbbing where it had struck the hardwood deck, Becca stumbled away. She did see figures ahead, retreating quickly before her. There had been witnesses to the bizarre scene, not members of the ship's staff who would surely have come forward to give aid but fellow passengers, unwilling to be involved. And who could blame them?

Sir. How foolish she'd sounded, and how ineffectual!

At least, the girl was safe now. At least, safe from throwing herself overboard.

Afterward Becca would wonder: had the girl's behavior been for the benefit of the father all along, to alarm and intimidate him? To make him regret his harsh treatment of her? Or—perversely—to invite more harsh treatment?

The girl would be returned to the family cabin. She would be heavily sedated, perhaps. She would be kept in seclusion until the *Bocca Brava* docked at the mainland the next day and then she would not be allowed out of the cabin until the other passengers had disembarked. Only then would the Diane Arbus family emerge from their place of refuge blinking in the sun like nocturnal creatures . . . But Becca would not be there to observe.

"MAX! THANK GOD."

She found him on the uppermost deck of the *Bocca Brava* but not where she'd imagined him. And not as she'd imagined him leaning against the railing but slumped in a chair turned to face the darkening ocean.

His hair was windblown. Ash-colored hair that had thinned at the crown of his head, the wife saw with a thrill of sympathy.

He will never recover from the loss of her. He is wounded, dangerous.

Nonetheless she came to him. He was her husband, she would claim him though she was trembling with fear of him. And so she laughed, to disguise her fear. She was covered in sweat, and smelled of the girl—the sharp rank animal-smell of female panic.

In a gesture that took them both by surprise she knelt beside the husband. She dared to touch his arm, in appeal.

"We can 'separate,' Max. I think that's what you want. I understand—I won't interfere."

Almost calmly she spoke, across the abyss. Almost gaily, and wanting again to laugh.

But the husband squinted at her, wincing.

"Jesus, Becca! What are you saying?"

"I was saying—only . . ."

"Don't be ridiculous. I don't want to hear it. You're upset, and you're not being rational."

She would tell him about the deleted message. She would tell him that the daughter's life might have been saved, if she had not deleted the message. She would tell him that she understood, she'd failed the daughter, and she'd failed him. She would fade from his life without protest. She could accept that now. But when she tried to speak the husband interrupted—"No."

It seemed clear to the wife that the husband wasn't well. His skin exuded a sickly heat. His eyes were bloodshot. The wife had not wanted to acknowledge having smelled, in the close confines of the cabin, the odors of the husband's sickness.

Yet, the husband managed to rise shakily to his feet. The husband reached for a chair to drag beside his, for the wife to sit in. For a moment he swayed on his feet—he had not quite caught his balance—or it may have been the rocking of the ship—one of those moments ever more frequently experienced with the passage of time, when one sees a tremor in the hand of another person, a quick and unwanted glimpse of physical intimacy, at once disguised—and then the husband sat back heavily in his chair, and drew the wife against him with a shudder, as if he were very cold and wished to protect the wife from the cold.

The first time the husband had voluntarily touched the wife in weeks. The first time he'd companionably slipped his arm around her, in months.

"But Max, if—"

"I said *no*."

The husband was furious with the wife—was he? His face flamed with heat like the face of one who has been exposed not in a lie but in a truth.

Yet, the wife dared to press the back of her hand against the husband's hot forehead. He did not fling the hand away but caught it in his and pressed it harder against his forehead for indeed, he was running a fever.

"Becca, just sit here. Sit still. We're here together—it's the last night—enjoy the ocean. It's only for now—but it is for now. Don't say another word."

Unaccountably, the husband laughed. His teeth chattered with cold.

She was aware of his arm, his heavy arm, around her shoulders. She was aware that he was gripping her hand, tight. She winced with pain, for her hand had been bitten, she hadn't realized that the skin had been broken in the fleshy crook between thumb and forefinger, already there was a dull throb of pain, and she could not tell the husband, of all sordid truths she could not tell the husband how she had come to be bitten and by whom and how reckless she'd been, to be so bitten, for the husband would be astonished and revolted, the husband would cease loving the wife again, in an instant; and the wife had not the strength to revive the husband's love another time; her soul swooned in utter weariness at the prospect of such renewed effort.

A long distance away the sun had vanished beneath the horizon. Most of the ocean was dark now, invisible. Waves lashed against the ship's sides. There was a chill, penetrating wind. Overhead the sky was fading-red, tattered like torn canvas. They were gripping hands, tight. Like swimmers drowning together, but gripping hands. Tight.

Les beaux jours

Daddy please come bring me home. Daddy I am so sorry. Daddy it is your fault. Daddy *I hate you.*

Daddy, no! I love you Daddy whatever you have done.

Daddy I am under a spell here. I am *not myself* here.

This place in which I am a captive—it is in the Alps, I think. It is a great, old house like a castle made of ancient rock. Through high windows you can see moors stretching to the mountainous horizon. All is scrubby gray-green as if undersea. The light is perpetual twilight.

Dusk is when Master comes. I am in love with Master.

Daddy, no! I do not love Master at all, I am terrified of Master.

He is not like *you*, Daddy. Master laughs at me, taunts me, twines his long thin icy fingers through my fingers and sneers at me when I whimper with pain.

Why did you come crawling to us, ma chère, if now you are so fearful?

Daddy please forgive me. Daddy do not abandon me.

Though it was your fault, Daddy.

Though I can never forgive *you.*

IT IS CALLED BY TWO NAMES. *Le grand chalet* is the official name.

Le grand chalet des âmes perdues is the unofficial, whispered name.

Indeed it is *très grand*, Daddy. The oldest part of *le chalet* dating to 1563 (it is said: such a time is not possible for me to imagine) and the desolate windswept land that surrounds it like a moat so vast that even if I could make myself small as a terrified little cat, if I could squeeze out one of the ill-fitting windows to escape across the moor, Master's servants would set his wolf-hounds after me to hunt me down and tear me to pieces with their sharp ravenous teeth.

Or, if Master is in a merciful mood, and not a mood of vengeance, the servants might haul me back squirming in a net to throw down onto the stone floor at Master's feet.

So I have been warned by the other girl-captives.

So I have been warned by Master himself not in actual words but in Master's way of laying a finger against the anxious little artery that beats so hard in my throat, with just enough pressure to communicate—*Of all sins, ma chère, betrayal is the unforgivable.*

I am not sure where *Le grand chalet des âmes perdues* is but I believe it to be somewhere in eastern Europe.

A faraway place where there is no electricity—only just candles—tall, grand candles of the girth of young trees, so encrypted with melted and hardened wax that they resemble ancient sculptures hacked out of molten stone. What shadows dance from such candles, leaping to the ceiling twelve feet overhead like starved vultures spreading their mammoth wings, you will have to imagine, Daddy—*le chalet* is nothing like the apartment in which we'd lived on Fifth Avenue at Seventy-Sixth Street, overlooking Central Park from the twenty-third floor though (as Mother said) those rooms were haunted too, and the souls that dwelt there wandered *lost*.

Here are six-foot fireplaces and great, soot-begrimed chimneys in which (it is whispered) girl-captives shriveled to mummies are trapped in their foolish yearning to escape Master. *Which is why Mas-*

ter is furious when smoke backs up into the room and a beautiful stoked fire must be extinguished so that the chimney can be cleared.

A faraway place, Daddy. Where the automobiles are very old but elegant and stately and shiny-black as hearses.

There is no TV in *le chalet.* Unless there is a single TV in Master's quarters which none of us has ever been allowed to glimpse as none of us has ever been brought into Master's quarters but this is not likely as Master scorns the *effete modern world* and even the *twentieth century* is vulgar to Master as a sniffling, snuffling, sneezing girl.

But there is an old radio—a "floor model." The servants call it a "wireless"—in Master's (downstairs) sitting room where we are brought sometimes if we have pleased Master that day in his studio.

In Master's studio it is often very drafty. Wind like cold mean fingers pries through the edges of the tall windows and strokes and tickles us, and makes us shiver and our teeth chatter for we are made to remove our clothing quickly and without protest and to cover our shivering naked bodies with silken kimonos that are too large for us, and fall open no matter how tightly we tie their sashes.

In *le grand chalet* we are often barefoot for Master is an admirer (he has said) of the *girl-child-foot.*

Also, the bare *girl-child-foot* cannot easily run through brambles, thorns, pebbles outside the *chalet* walls.

In Master's studio we are made to pose by sitting very straight and very still for hours or by standing very straight and very still for hours or (some of us, the most favored) lying with naked legs asprawl or aspread on *chaises longues* and our heads flung back at painful angles. And some of us, rumored to be the most favored, made to pose by lying very still on the freezing-cold marble floor in mimicry (Master says) of *le mort.*

It is forbidden to observe Master at his easel. It is forbidden to glance even fleetingly at Master contorting his face in a paroxysm of anguish, yearning, ecstasy as he crouches at the easel only a few feet away from us scant of breath, weak-kneed. For art is a brutal master, even for Master.

Sometimes, Master who is the very essence of gentlemanly decorum curses his brushes in a language most of us do not know. Sometimes, Master throws down a brush, or a tube of paint, like a furious child in the knowledge that someone (an adult, a servant) will pick it up for him, at a later time.

Fortunately, the marble floor beneath Master's easel is covered with a stained canvas.

It is shocking to us to glimpse Master's many tubes of paint, that appear to be flung haphazardly onto a table beside his easel; myriad tubes of paint of which most are very messy, some are skeletal and squeezed nearly dry, a few are plump and newly purchased; for elsewhere in *le grand chalet* all is chaste and orderly as a geometrical figure.

Master's studio with its high ceiling and white walls is one of the most famous artists' studios in the world, it is said. Long before the oldest of us was born, the studio existed at *Le grand chalet des âmes perdues,* and of course, long after the youngest of us will pass away, Master's studio will endure for it is enshrined in legend, like Master himself who (it is said) is one of the very few living artists whose work is displayed in the Louvre.

Master has shunned fame, as Master has shunned commercial success, yet, ironically, Master has become famous, and Master has become one of the most successful painters of what is called the "modern era"; his paintings are unusually large, fastidiously painted and repainted, formal, rather austere, "classic"—even if their subjects are nude or minimally dressed young girls posed in languid postures.

Master insists upon the impersonality of art. Master has chosen to live far from the clamor of capital cities—Paris, Berlin, Prague, Rome. Master scorns the elite art world even as Master scorns the media that nonetheless pursues him with *paparazzi*. Master is revered for the severity of his art and for his perfectionism: Master will spend years on a single canvas before releasing it to his (Parisian) gallery. With each of his rare exhibits Master has included this declaration:

LIFE IS NOT ART
ART IS THE LIFE OF WHICH NOTHING IS KNOWN
TURN YOUR EYES TO THE PAINTINGS
"THE REST IS SILENCE"

Yet, the media adores Master as a *nobleman-artiste living in reclusive exile in a romantic and remote corner of Europe.*

In Master's studio time ceases to exist. In Master's studio the spell suffuses me like ether. My arms, my legs, my supine being on the green sofa—so heavy, I cannot move.

Master has posed my arm in a tight sleeve, Master has tugged open the tight bodice so that my very small, right breast is exposed; Master has positioned my bare legs just so, and Master has placed on my *exquisite girl-child-feet* thin slippers made of the most fragile satin, one could barely walk in them across a room; Master has fastened a necklace around my neck, of small gems worthy of an adult beauty (as Master has said: the necklace may have belonged to one of Master's wives).

And Master has given me a little hand-mirror in which to gaze, mesmerized at what I see: the pretty doll-face, the pert little nose and pursed lips that are *me*.

HOW DID I COME TO this captivity?—I think of nothing else.

Daddy, I ran away from you. I ran away from *her*.

Yet first it was with Mother, those restless hours in the great Museum visible from our Fifth Avenue windows. Mother in dark glasses so that her reddened eyes were not exposed and no one who knew her (and knew you) would recognize her. Mother pulling my sister and

me by our arms, urging us up the grand stairs, in seek of something
she could not have defined—the consolation of art, the impersonality of art, the escape of art.

The mystery of art, which confounds us with the power to heal
our wounds, or to lacerate our wounds to greater pain.

Soon then, I slipped away to come alone. A novelty at the Museum, a child so young—alone . . .

But I was mature for my age, and my size. It was not difficult
for me to single out visitors whom I would approach in the usually
crowded lobby to ask to purchase a ticket for me, and take me inside
with them as if I belonged with them . . . Of course, I gave them
money for my ticket. Very cleverly, I even lent them Mother's mem-
bership card (appropriated for the occasion), to facilitate matters.

Usually it was women whom I approached. Not young, not old,
Mother's age, not glamorous (like Mother) but motherly-seeming.
They were surprised by my request at first, but kindly, and cooperative. It was not difficult to deceive these women that you or Mother
were waiting for me in the café in the American Wing, and then to
slip away from their scrutiny once we were inside.

Soon then in the great Museum I began to linger before a row of
paintings by the twentieth-century European artist whom I would
come to know as Master.

What a spell these paintings cast! I could not know that it was the
spell of enchantment and entrapment, of inertia, that would one day
suffuse my limbs like an evil sedative . . .

These were large dreamlike paintings executed with the formal-
ity, stillness, and subdued beauty of the older, classical European art
Mother had professed to admire, yet their subjects were not biblical
or mythological figures but girls—some of them as young as I was.
Though in settings very different from the settings of my life the girls
seemed familiar to me, more sisterly than my own sister who was too

young and too silly for me and was always interrupting my thoughts with her chatter.

Especially, I found myself staring at a painting of a girl who resembled me, lying on a small sofa in an old-fashioned drawing room. (I did not yet know the word for such an item of furniture—*chaise longue*.) The girl was like myself yet older and wiser. Her eyebrows were thin as pencil lines artfully drawn while mine were thicker, yet not so defined. Her eyes were exactly my eyes!—yet wiser, bemused. Her coppery-colored, wavy hair resembled my own, though in an old-fashioned style. Her doll-like features, delicately boned nose and somber pursed lips—like mine, but she was far prettier than me, and more ethereal. And she was gazing at herself in a small hand-mirror with an expression of calm self-absorption—impossible for me, who had come to dislike my face, intensely.

What was strange about the painting was that the girl on the sofa seemed to be totally oblivious of another presence in the room, only a few feet away from her: a stooped young man stoking a blazing fire in a fireplace, that so pulsated with heat and light you could nearly feel it, standing before the painting.

In fact, when you approach the painting from a little distance it is the "blazing" you first see that leaps out to strike your eye, before you see the small supine figure on the sofa gazing dreamily at her reflection.

Isn't that strange, Daddy? Yet, if the girl on the sofa is a girl in a dream, and the dream of the girl is her pretty doll-face, it is natural that she is unaware of another presence, even close by; the stooped figure is male but it is *stooped*, a servant surely, and not Master.

Each day after school I came to the Museum. Each day I lingered longer by this painting—*Les beaux jours*. At first I'd thought that the title might mean *The Beautiful Eyes*—but *jours* means "days," it is *yeux* that means "eyes."

And so the title is—*The Beautiful Days*.

Days of enchantment, entrancement. Not yet days of entrapment.

Beautiful days of perfect calm, peace. Enough just to gaze into the little hand-mirror and to pay no heed to your flimsy satin slippers that will impede your flight if you try to escape and to the hot bright-blazing fire being prepared a few feet away by a stooped and faceless servant.

Other paintings by the artist whose name I must not speak—(for to speak of Master in such a way is forbidden to us, as to the servants of *le grand chalet*)—were fascinating to me as well and any one of these might have held me captive: *Thérèse rêvant—Jeune fille à sa toilette—Nu jouant avec un chat—La victime—La chambre.*

Faintly, I could hear their cries. The captive-girls in the paintings who were (not yet) myself.

So faintly, I could pretend that I had not heard. Glancing around at others in the Museum, casual visitors, uniformed guards who took little notice of me, a child of eleven seemingly alone in the gallery, shivering with apprehension for what precisely, I could not have guessed.

(And what is there to say of the Museum guards?—did they not hear, either? Had they grown indifferent, bored with beauty as with suffering, as if it were but mere paint on canvas, a veneer and not a depth? *Will they not hear me, when I cry for help?*)

OUTSIDE THE MUSEUM, the clamor of New York streets. Tall leafy trees, the enormous green park. On Fifth Avenue taxis queuing up at the curb in front of the Museum, at the foot of the great pyramid of stone steps.

Vendors' carts, stretching along the block. These are owned exclusively by U.S. veterans, it is decreed. The smell of hot meats is almost overwhelming to us, who are faint from malnutrition.

Our apartment at Fifth Avenue and Seventy-Sixth Street. Overlook-

ing the park from the twenty-third floor. So high, we heard nothing. No
sounds lifted to our ears from the street. When I pressed my hands over
my ears, I did not hear sobbing. I did not hear even my own sobbing, or
the wild beat of my heart.

ELEVEN ON MY LAST BIRTHDAY. When you were still living
with us, Daddy, though often you stayed away overnight. And your
promise was—*Darling of course I am not leaving you and your sister*
and your mother; and even if I left—temporarily!—your mother, that
would not mean that I was leaving you and your sister. No.

But when you left we were made to move to another apartment on
a lesser street, on a lower floor. You left us for another life, Mother
said. She wept bitterly. She inhabited her (sheer) nightgown for days
in succession.

Men came to stay with Mother but never for long. We heard their
loud barking laughter. We hear the clatter of glasses, bottles. We
heard our mother's screams.

We heard the men depart hurriedly in the early hours of the morning: stumbling, cursing, threats. Laughter.

Jenny whispered wide-eyed—*One of them will murder her. Stran-*
gle her.

(You are thinking that is not likely, a child of eight or nine would
say such a thing? Even in a whisper, to her eleven-year-old sister? Do
you think so, Daddy? Is that what you have wished to think?)

(A daddy is someone who wishes to think what protects him. Not
what protects his children.)

We knew nothing of adult lives. Yet, we knew everything of adult
lives.

We watched TV. Late-night when we were supposed to be in bed,
the volume turned low. We were thrilled that women with dishev-
eled hair and mascara-streaked faces wearing sheer nightgowns were
raped, strangled, murdered in their beds. NYPD detectives stared

rudely at their naked bodies. Photographers crouched over them, bending at the knees so that their groins were prominent.

But Mother did not die, as you know. Mother's screams prevailed. Even here, in *le grand chalet,* I hear those screams at a distance. Unless they are the screams of my sister-captives, muffled with cushions or the palm of Master's hand.

The men brought whiskey, bourbon. Cocaine.

Out of Mother's refrigerator, soft, smelly brie. Hard Italian provolone. Snails and garlic, hot butter. They ate greedily. They ate with their fingers. We ran away to hide, we hid our eyes. Nothing so disgusted us as snails like the tiny ridges of flesh between our thin girl-legs we could not bear to touch even in the bath, the sensation came so strong.

Daddy, you dared not touch us there. In those days when you were a new, young Daddy, and you bathed us. When we were very young girls, scarcely more than toddlers, babies. That long ago, you have (probably) forgotten.

Daddy, we have not forgotten. How your eyes glistened with knowledge of what lay secret and hidden between our legs that you did not (allow yourself to) touch.

Master touches us everywhere. Of course, Master touches us *there.*

DADDY WHY DID YOU GO AWAY. Why was your life not *us.*

Mother never knew how once, we saw her—the girl slipping from your lap, giggling.

Young enough to be your daughter, Mother had accused, furious. I wanted to protest, I am your daughter!

It had been an accidental encounter. Jenny and I had been delivered too early to the apartment by your private car, or your friend had stayed too late. Slipping from your lap giggling and blushing, stammering—*Oh hey. Don't think badly of me. I am not a bad person . . .*

She'd been drinking. Both of you drinking. It was surprising to us, she was so tall, and not so thin, not so very pretty really, and not (probably) so young as Mother believed her to be though much younger than Mother of course.

Her tight, short skirt pulled up from her firm, thick thighs. The front of her shirt pulled open.

Not a bad person. Please believe me!

IN THE GREAT MUSEUM quickly I made my way up the grand steps, along the high-ceilinged corridors, to the dimly-lighted gallery that contained Master's paintings.

Unerring through the maze of the Museum like a blind child navigating by smell, or touch. And there it was, suddenly before me—*Les beaux jours.*

Stunning to me, nothing ever changed in the painting. The girl lying on the green *chaise longue* with legs askew, the girl gazing at herself in the little hand-mirror. The girl so like myself yet older and wiser than I, and (seemingly) content with that knowledge.

The girl oblivious of the hot bright fire blazing only a few feet from her.

For the first time I heard the faint, yearning voice, or voices— *Hello! Come to us.*

Or did they cry—*Help us* . . .

On weekday afternoons the gallery was often near-deserted. Visitors trooped through the special exhibits but did not make their way to this gallery.

No one heard the cries. Except me.

How strange, the Museum guards never heard. As the stupefying dullness of their guard-lives had made them incapable of seeing the wonder of Master's art though it was hanging before them, triumphant and transgressive.

Which is why it is so lonely, Daddy. If *you* do not hear.

And back in the apartment which was on a floor lower than the twenty-third but still high above the pavement, high enough to stir dread in the pit of my belly, I crawled out onto the dwarf-balcony, I dared to lean over the railing that was encrusted with pigeon droppings, waiting for you to discover me, Daddy, and scold me as (rarely) you'd done—*What are you doing! Get back in here, darling!*

Master never scolds. Master (rarely) betrays emotion in our presence for we do not merit emotion only just vexation, disappointment, displeasure.

Daddy, come soon! I am afraid that if Master is displeased with me, if Master becomes bored with me, that Master will dispose of me as he has disposed of the others.

So lonely! Yet, I love Master. I love this heavy spell that falls upon me in Master's studio even when my limbs ache and my neck strains to bear the weight of my head, posed and unmoving for hours.

If you do not come to bring me home, Daddy. If you abandon me to Master I will sink ever more deeply into the spell, and Master will tire of me, and a collar will be fastened around my neck, and a chain to the collar, to bind me fast in the lowermost dungeon of *le chalet*.

COME TO US, *help us.*

Help us, come to us.

As I drew nearer the paintings in the great Museum the spell began to work upon me. Like ether, in the air.

There was no guard near. No other visitors. Trembling I leaned close to whisper *Yes! I will come to you.*

For what I could see of the drawing room of *Les beaux jours* was very beautiful to me, if strange and sepia-colored, not altogether clear as the details of a dream are not altogether clear and yet seductive, irresistible.

More and more in the lonely afternoons after school I found myself in that other world. I did not (yet) realize it was Master's world for you do not see Master in the paintings, you see only yourself painted with such ardor, such yearning, such desire it is like nothing else in the world you have ever known, or could imagine.

Each of the girls, in each of the paintings: their stillness, their perfection. For even the awkward girls, even the girls whose doll-faces were hidden from view, were cherished, beloved. That, you could feel.

Without you in my life, Daddy, there was not a promise of such happiness anywhere I knew.

Come to us, you are one of us—the voices whispered; and my reply was—*Yes. I am yours.*

MA CHÈRE, BIENVENUE!—so Master greeted me.

Ma belle petite fille!—Master exclaimed in delight at the sight of me as if he had never seen anyone so exquisite.

For I had been discovered by a servant wandering lost and tearful in one of the dim-lighted corridors of the great old house I did not (yet) know was *le grand chalet des âmes perdues.*

Master made me blush, and my heart beat so rapidly I could not breathe, covering my face, my hands, my bare arms with his sharp damp stabbing kisses that left me faint.

How far you have come, ma chère!—*across the great ocean, to your Master.*

I could not (yet) know that each of the girl-captives was greeted so lavishly by Master, and made to feel *You are the one. Only you.*

IN THAT OTHER LIFE it had come to be, I could not bear to look at myself in a mirror.

For when you'd left us, Daddy, you took away with you so much—you could not know how much.

But in Master's studio, posed by Master on the green *chaise longue* I am allowed to see that my face is not homely, not despised, but a pretty doll-face. I love gazing into the mirror that Master has given me, at the pretty doll-face.

It is like sleep, gazing at the doll-face. Very hard to wake up, to look away from the doll-face. My lips scarcely move—*Is this* me? The wonder of it is hypnotic, like caresses that never cease.

Though I know—I think—there is someone in this room with me . . . It is heat that I am beginning to feel, an uncomfortable rising heat in this drafty place.

The heat of a *blazing fire*. Somewhere close by.

Master tugs at my tight-fitting sleeve, pulling it off my shoulder to expose my right breast that is small and hard as an unripened apple. The skirt of this (tight) dress which I have been given to wear is very short, and falls back to reveal much of my legs. In other paintings, in other rooms, the stark white of my little-girl panties is revealed as Master has positioned my legs, spread my legs just so. But in this painting you cannot see the narrow band of white cotton between my thighs.

In Master's studio time ceases to pass. In Master's studio we never age. That is the promise of Master's studio.

Master laughs at us but not unkindly. *You know you have come to me of your own volition, do not be hypocritical, mes chères. Hypocrisy is for les autres.*

Long hours we must pose. Our lives spill out before us heedless as spools of thread rolling across a slanted marble floor. Some of us are new to *le grand chalet,* some of us have been here entire lifetimes. For long hours we must pose in the drafty studio or we will not be given food. We must not interrupt Master's concentration for Master will be choked with fury, and Master will punish by withholding his love.

To quench our terrible thirst we are given small sips of water by a servant who crouches at our side. Master is particularly furious if we beg to be "excused" to use a bathroom.

Water-closet is the word they use here. I am embarrassed at this word. The flushing mechanism is very old-fashioned, pulled by a chain. Old pipes clang and shudder in the great old house like demons.

You disgust me. You!—Master's thin nostrils quiver with indignation.

It is hard to live in a body, we have learned. The body betrays the pretty doll-face and makes of its prettiness a mockery.

Bitterly Mother told us, as soon as she'd become pregnant for the first time, it was the end of your love for her, Daddy. My belly, she said. My breasts. So big, swollen. No longer a girl, he'd felt betrayed. Poor man was not *turned on*.

We did not want to hear this! We were too young to hear of such ugliness.

Of course, the marriage continued. Your father would not have admitted even to himself the limits of his—of a man's—desire.

AND ONE DAY MASTER SELECTS ME for a special scene to which he will give the title, succinct and appalling—*La victime*.

I am hoping that you will see this portrait, Daddy. It is the very painting I had seen on the wall in the Museum, without guessing that the girl lying in a limp, lifeless pose does not merely resemble me *but is me*.

La victime is not so dreamlike and beautiful as other paintings of Master's, that are more celebrated. *La victime* is the blunt, irrefutable image—the *girl-victim*. Patiently, almost tenderly Master urged me to the floor, to lie on my back on a stone slab; almost lovingly Master molded my bare limbs, turned and positioned my head with his steely-strong fingers.

In *La victime* I am not so pretty, I think. I am very pale—as if bloodless. Nor am I provided with a little hand-mirror in which to admire my pretty doll-face. My eyes are shut, the vision has faded from them. Except for thin white cotton stockings and tiny, useless slippers I am nude—*naked*.

Slowly as if in a trance Master executes this portrait. After long hours, when Master has finished for the day, and exited the studio in wraithlike silence, I am roused from a comatose state by one of the servants, a dwarf-woman who flings open heavy drapery to let in sunshine like a rude blow—*Wake up, you. Don't play games. You're not dead—yet.*

WHEN FIRST I ARRIVED at the chalet, I was treated like a princess.

As, when I was born, and for years when I was your only child, Daddy, I was treated like a princess by you.

Lilies of the valley in a vase, in my room at the chalet. Beside my bed which was perfectly proportioned for a girl of eleven. Sweet fragrance of lily of the valley which is mesmerizing to me even now, to recall.

A woman-servant bathing me, washing my hair and brushing it in slow fierce strokes as Master looked on with approval.

Très belle, la petite enfant!

And sometimes, at first, in those early *beaux jours* I'd thought would continue forever, Master took the hairbrush from the woman-servant, and brushed my hair himself.

And sometimes, vaguely I recall—Master bathed me, and put me to bed.

I am ashamed to confess, Daddy—I did not really miss you then. I did not think of you. It was only Master of whom I thought.

In Master's studio Master wears a smock that is stark-black like a priest's cassock. By the end of each day Master's smock becomes stained with paint, and so, each morning, Master must be provided with a fresh clean black smock.

On his slender feet, black silk slippers in which Master moves silently as something that is upright, a wraith.

I have never looked fully at Master's face, Daddy—it is not allowed. And so I have not really seen Master except to know that he is older than you, and very dignified, with a pale austere face like something that has been sculpted, and not mere flesh like other, lesser beings.

(Has your face grown coarse, Daddy? I don't want to think so.)

(*I will not think so* though Mother tried to poison us against you.)

Some of us have come to realize that Master does not love us because we are not Master's children. This was hard to comprehend, and hurtful, and yet it is obvious: none of us, Master's girl-captives, are the children of Master's loins. For Master's own precious seed (it is said) was not spilled carelessly into the world but planted well, and thrived, and Master has a son, a singular being (it is said) whom we will never see, for he lives in Paris and is, like Master, an *artiste* though not a world-famous *artiste* like Master.

Wildly it is said, Master's son will one day come to *le grand chalet* to free his father's girl-captives, for Master's son does not approve of Master's way of art.

Yet the years pass, and Master's son does not appear.

Instead, photographers dare to journey to this remote region in eastern Europe, somewhere beyond the Alps. There are reporters, would-be interviewers. Master has instructed his servants to turn away most visitors from the gated entrance of *le chalet* but from time to time, unpredictably, for it is Master's way to be unpredictable, Master will allow one or another stranger entry, if he (or less frequently, she) is working for an impressive publication, or is a fellow *artiste* with impressive credentials.

These privileged individuals are not allowed beyond the formal rooms of the great old house. Servants observe them carefully at all times and (it is said) Master's wolf-hounds are stationed at a little distance, charged with watching the strangers' every move and poised to attack if a signal is given.

Most visitors see only opulently furnished rooms with heavy furniture, heavy Persian carpets, heavy velvet drapes of the hue of burst grapes, that have faded in swaths of sunshine, unevenly. They are allowed to photograph Master in such settings, which Master prepares in every detail, as in a stage set, for Master takes (occasional) delight in such scenes; in Master's apprentice years, Master was at the periphery of the Dadaist movement, and was a close friend of Man Ray; visitors are forbidden to photograph begrimed marble floors, cracks and water stains in ceilings, a patina of dust on Master's antique Greek statuary, the shocking interior of a *water-closet*. Except on very special occasions when Master's studio has been scrupulously prepared for such an invasion—a German public television documentary, an American celebrity-interviewer for prime-time American TV—they are not allowed in Master's studio.

Very graciously Master answers questions at such times, that have been approved by Master beforehand. For Master is the most eloquent of *artistes,* whose every remark is carefully shaped, like poetry.

Art is not the truth. It is art that shapes truth.

Art is not "beauty"—art is greater than beauty.

Art is the shadow of life that soars above life, and can never be contained by (mere) life.

At such times no one hears our cries from the back rooms of the chalet, or the (terrible, unspeakable) dungeons in the cellar.

MASTER HAS MANY OF US HERE, Daddy. Of our free choice we came to Master, and to Master we surrendered our freedom like children who have no idea what they are doing. You cannot blame the servants for laughing at us—one day *ma chérie,* the next *ma prisonnière.*

In many rooms of the chalet Master has imprisoned us. Some of us are "servants"—that is, slaves. Some of us have collars around our necks, attached to chains. We are made to eat leftovers from bowls on the floor, as Master laughs at our desperate animal hunger.

Mes chères, you are petits cochons *are you? You are not angels! We know this.*

Especially, no one hears our cries from the dungeons. The locked chambers, that servants avoid. Here is a smell of rusted iron, cobweb.

No one wishes to hear, invited to a spare but elegant tea with Master in the most opulent of the front rooms, where a Broadwood piano (1813) is displayed, reputedly once owned by Beethoven.

No one wishes to penetrate the mystery of *le grand chalet* despite rumors that have circulated for decades in such European capitals as Paris, Berlin, Prague, Rome. No one has the courage to confront Master, to risk Master's wolf-hounds and servants and throw open the locked doors of the house, to release Master's girl-captives from their misery.

Help us! Please help us.

Release us from Master . . .

In the most notorious of the dungeon rooms girls have died in their chains, their bodies shriveled like the corpses of the elderly. These were once living girls, girls with pretty doll-faces and coppery-colored, wavy hair, withered to the size of four-year-olds.

We who are still living beg for food which Master's servants give out grudgingly for Master is very clever, and very cruel, restricting the household food so that the more that is given to the girls, the less the servants will have for themselves.

Like all tyrants Master knows how to set individuals against one another—*It is a finite universe in which we live. The more you give away, the less you will have. Give away too much, and you will starve.*

I am ashamed to say, Daddy—at the very start I was ignorant, and naïve, and had no idea what lay in store. As a new arrival I was treated like a princess, and so I took pity on some of the other girls, who had been here longer, and seemed to be less favored than I was; I gave them food of mine, for each of my meals was a small feast, and I could not finish so many delicacies. You know, we can be generous when our bellies are stuffed, and so I was generous, but this did not last beyond a few months. It would not have seemed possible that Master would so turn against me, after he had so flattered me. This was my error, Daddy. But having come here at all, having lingered so long in front of *Les beaux jours* until one day I found myself inside the painting, in the drawing room with the blazing-bright fire, giddy with happiness—already that was my error, for I could not so easily crawl back out of Master's house and into my old, lost life.

You begin by being adored. In Master's adoration, you bask in your power. But it is a short-lived power for it is not yours, it is Master's. That is the error.

AND THEN ONE DAY, a camera crew arrives at the chalet in a modern-looking vehicle—a *minivan*. Strangers from London are welcomed into the chalet. There is a silken-voiced interviewer, himself a *celebrity of the art world*.

How renowned Master has become! How many honors has his art garnered! Major museums have hosted major exhibits. His name is "known"—by the discerning few, if not the multitudes. He has outlived all of his great contemporaries—he has outlived many younger artists, whose names will never be so extolled as his; he is an elderly man revered like a saint. With age his face has only grown more beautiful, and what is *aged* in his face—discolorations, lines—can be disguised by makeup, that makes of the sallow skin something marmoreal; his somewhat sunken eyes are outlined in black, each lash distinct. His thinning silvery hair is combed elegantly across his high skull. In his black cassock of the finest linen Master is a priest of art—the highest art.

Master says—*But we live for our art. There is no life except our art.*

The interviewer says—*Excuse me, sir?—I think I hear something— someone . . .*

(For the interviewer has heard us. He has heard us!)

But Master says laughingly—*No. You are hearing just the wind, our perpetual wind from the mountains.*

(Wind? These are cries, and not the wind. Not possible, these cries are but *wind*.)

The interviewer hesitates. The silken-voiced interviewer is at a loss for words, suddenly chilled.

Master says more forcibly, though still laughingly—*This is a remote region of Europe, mon ami. This is not your effete "civilization"— your Piccadilly Circus, Hyde Park and Kensington Gardens. I am very sorry if our melancholy wind that never ceases distracts you and makes you sad!*

Master is so very charming speaking with a mock British accent, no one detects the quaver in Master's voice that is a sign of incipient rage; but the interviewer exchanges glances with his assistant, and does not pursue this unwelcome line of questioning.

It is so: Master is a great artist. A great genius. To genius, much is allowed.

As other interviews have proceeded at *le chalet,* this interview proceeds without further interruptions: just one hour, but a priceless hour, to be scrupulously edited, and not to be broadcast on the BBC without the approval of Master and Master's (powerful, Parisian) gallery.

But the silken-voiced interviewer disappoints Master by declining his invitation to stay for tea, pleading exhaustion. And he and his crew must hurry away in the *minivan,* to catch a flight back to "effete" London.

Well! There is some laughter. There are handshakes.

Master has been placated, maybe. But Master is still irritable, and (as some of us know) still dangerous.

In the nether regions of the chalet we tell ourselves that the celebrity-interviewer from London heard us, and understood—it is not possible that he did not understand. One need only examine Master's famous paintings to understand. He will seek help for us, he will save us.

Such tales we tell ourselves to get through the long days and interminable nights in *le grand chalet des âmes perdues.*

WIND ON THE MOORS, wind from the mountains. Perhaps the mountains are not the Alps but the Carpathians.

It is not so far a distance to come, Daddy! Please.

It is not too late yet, Daddy. I have not yet been dragged to the lowermost dungeon, where the door is shut upon us, and we are forgotten.

You have not forgotten me, Daddy. I am your daughter . . .

In *Les beaux jours* you will see me for I am waiting for you there. Come to the Museum! Come stand close before *Les beaux jours* where I await you.

Help! Help me!—I whisper.

If I could call out more forcibly I am sure that someone would hear me. A visitor to the Museum, one of the vacant-eyed guards. They would wake from their slumber. They are all good people, I know—at heart, they would *help me if they could.*

If you could, Daddy. I know you would help me. Will you? It is not too late.

I have set aside the little hand-mirror. I have gazed enough at the pretty doll-face. Sometimes I can see—almost see—out of the frame, Daddy—and into the Museum—(I think it must be the Museum: what else could it be?)—in the distance, on the other side in the land of the living—slow-moving figures, faces.

Daddy, are you one of them? Please say *yes.*

If I had my old strength I could crawl out of the frame, Daddy. I would do this myself, and would not need you. I would crawl out of the drawing room, and I would fall to the Museum floor, and I would lie there stunned for just a moment, and maybe someone, one of you, Daddy maybe you, would discover me, and help me.

Or maybe I would simply regain my breath in the land of the living, and my strength, and manage to stand on my weakened legs, and walk away, leaning against the wall—past rows of paintings in hushed galleries—to the familiar stone steps, where Mother would pull Jenny and me, gripping our hands in hers—and I would make my way to the front entrance of the great Museum, and more steps, and so to Fifth Avenue and the clamor of traffic and life—if I had my old strength—almost . . .

Daddy? I am waiting. You know, I have loved only you.

Balthus, *Les beaux jours*, 1944–45

Fractal

I

At eleven, the child was *into fractals*. Naturally then, the mother agreed to drive him to the Fractal Museum in Portland, Maine— "The Singular Museum of Its Kind."

One blustery November morning when the mother might have been doing other things, more homey/domestic things (for it was a Saturday), virtually anything she'd have preferred to driving two hours twenty minutes from New Haven, Connecticut, to the Fractal Museum north of Portland, Maine, the (fatally unwitting) mother found herself, in fact, driving the (doomed) child for two hours twenty minutes north on I-95 from New Haven, Connecticut, to the Fractal Museum outside Portland, Maine, which the child had discovered online and had begged the mother to let him visit.

Well, *begged* was an extreme word. This delicate child who wanted so little that adults could provide him, usually so absorbed in his architectural drawings, or a science book, or an electronic gadget, and so often (you would not want to acknowledge aloud) *withdrawn*, wasn't it a good sign, a healthy sign, an encouraging sign, Oliver had actually made a rare request of the mother: would she drive him to the Fractal Museum in Portland, Maine? Sometime? *Please.*

She'd been flattered, he hadn't asked the father. (Of course, the father would have been *too busy.*)

She'd been flattered but she hadn't wanted to say *yes.* Oh, why *her*!

Yet, being a (good) mother of course she'd said *yes.*

For weeks then, after the date had been marked on the calendar, plans began to be made including where even to stop for restrooms along I-95 (for the child was prone to anxieties about toilets, sanitary conditions, access to bottled water, etc.), and these plans the mother and the child shared, and the father looked on, listened, at a little distance, bemused and just slightly envious, or seeming-so.

And so, this fierce cobalt-blue November sky. Cumulous clouds with puckered cheeks blowing in such gusts, the Toyota SUV at sixty-eight miles per hour quaked and came near to drifting out of its lane.

"I wish you would talk to me, honey. To keep me company. Always absorbed in that damned iPad of yours."

Of course the mother wasn't jealous of a damned *iPad.* Not really. Not much.

Yet to the child, *damned* was a swear word. Not an extreme swear word like some (which he'd heard in the mean mouths of older and coarser classmates but had not dared enunciate to himself) but yes, *damned* struck the child's sensitive ear like fingernails drawn against a blackboard; for if a parent or indeed any elder complained of *damned. iPad* it was anger that was the motive, and an elder's anger was/is wounding to a sensitive child.

Neither the mother nor the father of the child would ever have struck him. Not a slap, not a nudge or a shove—never! Not a pinch! If in a blind fury at the child's taciturnity/stubbornness the father had ever struck Oliver he, the father, would've gnawed off the offending hand. He swore!

They were not that sort of parents. Not that sort of people. Not ever.

But words too can lash. Words too can sting.

Often too, to draw the preoccupied child's attention to her and away from the iPad in his lap, the mother would do something playful: thrust out her lower lip and blow air briskly upward stirring the fluffy-faded-red-bangs on her forehead, a clownish gesture copied from a grade-school classmate decades ago. The gesture was to make the child who did not readily giggle, giggle.

For the child was insufficiently *childish* and this creates a vacuum in a parent-child relationship which a guilty adult may feel the obligation to fill.

However, the child took no notice of this goofy-silly antic which another child (the mother doesn't want to think) would've found hilarious; instead feeling the rebuke, worse than if the child had sneered at her.

"Are you even listening, Olly? I'm beginning to wonder—why am I here? *Why me?*"

Olly and not *Oliver* meant that the mother was not scolding, not really. Chiding, teasing. Though there was an edge to the mother's voice—*Why me?*

Which could mean *why* the mother and not the father; or *why* either parent, driving north on I-95 in such a ferocity of wind. And perhaps too there was another *why*, beyond the reach of the mother's mental grasp.

That *why* you must not ask. Nor *why* you must not ask *why*.

In the passenger's seat beside the mother, safely belted-in, the child had been immersed in an interactive topology game on his iPad for the last thirty miles, yet, uncannily, for the eleven-year-old who was *into fractals* and had at the age of nine declared his intention of being *an architect* was at the same time enough aware of his mother's ranting to call her bluff, and to answer her seriously.

" '*Why me?*'—because there is no one else."

Very solemnly the child spoke as if issuing a decree. In his voice which the mother worried was *too thin, too soprano* for one soon to enter the maelstrom of middle school.

"What do you mean, 'no one else'? I don't understand."

"From the beginning of the universe. Determined to be *you*. It could not be anyone else in the driver's seat, because it is *you*."

In his solemn methodical way Oliver spoke to the mother as one might speak to a classmate who is having difficulty with a homework assignment. Sweetly patient, not condescending.

"That doesn't make sense, Olly. Of course it could be someone else, and I could be somewhere else. Why on earth not?"

"It isn't like that, Mom. Because if the person driving this vehicle is *you* that is all the proof you need that there is no one else it could have been, and there is nowhere else *you* could be except here. And the same is true for me."

"You mean—here with me. Beside me."

"Yes."

Well. The mother had to concede, that was probably correct. She would certainly not be driving on I-95 on this blustery Saturday morning if not for the child beside her.

"And I suppose it would have to be 9:27 A.M.? It couldn't be some other time, earlier or later?"

"Not if it's *here*. Has to be"—with a glance at the countryside through which they were moving, of the hue of bleached chlorophyll, stubs of undergrowth and featureless trees like a papier-mâché stage set—"here."

The mother didn't know whether to laugh at the child's certainty, or be impressed. Or annoyed. She wondered if Oliver dared confound his math teacher with such paradoxes, or whether it was his math teacher who provided the eleven-year-old with such paradoxes. (For the child, officially in sixth grade at New Haven Day, was allowed to take an advanced math course taught in the high school.)

"It was of my own free will that I agreed to drive us to Portland, Olly. You forget. I might have said 'no—too busy.' And it was an accident more or less that we left when we did, at that precise moment, so that it's 9:27 A.M. now, when we're passing the exit for—what is it—'Biddeford.'"

Oliver was not persuaded. "Mom, no. There are no 'accidents.'"

"You're being ridiculous—an eleven-year-old who doesn't believe in free will! Do you really feel as if you're enclosed in a sort of cobweb, or you're a puppet on strings, being manipulated? *Determined?*"

"What we 'feel' doesn't matter, Mom. A 'feeling' is just—nothing."

Of course, this was so. The mother knew that this was so. Yet, in her role as *mother,* she could not let things lie there bleak and forlorn as a pile of twigs.

"Well, then—'think.' Not 'feel' but 'think'—'reason.' We can *reason* that we have free will. It just seems so—obvious . . ." Her voice trailed off, as if that were an argument.

But the canny eleven-year-old persisted: nothing could be accidental, for all things are determined. If you could wind time backward, tracing things to their causes, you would see—"There's no chance of something just swerving off on its own."

The grim prospect seemed to please Oliver unless—possibly—he was joking? For sometimes Oliver seemed bemused by his mother's obtuseness.

Oh, she hoped so! She'd have welcomed the child's joking, *joshing.*

What is a family without good-natured joking, teasing, *joshing?*

"D'you know what?—you're too smart for your own good. There are plenty of 'accidents' in life—you'll see."

You yourself are an accident. Were.

What d'you think of that, smartie?

(But no. They'd decided no, they would have the baby. That is, they *would not* not have the baby.)

(Unexpected/unwanted pregnancy a nightmare before they were married at the very worst time in the father's life preparing for law exams and not a great time in the mother's life while her own mother was undergoing chemotherapy but decided not to delete/abort. Deciding *yes all right. Yes. We will. We can.* Scarcely guessing how the [unexpected/unwanted] pregnancy would turn out: the extraordinary child whom both the mother and the father loved deeply and without whom they could not imagine their lives.)

Of course, the child would never know. No one except the mother and the father could know this secret and when they cease to exist, the secret will die with them.

He was a beautiful if fragile child with a chronic asthmatic condition susceptible to pollen, dust, danger, heat, aridity and wind, excitement and agitation. His skin was slightly feverish to the touch; the mother wondered if this was the result of his medication, steroids, which quickened his pulse. She wondered if other children, and most adults, seemed dull to him, slow-paced in their thoughts, predictable and lacking in complexity.

In her handbag she carried the child's "rescue inhaler"—as it was called. The child had not required this inhaler in years and could not bear to see it in the mother's handbag.

His vision was myopic, often his eyes squinted behind round, wire-rimmed eyeglasses that gave him a scholarly look. His chin seemed to melt away as if lacking sufficient bone. His hair was a fine, fair gingery color, lighter than the mother's, and his skin was splotched with freckles as with droplets of water tinged with cinnamon, or turmeric—a beautiful smooth skin the mother felt a need to touch, perhaps too frequently, as she felt the need to lightly kiss his temple. Where the child had tolerated such motherly affection when he was younger by the age of eleven he was beginning to stiffen and flinch away.

Trying to reason with him, for she loved talking seriously with her son, and being taken seriously by him.

"But we are always somewhere, aren't we? I mean—if we exist at all . . . Why is any *where* we find ourselves a *where* that had to be? Why—*had to be*? That's what I don't understand."

Felt as if her tongue was twisted. Not sure what she was trying to say.

And where are they? Just beyond an exit for Biddeford, Maine?

Otherwise, nowhere. New England countryside, dense-wooded, mixture of deciduous and evergreen trees, thunderous trailer-trucks rushing past, a *here* interchangeable with any *there*.

Oliver murmured *OK, Mom*.

"Am I correct? Or are you just humoring me?"

Oliver murmured *OK, Mom*.

Returning his attention to the damned iPad in his lap that had been there all along, waiting.

2.

Offhandedly the child had remarked at the age of nine that he guessed he wanted to be *an architect*.

The astonished parents weren't sure they'd heard correctly. Had their very young son remarked that he wanted to be *an architect*?

Exchanging a glance. Really! How—*funny*!

Or rather, how impressive. And rare, a child of nine would express such a wish . . .

There was an air about their singular child of intense curiosity, wonderment, as if he were a fairy caught in a net, his fairy-wings fluttering but not (yet) broken— (so the mother thought, with much tenderness and concern). He'd been a premature baby and had not thrived as an infant; eventually he'd grown, but remained small for his age, and his bones seemed thin, everything about him gossamer-light, provisional. There had been some frightening asthmatic episodes when he'd been a small child but the condition seemed now controlled by medication, or nearly.

So far as the parents knew Oliver had never met an architect, nor had he heard them talking of architecture. The mother had a degree in art history and had hoped at one time in her life to be an artist but there were no other artistically inclined persons in her family, and no architects. The father was a (Yale) university attorney. For each, the marriage was the first and the child was the only child.

Vaguely Amanda and Peter wished to have a second child. Possibly, a more ordinary child. For it did not feel quite right, Oliver was such a *precious child.*

Since he'd been capable of gripping a Crayola in his (left) hand the child had loved to draw. He'd had little interest in toys, children's books, but rather adult books, particularly oversized books with photographic plates. Any subject seemed to interest the inquisitive child—ancient Egyptian pyramids, constellations of the night sky, Himalayan mountains, medieval fortifications, twentieth-century "skyscrapers," Arctic marine life, meteors, bird life, "earliest forms of organic life" . . . Before Oliver could read he was drawn to such books, and to copying from them onto sheets of tissue-thin paper with a fanatic concern for accuracy.

The mother looked on, fascinated. The child seemed to be in a trance, exuding an air of feverish intensity.

The mother wondered—*What is he doing? Is he—"taking possession" of what he draws?*

Concentrating on visual images the child was late in speaking. But when Oliver did begin to speak it was in phrases and not in single, monosyllabic words like the speech of most toddlers; soon too, his vocabulary flourished with such words as *design, wish, depending-upon, accelerating.*

For a brief while, when he'd been very young, Oliver had been captivated by the word *other.*

For what did *other* mean, really? When you pondered upon it.

Other was not-this, and (possibly) that. Or (possibly) not-that.

Other other other other.

Once, he'd screamed and laughed—*Oth-er!* The mother had been alone with him at the time and had felt a moment's faintness, the child was mad.

But of course, the moment passed. Such moments pass.

One thing was clear, the child was indeed *other.*

And then one day the child (who was an inquisitive child but not as other children are inquisitive, rather as adults are inquisitive, "nosing" about a household) discovered in a storage closet the architect's plans for the house in which the family lived, that had been built forty years before. It was a stucco, stone, and glass house constructed in a style made popular by Frank Lloyd Wright in an earlier era, though not so starkly beautiful as any house by the great architect, rather more resembling an upscale American "ranch" house. The child was excited by the architect's plans which he'd examined with a magnifying glass and copied in colored pencils on tissue-thin sheets of paper. This became his play, his preoccupation. Soon he believed he'd discovered a secret passageway in the basement—a kind of large cupboard or crawl space opening from an obscure corner of the room. This, to the mother's distress, he insisted upon exploring with a flashlight and emerged covered in cobwebs and blinking his eyes like a nocturnal creature thrust too rapidly into the light.

Other parts of the house too, the child determined to be "secret." A ghostly doorway in a corridor, a passageway of only six inches width inside a wall. You could not see these features of the house with just

your eyes; you could only discover their existence through examining the architect's plans, which were unfortunately now badly faded
and creased. "But what are you seeing, Oliver?"—the mother would
ask; and Oliver would direct her to look through the magnifying
glass at the sketch of a door, or a passageway, or a "false ceiling" in
the house plans which he'd discovered.

But why is it so important?—the mother wondered. *Is this some
other—world?*

Neither she nor the father could comprehend the child's preoccupation with this sort of "architecture." Neither had troubled to
glance at the architect's plans and had long forgotten their existence.
The house they'd purchased was the physical house and not the architect's plan of a house that did not exist except on paper. At the
closing they'd been given the architect's plans in a folder that tied
with a ribbon, as if it were a precious document; but neither had
untied the ribbon.

Twelve years later the child discovered the folder in the closet,
which intensified his wish to become, one day, *an architect.*

For each house designed by an architect, Oliver explained, was
actually two houses: the one people lived in, and were meant to see;
and the other, which they were not meant to see but which was preserved in the architect's plans.

This remark left the parents baffled. What on earth did their son
mean?

Whatever, it was not the sum of his words. For they repeated his
words to each other, and were not illuminated.

"What interests you about being an architect, Oliver?"—relatives
asked the little boy, not sure whether they should be amused by him,
or somewhat alarmed by his precocity, which marked him as very
different from their own children; and Oliver said in a shy murmur
that he wanted to draw "special houses," which only an architect
could draw.

"The architect is the one looking *down*, and *in*."

In the child's room there came to be an accumulation of books, glossy magazines. No design of any house or building that included detailed floor plans failed to captivate him. His favorite architects were Gaudi, Kahn, Wright, Graves, Gehry. There came to be a new word in his vocabulary—*deconstruction*. (The [controversial, disorienting] architecture of Gehry.) His many pencil drawings were of houses that did not (yet) exist. And he continued to draw plans of the family house with "special"—"invisible"—features added.

It was bittersweet for the mother, to see in the child some of her own, inchoate yearnings. She'd tried to paint in her early twenties but had lacked confidence. Luminous visions in her head were crudely parodied by brushstrokes on canvas. She'd come too late for "figurative" art—too late for "abstract" art—too late for "pop" art and "conceptual" art. The child had no awareness of art as history, it was all one to him, present tense. He had no concern for being belated. The mother was thrilled by the child's skill at drawing though he rarely drew figures (animals, people) as other children tried to do; his obsession was with the interiors of buildings, the skeletal outlines of material things, which never seemed to bore him. If human figures appeared in Oliver's drawings they were positioned for practical reasons of scale, and had no identities.

Oliver acquired notebooks, and made sketches of the interiors of places he visited, the homes of relatives and friends, transcribing what he saw (which was not likely to be what others "saw") as others chattered around him. And then, he might point out to the homeowners some oddity, some imbalance or error in the architecture of their house with the suggestion that a door, a window, a staircase was in the wrong place, a ceiling too low or too high, a room too small or too large, and should be "rebuilt."

A wall should be removed—"It is blocking the spirit of the house."

A roof should be raised—"The house wants to be taller."

Such suggestions were met with blank faces, incomprehension or annoyance. "Well! Thank you, Oliver."

Or, the child would say nothing to the homeowners but remark to the parents on their way home that something had happened in the house that had left its ("invisible") mark, which was evident ("visible") only in his sketching.

Did they see what he meant?—Oliver would try to show them in his sketches of the house; but the parents could never see.

Easier to dismiss the child's notions as *play, imagination.*

It was also Oliver's belief, explained to the bemused parents, that there were places (homes, school) in which the texture of the very air might become "denser" depending upon what was happening, or not happening: a "boring" space (school classroom, for instance) became a "dense" space requiring literally more effort to endure, thus literally more time to endure than if it were not boring. The equation for this phenomenon was

$$\text{T (time)} = \text{D (density)} \times \text{E (effort)}$$

Oliver's father laughed saying of course, it was common knowledge, emotions affect our experience of time; boredom makes time seem to pass slowly, as in an excruciatingly dull lecture on torts, while a pleasurable time may seem to end too soon. But the child frowned, saying with an air of rebuke that he did not mean *that.*

Nothing so obvious, so commonplace as *that.*

With infinite patience, over a period of months, Oliver copied the architect's plans for the family house, until he could draw them without consulting the original. Then he began to experiment with additions of his own introduced into the drawings, that seemed to have the effect of altering features of the house.

The mother began to notice that the house "felt" different, in some rooms; its ceilings were at unexpected angles or its floors slanted; its windows appeared to be smaller, or larger, or unexpectedly shaped;

through glass panes the exterior world looked different even as it was (evidently) unchanged. The very air in certain parts of the house seemed "denser"—exuding a faint, sepia cast—than it had been even as in other parts of the house the air seemed lighter, purer.

Were these changes the consequence of the child's alterations to the house plans, or had the child perceived discrepancies in the house in which the family had been living obliviously, which his attentions had made evident? Had the strangeness in the house been but *implicit* previously, and was now *explicit*?

The mother wondered if, gazing at her, the child might see something in her, in her (invisible) soul, unknown to her, unfathomable.

Feeling a wave of something like panic, fear. That the child who was *her child* yet might acquire a perspective from which he could view her as dispassionately as he viewed the interiors of houses.

One day Oliver asked the mother to participate in an experiment he called the "Zone of Invisibility." This involved the mother waiting in the hall outside his room and knocking on his door several times; each time she knocked, if he answered *No!* she was not to come inside, but just to wait a few minutes and then knock again; only when the mother knocked and received no answer was she to open the door, and come inside.

These instructions the mother followed, at least initially. It was not often the boy requested anything from her, let alone her involvement in his life, or rather in the life of his architectural imaginings, that were usually kept private and secret, and certainly not shared with the father. But after she'd knocked on his door several times she couldn't determine whether she heard the boy's voice, or just imagined it, and so she opened the door impulsively—discovering that Oliver wasn't in the room after all, so far as she could see.

"Oliver? Where are you?"—the mother tried not to sound alarmed.

It was some sort of game, she supposed. Though the child had never cared for children's games like hide-and-seek.

The child had never cared for *pranks*. His play was serious play, and not ever a waste of his time.

"Oliver? Oli-ver?" The mother looked in the child's closet, and stooped to peer beneath the child's bed, and even lifted the comforter on the bed though (certainly) she could see that no child was lying flattened beneath it and hiding from her.

"Oliver?—where on earth . . ."

She had to laugh, if nervously. The child was (certainly) in the room somewhere.

There were two windows in the child's room but these were shut tight, locked. If Oliver had crawled through a window to jump down to the ground outside he could not have shut the window behind him, still less locked it.

Not that Oliver would have played so crude a trick on the mother. He was far too fastidious for such behavior.

"Oliver! This isn't funny . . ."

Was it possible, the child had the power to create, somehow, an actual *Zone of Invisibility* in his room? But what did this even mean? A kind of hypnosis, a mirage that obscured the mother's vision so that Oliver might be actually present, but she could not see him?

"Oliver? I—I don't like this. It isn't . . ."

How could it be, Oliver seemed to have vanished in his own room? That was not possible.

Desperately the mother yanked open drawers in the child's Maplewood bureau, as if Oliver could have squeezed inside one of these and shut the drawer upon himself!

The mother took note of light fixtures in the ceiling. These were of ordinary dimensions yet the mother found herself wondering fantastically if the child had somehow *shrunken himself* to a miniature size, to hide inside one of these?

It was not likely, and yet—the proof of *Invisibility* seemed to be that the child had become *not-visible*.

Nor did the mother sense the child. Surely a mother would sense her child, if he were present . . .

As, years ago, the mother had felt her hard-swollen breasts ache with milk, hearing the infant begin to whimper, in another room.

How brainless she'd been, in those (happy, unquestioning) days! Like a creature with its head cut off, sheer instinct, breasts and womb, female body.

However, it had not lasted. The fever-trance of motherhood had lifted, faded. Now and then she yearned for its return as one might yearn for ether, a fat thumb to suck in one's mouth.

But no, the prospect filled her now with revulsion. Really, the mother was eleven years beyond that stage in her life and did not want its return.

Of course, the parents spoke vaguely, smilingly, of another child. In conversation with others, especially relatives, they were prone to say how nice it would be, how ideal, if Oliver had a baby sister. *He is too much the center of our lives, that is not good for him or for us.*

Once upon a time, a man and a woman had as many children as God sent them. That is, the woman had as many children as God directed the husband to afflict upon her.

There was no refusal. Not of the man, and not of a woman's task.

"Oliver? Please don't scare me, honey . . ."

A spell of vertigo overcame her brain. Sat down hard on the child-sized bed, that yielded to her weight. The wild thought came to her that cunning Oliver had attached himself monkey-like to the box springs below the mattress and was hiding beneath the bed but not on the floor, so she'd failed to see him . . . But when she knelt panting to peer beneath the bed another time, of course there was no one.

A world without the child. A world depleted of the child.

The child who held the marriage together like cartilage in the (shared) spine of conjoined identical twins.

"Oliver! P-Please . . ."

Realizing that she lived for those moments when Oliver was (again) hers. When the child would smile spontaneously at her.

It could not be, that this vivid presence might vanish from the world. As you'd switch off a lamp and be plunged into darkness.

But then, suddenly: "Mom? Hi."

Out of nowhere the child appeared. Behind her, on the farther side of the bed.

Smiling at the astonished mother, pleased and excited. The experiment had been a greater success than he'd expected.

"Oh, Oliver! You frightened me . . ."

She would chide the beaming child, she would strike her hands together in a display of motherly exasperation, but also motherly pride, vanity. He'd been naughty, hiding from her; but he'd been very clever too, for he had fooled her utterly, because he was such a clever child.

Quite the most clever child she had ever encountered.

She embraced him, kissed his fevered forehead. Later she would think—*He must have been hiding in the closet. Of course.*

3.

"Oh, Oliver. Oh *no*."

The Fractal Museum was closed! Closed Saturdays and Sundays, November through April.

What a disappointment! All the way to a desolate interstate exit on the northern outskirts of Portland, Maine—to discover the damned museum closed . . .

The website that had posted Saturday and Sundays as *open* had not been updated since September—that was the explanation. The child could not be blamed but the mother blamed herself: why hadn't she telephoned ahead, just to make sure the Fractal Museum really was open?

It is the *off-season* now in Maine.

But there is a good side to the disappointment: more time to explore the beautiful Atlantic coast a short drive away. Walking with the son, just the two of them. Rare for the mother and Oliver to be alone together in a place like this.

Arm in arm, when the walking is treacherous. Rocks, boulders. Crashing surf. She will take pictures of the rocky coast, white-capped frothing waves pounding against the shore at Prouts Neck, that Winslow Homer depicted in his extraordinary drawings, watercolors, and oil paintings.

They will visit the Winslow Homer Studio at Scarborough, which is on the way home.

Out of a kind of shyness the mother has never told the child about her love of art and her hope to be an artist, before his birth. Her awe at the work of Winslow Homer in particular. She is excited now at the prospect of sharing Winslow Homer with him . . .

4.

In fact, the Fractal Museum is open. It is a Saturday morning, and the Museum is closed on Mondays and Tuesdays: the website was correct after all.

Thank God! Oliver would have been disappointed, sullen and sulky. The mother would have had to find some other quasi-intellectual diversion for him, museum or otherwise, in Portland, before daring to suggest walking along the coast at Prouts Neck or stopping at the Winslow Homer Studio in Scarborough.

"Well—here we are!"—for her own sake as well as the boy's the mother is trying to sound upbeat, cheerful.

It is rare for Oliver to scramble out of a vehicle so eagerly. Usually he is scarcely aware of having arrived at a destination reluctantly looking up from his iPad.

"Oliver—don't *run*."

Parking the vehicle the mother feels something like a (ghost) hand pressing against her chest in warning—*Go back. This is wrong. It is not too late.*

5.

You may enter at any door. All doors lead to the same place.

(The reverse is not true.)

HOW STRANGE, THE FRACTAL MUSEUM looks as if it is comprised of several buildings, simultaneously!

Oliver tells the mother *no*. That is an illusion—"simultaneity."

But—what does he mean? The mother is perplexed.

Politely Oliver explains: "We don't see all sides of the Fractal Museum simultaneously. We see just one side at a time—the Museum is deliberately constructed so that we 'see' what is being presented to us to be seen. It's 'fractal architecture'—there are sides of the Museum that appear to us in sequence but our perception is that they are 'simultaneous.'"

Adding, as the mother ponders what he has said: "Nothing is 'simultaneous' with something else—that's an optical illusion."

Oliver is eager to take pictures of the Fractal Museum. He has been planning this, the mother assumes, for weeks.

Seen from the front the Fractal Museum appears to be made of some attractive but commonplace material like sandstone, with narrow vertical plate-glass panels in a pattern that repeats itself (one would assume) on all sides of the building; it is foursquare, three stories high, set back from a state highway. Seen in a partially filled asphalt parking lot, and resembles a moderately well-kept medical office building.

But that is only the façade.

From the (west) parking lot the Fractal Museum is revealed to be, behind the sandstone façade, a private house, or what had once been a private house: a renovated old Victorian shingle board painted dark purple with lavender trim, bay windows, steep slate roofs, lightning rod and weathervane—exactly the sort of distinctive old property given away by heirs to townships for charitable purposes, to escape property taxes. Overlapping shingles suggest a fractal pattern that repeats itself top to bottom, bottom to top, impossible to measure with the eye as a result of its repetition; as the visitor's eye moves about this (visible) portion of the house it comes to seem, uncannily, that there are more tall narrow windows here than could possibly fit into the limited space; it is an effort to move the eye horizontally, left to right, right to left, and not rather vertically, as if something in the structure of the building is an active (if subliminal) impediment to the visitor's curiosity.

Seen from the (east) parking lot the Fractal Museum is revealed to be, behind the sandstone façade, another private house, very different from the Victorian: a large Colonial with weatherworn white shingles, dull-green shutters, a greeny glimmer of moss on its roof, exactly the sort of distinctive old property given away by heirs to townships for charitable purposes, to escape property taxes. Here too there is something uncanny about the windows—there are not enough windows for the space and they appear to be of differing sizes; the observer is led to glance quickly from window to window, to see how they differ, yet there is some sort of impediment (instant amnesia?) preventing "seeing" the windows in relationship to one another, so that each sighting of each window is distinct from its predecessor, and forming a comparison is not possible.

Also, there appear to be in the windows remnants of holiday decorations, candles or Christmas lights, unless these are but (fractal-like, repetitive) reflections in wavy glass.

The rear of the Museum is a blank freshly-painted (beige) stucco wall that might be the rear of a fast-food taco restaurant—blunt, pragmatic, windowless, and so textured that if you look closely you can see the suggestions of fractal designs in the material, leaf-like, overlapping in seemingly infinite repetition. There is a single large metal door marked EXIT and below this a smaller sign: NO RE-ENTRY. From a stoop, a short flight of concrete steps and a ramp to the parking lot.

As he has been taking pictures of the Museum with his iPad Oliver has been trying to explain to the mother that the Fractal Museum is considered a "living paradox"—a "living conundrum." Measured from the outside its square footage is (reputedly) considerably less than the square footage measured from the inside—"Interior fractal space." Oliver plans to take pictures inside the Museum to determine for himself the authenticity of *interior fractal space,* at which online commentators have marveled.

The mother has listened, or half-listened, to the child chattering about the Fractal Museum for weeks. But this is new to her. How can the Museum be smaller on the outside than on the inside? And how can a museum, which is nothing but a building constructed of wood, brick, stone, stucco, *unliving* materials, be *living*?

The mother hesitates to ask the child another time to explain what he is talking about. (Especially, the mother hesitates to ask the child to explain what the hell he is talking about. *What the hell* will be registered by the child as exasperation, dismay.) The mother is self-aware enough to dread that hour when she hears in the (prepubescent) boy's voice the equivalent of *Oh Jesus, Mom! Please.*

At the entrance of the Fractal Museum a woman of about Amanda's age, looking both harried and flushed with a mother's eagerness to please, is ushering inside several children of whom the eldest, lanky-limbed, with round eyeglasses, resembles Oliver to an uncanny degree.

The mother holds her breath waiting to see if the two boys notice each other: they do not.

6.

It is just 10:28 A.M. The Fractal Museum has opened at 10:00 A.M. Inside, there is a surprisingly long line for tickets. Families with young children, a predominance of mothers. The Fractal Museum advertises itself as a *family-friendly museum*.

While the son studies an interactive floor map of the Museum that bristles with lights and animation like a casino game the mother purchases their tickets. She is surprised that this obscure museum in a quasi-rural suburb of Portland, Maine, is expensive: thirty-five dollars for adults, thirty for seniors, twenty for children under twelve. *Twenty for children under twelve.* Is this even legal?

"Another year, and I'd be paying the 'adult' price for my son here."

Just a mild observation. Not a complaint. The mother understands that the Fractal Museum is privately owned and probably isn't subsidized by the state.

"Eleven? Your son is *eleven*?"—a query from the woman selling tickets isn't intended to be rude but yes, it is tactless.

"Yes. He is eleven."

With a pang of dismay the mother sees that the child who so often seems to her immense in his intelligence and imagination and willfulness is indeed small for his age. Not short, as tall as an average eleven-year-old perhaps, but painfully thin, with underdeveloped shoulders and arms, the slender neck of an aquatic bird, and that pale, skim-milk, cinnamon-freckled skin—*vulnerable* is the word that comes most readily to mind.

In his dark red flannel shirt he'd buttoned crookedly, and she'd had to rebutton. In wire-rimmed eyeglasses that enlarge his eyes that glow like bees.

Fiercely the mother thinks—*I will protect him with my life.*

But Oliver isn't so frail, to himself: Oliver is strong-willed, even defiant. He has been an only child for eleven years—a lifetime!

Edging away from the mother frowning as he struggles to clip the bright blue Fractal Museum badge (which is in fact several fractal-leaf-badges conflated as one) onto his shirt without her assistance. Though he hasn't heard the exact exchange between the ticket seller and his mother, the mother's friendly chatter with strangers is embarrassing to him.

Especially since the child knows that the friendly chattering mom is not really *the mother*—just some silly mask and costume the mother puts on, in public.

Adjacent to the foyer is the gift shop. Adjacent to that, a planetarium with hourly showings—*Our Fractal Universe.* Also a café that is brightly lit and buzzing with customers.

Oliver suggests that the mother have coffee in the café and meet him afterward in the third-floor exhibit—for he knows how badly she would like coffee (very black, strong!) after the stress of the drive—but the mother quickly demurs. "No! I'm not letting you out of my sight in this weird place." Adding, as if it were an afterthought, with a smile, "Sweetie."

It is the mother's nightmare, that she might lose the child in some unfamiliar place like a museum, airport, subway. Perhaps an outdated nightmare since the child is not of an age to be easily lost any longer.

Sweetie is a signal, the mother is pleading with him. The child is stiff-backed, not in a mood to be pleaded-with.

If she didn't know that the child would ease away from her like a cat not wishing to be stroked she'd have taken his hand. Just to feel the small, hot-skinned hand in her own and to claim—*See?*—*I've got you. Safe.*

"oh, oliver! *Look.*"

Their first exhibit is on the third floor: *Naturally Occurring Fractals.* This is a massive and dazzling display that winds its way in brightly lighted glass cases and interactive presentations through the entire third floor. Crowded with visitors (including the harried-looking young mother with a son who resembles Oliver) this exhibit appears to be at least twice as large as the mother would have anticipated, given the (apparent) size of the museum from the outside. Just to gaze into it, to the farther walls of the museum that seem to dissolve into the ether, is disconcerting.

Giant illuminated photographs of seeds, leaves, flowers. Feathers, hairs, fur, scales (snake, fish, lizard). Many-times-magnified snowflakes, crystals. Magnified cells, neurons, ganglia so tangled and so beautiful, they evoke a sense of vertigo in the brain. And there are, scarcely less startling and strange, skeletal trees with fractal-branches, fractal-twigs, fractal-veined leaves. Fractally dense evergreen cones looking sharp and lethal as spikes. With his iPad Oliver takes multiple pictures. He is particularly interested in a sequence of highly magnified photographs of the New England coastline, in ascending order of magnification.

No matter how many times magnified, the fractal pattern of the coastline recurs. The mother can see this but can't quite see the point of magnification. Is there to be no end of things?—no *end*?

"What you think is a straight line," Oliver says, "actually isn't. There are all these little breaks and creases, that go on forever." The child speaks with a sort of grim glee as if *forever* were not a terrifying prospect.

"Oh. But—why?"

"Just *is*, Mom."

"I mean—why pursue it? Why would you want to know so much that has no use?"

Oliver retorts that most of science is "useless"—plus math, fractal geometry. That something is *useless* is not a description of its essential properties but is irrelevant. *Useful* is also irrelevant.

The mother feels rebuked. For a mother is of all things meant to be *useful*.

Before each dazzling display the mother lingers. She is (half-) aware of time fracturing, fractal-ling. Unlike Oliver who seems to be familiar with much of this information the mother needs to carefully read, reread the descriptive passages on the walls. Her brain feels gluey. Her eyes feel the strain of so much to see.

Her arms ache from the effort of having held the damned steering wheel steady for so long, to keep the SUV in its proper lane and prevent a sudden catastrophe, crash into an abutment (just beyond exit nine at a place called Elk River) and two lives *snuffed out just like that.*

But no, that did not happen. Without incident they'd passed the exit where they'd been most at risk, at about 9:05 A.M. Arms trembling with effort the mother held the steering wheel firm as an enormous tractor-trailer truck thundered by in the adjacent left lane.

The child had not even noticed. Absorbed in the intricate puzzles of the iPad.

The mother wonders: is there such a thing as fractal-time? She feels a thrill of dread that this must be so. Each hour, each minute, each second broken down into its components, to infinity; and in each, an alternative fate of which she knows nothing.

Up close, life is but life. At a little distance, life is fate.

Crushed, broken amid the wreckage. Steam lifting, stink of gasoline. Snuffed out just like that: two lives.

To the husband she'd have said *Serves you right! You have aban-doned your child and your wife and now you have lost them.*

Something is staring—glaring—into her face. Another of the giant illuminated magnifications. Reduced to its fractal components the photograph (rock, lichen) is unrecognizable as a swirl of molecules.

Yet, the fractals abide. No matter the degree of magnification.

The mother has certainly underestimated the Fractal Museum, she is thinking. She'd meant simply to humor the child, driving him here. She'd hoped that, if there was an extra hour, on the way home she could stop at the Winslow Homer Studio at Scarborough about which she has read in the *AAA Maine Guide*, and that would have made the long trip worthwhile for her.

But now, she is quite absorbed in the exhibits. It is a new world to her, close beneath the surface of the world she believes she knows without needing to examine how she knows.

Naturally occurring fractals seem to encompass virtually everything in the physical world—all that the mother has been seeing with her eyes (and not with her brain) through her life.

The fractal is the basic unit of design.

The fractal repeats itself endlessly and yet each fractal is unique and unlike any other.

Trying to grasp this. Like stepping out onto ice. Possibly it is rock-solid and will support your weight. Possibly it is not.

"SHALL I TAKE YOUR PICTURE, Olly?"

Shakes his head *no.*

Ducks his head. Smooth-freckled pale skin reddening as if slapped for certainly the mother must know that the child hates being called *Olly* in a public place.

Well, in fact—the child isn't comfortable being called *Olly* at any time, this past year.

Stubbornly resisting. No picture!

The mother feels a surge of something like fury and wants to take hold of the child's skinny shoulders, give him a shake.

But consider: she is *the mother*, she is not *the child*.

In a contest of wills *the mother* does not need to vanquish *the child* to establish her power over him.

"Come on, sweetie. Please. Just stand here. We can mail the picture to Daddy, to make him envious he isn't here with us."

This is very mild sarcasm. This is not actually a condemnation of the father who is oblivious of much in the household.

"Actually, Daddy asked me to take your picture. And send it to him. So he knows we got here safely. OK?"

None of this is true. But the mother exudes such sincerity, the most icy-hearted child could not resist.

And the mother has exerted her authority by taking the iPad from the child—virtually unhooking it from his fingers—and positioning him against a wall, as if he were a much younger child.

(The wall display is one of the gorgeously colored magnifications of—is it a nebula? a multifoliate rose? a neuron in the human brain?)

"There! That wasn't so bad, was it?"

The child has allowed the picture to be taken, to humor the mother.

The fear that our likenesses will outlive us. The image of a being in a (future) time in which the being has ceased to exist.

This is a morbid thought that has leapt into the mother's brain like a sly louse or tick, out of the gorgeous fractal display on the wall. But the mother casts the morbid thought off as she always does such thoughts, by ignoring it.

The time is 10:31 A.M. But—how is that possible? The mother stares at her (digital) watch, baffled and uneasy. She has given the iPad back to the child, or she would check the time on the electronic gadget as well.

Hadn't they arrived at the Museum shortly before 10:30 A.M.? The mother is sure she remembers the time correctly. And if so, if at least forty minutes have passed in the exhibit, it would now be 11:10 A.M., approximately; how then can it be only 10:31 A.M.?

Something is very wrong. The mother's brain reels.

If time moves with such glacial slowness in the Fractal Museum they will never be released from it. They will never return to their home in New Haven where someone, the third party of the triangle of which they constitute two-thirds, awaits them.

The mother gives her watch a shake. Damned battery must be slowing down.

"Oliver, wait!"—the child is eager to move on.

Culturally Appropriated Fractals is an equally massive and dazzling display sprawling through the Museum's second floor. Here are walls of illuminated mandalas, rose windows. The mother will spend many minutes here entranced as one who has been deprived of beauty and is now blinded by it.

Astonishingly elaborate, intricately designed Hindu mandalas. In these you can lose yourself. That is, *self.*

The mother is mesmerized by the great illuminated mandalas. These are as different from one another, and alike one another, as fireworks in a night sky. Seeing one, you have seen them all; seeing many, you have seen one.

Like the infinite faces of God.

The child is less intrigued by (mere) visual beauty. The child is drawn to the cerebral component—the fractal structures that underlie beauty.

In the beige tile floor of the Museum are several stripes: green, red, blue, yellow. Each leads to an exhibit. It is the green stripe that Oliver wants to follow to bring him to more cerebral exhibits, video puzzle-games and interactive robots that mimic/mirror the individuals who stand before them typing on keyboards. There is the promise of the Sierpinski Triangle Labyrinth which is a "challenging" maze-game in the form of a triangle containing countless triangles in which time as well as space has to be navigated.

Oliver plucks at the mother's wrist to move her along but the mother finds it difficult to break the spell of the mandalas. The exhibit area is enormous, the size of a football field. Always there is more to see: another gorgeous dazzling intricately wrought mandala that seems to hold a secret—a secret meaning. Beauty exudes a powerful spell upon the mother, like a heady perfume.

The mother becomes aware of an agitated hubbub of the air about her as of a crowd pressing near but when she looks around, there is virtually no one else (visible) in the enormous room.

At the farther end of the room a Museum guard motionless as a mannequin. His face is generic and friendly, of the hue of skim milk.

Oh, where is Oliver?—the mother hurries to locate him. And there Oliver is, around a corner, in a corner, absorbed in an interactive video that makes him laugh.

Something about fractals, of course. Fractal topology? Vivid colors, like explosions in the brain.

The mother tells the child please don't move away from her. It is crucial for them to stay in each other's sight. The Museum is much bigger than she'd thought, and—(how to express this)—"Time moves differently here."

The mother dislikes video games which she interprets (correctly) as an alternative reality not congruent with her best interests. *She* would like to imagine herself the emotional center of the child's life, and not a brain-exhausting game.

(Can a machine love her son, as she loves her son? Of course not.)

Being of an older generation to whom such antic video figures will never exude familiarity or comfort the mother instinctively distrusts humanoid figures. She knows that they are "programmed"—(she thinks that "programmed" means "safe")—but this makes no difference to her. She *cannot trust* any machine.

As Oliver interacts with the video game the mother loses herself in an exhibit of eerily incandescent, shimmering flowers of diverse varieties and colors. These too are fractal-mandalas. Peering into them is like peering into the soul.

From all sides, Ravel's *Bolero*. Ever faster, ever louder, musical notes turning frantically upon themselves like snakes in a cluster.

7.

"It's OK, Mom. I can go alone."

"Oliver, no. I don't think so."

The Sierpinski Triangle Labyrinth, located on the mezzanine floor of the Museum, takes up the entire floor.

The child cannot think of anything more disappointing than to have journeyed to the Fractal Museum only to be forced to undertake the Labyrinth, the Museum's major interactive exhibit, about which he has been reading online for weeks, in the company of his timorous and uninformed mother. No!

And yet there is a warning posted above the entrance: *Children Under Twelve Must Be Accompanied by Adults into the Labyrinth.*

Though Oliver is hardly a small child the mother intends to enter the Labyrinth firmly gripping the boy's hand. It isn't likely that he would run ahead of her, or become lost, for after all the Labyrinth is finite—(no larger than the mezzanine floor, you can see)—still the mother is reluctant to let the child push ahead and leave her behind. She is still somewhat dazed by the effect of the mandalas and rose windows in the preceding exhibit and feels reluctant to leave them so soon.

Amanda has not been a religious person and has not (consciously) felt the need for spiritual solace. A great hunger is opening in her, in the region of her heart, that will never be filled.

And yet—she is obliged to use the women's restroom. This is not so spiritual.

Instructing the child to please wait for her in the corridor. Or use the (men's) restroom himself, which is just across the hall, and wait for her. And then they will proceed—together—to the Sierpinski Triangle Labyrinth just a few feet away.

The child agrees. Seems to agree. *OK, Mom.*

Standing very still, deceptively. With an expression of utter innocence.

On surveillance cameras it will be recorded: the mother addressing the child, the child seemingly docile, a lanky-limbed boy of about ten?—with ginger-colored hair, in a dark red, or maroon, shirt buttoned to his throat, jeans, sneakers.

Mother disappears into women's restroom. Child waits obediently for two seconds before edging away into the entrance to the Labyrinth.

(Not that Oliver was a rebellious child. Rather, Oliver was oblivious of the fact that while he *was* he was a *child*.)

In the Sierpinski Triangle Labyrinth each individual who enters is designated a *pilgrim*, overtly; covertly, from the perspective of the program that governs the Labyrinth, each individual is a *subject*.

There is (allegedly) a direct path that leads from the entrance of the Labyrinth to the exit, at which there is posted *EXIT: NO RE-ENTRY.* If you make the right choices each time you are confronted with a choice (that is, a fork in the path) you will exit the Labyrinth after a breathless forty-fifty minutes.

Has anyone ever exited the Labyrinth in this relatively short period of time? Legend is, no one has (yet). Thus, each *pilgrim* imagines himself potentially ranked #1 in the Labyrinth competition; the child Oliver is, or was, no exception.

Like human intestines that might measure, if stretched out, more than twenty-five feet, yet are condensed into a much smaller abdominal space, the devious path of the Sierspinski Triangle Labyrinth is far longer than one would guess; calculating the numerous (fractal) turns, each of which involves an equilateral triangle replicating the larger equilateral triangle that constitutes the outermost limits of the Labyrinth, and factoring in the time-fractal as well, the Labyrinth is many miles long, perhaps as many as one thousand. Examined minutely, however, the Labyrinth might be said to be infinite, for each smaller triangle in the path might be deconstructed into its parts, to infinity.

The *pilgrim/subject* makes his way into the Labyrinth, confronted with forks in the path at intervals of only a few seconds; he must choose to go right, or left, for he cannot go backward; having made his choice, he will be confronted with another fork within a few seconds, and must choose to go right, or left; and so on. As soon as he has entered the Labyrinth the *pilgrim/subject* is moving through time as well as space, and this movement into both time and space is irrevocable—though it is not likely that the *pilgrim/subject* realizes it, as none of us do.

Having calculated a route beforehand, Oliver has a plan to take the left fork of the path, then the right, and again the left, and the right, in a pattern of strict alternation, in this way (he deduces, plausibly) he will always be hewing to the center, and will not be drawn off into peripheral, fractal branches that may culminate in dead ends. Oliver is very bright and quick and has a near-photographic memory and so tells himself—*I can't become lost.*

It has been Oliver's aim—his dream—to complete the Labyrinth in record time, or at least to tie with the previous #1 *pilgrim* whose likeness he has seen posted on the Museum's website: a seventeen-year-old boy from Manhattan's Fieldstone School who intends to major in cosmology at MIT.

And so, the bold child enters the Labyrinth without a backward glance. At once the atmosphere is altered—he finds himself almost weightless, disoriented. Surprised too to see that the maze-walls are not solid as he'd anticipated, but rather translucent, or giving an impression of translucence, opening onto sunlit areas, fields of poppies, Shasta daisies, wild rose that seem to stretch for miles. There are high-scudding clouds. Fleecy, filmy cirrocumulus clouds in a cobalt-blue sky. Cries of birds, or perhaps they are human cries—a young family at the beach, laughing together. All is vivid and then fleeting, fading. Forks in the path come rapidly—more rapidly than Oliver has expected—but each fork seems to lead into an identical space so that it is possible to forget one's strategy and make a blunder, "choosing" randomly, with the assumption that *left* and *right* are interchangeable; and since the *pilgrim* can't reverse his course he has no idea if *left* and *right* are in fact interchangeable, or in fact very different—as radically opposed as *life* and *death*.

Once a choice has been made it is irrevocable, for a powerful momentum draws the *pilgrim* forward, as a mist of amnesia trails in his wake.

Soon then, the child has entered an industrial landscape. Factories in ruins, dripping water. The sky is leaden, sinking. All color has vanished. Suddenly he is in dark rank water to his ankles. (Is the water *real*, or is the water *virtual*? In the Sierpinski Triangle there is no clear distinction between the two states.) A strong chemical odor makes his nostrils pinch for the water is poisoned. It is the reeking landscape of the Russian film *Stalker*—Oliver's favorite film since he'd first seen it at the age of ten.

How many times Oliver has seen *Stalker*! He has been mesmerized by the long dreamlike excursion into the Zone in which all wishes are fulfilled including those wishes we do not know we have. Recalling how a black dog suddenly emerges from the contaminated water, to befriend one of the pilgrims . . .

There is no doubt that Oliver must continue forward, ever deeper into the Zone. Dank dripping water, a tightening in his chest. No friendly German shepherd appears (yet). Oliver has no time to wonder how so abruptly he has stepped out of the comfort of the Fractal Museum with its clean restrooms and brightly lit café buzzing with customers and the planetarium show—*Our Fractal Universe*—which he might now be seeing safely with his mother, except the line of mothers and children was too long, and the lure of the notorious Sierpinski Triangle Labyrinth irresistible. For weeks Oliver has planned how, if he follows his plan unfailingly, he will exit the maze in "record time"—his name and likeness posted on the Fractal Museum's website for all to see.

For the father to see. For kids at school to see.

Yet Oliver has a strong feeling that he should turn back. Even if it is against the rules— perhaps the program that drives the Labyrinth will make an exception for him. (He is a special child, isn't he? The fuss his parents have made over *him*.) He has made a mistake to push ahead into the exhibit without his mother—they will make an exception, for he is just a child. He has deceived his naïvely trusting mother.

She will be upset. She will be angry. Her eyes will smart with tears. Her lower lip will tremble. *Oliver how could you! You must have known that I would be looking for you, I would be sick with worry over you . . .*

Hesitating on the path, uncertain which fork to take. Now there is not only a right-hand fork and a left-hand fork but a middle-fork. Three!

Oliver had not known that some of the choices would involve three forks in the path. He is confused, uncertain. How deeply has he penetrated the Zone? Will there be a way out?

Always there is the promise, if you are an American child and your parents love you, there will be a *way out.*

Even if you have rejected your parents there is a *way out.*

The polluted air is difficult to breathe, the child's chest begins to tighten. Airways in his lungs begin to tighten. He begins to choke, wheeze. He is panicked suddenly. It is a violent asthmatic attack of a kind he has not had in years. In another few seconds his eyesight will blotch and blacken and he will sink to the floor gasping for breath, unconscious . . .

Oliver darling! Here.

He feels the mother's hand on his shoulder. He feels the mother's panting breath on his cheek. The mother has brought Oliver's rescue inhaler in her handbag. Of course, the precious rescue inhaler, the almost-forgotten inhaler, the despised inhaler that will save the child's life.

I've got you, darling, you are all right. Your mother has you now, just breathe . . .

8.

At the entrance to the Sierpinski Triangle Labyrinth the warning cannot be clearer: *Children Under Twelve Must Be Accompanied by Adults into the Labyrinth.*

Yet, when the mother emerges from the women's room to glance about inquisitively the child is nowhere in sight.

Oliver has entered the Labyrinth by himself—has he? The mother is exasperated with the son but not (yet) upset.

Noting the time: 12:29 P.M.

Reluctant to enter the Labyrinth, for the mother knows that it is the most challenging of the Fractal Museum exhibits, indeed an "ingeniously" difficult maze, the mother looks prudently about to see if, in fact, Oliver might be somewhere else. Perhaps he has wandered into another exhibit, around a corner. Into the men's restroom? With mounting anxiety she waits outside the restroom. In case Oliver is inside. Oh, she hopes so! If he appears, she will not scold him. *Oliver! Thank God.*

Though she is not by nature an *anxious mother*. Minutes pass, Oliver does not appear. Other boys emerge from the restroom, one of them closely, uncannily resembling Oliver, the boy who'd worn the dark green Newtown Day hoodie, coming to join the mother waiting for him outside the Labyrinth; but Oliver is not among them. Finally the mother asks a Museum guard if he will please go inside the restroom to see if her son Oliver is in there—eleven years old, "small for his age," gingery-red hair, wire-rimmed glasses, dark red shirt, jeans, sneakers. The Museum guard is willing to oblige but returns from the restroom without Oliver.

Is she sure he hasn't entered the Labyrinth?—the guard asks.

The mother confesses that she doesn't know. She'd asked the son to wait for her, but . . .

At 12:36 P.M. the mother again approaches the guard: should she enter the Labyrinth to search for the child?—or should she assume that he will emerge at the exit, when he completes the maze?

The Museum guard is a skim-milk-skinned individual of no discernible age with an affable smile, Museum uniform and badge. He does not appear to be armed except with a device that might (the mother thinks) be a Taser. He assures the mother that the maze is a "challenge" but it is "finite"—"It is guaranteed to come to an end." He recommends that she wait for her son at the exit, which she can access by taking the stairs or elevator to the first floor, walking to the rear of the Museum, then taking the stairs or elevator back up to the mezzanine. She will encounter *pilgrims* leaving the maze there, and possibly someone among them will have seen her son.

This, the mother does with some misgivings for it seems not a good idea to leave the Labyrinth entrance in case Oliver shows up there after all. Bitterly she regrets not having insisted that the child carry a cell phone so that she can contact him easily but Oliver (who does not want to be contacted easily by his mother) is interested only in the damned iPad.

At the Labyrinth exit the mother waits. Surely, Oliver will emerge from the maze soon!

Each person who appears at the Labyrinth exit—many of them boys Oliver's age, or older—looks familiar to her, for a brief moment. Her heart is suffused with hope even when she has seen a face clearly and knows that the person cannot be Oliver: the child out of all the universe who is precious to her as her very life, perhaps more precious, for he is *her child*, and the promise is—*Our children must outlive us, and remember us, else we cease to exist utterly.*

An older, white-haired gentleman exits the Labyrinth appearing distracted, distraught. It is unusual to see an individual of such an age in the Labyrinth. The mother tries to speak to him, to ask if he might have seen Oliver inside the maze, but the white-haired man seems reluctant to meet her eye, and hurries unsteadily away.

The mother tries to reason with herself: it is (probably) foolish to worry about Oliver—the Labyrinth is only a Museum exhibit, a maze for children to navigate, nothing like a Ferris wheel or roller coaster; a child is obviously not in danger of his life in the maze, nor is it likely that a child could become *lost*. She knows this, certainly.

Strangely, it is only 12:29 P.M.—how is this possible? Amanda could swear it would have to be an hour later, at least. She is becoming increasingly anxious.

At the Labyrinth exit is a sign in emergency-red letters: EXIT ONLY DO NOT ENTER. Amanda hesitates, wondering if she should try to enter; or, should she return to the entrance, and try to make her way through the maze, to find Oliver? Reaches out her hand to the doorway—her hand is confronted by a very slight resistance in the air. (Is this real? Imagined? She feels a sensation like a mild, warning shock.) A Museum guard approaches her to inform her politely but firmly that visitors are not allowed into the maze at the exit; if they wish to enter they must return to the entrance.

She stammers that her son is somewhere inside the maze, she's afraid that he is lost, that something may have happened to him— "Please? Please help us."

On his walkie-talkie the guard summons an aggressively friendly woman in a Museum uniform (jacket, pleated skirt), badge identifying her as *M.W. Pritt,* who assures the mother that of course it is natural to be worried, for some children get "mired" in the Labyrinth and take longer to complete it than others, and it is natural— understandable!—for a mother to *worry.* But there is (after all) only one way out of the Labyrinth, even if the Labyrinth turns upon itself, in mimicry of a fractal universe, in ever-tighter "pathways" within ever-smaller triangles, and even if, as all visitors to the Museum are clearly informed, in fact it is printed out distinctly (if in a very small font!) on the reverse side of all Museum tickets, that the Sierpinski Triangle Labyrinth is also a maze *in time.*

What does that mean, the mother asks—"A maze *in time?*"

"It means that the maze is ingeniously imagined as a maze *in space* and *in time.*"

"*In time . . .*"

"The *pilgrim* who undertakes the Labyrinth is moving through space but also, inevitably, through time."

"But—why is that different from what we are doing, just standing here? Aren't we moving *through time?*"

"Of course. It is not possible not to move *through time.* But *time* is a kind of spectrum, and there are different rates at which one moves. The Labyrinth experiments with 'time'—at least, that is what the inventor claims. Very few of us, on the staff, have actually *gone inside* our interactive exhibits."

"You've never gone into the Labyrinth? Why—why not?"

"But why would we?"—the woman regards the mother with a quizzical smile. "We are here to 'manage'—not to be entertained."

Seeing that the mother is looking distressed and confused *M.W. Pritt* repeats again that the Labyrinth is *finite*, and if the child is still in the Labyrinth he will be found.

The mother asks what does she mean by *if?*

If. If the child is still in the Labyrinth, or *if* the child ever entered the Labyrinth.

The mother asks if there are security cameras inside the Labyrinth and is told that there are not, for reasons of privacy, as there are not cameras in restrooms; though there are security cameras in the Museum generally, in the exhibit rooms and corridors.

"But—I don't understand. 'Reasons of privacy'—what does that mean? In the maze?"

"Ma'am, I am just relating Museum policy to you. I did not set the policy!"

M.W. Pritt escorts the mother downstairs and into the security office where she is allowed to observe a wall of TV screens. On each screen humanoid figures are moving at a distance, blurred and indistinct, with only intermittent colors, as if seen undersea. It is very difficult to distinguish faces. In fact—are there faces? A preponderance of children, young adolescents, some adults, a white-haired older man drifting about like sea anemones in an invisible current. When the videotape from the Labyrinth entrance is rewound and replayed the mother stares so intensely she almost cannot *see*—"Wait! Is that Oliver?—is that me? Or, maybe not . . ."

A mother and a boy, obviously her son, yearning to slip away from the mother, listening to her anxious prattling with an air of barely restrained impatience; a young boy, not yet an adolescent, in what appears to be a jacket or a hoodie, standing very still.

The mother enters a women's restroom, and vanishes from the TV screen; the son remains for a beat, two beats, before turning away decisively and entering the Labyrinth.

Last glimpse of the son, a defiant little figure, entering the Labyrinth without so much as a backward glance.

The mother stares at the screen, perplexed. Again, she is so agitated she has difficulty seeing.

"I—I think that might be us. Though that doesn't actually look like us. Especially me . . . That isn't *me*. But the boy resembles Oliver. Oh—I just don't know."

The recorded time, noted on the screen, is 12:25 P.M.

The head of Museum security is very sympathetic with the mother. He rewinds the videotape, replays it. The mother stares avidly, as a starving person might stare at (a representation of) food, imagining it in three dimensions, smelling it. She is thinking how human beings recorded by such cameras are diminished, soulless. Flattened and distended like sea creatures of so little consequence they would not require names. Their limbs grow stubby, flaccid. Their faces are melting like wet tissue. It is particularly curious that on some of the screens you can distinguish adults from children only by height, and even that is not a reliable measure.

The mother demands that she be allowed to enter the Labyrinth, that a security officer escort her, that they find Oliver, immediately. She is excited, her voice rises. Calmly it is pointed out to her that the boy has not been in the maze very long, by their calculation less than ten minutes, and that, if he is making his way through the maze as the brighter children do, he will need at least forty or fifty minutes to complete it.

"You don't want to disappoint your son, ma'am. He may make excellent time and be a top-ranked *pilgrim* posted on our website. Why don't you wait here in our security office for a few minutes at least, before we enter the Labyrinth and create a commotion? Maybe your 'Oliver' will show up on camera, at the exit."

The mother is about to burst into tears—*No! You are lying to me. Something terrible has happened to my son, I want to see him at once.*

But hears herself saying weakly yes, all right. Suppose that is sensible. Probably the child in the video was Oliver, though the woman did not much resemble her, the mother, in which case if Oliver entered the Labyrinth at 12:25 P.M., it is only 12:38 P.M., and not much time has passed.

Many hours have passed. The mother is exhausted, her bones melting like wet tissue.

"Why don't you have a seat, ma'am. Try to relax. We will watch the camera trained on the Labyrinth exit, and see when your son emerges. And we will station a guard there, to bring him immediately to you. Shall I get you a coffee from our café?"

9.

In the Labyrinth there is no *time.* There are many *times.*

The child is beginning to suspect that each *time* he chooses a fork in the path he is choosing a *time* that does not "differ from" but has no relationship at all to other *times.* His experience in the Labyrinth is not (he supposes) synchronous with the *time* preceding his entry, which has continued in his absence, nor with the *time* in which (he supposes, guiltily) his mother is now looking for him.

Beginning to appreciate the ingenuity of the Labyrinth, which is more properly described as a *Labyrinth of Infinitely Receding Triangles.*

For when the child makes a choice—left, middle, right—right, right-middle, left-middle, left—there is the alternative child-self who takes alternative paths. And each of these selves has engendered, or will engender, alternative selves.

Already the (defiant) child is lost to the (overly-trusting) mother.

As soon as he'd stepped into the Labyrinth loss suffused them each like a smell of brackish water.

In the Zone, the child has been alone. The friendly black German shepherd dog has yet to appear.

And then, at a subsequent fork of the path, the child is greeted by the friendly black German shepherd dog!

Delighted, with childish relief. The child takes a seat in front of the German shepherd who is (obviously, the child can see this) a robot, though a very realistic-looking dog. The child pets the dog, wanting to think that the stiff synthetic fur is actual fur, coarse from the brackish pools. The tawny-golden eyes shine.

The child is invited by the Friendly Dog to participate in an interactive game. *Your Fractal Twin.*

Though the Friendly Dog is a "dog" he/it is also more essentially a mirror of the child.

Oliver laughs, the Friendly Dog has made him very happy. Though he is eleven years old and not a young child yet he is not thinking so clearly now, to be made very happy by the Friendly Dog, and to trust the Friendly Dog when (he can see) the Friendly Dog is but the carapace of a machine that has (probably) not been programmed in the child's best interest.

Sierpinski triangles within triangles. Oliver tries to calculate how far inside the Labyrinth he actually is, how many triangles *in*. Five? Six? More? He'd intended to navigate the maze by reverting always toward the center but has been distracted in the Zone.

Begin with any key.

Oliver strikes the return key. On the screen instructions appear. These, he follows. Questions appear, he answers. Almost Oliver laughs, the game is not so difficult as he'd expected.

Strike any key. For all keys are a single key and no single key matters.

Oliver hesitates. Which key to strike? But of course, it does not matter—all keys, like all doors, lead to the same place.

Oliver strikes the letter O, as a capital. For *O.* means *Oliver.*

In that instant the Friendly Dog reaches out in a swift unerring gesture of a foreleg, seizes the child by his upper body and with a powerful wrenching snaps the child's upper spine and neck, as one might snap the vertebrae of any small mammal. There is no resistance, the child had no idea what was coming, and in the next instance the child *ceases to exist.*

The small limp body lies broken on the floor. Still warm, though no longer breathing, within seconds it is liquefied. Through vents in the wall a vacuum sucks the remains away and within thirty seconds nothing remains of the child except shreds of clothing, pieces of a sneaker, a glaring-white fragment of bone. A smashed iPad.

By the time the next *pilgrim/subject* takes a turn in the path, and discovers the Friendly Dog, these pieces of debris too have vanished.

10.

It is 12:47 P.M. The anxious mother has returned to the entrance of the Labyrinth and is making a spectacle of herself, as visitors to the Museum look on gravely.

Demanding again to be taken into the Labyrinth by Museum officials. Threatening to call the police.

But is she *absolutely certain* that her child entered the Labyrinth?

Yes, she is certain. Yes!

Doubt is being raised. Witnesses have been discovered who do not agree with the mother's charges. A Museum guard says that he'd seen the mother with a small boy, a "sweet-faced, shy" boy with eyeglasses and a school hoodie, but not in the vicinity of the Labyrinth: in the Museum café.

A middle-aged man whom the woman is certain she has never

seen before steps forward to volunteer that he'd definitely seen a "red-haired boy, a little mischievous scamp, ten or eleven years old" playing the *Fractal Topology* video game—but that had been on the first floor of the Museum, at least two hours before.

Weakly the mother protests, that could not have been Oliver. There is only one Oliver, and he must be in the Labyrinth, except the Museum officials won't allow her to look for him, she will have no choice but to go to the police . . .

Rehearsing how she will plead with the father—*Our son has disappeared. I have lost him. Forgive me, our son is lost in the Fractal Museum.*

II.

"Ma'am."

A kind person is pressing damp towels against her forehead. She has no idea what she looks like. In the security video her features seem to have melted, her face is a blur. She is of an unknown age: somewhere between twenty and forty. But no, she has not been twenty in a long time. Her hair is faded-red, possibly it is laced prematurely with silver. Her skin is drained of blood, the redhead's pallor, an Irish complexion perhaps, freckles like splotches of rust-tinged water.

"I don't know why I am here. I'm not sure where I am. Though I have been drawn to—fractals."

This is hardly true. She isn't sure what fractals are. Something to do with—math? physics? computers?

". . . mixed up with black holes. Gravity—events."

She has been a wife, and a mother. She has wrestled with the conundrum: inside the laundry dryer which is a (finite) space, how can articles of clothing disappear?

If a pair of socks disappears, you do not notice. Only when one sock disappears do you notice. So possibly there are more disappearances than are perceived.

In the black hole, gravity sucks light inside. You must imagine for you can't actually experience or measure non-being. Indeed, the universe may be mostly non-being.

She is feeling better. She has forgotten what it is she has forgotten.

Amnesia! It is a rare malaise of the spirit that amnesia cannot heal.

Strangers are whispering about her. She is both anxious to leave and yet reluctant to leave. She is desperate to flee this place of confinement yet she is wary of being excluded, expelled. She knows: if you exit the Museum, there is NO RE-ENTRY.

She has come to loathe and fear the atmosphere of the Fractal Museum which is a constant murmur of fans, air vents, machines. A constant murmur of voices. Children's complaints, small ticking sounds like the manic heartbeats of crickets.

She hears too acutely. All of her senses are too acute.

Needs a tissue. Her nose is running, eyes leaking.

In the tote bag are receipts for many (old, recent) purchases. Two tickets to the Fractal Museum. Adult, child.

Obviously a receipt for two tickets must belong to someone else for she'd come to the Museum alone. Must've fluttered into her tote bag or been given to her by mistake. She crumples the receipt and sets it aside as if it were an annoyance.

"Are you feeling better, ma'am? You are looking a little better—not so pale. Still, we should call an ambulance . . ."

"Please don't call an ambulance!" Suddenly she is begging.

She will not sue the Museum, she promises. Oh please!

Can't imagine why she is here. Whatever this place is.

It is explained to her that she is approximately two hundred and fifty miles from her home. If indeed she has come from New Haven, Connecticut, which her driver's license indicates is her home, as it has indicated that her name is Amanda.

Directions to her address by car have been printed out for her by the kindly Museum staff. (As if, having gotten to the Fractal Museum, she could not simply reverse her route, to return home!)

But she is polite. She is a polite person. Trained to be polite, and by nature polite. Thanking the Museum people. The woman with the *Pritt* badge. Courteous Museum guards. Individuals practiced in dealing with hysterical visitors. Mothers who have lost their children. Adults who have lost their elderly parents in the Fractal Museum. Husbands who have lost their wives. Miscarriages?

A stillborn baby is not a fetus. A fetus is not a baby. A fetus has no history.

They have been very kind: they have brought her to this warm, interior room where it is quiet. She can lie undisturbed on a sofa, she can rest. For if she tries to stand too quickly the blood will drain from her head, and she will faint. It is an effort to keep her eyes open.

Gradually she becomes aware of something strange about the room. The walls. On all sides, walls that are not covered in wallpaper, or with a coat of paint, but rather with something like—could it be *skin*? Soft-leather skin like the skin of a (not-yet-born) creature.

Exuding an air of warmth. Blood-warmth. Thinnest of membranes, lightly freckled.

"Ma'am?"—smiling *M.W. Pritt* stands before her with tawny shining eyes, offering a very black cup of coffee from the Museum café.

12.

Days dark as Norwegian nights. Rain pelting against windows, rushing down drainpipes. The husband away and the wife, the mother, at home with the baby cuddled in her arms. Both naked.

Flesh of my flesh. Blood of my blood.

Before the birth, cells from the embryo made their way through the placenta into the very marrow of the mother's bone. After the birth, cells remain in the mother that might one day be required for the restoration of the mother's health.

How happy she is! Suffused with joy.

He'd told her *no*. That is, he'd told her *yes*.

PREGANNT.

No: *pregnent*

No: *pregnant.*

Her tongue was numb. Her tongue had become a desiccated old sponge. Her tongue could not manage speech.

"Amanda, what did you say?—*preee*—"

Fear. Wariness. Caution. The (instinctive) male response.

They'd made their (his) decision. Well, it was hers (his), too.

Will you love me, she'd asked.

Will you love *me*.

He took her to the Clinic. Of course—he'd driven.

Waited with her. Held her hand. He'd brought work to do. He always brought work. His eyes danced with work. His soul festered with work.

He was/was not the father. Yet.

At that age, has the fetus a soul? No.

The correct term is not "age"—I think. The terminology is weeks: how many.

The crucial thing is, you don't name them before birth. That is not a good idea.

Primitive people often do not name babies/children until they are several years old. So that if they die, the loss is not so great.

An unnamed child is not mourned as a "named" child would be mourned?

Her name was called. A name was called, beginning with *A*.

A was unsteady on her feet for they'd provided her with a round white pill and she had not slept the previous night nor many previous nights lapping leaden against a hard-packed shore. Her companion who was/was not the father walked with her to the door gripping her icy hand and his eyes were damp with tears hot and hurtful as acid. Asking her yet another time if she was *all right* and what could she say but *yes of course.*

Stumbling back to his chair in the waiting room. He would wait, how long. The actual surgical procedure was not more than a few minutes. They knew: they'd researched the procedure. They were the type to (carefully, exhaustively) research all things that touched upon their lives which challenged their control.

Prep took a while. Anesthetic is recommended. Absolutely. Cervix is forced open wide with a speculum, very tender, interior of the body, best to be numb, asleep. Suction.

Oh Peter—I took a tranqizziler. Feels so funny . . .

Tran-lil-lizzer?

On the gurney, legs spread. Shoes off, in stocking feet. Naked from the waist down. Very cold, shaking. OK to keep the bra on. Otherwise, naked. Paper smock, pale green like crepe paper.

This will pinch a little. Hey—that vein just wriggled away . . . .

. . . small veins. Maybe use a children's needle . . .

. . . will take twice as long. Let me try.

Suction. Suck-tion. It did not hurt, she was miles away. If there was hurt in the room it was not hers. Head was a balloon bobbing against the ceiling. Heels pressed hard against stirrups.

The vacuum sucked thirstily. The gluey remains vanished.

In the other room the distracted father was logging into his laptop.

Password, invalid. What the hell?—he types it again, alarmed. This time the screen comes alive.

∽

In another story, the son hopes to be an architect.

"An architect is the one looking *down*, and *in*."

13.

"Ma'am? You are looking as if you have lost something."

Yes, she has. She has lost something. She laughs awkwardly for she isn't sure what.

Is it so obvious—the terrible loss in her face?

The uniformed woman is smiling at her. A smile stitched into the face. *M.W. Pritt* is the name on the plastic badge.

"He was just here with me, a few minutes ago. He—I think—went into the Labyrinth . . . I suppose he must still be in the Labyrinth."

It had been a child. Or, an elderly white-haired gentleman with kindly eyes that would not engage with hers.

Uncertainly Amanda speaks, almost apologetically. Her heart is beating rapidly as if hoping to outrun her anxious thoughts.

He is gone gone gone. You have lost lost lost him. You are damned damned damned and this is hell hell hell.

"Ma'am—'Amanda'—I'm sure that I saw you come into the Museum about an hour ago, and I'm very certain you were alone. In fact you'd come into the Museum at the same time another woman came in, a woman of about your age, who had several children with her, and I'd thought at first that you were together, friends who'd brought their children to the Museum together. But that wasn't the case, evidently. You were alone. You are alone. You bought your ticket and you made an awkward joke about the tickets being expensive—

'for such an obscure museum.' And our ticket seller Mary Margaret said: 'Distances are deceiving in the Museum, ma'am. Visitors are often surprised.' For some reason, you laughed at Mary Margaret's remark."

It might be her passport Amanda was afraid of losing. Many of her dreams are of losing her passport in a foreign country where she doesn't know the language. Often she'd lose her plane ticket as well.

"But—this isn't a foreign country, thank God!"

Laughing nervously. *M.W. Pritt* in boxy jacket and pleated skirt, bosom hard as armor, regards her with something beyond pity but does not join in her laughter.

"There are many variants of 'foreign,' Amanda. Some people are surprised to learn."

And: "I don't think you quite realized why you were laughing, Amanda. Sometimes it's better to think before you laugh."

That is certainly correct. Amanda has no idea why she'd laughed that morning purchasing a single, overpriced ticket for the Fractal Museum in Portland, Maine.

14.

After the Fractal Museum she will drive to Prouts Neck at the shore, to hike along the beach in a swirl of icy froth. The Atlantic has been whipped to savagery by rushing winds on this November afternoon. Scarcely is it possible to imagine another season, a warmer light— waves peacefully lapping to shore, expelling foam like harmless tongues lolling on the beach.

Perhaps this afternoon she will hike out beyond the crashing waves, beyond the seaweed-shrouded boulders. Icy waves pummeling her slight body against the hard-packed sand. The end will be swift, merciful—her (unprotected) skull cracked against a great rock puckered as if for a kiss.

But no: she has brought her small inexpensive camera, she will take pictures of the sea, the sea shore, the November sky ragged with clouds. Ocean debris, seaweed and rotted things, desiccated fish, corpses of unnamed creatures, skeletal remains like lace. When the husband sees the digital images he will squeeze her hand and say half in reproach—*You see, darling? I've always tried to encourage you. Everyone has tried to encourage you. You have an eye for beauty in the least beautiful things.*

Also: she is thrilled at the prospect of examining close up Winslow Homer drawings and paintings she has never seen before.

There is beauty, and it is outside us. Yet, it is us.

That is why she'd driven so far that morning, she realizes. Rising early in the dark, driving against the wind until her arms and shoulders and head ached. A purpose to her most impulsive acts, she must learn to have faith and to combat depression settling like a shroud of mist around her, through which only the sharpest and most corrosive sun-rays can break.

Yet she is reluctant to leave this place. For still, after so many hours, she is in the Fractal Museum.

A warm room, if slightly airless. No windows. No security cameras. (That she can detect.) No one to observe how strangely she is drawn to the wall beside her, to what covers the wall, taut and tight as skin.

A thrill of horror comes over her. For it does seem to be—the wall's surface is neither paint nor wallpaper but a sort of membrane, a skin, soft, heartrendingly soft, exuding a barely discernible warm pulse like a living thing. It is lightly freckled, like droplets of water tinged with cinnamon, or—turmeric . . . In wonderment she touches it—just the lightest touch, with the fingers of her right hand.

"Ma'am? We're sorry, the Fractal Museum is closing now."

Yes! Of course. It is time for her to leave.

By the rear exit with the blunt admonition *EXIT: NO RE-ENTRY.*

Only one vehicle remains in the parking lot. If the key tightly gripped in her hand fits the ignition, obviously that vehicle is hers.

Undocumented Alien

PROJECT JRD
Lost in Time

TEST SUBJECT #293199 / JOSEPH SAIDU MAADA
(UNDOCUMENTED ALIEN, HOME COUNTRY NIGERIA,
B. 1990 D. 2016)

Most immediate and long-lasting effect of the neurotransmitter Microchip (TNM) inserted in the cerebral cortex of the human brain appears to be a radical destabilization of temporal and spatial functions of cognition. (See Graz, S.R., "Temporal and Parietal Functions of the Human Brain," *Journal of Neuroscience Studies* 14: 2 for a detailed description of normal functions.)

In test subject #293199 temporal destabilization was immediate and (seemingly) permanent; spatial destabilization was sporadic and unpredictable.

For instance, upon several (videotaped) occasions in the PROJ-ECT JRD laboratory (Institute for Independent Neurophysiological Research, Princeton, NJ) test subject #293199 J.S. Maada demonstrated confusion and panic when asked to list events in a chronological sequence. Even those events which were made to occur within a single hour in the Institute laboratory, which he had observed, were virtually impossible for Maada to "list"—(it was noted that the subject seemed to have lost comprehension of what the term "list" means). If subject was allowed to view a videotape of the hour he could list events on a sheet of paper as he observed them occurring, though after the elapse of a half hour, he would not remember their sequence except by consulting the list. Also, Maada did not appear to recognize himself in the video, or would not acknowledge himself. (*Who is that black face?*—Maada would ask, sneering and anxious. *I see him. He does not see me.*)

In the last several months of Maada's life, partly as a consequence (it is believed) of deteriorating vision, hearing, and cognitive functions, subject's paranoia was heightened so that he became convinced that a team of *black spies* had been sent to abduct him and return him to Nigeria to be imprisoned and tortured in collusion with the CIA. (See Lehrman, M., "Learned Helplessness and Conditioned Paranoia in 30-Year-Old African-American Male," *Johns Hopkins Neurophysiological Journal* 22: 17. Though this paper [attributed to Dr. Lehrman but in fact 90 percent of it the work of his post-doc staff at the Institute] is based upon PROJECT JRD classified experiments it does not contain information that reveals the identity of the test subject or the laboratory in which the cycle of experiments took place. Thus, the age of the subject has been altered as well as other details pertaining to the subject's ethnic identity and legal status in U.S., in conformity with Department of Defense regulations stipulating classified

scientific material revised for publication in non-classified journals.)
Simultaneously, and with no awareness of the contradictory nature of
his assumptions, test subject Maada was made to believe that he was
a "privileged alien agent" sent to Earth on a "secret stealth mission"
from one of the orbiting moons of Jupiter and that the nature of this
mission would be revealed to him at the proper time, and not before.
Am I a ticking bomb?—Maada would ask slyly. *Or am I just a ticking
clock? A heart?*

Over a duration of several months Maada so lost his ability to
register the sequence of what we call "time" that he was continu-
ally expressing surprise at encountering members of the S___ family
(with whom he was living in Edison, NJ; their name is redacted, at
least in this rough draft of our report, since the entire S___ family
is "undocumented"/"illegal") in their cramped quarters in a brown-
stone tenement on Ewing Street, Edison. When the older children
returned from school, if Maada was in his room and heard their
voices he would rush at them demanding to know why they weren't
at school, for it seemed to him (evidently) that they had just left, or
had not left at all; concepts of "earlier"—"previous"—"subsequent"—
"consequent"—were no longer available to him. The several children
in the S___ household, ranging in age from three to eleven, were very
fond of "Saidu" (as they called Maada), because he was "kind" and
"funny" with them, like an older brother, and "very smart," helping
them with their homework; but over the course of PROJECT JRD,
as Maada's personality was made to "plasticize" (i.e., alter in a "melting" way) and other features of the experiments were initiated, the
children did not know what to expect from their "Saidu" and began
to avoid him.

When the several adults in the S___ household returned from their
low-income jobs in the Edison area Maada frequently expressed great
anxiety for them, and occasional impatience, that they had failed to
go to work at all, and were risking their jobs, thus their livelihood

and ability to pay rent which would lead to their arrest and deportation, and his own.

For the "undocumented alien"—"illegal alien"—it is arrest and deportation that is the prevailing fear, and not, as it is for others of us (who are U.S. citizens) a more generalized fear of the impenetrability of the future: *Death,* we can assume; but not the *how of Death,* still less the (precise) *when of Death.*

As early as 6/11/15, within three weeks of the start of his participation in PROJECT JRD, #293199/J.S. Maada began to have difficulty listing the chronology of events in his previous life: his arrival in the U.S. as an engineering student at Harrogate State University, Jersey City, NJ, at which time a student visa was granted in his name by the United States Department of State (8/21/07); his withdrawal from Harrogate on "academic grounds," at which time his student visa was declared null and void and he was issued a summons from the Department of State ordering him to report immediately to the Newark Immigration Authority (2/2/08); his (unlawful, unreported) move to Edison, NJ, as an "undocumented alien" given temporary shelter in the small, fiercely protective Nigerian community; his sporadic (and undocumented) employment in the Edison/Newark area as a cafeteria worker, busboy, hospital and morgue custodian, sanitation worker, construction and lawn service worker, etc.; his (first) arrest by law enforcement officers (Newark) on grounds of creating a public disturbance, refusing to obey police officers' commands, and resisting arrest (5/21/15); his release from police custody dependent upon agreeing to participate "freely and of his own volition" in the National Defense Security (Classified) PROJECT JRD (5/24/15); his (second) arrest, Montclair, NJ (6/19/16), on more serious charges of sexual assault, aggravated assault, assault with a deadly weapon (teeth, shovel), assault with the intention of committing homicide, and assault against (Montclair) law enforcement officers.

Following the altercation with law enforcement officers in Montclair test subject J.S. Maada did not return to participate in the
PROJECT. Injuries sustained at the time resulted in (emergency)
hospitalization at Robert Wood Johnson General Hospital, New
Brunswick, NJ, with the (federally mandated) proviso that no medical information regarding the patient could be entered in any hospital computer, and that access to the subject's room was restricted.
Following the subject's death (6/30/16) his room was declared a
quarantine area accessible only to the PROJECT JRD medical team
which performed the autopsy establishing cause of death as "natural": hypothermia, brain hemorrhage, respiratory, cardiac, and liver
failure (7/2/16). Per the contract signed by the test subject at the start
of his participation in PROJECT JRD, his "bodily remains" became
the property of PROJECT JRD and are currently stored in the research morgue at the Institute for Independent Neurophysiological
Research on Rt. 1, Princeton, NJ.

(Information concerning TNM inserts, shunts, surgical and chemical alterations to J.S. Maada's brain and body are not indicated in
the [official] autopsy which has been sent to the test subject's family
in Nigeria but are to be found in the [classified] autopsy on file with
NDS [National Defense Security].)

Though the equivalent of hundreds of pages of data have been
recorded in PROJECT JRD computer files, the participation of test
subject #293199/Joseph Saidu Maada in the cycle of experiments at
the time of his demise is considered incomplete and unsatisfactory.

NOTE: As indicated above, this report is a rough first draft, a com-
pilation of lab notes with some expository and transitional material
put together by a small team of post-docs assigned to Dr. M. Lehrman
working late at night in the depressing and ill-smelling quarters of the
Institute. If you have read this far please do not be offended by our
plea (of a sort) that allowances might be made for our (relative) lack of
data concerning test subject #293199/Joseph Saidu Maada whose full

name was not available to us until this morning when we arrived at the lab to learn to our surprise that (1) #293199 was not coming today, as he had been coming every Thursday for months; and (2) #293199 would not ever be coming again, for any scheduled Thursday.

Oh. Shit—one of us murmured.

Weird. We'd got to know the guy kind of well, and now—

It is common practice in laboratories under the auspices of PROJECT JRD to refer to test subjects by their (classified) ID numbers and not by their (actual) names; so too test subjects are not told the (actual) names of the research scientists and medical authorities who work with them over the course of the cycle of experiments. (So far as Joseph Saidu Maada could know, the names on our badges—*Dr. R. Keck, Dr. M. Lui, Dr. J. Mariotti*—indicated who we actually are, and in addition to this [quasi-]information we encouraged the subject to call us by first names closely resembling our own, actual first names: "Rick" for "Rich"; "Michelle" for "Millicent"; "Jonny" for "Jonathan.") In this way, a desired *atmosphere of trust* was established, a crucial goal for all PROJECT JRD labs.

Also, as post-doc assistants to Dr. M. Lehrman, director of our Institute lab, and not director of PROJECT JRD itself, we could not access some essential files without arousing suspicion. Each rank at the Institute, as at PROJECT JRD, as at the Department of Defense, carries with it a degree of "classified clearance," and post-docs are of the lowest rank. (Just above lab technicians—we are sensitive about being confused with lab technicians who do not have Ph.D.'s as we do.) Hence the haphazard nature of this report, which we intend to correct in subsequent drafts, before submitting it to Dr. Lehrman, who will slash through it with a red pencil, correcting our mistakes (as he sees them), revising and excising, and providing (restricted) information of his own (which we will never see), to the director of PROJECT JRD whose very name is not known to us but whose office is in the Department of Defense, Washington, DC.

(Unfortunately, the final draft of this report is due on Monday morning. If only we were outfitted with the more potent neurotransmitter chips inserted into J.S. Maada's brain, or, at least, one or two of the amphetamine biochemical boosters that kept the hapless test subject awake at night!)

RADICAL TEMPORAL DESTABILIZATION seems to have intensified the subject's confusion about his (classified) role as a "privileged alien agent" with special powers (invisibility, ability to read minds, to pass through solid walls, and to perceive the shimmering molecular interiors of all things; to "detonate"—"demolecularize"—when directed by his Commandant) and his (actual, literal) life as a manual laborer in the not always reliable hire of Adolpho's Lawn Care & Maintenance of Montclair, NJ.

From the perspective of Institute research scientists it would have been preferable that the test subject had not worked at all, and that he was available for their purposes at all times, like a laboratory animal that is kept, for his own safety as well as for the convenience of experimental researchers, in a cage; but J.S. Maada's disappearance from the Nigerian enclave in Edison would have aroused suspicion, it was believed. And so, inevitably, J.S. Maada's real-life activities impacted upon his role as an experimental subject, and presented serious limitations, which resulted in the tragic events of 6/19/16.

Precipitating factors include extreme heat on the day of the "assault" (a high of 96°F in Montclair, NJ, by noon), protracted labor (the lawn crew had begun work at 7:00 A.M. at the E___s' large, three-acre property; the assault occurred at 11:00 A.M.), and an evident miscommunication between Mrs. E___ and J.S. Maada that ended in a "violent outburst" on the part of the test subject, bringing to an abrupt and unforeseen halt the subject's participation in PROJECT JRD.

Possibilities accounting for Maada's extreme reaction following an exchange with Mrs. E___ are: the shunt in the subject's cerebellum had begun to work loose and/or one or another of the inserted Microchips may have been malfunctioning. Usually "docile, reticent, cooperative, and naïvely unquestioning" the test subject allegedly became "excitable, belligerent, and threatening." According to witnesses Maada lifted his shovel as if to strike the terrified Mrs. E___ but decided instead to attack the Floradora bush, rendering it into pieces; he then threw down the shovel, seized Mrs. E___ by her shoulders and shook her violently as one might shake a doll with the intention of breaking it. Further, according to Mrs. E___, Maada bared his "wet, sharp" teeth and lunged as if to bite her in the (right) breast.

By this time two of Maada's co-workers came shouting to the rescue of Mrs. E___. Inside the house, a housekeeper called 911 to report the attempted sexual assault/homicide.

When Montclair police officers arrived at the E___ residence they discovered the agitated (black, Nigerian-born) laborer "cowering at the foot of the property, by a fence"—"foaming at the mouth like a mad dog"—"rushing at us with a shovel"—after "repeated warnings" no choice but to open fire seriously wounding but not (immediately) killing subject #293199.

TRANSCRIPT OF TESTIMONY OF MRS. E___,
TO THE ESSEX COUNTY PROSECUTOR. 6/28/16

I did not condescend to Mr. Marda. I did not provoke him.

You can ask any of Adolpho's men—I am always very friendly when I see them. I will admit, most of the time I can't remember their names—their names are so exotic!

We couldn't possibly—personally—know which of the workers are undocumented—illegal. I would never dream of questioning anyone who works for us, who is obviously working very hard to send money back home to a wife and seven children, or a mother and eleven siblings, in God knows what poverty-stricken African or Central American country, still less would I register suspicion of their legal status. I suppose that some are Mexicans, and some are Filipinos, and some are African, and some are—Pakistani? Well, I don't know. They are all foreign.

Mostly, they are excellent workers. Sometimes, in the house, I see them working out in the sun, and start to feel faint watching . . . Of course, as Adolpho has said, they are not like us. They don't mind sun and heat, they have been born nearer the equator.

So in all innocence I approached "J.S. Marda"—this is the name I would afterward learn—I will never forget!—to whom I had spoken the week before, at least I think that I had—(it's hard to keep them straight, they look so much alike especially hunched over in the rose garden), and I told him that the Floradora rose had not worked out well where he'd transplanted it, so he would have to move it again, back to where it had been originally, except now there was an azalea bush in its place which he'd planted, and that would have to be relocated . . . I was not speaking rudely. I am not a bossy person! I was speaking slowly and carefully as you would speak to a child or a retarded person. For the man did not seem to comprehend my words. I could see his mouth working—but no sounds came out. He was sort of hunched over in the rose bed like a dwarf, with a back like a dwarf's back, but he was not small like a dwarf, and sweating terribly, and "smelling"—(well, I know he could not help it, none of them can help it which is why we don't allow them to use the bathroom in our house or to come into the house for any reason)—it was a strong smell—and was making me feel sickish . . . He was not looking at me, his eyes were averted from my face. He had a very dark skin that seemed to suck in all the light, like an eclipse in the sky. He was polite and stiff and he was trying to smile but his face was contorted like a mask and I could see that he had cut his arm on some of the rose thorns but he did not seem to be bleeding like a normal person. It was like some kind of mucus leaked out, with a strange, sharp smell. And now I could see, his eyes were not matching colors. The iris of one eye was a strange bright russet-red and it was larger than the other iris, which was mud-brown. Though his face was very dark it seemed to have begun to splotch with something like mange, or melanomas. It was very frightening to see—the black, "Negroid" skin seemed to be peeling off, but what was beneath?—a kind of pinkish skin, like our own skin if the outermost layer is peeled off, an unnatural pink, like raw meat. And now, the man was furious—at me. I could not believe how he lifted the shovel to hit me—screaming at me in a strange, brute language like the grunting of an ape—and then he struck the rosebush with the shovel—like a crazy man—and then he took hold of me and shook, shook, shook me and bared his wet, sharp teeth to b-bite . . .

(So agitated did Mrs. E___ become, the prosecutor excused her from further testimony.)

CONSEQUENTIAL, SEQUENTIAL. WITHOUT TEMPORALITY, i.e., the measured unfolding of time, the human is reduced to something lesser than human.

J.S. Maada's first arrest, one day to be conflated with his second arrest, and yet a *causal factor* in the second arrest, had been in New Brunswick (5/21/15). Subject was waiting for a bus at State Street and Second Ave. at approximately 9:20 P.M. when two New Brunswick PD squad cars braked to a stop and police officers swarmed upon several "black youths" on the sidewalk. Subject demonstrated "suspicious behavior" by running panicked from the scene; after a scuffle, during which subject was thrown to the sidewalk and handcuffed, subject was arrested and taken to precinct with other young men.

Jailed in the New Brunswick Men's Detention, subject was ignored for forty-eight hours despite requests for medical attention (broken ribs, lacerated face, possible concussion), then discovered to be an "undocumented alien" from Nigeria whose student visa had expired.

NOTE: "Undocumented aliens" have no immigration status in the United States and may be arrested at any time and "removal proceedings" initiated. Legal help may provide options but these are temporary. Until individual is issued a green card (providing permanent residence, but not citizenship) or a student visa, he can be deported at any time.

Marriage with a U.S. citizen automatically confers immunity to deportation by the State Department but does not confer citizenship.

Distraught subject was visited in the New Brunswick Men's Detention by a PROJECT JRD officer who explained to him that deportation for undocumented aliens was mandated by the U.S. State Department with one exception: if subject volunteered for a federal medical research program which he successfully completed, he would be issued a new student visa with which to attend "any university of his choice" and he would be eligible for a green card—that is, permanent residence in the U.S.

Gratefully then, subject Maada agreed to participate in the project, which was explained to him as funded by both the United States Department of Defense and the United States Department of State. Contracts pertaining to Maada's willingness to waive his rights were signed with a flourish though (strictly speaking) the undocumented alien does not share "rights" with U.S. citizens. The seal of the State of New Jersey lent to these documents an authentic air. Among the test subject's personal remains, after his death, these documents were found, and reclaimed by the PROJECT.

According to the S___ family who had taken in the young man in his hour of need, after his expulsion from Harrogate University, Maada seemed certain that his application for U.S. citizenship was being processed by a "special, secret court," and that he would soon become a citizen, and when he did, he would help the entire S___ family to apply as well. *Saidu was a very kind young man, very helpful and loving with the children especially our three-year-old Riki. When he first came to live with us he was not so talkative and suspicious of everyone at the door but then, later, he became nervous and excitable and loud-laughing when there was nothing so funny we could see. With a wink he would say how he would pay us back one hundred times over for he was a "special-mission agent," one day we would be surprised.*

Maada had enrolled in the engineering program—"One of the Finest Engineering Programs in the World!"—at Harrogate University but his background in mathematics was inadequate and his ability to read and write English was substandard. He had difficulty with all of his first-year courses but particularly Introduction to Computer Engineering in which he was given a grade of D- by a (Pakistani-American) teaching assistant who, he claimed, had taken a "hate" of him and whose heavily accented English Maada could not comprehend. His tuition to Harrogate had been paid by an international non-profit agency and would not be continued after his first year. *It was kind of pathetic, these African students they'd recruited from God knows where. They weren't the age of college freshmen. They could speak English—sort of. Their tongues were just too large for the vowels. They had the look of swimmers flailing and thrashing in water hoping not to drown. They sat together in the dining hall, trying to eat the tasteless food. Their laughter was loud and kind of scary. White girls were particularly frightened of them for the way the Africans stared at them with "strange hungry" smiles, they could feel "intense sexual thoughts" directed toward them especially if they wore shorts and halter tops or tight jeans which (they believed) they had every right to wear and were not going to be "intimidated."*

Along with several other universities Harrogate has been charged with fraud in soliciting young persons from abroad with "enticing and misrepresentative" brochures, "unethical waivers of basic educational requirements," and "worthless scholarships"; presidents of these universities travel to Africa, India, Korea and China to proselytize shamelessly for their schools, which attract only a small percentage of (white-skinned, above-average-income) Americans and are not accredited in the U.S. The university does not clearly state that tuition and costs are non-refundable as soon as the term begins and that "undergraduate living fees" are considerable. Harrogate University in Jersey City, NJ, has been several times indicted as perpetrating fraud—yet, even as a half-dozen lawsuits pend, it is still operating in New Jersey.

After being asked to leave Harrogate Maada was deeply shamed and disconsolate. With several other ex-engineering African students he made his way to Edison, NJ, where he lived with the S___ family, fellow Nigerians who took pity on him and made room for him in their small, cramped apartment on Ewing Street. In Edison Maada looked for employment wherever he could find it. He was paid in cash, and took pride in paying the S___s whenever he could; they did not know details of Maada's personal life but registered surprise that Maada had been released from men's detention so quickly after his arrest, with no charges against him. Not only was Maada spared a prison sentence but he was guaranteed payment from the U.S. government each month, in cash, that, combined with the cash he received from his numerous jobs, allowed him to pay the S___s usually on time, and even to send money back to his family in Nigeria.

By a 2012 mandate of the Department of Defense payments received by all participants in (classified) research projects throughout the United States are to be "at least one and a half times" the wages earned by the participant in his primary civilian job; this has been emphasized, for PROJECT JRD has committed to "zero tolerance" of exploitation of any of its subjects domestic or foreign.

LOST IN SPACE

As stated at the outset of this report, the destabilization of spatial functions of cognition in test subject #293199/Joseph Saidu Maada as a consequence of neurotransmitter Microchips inserted in his cerebral cortex did not appear to be so extreme as the subject's temporal destabilization, though it was frequently a contribution to his general "disorientation."

Essentially, subject did not know "where" he was in the basic ontological sense of the term. He had exhibited some natural curiosity before leaving his homeland to fly (to Newark International Airport) and then to take ground transportation (bus) to Jersey City, New Jersey, to the campus of Harrogate University; but, if examined, he could not have said where these destinations were in relationship to one another let alone to his homeland or, indeed, to any other points on the map; nor did Maada, like many, or most, foreign visitors, have anything like a clear vision of how vast the United States is and of how staggeringly long it would require (for instance) to drive across the continent. Maada had no idea of his proximate position in the universe—he had no idea of the universe. When it was revealed to him via the Commandant (NTM) that he was a native of a distant planet (Ganymede, one of the moons of Jupiter) sent to Earth on a mission that involved amnesia (no memory of Ganymede) and "surrogate identity" (quasi-memory of Nigeria), he was initially eager to be shown photographs of Ganymede and Jupiter but soon became discouraged by the distant and impersonal nature of the images provided him at the Institute. For—where did the people *live*?—Maada wondered. All you could see was strangely colored rock and blank, black space that was very beautiful but did not appear to be habitable.

Before this, Maada had had frequent difficulty with his physical/spatial surroundings in his "adopted" country. He could not begin to comprehend the New Jersey Turnpike with its many lanes and exits

that seemed to repeat endlessly and to no purpose; if he was obliged
to ride in a vehicle on the Turnpike, being driven by Adolpho to a
work-site, he shut his eyes and hunched his head between his shoulders and waited to be told that he had arrived. Even on the Harrogate
campus he was easily confused. Not only did the blank, buff-colored
factory-like buildings closely resemble one another but walkways and
"quads" appeared to be identical. Many of the (multi-ethnic) individuals whom he encountered at the university appeared to be identical.
Often he became lost looking for a classroom; by the time he arrived,
the class had ended, or perhaps it had never existed. Tests were administered like slaps to the head—he could not grasp what was being
demanded of him, and he did not like the way his professors and TA's
("teaching assistants"—a term new to him) smiled at him in scorn,
derision, and pity. For amid so many dusky-skinned persons, Joseph
Saidu Maada was decidedly *black*.

Somehow then, it happened that he was barred from the dour
asphalt dormitory to which he'd been assigned, to share a "suite"
with several other first-year engineering students from scattered parts
of the globe. He was served a warrant: a notice of expulsion signed
by the chancellor of Harrogate University and affixed with the university's gold-gilt seal. African-American security officers, taller than
he by several inches, burly, uniformed and armed with billy clubs,
arrived to forcibly escort him off campus with a warning that if he
dared return he would be arrested and deported. His student visa
had been revoked, his scholarship had been terminated. So quickly
this happened, Maada had difficulty comprehending that he was no
longer a *student* with much promise enrolled in one of the great engineering programs in the world but an individual designated as *undocumented, illegal* who was shortly to be *deported*.

In "New Jersey" there was nowhere to go *on foot*. You could not
use *instinct*. Blows to the test subject's head caused by the booted
feet of enraged New Brunswick police officers contributed to his

diminished sense of place and direction. In an apartment of three cramped rooms Maada could become hopelessly lost; as in a hallucination he might encounter his own self emerging through a doorway. A dingy mirror or reflecting surface told him what he already dreaded to know—there was "another" on the farther side of a glass whose intentions could not be known.

Later, the Commandant would quell such fears. *You are one of many, and you are many of one.*

Since Maada had no idea where the Institute was, how many miles from the apartment he shared with the S___s in Edison, there was a kind of comfort in not-knowing and in the certitude of not-being-able-to-know where he was taken. No one could possibly expect Maada to draw a map of where he was taken—he had virtually no idea where he *was,* before he was *taken.* Each Thursday, according to schedule, and in fulfillment of his contract, Maada was picked up by an (unmarked) van, to bring him to the Institute for approximately twelve hours of neurophysiological experiments; soon after the onset of the TNM insertions in the parietal lobe of his brain, Maada had but the vaguest sense of direction, like a child on a fun house ride who is dazed and dazzled and frightened and yet strangely comforted that the ride was after all a *ride,* prescribed by adults whose wisdom far surpassed his own.

On a typical Thursday, the test subject was instructed to wait in the early morning at a designated place, usually in the parking lot of a fast-food restaurant on Route 1, though sometimes in the parking lot of a discount store on Route 27; there was a busy intersection near the campus of Edison Community College on Route 27 which was a convenient place for Maada to await the van, for here he could easily blend in with other young men like himself, drawn to the college with a hope of bettering their lives and being granted U.S. citizenship as a reward. Maada had been warned never to speak of waiting to be picked up by any vehicle. So zealous to obey the Commandant, he did not speak to anyone at all, gesturing at his throat and shaking his head bemusedly to indicate that (possibly) he had a sore throat, laryngitis, if anyone tried to initiate a conversation with him. It was a continual surprise to the subject to glance around and discover the (unmarked) van gliding to the curb beside him like a vehicle in a space film, and braking silently to a stop. The driver, only just distinguishable through a tinted windshield, wore dark glasses, and gave no sign to Maada that Maada should make his way with seeming casualness to the rear of the van, where the doors would be opened for him, quickly, and quickly shut behind him.

It was with a sense of excitement and exhilaration that Maada climbed so trustingly into the van, to be borne however many miles to the Institute, in the company of mostly dark-skinned men of about his age, sometimes younger, rarely older; these were individuals dressed like himself, in nondescript dark hoodies provided by the PROJECT and good-quality running shoes; at a glance you saw that their wrists were not cuffed and their ankles not shackled, for they were here voluntarily, as J.S. Maada was here voluntarily. There was little need to warn these men (they were all men) to remain silent, and to keep to themselves, for each believed the others to be spies who would report them to the CIA. Also, each knew that a surveillance camera was trained on the interior of the van, for (they knew) all U.S. citizens were under surveillance at all times. The van was windowless, of course. There was no way to *look out*. The driver took the silent, slightly apprehensive men who avoided eye contact with one another on an ever-shifting, improvised circuit that might have taken them twenty miles from their pickup site, or five hundred yards. Their destination was the Institute for Independent Neurophysiological Research on Route 1, Princeton, NJ—a windowless three-floor rectangle that looked as if it were covered in aluminum foil, blindingly reflecting the sun—but of course none of the men ever saw the exterior of the Institute, and those (of us) who toiled there had ceased to see it almost immediately after beginning to work there.

(It is only with effort that I summon a vision of the exterior of the Institute, not as I'd glimpsed it today, or in recent months, but rather when I'd first seen it, approximately twenty months ago, when I'd come directly from Cambridge, MA, with my newly granted Ph.D. in neurophysiology to be interviewed by Dr. Lehrman for one of the highly coveted post-doc positions with the PROJECT.)

The van passed into an underground garage and came to a halt. The rear doors were unlocked by unseen, deft hands. As Maada and the others disembarked, always very polite with one another, and maintaining their discreet eye-evasion, PROJECT assistants were waiting to check their IDs (eyes, fingerprints) and to take them to their assigned laboratories. They had not a moment to glance about, to "get their bearings"—indeed, in the dim-lighted interior of the garage, that smelled of nothing more ominous than motor oil, there were no bearings to *get*.

Inevitably, the test subjects had no way of exercising any residue of a natural sense of space and direction for they had no more information about where they were than blindfolded children forced to turn in circles until they were dizzy and in danger of fainting might have.

Joseph Saidu Maada was usually eager to cooperate with researchers. He was boyish, even energetic. He laughed often, if nervously. At the Institute it was said of him that he resembled the youthful Muhammad Ali—so tall, so handsome, and so good-natured!—but that was at the start of his participation in the PROJECT.

After disembarking from the van the test subjects were quickly taken to individual examination rooms in the Institute. Their blood was drawn, and lab tests run. Some, like J.S. Maada, often volunteered to give more blood, for which they were rewarded with cash bonuses; but this was not required.

(Of course, after several months, when our research team began to replace Maada's blood with an experimental chemical solution mimicking the molecular structure of the blood, it was not "blood" drawn from his arm but a surrogate material designated as *blood [patent pending] in the reports. See also *plasma, *bone marrow, *nerves, *ganglia.)

From the examination room the subject was brought to Dr. Lehrman's laboratory where the staff awaited him. Assiduous lab notes were kept by all, to be subsequently conflated; each session was videotaped, and copies sent at once to PROJECT JRD headquarters.

One of the consequences of the initial brain (Microchip) insertions was a flattening of vision, so that to the subject much of the world looked like "walls"—"wallpaper." A three-dimensional world is a visual habit that can be broken readily in the human brain, if one knows how. Maada was more perplexed by this phenomenon than disturbed, for there was, in line with the simplification of images, a cartoon-like simplification of "depth"—you could feel that "depth" was missing from your visual field but you could not comprehend that it was "depth" that was missing.

Soon, without understanding what was wrong, and that it was his perception that was amiss and not the actual world, Maada began to puzzle over the S___ children, who did not seem (to him) to be the "right sizes." Especially his favorite Riki, a lively three-year-old, appeared to be "different sizes" depending upon his physical proximity to Maada. For Maada might sight Riki at a distance, without realizing that it was a distance, and so the child would appear to Maada much smaller than he was, like a doll; without three dimensions to suggest depth all was flattened, cartoon-like. Such experiences bewildered Maada who could not have explained them, even before the impairment to his cerebral cortex, in clinical or intellectual terms. The diminution of the children in size was particularly frightening to Maada who soon became convinced that Riki, the smallest child, was in danger of *going out*—as a flame is blown out.

Conversely, adults who seemed, to Maada, of a comfortably small, contained size at a distance, loomed large up close, and could be terrifying. The overall shifting sizes of persons and objects was disorienting to Maada, and eventually exhausting, but he learned to shut one eye so that the expectation of three dimensions (whatever "three dimensions" had come to mean) was not an issue.

In all, there would be eleven surgeries performed on Maada's brain, each for a distinct purpose. One of the more successful was the instillation of selected amnesia, through "erasures" of certain clusters of neurons in the brain matter surrounding the hippocampus, with the result that the subject could not remember that he'd had surgery, along with much else. To account for his part-shaved head, the subject was told that he'd had an infestation of head lice—his hair had had to be cut off and his head shaved in the affected area. The surgery left wounds and scars which had to be disguised with a scalp covering, in this case a "wig" that was a patch of hair matching the subject's own hair, which he could not remove from his head, and would not try to remove, under the impression that it was a "scalp flap" that had been secured with stitches. In addition, Maada was told that the patch contained toxin to repel lice. All this, he seemed to accept without question.

Another of the surgeries concentrated on the agency of *will, willfulness*. With neurons in these areas "hosed clean," these were subdued.

Eventually, the "scalp flap" was enlarged, and a more serious, systematic neurosurgery was performed on the subject. (Of course, the subject was kept in an anesthetized state for such surgeries which could require as long as nine or ten hours.) Exposed as a clockwork mechanism, the brain was readily examined by a team of experimental neuroscientists involved in the TNM project. Could one communicate with a region of the subject's brain without involving the subject ("consciousness") at all? Could one give contrary signals to parts of the brain, and force upon the brain a quasi-consciousness, born of desperation? Could "consciousness" be chased into a region of the brain, like a rat into a cage corner? Maada, in his state of suspended animation, barely breathing, bodily functions monitored minutely, was an ideal subject, for he was in excellent physical condition and, in recent months in particular, inclined to *passivity*.

In a sequence of surgeries parts of the subject's brain were excised and replaced with artificial devices—chips, stents. Such experimentation is crucial, for one day—and that day not far in the future—neurophysiological "enhancements" will be necessary to provide longevity to humankind; at least, to world leaders and members of the ruling classes. One of the most innovative experiments developed at the Institute has been the gradual replacement of a subject's blood with a chemically identical *blood that was not red but near-transparent, a more practical blood-composition in which white cells are better equipped to combat bacterial and viral invasions than "natural" blood.

In another yet more radical experiment, through electrical charges directly into the memory center of the subject's brain, circumnavigating conscious channels, the subject was informed in a vividly "mystical" dream that he was not an ordinary, mortal human being but a native of Ganymede, one of four large, beautiful moons of the sixty-seven moons of Jupiter. Given the code name "Joseph" the subject had been sent on a stealth mission to Earth, to the United States, in the guise of a youthful, male native of the African nation Nigeria; to throw off suspicion, the subject was outfitted with a very dark, purplish-black skin, hyper-alert senses (visual, auditory, olfactory) and "radioactive" eye sensors. In this guise, as "Joseph," the subject could see through solid objects; he could hear not only what was being said at a distance but he could also "hear" thoughts. He knew languages instinctively—without needing to think, he "translated" these languages into thought. In this superior being, the thin scrim between consciousness and unconsciousness had been penetrated.

Of course, there have been unanticipated side effects of such experimentation: in several test subjects these have included convulsions, psychosis, and death. (So far as we know, none of these have been subjects in Dr. Lehrman's lab.)

HERE, THERE. How do we distinguish?

Despite J.S. Maada's spatial destabilization, or perhaps because of it, the subject exhibited no difficulty in understanding, or imagining that he understood, how his cramped living quarters in Edison, NJ, were at the same time the open, unbounded atmosphere of Ganymede; he was not baffled that he could be *here* and *there* simultaneously.

Partly, this extraordinary mental feat was made possible by the near-total modification of the subject's basic memory—that is, the neural region in which were stored memories of the subject's earliest childhood and adolescence, altered to include purposefully vague "memories" of Ganymede. In a bold experiment the subject was shown photographs taken in Nigeria, initially landscapes of surpassing beauty, villages, celebrations, smiling children; suddenly, war-torn villages, hellish ruins, fires, corpses; men, women, and children strewn in the street, some badly mutilated, headless. Such powerful stimuli yet had a minimal emotional effect upon the subject, for an inhibitory Microchip governed the firing of neurons in his brain. Where neurons fail to fire there cannot be conscious "thought"; where there is not conscious thought, there cannot be the retrieval of "memory"; and where no memory, no "emotion." (See Lehrman, M., "Neurotransmitter Inhibitory Functions in the Subcortical Human Brain," *Neuroscience Quarterly,* I: 3. [Another paper of which 90 percent was written by Dr. Lehrman's post-docs, names grudgingly acknowledged in an obscure footnote.])

Yet more ingeniously Microchip neurotransmitters were activated at a distance in the subject's brain by (remote) electrical stimulation sending "voices" to the subject, with such auditory acuteness the subject could not but believe that they were in the room with him, and were *actual;* amid these, secondary "voices" could be sent to confirm, or contradict, or drown out the initial voices, leaving the hapless subject utterly baffled and catatonic. In one phase of the experiment the subject was made to hear voices in his original (Nigerian) language but with unusual inflections as if being uttered by computers, or foreign-born persons, which produced a particularly unnerving effect in the subject; in another phase, the subject was made to hear "Ganymede" speech—a computer-generated language with a scrambled syntax. At all times the voice of the Commandant could interrupt and redirect the subject. (This too was a computer-generated voice but its baritone timbre was soothing and "paternal.")

More recently developed has been a means of using the subject as a recording device without the subject's awareness, in Maada's case exchanges among Maada and some members of the S___ family, when Maada sat down to meals with them; these, in pidgin English or, presumably, Nigerian. No effort was made to translate these desultory conversations as they could have zero scientific interest.

Other sounds sent to the subject at a distance were thunder, music, dreams, an eerie whispering "breath" of outer space meant to simulate the sound of winds on Ganymede; each drew a specific reaction from the subject, ranging from fear to sorrow to intense, infantile joy, and each was experienced without question.

Electrical stimulations in the subject's brain stirred appetite and nausea, sexual desire and sexual repugnance, simultaneously. Shown photographs of (presumably) sexually stimulating images, like naked, nubile women and girls, the subject did not react as he might have reacted normally, when neurotransmitters blocked his reflexive reactions; conversely, shown photographs of (presumably) asexual images the subject was stimulated to react sexually. (Of experiments performed upon him without his awareness this was perhaps the most distressing to the subject as Maada could not comprehend why he was beginning to have "sex desire" for such bizarre and inappropriate objects as clouds, towels, doorknobs, infants and toddlers. Even in his diminished state the subject retained a residue of human shame and conscience, and came to feel agitated about losing control of his "soul.")

It was presented as a test to Maada's loyalty to his Ganymede stealth mission that he carry an explosive device strapped to his body, to be detonated by remote control at the direction of the Commandant. Of course, Maada did not question this mission though he was perceived to be "anxious" and "distracted" over it beforehand. Such detonations were planned when, for instance, the S___ family gathered for prayers, or when they and Maada were sitting together at a mealtime; when Maada was shopping in a 7-Eleven store, walking along a crowded street in Edison, or traveling with his fellow lawn crew workers in the rear of his employer's truck. Each time Maada was directed by the Commandant to the point of (theoretical) detonation he became highly agitated, but only inwardly; his heartbeat accelerated, and his sweat glands oozed sweat. (Eventually, in a later phase of the experiment, the subject's heart was adjoined to a fine-meshed mechanism that was immune to "accelerating.") Yet Maada did not cry out a warning to the S___s for he had been programmed to value the Commandant over any merely human beings; he would not betray his Ganymede destiny, though his vision of the (mythical) homeland was almost entirely abstract: a rugged rock-terrain of pitiless sunshine and shadows so sharp they registered to the eye as crevices.

In another, more controversial experimental mission the subject was directed to make his way on foot into a federal courthouse in Newark, passing through the metal detector and security checks without incident (since of course subject was not wired with actual explosives but only believed that he was). PROJECT observers stationed at the site noted that Maada did not behave suspiciously in

this public setting but pressed forward with the eager-to-please manner of a visitor to the U.S. who is hoping one day to become a citizen.
Here, too, the subject was convinced that he was a "stealth missile"
to be detonated by a remote control.

Even then, Maada retained some residue of dignity and conscience
from his former life. He knew himself innocent of knowledge of who
his enemies were, and why they, and he among them, were to be annihilated in a cataclysm of flames and rubble in this austere old government building. Federal Justice D___ was to be "executed"—but
why? An enemy of—whom? Was the U.S. government involved in a
stealth program to assassinate certain of its citizens, like Judge D___?
So long as Maada was innocent of such knowledge and merely following the directives of the Commandant he was innocent of the
acts he precipitated, and this appears to have been a solace to him.

(It is said that the president of the United States is the "invisible
man" on the PROJECT advisory board and of course, this adds considerably to the prestige and authority of the mission.)

(Yet, it has been said that the president of the United States is
excluded from Department of Defense policy on its highest plateau,
for there may come a time when it is unavoidable that the president
of the United States must be "executed" for reasons of "expediency.")

In the federal courthouse the subject was directed to be seated
in Justice D___'s courtroom, which was half-filled with participants
and spectators, to await the precise time for the detonation of what he
perceived to be explosives attached to his body; then abruptly, after
an anxious forty minutes, the subject was informed that the mission
had been suspended for the time being, and that he was free to leave.

In front of a vending machine on the ground floor of the courthouse Maada found himself trembling. So many choices!—soft
drinks, candy bars, chips. He could not decide if he was hungry, or
thirsty. In the euphoria of freedom he began to cry hot acid tears that
ran in corrosive rivulets down his cheeks.

AND THEN, MAADA BEGAN to misinterpret TNM signals. Willful neurons in the test subject firing *in ways contrary to directives*.

That this was happening in test subject #293199 after months of subject's cooperation was in itself a significant development. For no experiment is without valuable revelations!

Of course, *willfulness* in the subject Maada was intermittent and inconsistent. Resisting programmed directives did not represent an altered pattern of behavior in #293199 for there was no (discernible) pattern to it.

Subject began resisting PROJECT expectations in late winter/ early spring 2016. In the heat of a premature summer working with Adolpho's Lawn Care crew he was observed shivering violently while others complained of heat; subject perspired heavily, yet continued to shiver with (apparent) cold. When TNM activity was inoperative subject began to "hear" voices of a new and inexplicable sort. Though he could not have known of the microscopic stents in his brain, still less the cluster of strategically placed computer chips, or the artificial "scalp flap" beneath a patch of hair, he began to obsess that there were "things" in his brain—grains of sand, staple-sized bits of metal, lice that crawled and sucked his blood. He came to believe that his heart had been replaced by "a kind of clock that ticks." His blood was no longer red but of the hue and substance of mucus. His skin, that had always been so rich and dark, was lightening in splotches, like a kind of cancer—from working in the sun? Yet, Maada could not *not work* for he needed the money to repay the S___ family for their generosity to him and also to send back to his family in Nigeria (though his family had become distant and blank to him like faded faces on a billboard and several messages from "voices" had called into question his actual blood-relationship to them). Maada diverted his most anxious thoughts by scratching and peeling his skin, which seemed to give him an intense, sensual pleasure; beneath were patches of sickly pale skin, both repugnant and fascinating.

Even when no TNM activity was recorded, subject began to experience zapping sensations in his brain and through his body. Genitals were particularly sensitive, mutinous. "Sex desire" for inanimate objects like Styrofoam trash and gardening implements swept upon him at awkward times. He could not bear to touch that part of his body for such touch was forbidden yet his hands moved of their own greed and willfulness, and were shameful to him. In the S___ family there was little privacy, which was shameful to him. *You smell funny, Saidu*—one of the older children said, wrinkling her nose. It was terrifying to him, the S___ family would evict him from their apartment; a voice not (evidently) identifiable as that of the Commandant suggested that it might be wisest to slash the S___s' throats in their beds, some night when all were sleeping peacefully; and then, to slash his own. Yet an instant later, Adolpho was shouting at him: *Asshole! Wake up.* Losing his ability to see himself in relationship to other, spatial beings. Much was becoming scrambled, dismembered, dissected. It was repellent to him, to observe his own body dissected by (white) strangers with hand saws and blood-stained surgical instruments. So vividly he saw these strangers, he registered their fastidious revulsion at the smell of his sawn-open torso—*Jesus, what a stink!*

Had it already happened?—or, not yet? As if compressed on the head of a pin everything was prepared to detonate.

When Adolpho came for them on a street corner in Edison in the twilit hour at dawn Maada had to summon his strength to climb into the truck with the others. Where once he'd been the youngest member of the lawn crew, now his youth had drained from him. His back was stricken with pain. All of the nerves of his back had been *zapped*. His brain felt swollen. His left eye was fevered. He had slipped back in "time"—he had become his own ancestor, a slave. On the moon of Jupiter, slaves had revolted in open, deep, crevice-pits. It had been a slave uprising, that had brought him to Earth. Maada yearned to know more of his mysterious and forbidden origin but the words that would have brought him knowledge began to break and crumble like a column of ants when a booted foot descends upon them.

Moving the massive lawn mower, plugs inserted in his ears. Yet hearing a babble and crackle of voices and laughter. Seeing figures which (though lifelike) he knew were not really there for they were transparent like jellyfish, you could see things through them.

At the E___ estate working stooped in the sun. Digging in the sun. (White) woman with a pig face. Snout nose. Pig-eyes lewd and laughing. Pig-eyes dared to descend to the gnarl of misery at his groin.

What issued from the pig-mouth was confusing to him for he had already obeyed the pig-mouth. He knew. He was sure. Yet he was not sure for perhaps it had not happened yet.

Yet, *it had happened*. The Floradora rose was to be dug up another time and another time replanted.

Dug up, and brought to the other bed, that is/was the first bed. It seemed to Maada that he had just done this. He had done this several times. The pig-woman had commanded him, and he had obeyed. Yet, it was possible that the several times he had obeyed the pig-woman were collapsed to a single time and that time like the head of a pin, too small to see. Was there just one rose bed, and one hole?— but more than one Floradora rose? Trying to comprehend this was like trying to push inside his head an object that was too big for the space and also sharp-angled. Subject began to experience rapid zaps in brain, groin, fingers. Began to scream, grunt, tear like a ravenous animal with his teeth.

Pig-woman screamed, screamed. His co-workers screamed at *him,* pulling him off her.

It was the end. All of Ganymede would rejoice, a new martyr would enter the firmament.

The night before, this had happened.

Riki who'd loved to cuddle with Saidu shrank from him now seeing something in Saidu's face that was beginning to twitch, splotch, and peel like sunburn. The iris of one eye was inflamed, half again the size of the other iris. And the strange smell like something rotted.

Riki laughed uneasily, and sucked his thumb, and began to cry when Maada stooped to play with him.

Yet, Maada had no clear idea when this was. Riki was running away from him before he'd run toward him.

No! Go away, I don't like you.

Reached for the child who was screaming with laughter. Or, screaming. Reached for the child, and the child's legs thrashed wildly.

Far away, on a moon of the great planet Jupiter, a remote control was being pressed. The detonation would be instantaneous though traveling at the speed of light, it would take some minutes to arrive.

Donald Barthelme
Saved from Oblivion

"I often think that not enough attention is paid to dead writers."

Donald Barthelme

* **HIGH WIRE, DREAM OF.**

Climbing, he is. The steep ladder's steps. Up-upward climbing, thirty-seven, -eight, -nine feet with a gay reckless smile for the motley crowd below. Climbing upward in jester's red-striped costume, miniature bells on cap tinkling gaily. In triumph climbing the steep narrow ladder toward the "sky"—(of course he is not such a fool to think that that Kodak-cerulean papier-mâché sky could be "real")—and with remarkable agility managing to straighten his (creaking) knees and stand (shakily) erect on the small platform.

Pole in hand! Six feet six inches long, a very special wand with gilt monogram *D.B.*

And there, the tight-strung high wire he must cross—(why?)—to a small (identical) platform forty feet away.

Cheers, whistles from below.

Isolated handclaps, each distinctive.

"We're with you, Don! You are the greatest—we love you!"

* **THE ART OF ART, IN ARTIST'S OWN UNMINCED WORDS**

"Nothing to it. Just open an artery and bleed."

* **TECHNIQUE OF THE ARTIST**

Tell your story in iambs. Then remove the "ambs."

Tell your story in *sequiturs.* Then insert *non.*

Tell your story in "collage"—i.e., the juxtaposition of discrete
and banal ideas, images, words and things that, "artfully juxta-
posed," achieve a startling freshness and originality.

* **AWKWARD MATTER OF ARTIST'S REMUNERATION**

Prose is (normally) typed to the right-hand margin of the page
while poetry (though not a "lesser" thing) is (normally) centered
on the page, with wide left- and right-hand margins as required;
for that reason, prose is *paid more-for.*

* **ANATOMY OF THE ARTIST**

Don is a force of nature. Don is a born rebel. Don is a prodigy.
Don has "squandered his gifts." Don is a genius. Don is an *idiot
savant.* Don is a raving lunatic. Don is a saint. Don is a con-man.
Don is an *artiste mauve.* Don exudes *sand freud.* Don is inimitable
and Don is unfathomable—except at those times when Don is
fathomable and those are times you do not, repeat *do not* want to
be around him. And sometimes Don is imitable and sometimes
Don is the "ept" of "inept." Don is a consummate fraud. Don is
an imposter. Don's drivel is pure, but also (sometimes) impure.
Don has sacrificed his sanity to his art. "Art for art's sake" has
dried up Don's (once juicy) heart. "Still waters run deep." "You

can't make an omelet without breaking legs." Don is both the knife in the back and the knife'd back. Don is the wolf in sheep's clothing and Don is the sheep in wolf's clothing. Don is a man of short "fiery" temper. Don is a scalawag in Mephisthophelean beard. Don does not suffer fools gladly. Don is the soul of modesty. Don is self-effacing to a fault. Don is generous to a fault. Don can't say "no"—to a fault. Don will not turn his back on you in your hour of need. But if you turn your back on *him*—well, don't! Don will not hurt a fly—but Don *would* give you the shirt off his back. Don is honest, Don is kind. Don is devious, Don is deep. Don is polar. Don is bi-, tri-polar. Don is old beyond his years but Don is young at heart. Don is happy-as-the-day-is-long. Don is deep, inscrutable. Don "broods." Don is *toujours gai*. Don is the saltpeter of the earth. Don is a regular guy. Don is an irregular guy. Don is a mensch. Don is "quite a character." Don is a man among men. Don is a man among women. Don is a man among children. Don is a man's man. Don is a woman's man. Don is a *womanizer* and Don is a *manizer*. Don is a titan. Don is a pygmy. Don "does not know his own strength." Don is a postmodernist without having been a modernist. Don is the Avis of *avant-garde*. Don is not to be underestimated and Don is not to be trifled with. Don "puts himself last"—except when Don "puts himself first." Don is both both archy & mehitabel of *archy & mehitabel*. Don is both Abbott & Costello of *Abbott & Costello*. Don is *Kukla, Fran & Ollie*—all. Don is all Three Stooges. If he has but one bottle of port, in a storm Don will give it to you. Don has gotten to the A of AA—and back. Don has lived to tell the tale. Don has helped an undisclosed number of women and children into lifeboats during the course of his "controversial" career. Don has swum in icy waves with a prayer on his lips. Don has not ever "jumped ship." Don is said to have jumped queues in ambiguous circumstances like lining up for

movie tickets when (it appears) there are two loose-formed lines
and it isn't clear who is in which line. Don is burning hot. Don
is icy cold. Don is a gentleman *par excellence*. Don is *je ne sais
pas*. Don is a *fête accompli*. Don is a one-man *folie à deux*. Don is
a feast for the eyes. Don is above, beneath, and beside reproach.
Don is "too smart for his own good"—except when Don "can't
see his nose for the trees." Don is an outlier—when Don is not a
maverick. Don's smile is disarming. Don's smile is armed to the
teeth. Don's smile twinkles. Don's smile is ruthless. Don's smile
is artless. *Don* is artless.

   Has it been said that Don broods?

*   **A PORTRAIT OF THE ARTIST**
Don broods.

*   **FUNAMBULISM I**
Oh is Don again on the high wire?
   Yes Don is again on the high wire.
   Why is Don again on the hire wire?
   We are so afraid for Don on the high wire . . .

*   **DETRACTORS OF THE ARTIST**
"Dreamed my father told me my work was garbage."

*   **SOUL OF THE ARTIST**
"Try to be a man about whom nothing is known."

*   **THE SLEEP OF REASON**
Recycled fairy tales. Fable, farce.
   "Narcissist culture." "Private realm of . . . self."
   At first the artist is shocked to be blamed for the "moral rot" of
"moral relativism" contributing mightily to the "decline of Western

civilization"—then, thinks Heigh-ho! and you'll see him rubbing his hands together gleefully and gloating.

Believing himself unobserved on one of those "assault days" Don would run and skip to his car in the parking lot, on the most gleeful days we would observe him sniggering and chortling like the little boy he was in his heart.

* ## RESPONSIBILITY OF ARTISTS FOR 9/11
Has to be considerable. "Moral rot"—"moral relativism."
Repeat.

* ## THUMBNAIL SKETCH OF THE ARTIST
Frankly, it was difficult to "see" him. You'd look but Don wasn't actually there. Sometimes he'd walk behind us—we *thought* Don was walking behind us. But when we turned—he wasn't there!

Of course being MFA graduates we are tempted to allude to quantum physics—"quarks"—that when you fix on them, assuming that there's a "them," they are not there; so too with Don. But we don't know the first thing about "quarks"—(as, it should be conceded, we don't know the first thing about "black holes" either)—so it is difficult to communicate the uncanny *gravitas* of Don.

Some said that Don was very *handsome.* Especially women and girls would say this. Others had never actually "seen" him. (See above.)

With your thumb smear the *handsome* face. That blurredness is the essence of Don.

Moderate height. Moderate features—"Nothing to jump out and grab you." Moderate myopia corrected by lenses. Moderate weight—(but probably some flaccid flesh about the waist). Moderate hair loss by early forties. Moderate neat-trimmed bristly-saltpeter beard. Moderate male scowl, abashedness. Puckish.

All things in immoderation—he'd quote his favorite ancient philosopher Aristotle, first in the original Greek or Latin or whatever it was, then in English with a broad Texan drawl.

We loved him.

* **INSCRUTABLE MOTIVE OF THE ARTIST**
"Negotiating between the treacherous poles of *déjà vu* and *jamais vu*. That is the 'high wire' of art."

* **PLEA TO THE ARTIST**
Appealing to his reason, common sense, shame.

Why at your age, eighty-fifth birthday, another time climbing the ladder to the high wire, another time entertaining yokels not worthy to finger the hem of your jester's costume, scarcely worthy to hear the bright tinkle of the bells sewn to your cap, what is wrong with a rocking Ames chair, what is wrong with a motorized wheelchair, what is wrong with a respirator, what've you got (left) to prove, a hundred times you have crossed the high wire, a hundred hundred times you have crossed the high wire—and why?

Obvious answer to (stupid) question: *To get on the other side.*

* **THE CRUEL DANCE MASTER**
"I think at a young and malleable age Don had a, how to put it, unhealthy relationship with one of those older personages that figure so predominantly in all of our lives—a father. And then, after the primal, so to speak, father, a non-biological father who exerted a synergistic but symbiotic spell upon the young impressionable artist eventually equivalent to the influence of the original, biological father *who continued to exist, in fact.*"

The essence of the Cruel Dance Master—(there is one in the lives of all of us, I'm sure!)—is that the Master will reward the artist only when the artist performs to the Master's liking, and not to the artist's (own) liking; only when the artist performs according to the Master's formula will the Master approve.

Hey! The Master claps his hands and the artist dances.

One-two-three

One-two

One-two

One-two-*three*

Dip to the right.

Dip to the left.

Curtsy to your partner.

Allemande left.

Allemande *right*.

Fall flat on face.

Prostrate.

Repeat.

*   ## FUNAMBULISM II

With gusto—again—he climbs the (shaky) rungs of the ladder reaching to Heaven. Grin of reckless white teeth cast to the adoring fools below as he up-climbs to the platform, seizes the awaiting pole, begins the delicious/precarious *crossing of the high wire*.

Oh he is just slightly surprised—the caprice of the wind on this seemingly windless day.

Gusts not guessed by the yammering crowd below.

A hundred times he has crossed the high wire. A hundred hundred times. The danger is to forget what you have learned. The danger is to "lose" what is called "balance."

The danger is *hubris*. The danger is *classic, Attic*.

Grips the wire with his toes. In the thinnest-soled slippers, Don knows how.

Spine no longer a young spine (yet) retains its cheetah-elasticity.

Feet no longer "young" feet. Bunion on left big toe.

Trick is in the pole. Exquisitely calibrated motions of the pole to maintain center of balance directly below the body.

(Yes, Don has crossed the high wire without the magic pole. Many times before many of you were born Don crossed the high wire in triumph without a pole. In fact you are allowed to use arms and hands and torso to maintain *balance* on the high wire but the exertions and contortions of the human figure forty feet above the gaping crowd are distasteful to the eye while the more subtle, almost at times languorous motions of the wand-like pole are deeply aesthetically pleasurable to behold.)

Art of *funambulism* is maintaining balance on the high wire despite gusts of wind, swoops of incensed gulls, shouts and cat-calls from the (sparse, rowdy) crowd below.

"Give up, schmuck! Nobody gives a fuck about you."

* ### Black Square, Nostalgia
"All that a man wishes for himself, in which to dwell, is a black square, a three-dimensional representation of a two-dimensional existence most poetically rendered by Kazimir Malevich in *Black Square.* As for 'what do women want' . . ." Unexpectedly Don begins to weep, his beard grows scintillate with tears.

* ### Antiquarian of Drek; or, The Drek Reliquary
In his atelier on Eleventh Street the artist broods. Stark white walls, ceiling. Hardwood floor. Ascetic, acerbic, acidic. Except—in the white wall a (secret) door, and beyond the door a gigantic walk-in closet, and in the closet shelves reaching to the ceiling crammed (in scrupulous alphabetic order) a vast galaxy of original, unique, and unreplicable *drek*—from a plastic aardvark (circa 1951) to a plastic zither (circa 1939) with every sort of novelty in between: Hula-Hoop, plaster painted figure of the

Virgin Mary, TV "rabbit ears," "sack dress," *Baltimore Catechism*, poster for *The Moon Is Blue*, container of pungent mimeograph ink, skinny necktie, bouffant wig, blueprint and small model for "backyard bomb shelter," table-sized artificial Christmas tree, *Memoirs of a Klan Wife* (1969), (emptied) bottles of arresting colors and shapes formerly containing Scotch, rum, wine, vodka, well-worn copies of *Reader's Digest, Book of the Month, Saturday Review of Literature, Peyton Place, From Here to Eternity, Fear and Trembling* and *The Sickness Unto Death* (boxed set), stained hacksaw, chopsticks to which mysterious sentiment is attached, gilt "baby shoes" (size sixteen), a still from *Boudu sauvé des eaux*, clip-on polka dot bow tie, *Life* cover of President John F. Kennedy with rouged cheeks, poorly typed chain letter, report card (all A's except C+ in "Physical Education"), slick yellow rain-poncho, mood ring, "pet rock," snow globe with miniature Niagara Falls inside, *Librium* prescription, diploma from *Famous Writers School*, Hallowe'en masks of Salvador Dalí, Frankenstein, Charles Manson, Ross Perot—and much more. "It isn't madness if it's alphabetized"—this was Don's frequent observation, made with a sage stroking of his beard and a twinkle in his eyes, and just the slightest quaver of defensiveness—"and if it has been 'successfully transmogrified' into art."

*   ## Alcohol: A Celebration

    Don drinks to celebrate. Don drinks as a meditation. Don drinks as a medication. Don drinks as confabulation. Don drinks as consolation. Don drinks as prevarication. Don drinks as procrastination. Don drinks for inspiration and Don drinks in contemplation. Don is rueful. Don is "gigantic with gin." Don "hides his sorrow in gin." Don drinks to "feel better about myself." Don drinks "to feel better about the world." Don drinks whiskey, and Don drinks wine. Don drinks vodka, and Don drinks lime rickeys. Don drinks beer, ale. Don drinks what is offered. Don drinks in mourning for a misspent life. Don drinks in mourning for the world's misspent life. Don drinks in the morning, and Don drinks in the afternoon. Don drinks in the evening, and Don drinks in the night. "I'll drink to that"—"I'll drink to this." "Bottoms up!" Don drinks in moderation *and* Don drinks in immoderation. Don drinks alone and Don drinks in company. Don drinks you under the table. Don drinks himself under the table—to keep you company! Don drinks to celebrate. Don drinks.

* **DON'S GAIETY**
"He has given away his gaiety and now has nothing."

* **BLACK HEART OF THE ARTIST**
"I have a black heart."

* **DON'S POSTHUMOUS CAREER ON TWITTER**
Would've been King. Millions of tweets posted, and millions of followers and numbers mounting daily, hourly. *Don Barthelme lived before his time when his métier would've found its perfect cultural equivalent. Sad.*

* **GUILT OF THE ARTIST**
Bulletin: "An atheistic relativism has crept into our serious artists like a fungoid decay. Literature of the recent past (i.e., since I have left school) has been remiss in showing us the way out of the moral labyrinth. Poetry, that once rhymed, now sways and topples like a drunken clown. Good solid prose, that was once readable, has lost all sense of purpose and careens like a runaway eighteen-rig down a mountain roadway of twists and turns. The moral compass just spins and spins—like a dervish. There can be no good conclusion to any of this. The artist has withdrawn

into his cave and contemplates his entrails. The artist pares his toenails while Rome burns. The most sincere fragments of our time are found in Chinese fortune cookies."

* ### Chinese Fortune Cookie Fortune

Stately plump Don deftly rents the crinkly cellophane wrapper containing his fortune cookie at Chinese Pavilion, Seventh Avenue at Ninth as admirers look on raptly. There is an aura of the premonitory here. His fortune is revealed on a little strip of white paper—*Guilt is never to be doubted.*

Don laughs, laughs. The artist's incisors glitter.

* ### The Unfinished Masterpiece

A labor of love. Forty-two years in secret toil. Linked sestina epic to rival *The Faerie Queen.* A tragedy it was never completed to the satisfaction of the (perfectionist) artist.

In a fit of despair in the late spring of 1989 Don tossed the 2,463-page manuscript into a blazing fire. With somber poker prodded the flaring pages.

But—didn't acolytes retrieve the manuscript from the flames?

N-No . . .

You mean, you guys just stood there and watched the unfinished masterpiece of the late Donald Barthelme burn to ashes?

I—I guess . . .

For God's sake why didn't you save it? Wrench the poker from the despairing writer's hands, overrule his (evident, possibly insincere) wish for self-destruction as Max Brod famously did with his friend Franz Kafka?

I guess we thought . . . We just didn't think.

Didn't *think*?

(They glance at one another sheepishly.)

(Slow fade to dark. No curtain.)

* **A & Q**

A: "'I always wanted you to admire my fasting.'"

Q: "Single line from literature you'd most like to have written that you have not, in fact, written, Mr. Barthelme?"

A: "You tell *me*."

Q: "Where do you get your ideas, Mr. Barthelme?"

A: "No comment."

Q: "Are you happier in that place you are now than you were here, given that, while here, you were often unhappy, and drank to hasten the passage of time to bring you to that place you are now, Mr. Barthelme?"

A: "Missing the twenty-first century altogether. Missing the temptation of a terminal disenchantment. Being spared ignominy of inevitable equation in quantification of quality with popularity most painfully evidenced by artist's Amazon ranking (on a good day) hovering at 7,592,000."

Q: "What is the best thing about being there, rather than here with us, Mr. Barthelme?"

* **ARTIST, UNGUARDED MOMENT.**

An unusually small child reaches up to tug at his knee. "Where do you get your ideas, sir, for your strangely compelling 'surrealist' art?"

Crankily the artist prepares to say something mean but, seeing how unusually small the child-inquirer is, says instead, with a melancholy smile, "Oh, son. I am hoping you might tell me."

* **ARTIST, UNOBSERVED**

In his atelier on Eleventh Street he broods. His fingers move restlessly. His heart pounds in his chest like a metronome. Art for the sake of art, or for humankind?

How can there be art for the sake of *art*? It is a question that keeps him up at night and that no quantity of Gallo Chablis can assuage.

* ARTIST, INTERRUPTED

In his atelier on Eleventh Street the artist broods. Art for art's sake is his *cri de coeur* until one mild April evening on his way home from his cubicle-workspace just off Union Square "eponymous" Art drops by to visit Don. Turns out Art is a moderate-height Everyman of indeterminate age, class, skin-tone, off-the-rack Macy's Men's Shop, affably puzzled. Art's mysterious midtown Manhattan work involving numbers, computers, algorithms (which when Don hears he misinterprets as "Al Gore rhythms"— which seems to him worthy of André Breton) and data structures leaves Art with an "emptied-out" feeling but Art has never been one to think too deeply, still less brood. Says to Don who is staring at him with the famed Barthelme smile-sneer, "Well. I guess I am your Art, Mr. Barthelme, but I'm not sure why."

"'My Art'? What do you mean?"—Don is perplexed.

"'Art for Art's sake' has been your buzzword, I believe. I can't claim to have been keeping up with any of this 'avant-garde' art but I do know that—well, I am Art. Arthur Turnkey."

"You! You are—"

"Yes. So it seems."

The artist is stunned by this revelation. The artist has staked his art on startling juxtapositions and revelations but the artist has not—ever—expected this.

Still, the artist recovers. Shakes hands with Art for whose sake he has been toiling for so many years, and so often in vain, and so often for a piteous and unmanning remuneration, indeed the men laugh together abashed at first then more companionably, then Don asks Art if he'd like a drink and Art says, with a conspiratorial smile, "I guess that's why I've been summoned here—eh?"

* ## FUNAMBULATION III

Not quite so boldly this morning he climbs the shaky ladder. Is this a good idea?

The Cruel Master has decreed. The artist will not disappoint.

(Are there more rungs on the ladder? And is the ladder narrower than usual? His legs are very tired. The bells on his jester's cap tinkle less forcibly.)

The audience below is sparse but noisy and distracting. They have been wandering over from the dirt-bike racetrack to see what's what. Some have been waiting too long, they are clapping in unison, harsh jeering derisive clapping, a mockery of honest clapping. *Don-old. Don-old. Don-old.*

Yet zestfully the artist crawls onto the small platform. Gusts of icy wind. Ominous rustling of (desiccated) leaves, papery leaves, a sky of poorly painted brooding clouds like water stains in wallpaper, hint of infinite space beyond, hardly the silence of which Pascal spoke with such eloquence.

There, his pole! In his eager hands, the magic pole.

Eager a hedge against meager. No one must see!

He must cross the high wire. Another time.

"But each time is unique. There is no true replication in life."

Life does not lend itself to replication.

You are here once, then not. Hold your applause.

Don-ald! Don-ald! You are the man!

Chant of the crowd below not entirely mean. Isolated voices, tears leaking out of eyes, expressions of anguish, the agony of love of those who've drowned up with the artist, excuse me *grown up* with the artist. Shared birthdays in fact.

Melancholy of farewell. Even *l'ennui* has its *l'envoi.*

Don't worry—the artist has had a bracing drink. The artist has had two bracing drinks. His long narrow feet are equipped with a monkey's prehensile toes. In the thin-soled slippers not one of us gawking below would dare slip onto our feet the artist ventures out onto the high wire—another time.

For the last time? Or but the penultimate?

It is not accurate to say that the artist crosses the high wire in our place. The artist himself does not know why he crosses the high wire but he sure knows it is not *in our place*.

Not-so-taut wire. Dangerously swaying. The platform on the far side of those trees. Murky pavement beneath. Edge of dirt-bike track beneath. Artist's lips move in silence.

Only way to avoid sin is constant prayer. Constant prayer only on the high wire. Pray for me.

Stepping into the void that is the high wire. Where?

* **UNACKNOWLEDGED LEGISLATOR OF WORLD**
Well—this happens.

He has been avoiding the high wire, actually. Been avoiding the high wire for a while. Actually on his way to Mulroney's Wine & Liquor at Seventh Avenue and Ninth Street when an unusually small child tugs at his trouser-knee. Will you carry me across the Avenue, sir, the child begs. Though in a cranky mood but anticipating the first drink of the day—(to be accurate, the first drink of "daylight"—for he was drinking the night before, past midnight thus into the "next day")—the artist smiles indulgently and says, All right! If there's no other responsible adult to carry you across the wide dangerous Avenue I suppose I will have to. Picks up the small child to ride on his (still sturdy, not-bowed) shoulders across the Avenue, lets the child down gently on the sidewalk, the child thanks him and runs away and soon disappears from view as in a crowd scene in a film, often at the upbeat end of the film. Not yet at Mulroney's Wine & Liquor when to his vexation another unusually small child accosts him, and asks to be carried across the Avenue, and this time too the artist hesitates, and sighingly gives in.

"Look. I don't want this to become anything like a *habit*."

Yet it happens, who knows why, as such things happen, and after the second small child there is a third, and then a fourth . . . The upshot is, the artist does not get to Mulroney's until the sun has shifted radically in the western sky above the river, clouds overhead very like the soiled clothes of the homeless that have been blown skyward, and when the artist tries to open the damned door at Mulroney's he discovers that the store is darkened, and closed; and in its window a sign he has somehow not seen: CLOSED.

In this way, which is an alternate universe, the artist is spared his (obvious, imminent) alcoholic's fate and embarks upon a new life of self-abnegation and devotion to others.

In the near distance, the Cruel Master gnashes his teeth and clenches his jaws but is impotent, defeated.

* ALTERNATELY . . .

Alternately Mulroney's Wine & Liquor is open until 9:00 P.M. on Fridays. The small children have vanished. At dusk he sees their figures in the mists above the West Side Highway. Ghost-children, languid, yearning, vanishing.

"I'll drink to that."

* MISANTHROPY OF THE ARTIST

"Don didn't really like people all that much."

* PHILANDRY OF THE ARTIST

"He loved women, you know, and he had his vanity. He didn't really want me there at his deathbed."

* **Pessimism of the Artist**
  "We defended the city as best we could."

* **Optimism of the Artist**
  "We defended the city as best we could."

* **Defiant Optimism of the Artist**
  "I opened the door, and the new gerbil walked in. The children cheered wildly."

The Memorial Field at
Hazard, Minnesota

When I awakened from the anesthetic they were waiting for me. *Sir? It is time to come with us now.*

My eyes were so heavy-lidded! I tried to explain to them, my face had become stone, crudely carved. Those weatherworn faces you see in churchyards. No longer was I crass, craven—no longer callow and *young*. My lips moved numbly.

It was not my fault. "History" is not my fault.

A President is elected by a majority of individuals. The President *is* the majority of individuals. Our blame is evenly diffused.

Blame so evenly diffused among many millions of individuals is less than a thimble of blame for each.

The blame that is my portion is less than a thimble. A clear amber liquid like a child's urine.

THE MEMORIAL FIELD AT HAZARD covers eight hundred acres.

It is so composed to replicate Midwestern ordinariness, you would not distinguish it from any other Midwestern field used as a chemical waste dump.

A *triumph de l'oeil!*

By the terms of the warrant they are bringing me to the Memorial Field at Hazard, Minnesota. I have not been to this place before, I think.

When I awakened from the anesthetic, they were waiting for me with the warrant fully executed by one of my own federal justice appointees in the early, heady days of my administration.

Wake up. Try to wake up sir. Open your eyes sir.

Try to keep your eyes open sir.

There is that moment of great urgency when emerging from the anesthetic—you may take a sudden turn backward, and turn into Lot's wife in the sudden, solid calcification of stone. Or, if you are brave and heedless, and hopeful, you will continue forward, as I have done.

Very good sir President! Now, you will come with us.

At first, I did not recognize Chickie and Bruce! My own grandsons, I did not recognize for they have become young men now, taller than I could have imagined, and each stubbly-jawed, with wild hair and stark staring eyes in which a grandfather can discern little tenderness or mercy.

Several tall uniformed youths among whom Chickie and Bruce were not distinguished except that they were my grandsons whom I had not seen since they were small children.

Grandfather it's time.

Grandfather you have been granted more than enough time.

The Memorial Field at Hazard, Minnesota, is located approximately sixty-five miles north of Lake Caribou and a quarter mile west of Lake Superior. Here, there are powerful gusts of wind from the lake. Waves rise as high as fifteen feet crashing against shore like mania. The shore isn't a beach though there are stretches of gritty sand with a dull, sullen gleam mixed with mud. Debris is washed ashore here from landfills along the lake. The Memorial Field was first constructed as a chemical waste dump in the waning months of the Korean War, 1953. A wilderness place was required that would draw no particular attention for its ordinariness.

The Memorial Field at Hazard, Minnesota, is four miles off Route 29, a state highway. You would take exit 11 from I-91. You will be surprised, I think—I was surprised.

THEY CAME FOR ME in the hospital. Faintly I said, I don't think I can come with you, there is this shunt in my heart. But they had the warrant. They said, No problem. We can bring the gurney with us.

We drove. We came to the Memorial Field at Hazard.

The generations conspire in unexpected ways. My children—my sons—rarely speak to me any longer. But my grandsons have come to see me in the hospital. I am disguised, I have been registered here under another name. I have been granted a civilian identity: Charlie Chanticleer. (Is this a comical name? I believe that it is. But I have always confounded mockery by failing to recognize it.) IV fluids drip into my wasted veins. So many times have chemicals been leaked into my veins, I have few "usable" veins. You will feel pity for me but only recall: it will happen one day to you, too.

I am wearing paper slippers, a gown that ties loosely in back. I am a spectacle, my buttocks part-exposed! People smile at me pityingly. (Do they recognize me, despite my unshaven jaws? My haggard eyes? My emaciated frame? For once I'd been as stout and hearty as any of you.)

Don't laugh at me, please. I will confess—yes, I tried to appeal to my grandsons, to help me escape. But the tall uniformed youths turned faces upon me blank as scrubbed soapstone.

It is not that they denied me, they seemed scarcely to acknowledge me.

Or, it was pity that neutralized their contempt, and turned their faces blank and eyes unseeing.

Grandfather you have been granted more than enough time.

FROM THE TRUNK OF THE VEHICLE, the shovels. How crude—*shovels.* The Memorial Field is eight hundred acres of primarily marshy soil. A smell of decay. Sucking at our feet. My escorts are urging me forward. I am not a young man—I can't remember having been a young man. *Sir, take one of the shovels. Sir, here.*

I am not accustomed to being ordered about.

Why we must walk on foot in such underbrush, in such arduous landscape, I am not certain. I am trying to remain in good spirits, to be a "good sport"—this has been my personality since grade school. If you are a "good sport" you will be forgiven much. I have always had hopes of being forgiven much.

We are marching, tramping, through a marshy landscape. Yet strangely, there is no insect life here—no cries and calls of insect life. Our feet are sucked-at, but only by mud. Just a little farther, *Grandfather! Do not weaken now.*

Will you leave me here, if I fall? You will not, I hope!

The landscape, the dark, the Memorial Field in which, with each rainfall, the bodies are beginning to emerge. There are vapors here, columns of pale rising toxic air. There is a powerful subterranean stench. I have tried to explain, I did not know that burying the bodies was the Chief Executive's responsibility and so my office staff was worked very hard, and there were breakdowns, there were replacements. There were eleven suicides among our support staff, reported as "accidents." There were insurance compensations to the devastated families of course. There were pensions. There was a secret budget for these. I repeat that I had not known, until the bodies began to arrive in the United States. The bodies were shipped in containers that might have withstood radiation. Body bags inside containers. At first I had thought *This is a cruel trick, a typical political trick, my political enemies who want to embarrass me.* But then, it was revealed that my enemies here at home were wholly unaware of the bodies, no one knew about the bodies but a small fraction of the Capital workers, the staff associated with the Pentagon and with the Executive Office.

These are the loyal army that "runs" the Capital. All organizations of any size are "run" by individuals of this class, the great majority of them women. We could not have wars—we could not have peace treaties—if this loyal army did not perform as adequately and as enthusiastically as they do. Tonight, I am extending my gratitude to these individuals—I thank you, and I thank *you*.

The Memorial Field at Hazard was the final destination, once the bodies arrived at the Pentagon. They had come great distances, and had to be re-addressed to Minnesota. A flood of such bodies. Vast freight trains of upright cylinders, boxcar after boxcar, the delivery of the *wartime dead.* As I was the Chief Executive at the time, as I was the War President, I had little opportunity for such details, about which I knew virtually nothing. I am beginning to think yes, I was shielded from such knowledge. And so: is ignorance *blameworthy?*

But now that I am retired, and a new and younger administration has taken power, though I am not in good health I have been informed of the Hazard Memorial Field warrant which I am obliged to fulfill under the terms of my Presidency.

The warrant stipulates: I must dig up the bodies one by one. As these are singular deaths, one by one.

And then, the decree is that I must assign a name to each body; and I must be photographed beside each body. I must crouch down inside the makeshift grave, or what passes for a "grave." I must lie down beside each body.

There are thousands of bodies. Part-destroyed by explosives, or fires, or natural decay. Bodies that are parts of bodies, once living.

Hundreds of thousands of bodies, or is it thousands of thousands of bodies . . . And each body is the President's responsibility.

I am gripping the shovel in my hands, tightly. I am beginning to sink the dull blade into the muddy earth.

They are holding candles beside me. An oil lamp, held high.

Grandfather you are doing OK.

My grandchildren speak in such a way to communicate that they do not think that I am *doing OK.*

As I unshovel the first grave, a powerful stench lifts to my nostrils, grown sensitive with my safe, sequestered life. There are those (of you) who abhorred me, I know: you believed that my bland boy's face, as vacuous of expression as a baseball glove, was not the proper face of the highest ranked politician of our nation. You believed that I was not fit for such office but I repeat: *I did not elect myself.*

How many more, how many more bodies lie ahead. The Memorial Field at Hazard is eight hundred vast acres.

BENEATH THE ROCKY SOIL, a shape began to emerge—a human body. The shovel exposed the body of a shockingly specific person. A boy of ten or eleven years, thin face, thin arms, legs—a naked child. His face was barely recognizable as a face but you could tell by the eyes, what remained of the eyes, that he was "foreign"—even the light-skinned are readily identifiable as such. His body was partly destroyed—and partly decayed . . .

Oh God I am very weak, my guts are sick . . . I did not anticipate a child, I am very sick, I am tired. There is a shunt in my arm, that leads to my heart. I am not "heartless"—I was never given a chance to speak my "heart."

Wanting to protest bitterly: *Why are you doing this to me? I did not touch this person. I did not—ever!—touch a single person. My directives were not personal. It was the office—the Presidency.*

When I was wakened from the anesthetic, I could hear voices

speaking to me and of me—as you would speak to a dead person, to urge him not to despair. The President was a younger man than certain of his advisers. He respected his elders. He respected powerful men, who were very wealthy men. He did their bidding—he would have been very imprudent if he had not. (He would not have been President if he had not.) *I didn't want to kill this person, this person is not my fault.* He began to cry. He began to sob. He was helpless in the throes of such sorrow. He did not know what he should do but he'd found solace in the knowledge that, once it was done, it would become "history." It was not what he decided, or what his advisers had advised, or what our consultants had suggested, it was "history" and you could argue—it had been "meant" to occur from the beginning of Time.

THE MEMORIAL FIELD AT HAZARD is our final resting place. In the Memorial Field, our solid bodies yield to liquid, and when the liquid dries, to dust.

The photographs are taken one by one. For we must die one by one as we are born one by one for we are singular and not plural. And the truth is to know, *the one is not the many, and the many is not one. But the one can be as great as the many.*

The former President grinning amid the dead. He grips a shovel in one hand and in the other, the partly decayed hand and arm of a young child.

It is the first of the children. It will not be the last.

He must crouch down into the grave. He must embrace the broken body as his own.

SO MANY GRAVES! When you are told *casualty numbers, enemy death count* you do not think in terms of *bodies.* At least, I did not. My staff did not. We were presented with figures, and often we joked of these figures—good-naturedly not cruelly, for we are not cruel persons no matter how our enemies misrepresent us—but we were not joking of *actual bodies*. Because we had no perception of *actual bodies*.

And so it is unjust now, I think, that I am being punished in this way. I would register an appeal but it would be to the very same court that has so sentenced me, thus an unjust court. My staff and my aides they have been executed, and for these innocent men there can be no appeal.

Never will I come to the end of the unshoveling of the graves at the Memorial Field at Hazard. Barely have I begun my hellish task, and my arms are aching, and my guts are sick, and my eyes are weak and burning in my head. I have been stripped of my absurd hospital gown. Even the paper slippers have been taken from me. The young soldiers prod me with their bayonets, as one might prick a stymied bull, that has not yet comprehended that his death is upon him, no matter how he bellows defiance and no matter how bravely he fights.

I am gripping the shovel with weakening fingers. Soon, it will fall to the ground and I believe that it will be then, the young soldiers will pierce me with their bayonets, in deathly silence. Not one will utter a word of remorse, affection, or simple sympathy. Not one will utter *No! Stop! He is innocent, he was a fool.*

Forgive me, there is no more speech remaining. It is just me—I— your President—standing naked before you, shovel in hand.

I thank you. And I thank you.

And *you*, and *you*. *I thank you.*

I thank you for your faith in me, as your President. I thank you for your votes. And I thank you now for your applause, and your blessing.